OUR CHANCE

NATASHA PRESTON

Books by Natasha Preston

THE SILENCE SERIES

Silence
Broken Silence
Players, Bumps, and Cocktail Sausages
Silent Night (A Free Short Story for Christmas)

THE CHANCE SERIES

Second Chance
Our Chance

STAND-ALONES

The Cellar
Save Me
Awake
With the Band

All characters in this publication are fictional, and any resemblance to real persons, living or dead, is purely coincidental.

Visit my website at www.natashapreston.com
Cover Designer: Dalliance Designs
Editor and Interior Designer: Jovana Shirley,
Unforeseen Editing, www.unforeseenediting.com

ISBN-13: 9781508901266

For Chloe Meyer

ONE

NELL

I bit my lip as I read Damon's latest text.

What colour's your underwear?

Dirty bugger.

I couldn't concentrate on work, and it was all his fault.

Who goes on a lad's holiday for a week, knowing full well that your special *friend won't be able to have sex until you return, and then send said* special *friend the dirtiest text messages in existence?*

Even I'd blushed at some of them.

His messages made me hot and needy, and if every man I worked with didn't look like a troll, I would've dragged one of them to the bathroom by now. Damon and I had a friends-with-benefits agreement, one that had been running for about six years now and one that I couldn't wait to resume the second he got home.

It was the start of 2015, and it'd started with me watching Chloe and Logan suck each other's faces off while I exchanged a *Happy New Year* text with Damon. Now, two days on, I was back at work and wishing I were still watching my best friend getting dry-humped in the middle of a club. This new year was not looking good.

I replied to Damon.

> *Shut up, leave me alone, and enjoy your holiday.*

Then, I silenced my phone and chucked it in the top drawer of my desk. I began working for the haulage company not long after finishing university. I had a degree which said I could turn a business around like a fucking pro and debts that told me I needed to, but the job I'd landed was right at the bottom of the ladder. Actually, I was the dirt under the ground that held the ladder.

The company was super small. My dickhead boss was a disgusting pervert, and I got to be his PA. But it was a start. I had seen a career advisor who told me to go for this job, and in six months' time, I would have experience in the industry that would be taken more seriously from bigger companies. She'd better be right.

"Nell," Reg, the dickhead himself, barked, "I need East Coast Holiday Park's folder."

No *please*. Never a *please*.

Gritting my teeth, I pushed my chair out and went to get his sodding file from the storeroom—a storeroom that was closer to his office than mine. The girls in accounting winced at me as I walked past. One of them used to be his PA before moving over. I hated her for switching and creating my job opening.

Ignoring them, I ripped the door open and dug through the archives under E. I wanted to turn his shitty just-ticking-over company around, not make coffee and get things for the lazy, rude tosser in the next room.

He'd had two assistants in the past. One was now in accounting, and the other had left. The longer I was here, the more convinced I was that this wasn't the start of a career. He just wanted someone to take care of him at work.

Pulling the file out of the cabinet, I repeated in my head, *Four months to go, four months to go.*

It wouldn't have even been that bad if he wasn't so rude and didn't let his son—unsurprisingly, the Deputy Manager—talk to my breasts.

I walked into Reg's office. "Here you go," I said, smiling brightly behind an urge to punch him in the face.

The younger version of him stared at me from his chair by his dad's desk.

"Good morning, Harry."

A small smile spread across his face, and he raised an eyebrow. "Good morning, Nell."

I didn't like Harry. He looked too hard and would sneak up when you least expected it. He was a creep, and his dad never told him to stop. I liked really dark eyes. Usually, they were alluring and mysterious, but Harry's almost black ones were beady with an edge of stalker. With light-blond hair, the same as his father's, his mega dark eyes looked even odder.

"A coffee when you've got a minute. Harry, want one?" Reg said.

Please!

Harry's eyes never left me. And when I said *me*, I meant, my cleavage.

"I would love a coffee, Nell."

My fake smile grew to the point where it hurt. I was sure they must be able to see it was a fuck-you smile, but I didn't care. "Of course. I won't be a minute."

If I had laxatives, I would grind up one—or nine—and put it in their coffee.

Hurry up, five o'clock.

I made the coffee, dropped it off to the lazy arse and then went back to my office to busy myself with rubbish little tasks that I'd been putting off, but that meant I wouldn't have to leave my office and risk running into them for the rest of the day.

After work, I went straight over to my best friend's house. Chloe answered the door, and I felt the stresses of the day melt away.

Her smile faded when she saw my frown. "Good day then?" she asked, wincing and tucking her long, straight brown hair behind her ear.

"Not really, but I survived it. I'm starving."

"Dinner is almost ready."

"Will Logan be joining us?" I asked, walking inside as she moved over.

Logan was Chloe's fiancé and a complete sweetheart. He'd pined for her for years before they'd gotten together. Not to mention, he was drop-dead gorgeous.

She closed the front door and shook her head. "He's working late tonight. Wine?"

"A bottle of it, please!"

"What did he do?" she asked, leading me to the kitchen and grabbing two glasses.

I got the rosé out of the fridge, opened the bottle, and poured two generous glasses.

"Same as always," I replied.

Every day was the same. At this rate, the only experience I would be leaving with was filing and making coffee. Neither of those was difficult or would look particularly fabulous on my CV. I didn't mind doing shit for Reg. That was the point of a PA, but he wasn't interested in training me to do anything. He didn't value me as a human, let alone an employee.

"It's not forever. Hey, have you heard from Damon?"

All bloody day. "A little. Why?"

Chloe had fully entered annoying cupid mode and was determined to get me and Damon together properly, despite what we both wanted.

"Is he having a good time?"

"He says he is, yeah."

She leaned her skinny hip against the worktop and stirred a Bolognese that was bubbling away on the hob. "Hmm, that'll be with all those bikini-clad women on the beach."

I knew what she was doing, but I wasn't going to get jealous. Well, I was jealous that they were experiencing what I was so used to, but that was it. Damon and I were friends who shared orgasms, and that was how we liked it.

"Probably," I replied. "Seven sinfully good-looking guys in Kavos are going to get a lot of action. Add Damon's dark hair and tattoos to the mix…" He was getting laid, for sure.

"Have you met his brother?" she asked.

"No, but I've seen pictures. The Masters brothers were blessed in the muscles department—and just about every other department actually."

Damon had a picture of him and his brother and, oh, sweet Jesus, the muscular arms in those plain T-shirts. I wish I'd taken a copy of it.

She rolled her eyes. "You're terrible."

"Why? Because you want to be the only one who's done the brother thing?"

Narrowing her eyes, she muttered, "Bitch."

"Slut."

We both laughed, and she slapped my arm from across the counter.

Chloe had been with Logan's brother, Jace, in her early teens for a couple of years. Then, he was killed in a bomb attack in London—or so we'd thought. Fast-forward four years, and Jace had turned up very much alive after giving evidence to put the bombers away and when Chloe had finally allowed herself to love Logan, guilt-free. Things had gotten messy.

"Tell me again, why don't you want to make it official with Damon?"

I stuck my middle finger up and changed the subject. She already knew, and I didn't feel like going over old ground again.

After two solid hours of gossiping and dinner, the front door opened and slammed shut. Chloe's whole face lit up, and she hadn't even seen her fiancé yet. *Sappy cow.*

Logan's face mirrored hers, softening, yet his eyes darkened with hunger at the same time. Then, he saw me and paused. "Oh, good, you're here again," he said, fully walking into the room and grinning at me. He kissed my best friend's head and dodged her elbowing his crown jewels.

"Nice to see you, too, Logan." I nodded at his very naked, very rock-solid sweaty chest.

He was a fitness instructor and would go running all the bloody time. So far this week, I'd been over twice and in time to see him run home from work. I didn't mind the view one bit.

"I'm having a shower. Tell your pervert friend to keep her eyes on my face, sweetheart, yeah?" he said to Chloe. He flashed me a smile before leaving us to it.

Whenever Chloe saw him, her face was sickening. Love was stupid, but Chloe and Logan were going to make it. If anything happened and she got hurt, I was going to castrate Logan with a blunt, rusty handsaw.

"So, one more time, how's friends with benefits working out with Damon?"

"Fine. It's *fine*. Fucking hell, I can have sex with someone without it meaning anything."

"I know." She lowered her voice to add, "Just not with Damon."

"I think I want a new best friend."

"What do you think's going to happen here, Nell?"

"I think I'm going to use Damon's body as often as I can. Same game plan as his, so stop worrying."

"At what cost?"

"Sleep. I'm not getting anywhere near enough when he's around."

Sighing, she rolled her amber eyes. "All right, fine. It's your life. I just don't want to see you get hurt."

"Neither do I. Nothing is going to hurt me, Chlo-Chlo. We're friends and nothing more."

She didn't look like she believed me at all, and that was fine. As long as Damon and I knew the score, we'd be okay. If the roles were reversed, I'd be just as worried about her, so I couldn't give her that much shit.

"Anyway, I'd better get going."

"Are you sure?" she asked, her brown eyebrows knitting together. The look of worry was etched onto her pretty face. "It's not because of what I said, is it?"

"No, it's because I have work in the morning, and I'm sure you're dying to join Logan in the shower."

She pressed her lips together, and the lightest blush touched her cheeks.

"Go for it," I said, winking, as I stood up.

I let myself out and walked to my car, tying my annoying long hair into a ponytail as the wind had kept blowing it in my face. Just when I started the car, my phone beeped with another text.

The things I'm going to do to you when I get home…

Damon's message put a huge smile on my face. I chucked the phone onto the passenger seat and drove off, thinking about what to reply to really make him wish he'd never gone on holiday.

TWO

DAMON

I sat at home, stuffing my face with the Indian takeaway I'd picked up after leaving the airport. I was knackered and quite possibly still pissed from the fourteen-night bender in Kavos. There wasn't one of the six guys I had gone with whom I didn't fucking hate now, and I still had two hours before I would get to see Nell again.

My arsehole of a brother had not so wisely decided to make our annual lads' holiday also his engagement stag. There was no such thing as a stag for an engagement, but it'd seemed like such a great idea at the time. If I didn't feel like a human again by the time I had to leave, I was going to disown Lance.

We'd had a rule on holiday, just one that had also seemed like a good idea. Being sober wasn't allowed. It wasn't just my liver that was pickled. I didn't think I'd formed a full sentence in the last nine days—not one that had made the slightest bit of sense anyway.

There was only one thing I wanted more than to collapse in bed and sleep for days, and it had legs that went on for miles, long and wavy black hair, and beautiful, bright green eyes. Two weeks was a long time not to see her. It didn't help that I had blue balls and had been too wankered to do much about it in Kavos, especially toward the end.

I shovelled the lamb dish down my throat and cracked open a beer. I wasn't ready for the killer hangover yet, so I'd drink tonight. Tomorrow, I could die in bed. Thank fuck I would have a day to recover before going back to work.

At nine thirty, Nell texted, letting me know she was on the way to the club with Chloe and Logan. Her message couldn't have come soon enough. I was desperate to get to her. I wasn't, by any stretch of the imagination, a good guy, and I'd slept with well over thirty women before I'd stopped counting, but Nell was the only one I went back to again and again and again.

I called a taxi because I was probably about ten times over the limit, and then I went to have a quick shower and change. With only fifteen minutes before the taxi was due to arrive, I washed in a rush and changed into some clothes that didn't smell like booze, sleaze, and regret.

A car horn sounded just as I'd finished styling my dark hair. Thank God for that. I should've insisted that Nell meet me here, but I hadn't wanted her to see me in the state I was in. It was a surprise when the airline let us on the plane to come home. We had looked like shit, groaned like cavemen in reply to questions, and could barely walk in a straight line. But they'd probably just wanted us out of their country.

"Hey, man," I said to the taxi driver after locking my door and getting into the black car.

"So, you're off on a bender?"

Not another one. "Meeting friends," I replied. I gave him the name of the club. *Meeting up with a girl I've not seen for two weeks but solidly thought about.* I would never admit to Nell just how much I'd missed her while I was away, but it was an obscene amount.

I was dropped off outside the club after getting the driver's complete life story. I made my way inside, as there was no queue to get in. That was never a good sign, but it was still early. The club was half-full. Groups of women were dancing while a few men honed in on their targets for the night.

There was only one I was looking for, and it didn't take me long to spot her. She stood at a raised table with Chloe, laughing at something she'd said.

Nell was so goddamn stunning that, sometimes, I would have to check I wasn't dreaming. When she was around, I barely saw any other girl; they paled in comparison. She was a gorgeous chick who didn't want anything heavy or serious, and she was also cool to hang with. I'd hit the motherfucking jackpot.

I was ready to take her home right now, five seconds after walking in the club. Her sexy body was wrapped in a skintight silver dress that showed off her back and long legs. Waves of inky-black hair trailed down her bare back to the top of her pert arse.

Chloe nudged her arm, and Nell looked around. Her green eyes darkened. I had the same thoughts as her, and each one involved us being naked. She left the table, and I got a perfect view of those legs. My mouth went dry.

Unexpectedly, she leaped into my arms, wrapping said long legs around my waist. I didn't have much time to process what was going on before her mouth was on mine, her tongue probing through my lips.

Hell. Yes.

I kissed her back, curling one arm around her back and the other under that gorgeous butt. *Shit, she's addictive.*

Chloe muttered something about going to help Logan with drinks, and I assumed she'd left us to it. I really couldn't have cared less if she'd stayed.

"Welcome back," Nell said, looking real pleased with herself for giving me a raging hard-on in the middle of the club.

"It certainly is a good welcome back. Know what would top it off?" I asked, smirking.

She arched her eyebrow and pursed her lips, urging me to continue.

"If you blew me in the bathroom."

Laughing, she untangled her legs from my waist and hopped down. "I'm sure it would be, but I bet you've had enough blow jobs for the last two weeks."

I held my finger up. *What crap is that?* "First, you can *never* have enough blow jobs, and second, no one gives them like you."

"Well, thanks, but I think I'll pass for now. You need to get yourself screened before any bare part of you is going in any bare part of me."

"What? I don't have anything, Nell."

"You went on a lads' holiday to Kavos. Do you really expect me to believe you spent two weeks looking at the architecture?"

"I wrap up; you know that."

To be honest, I'd failed miserably in the screw stakes in Kavos. The rest of the lads—the single ones—had had over five women each. My number stood at two, and I hadn't even *done* the second one. She'd just given me head in the alley between a kebab shop and another club.

"I don't care. Test or no blowies."

Is she serious? How long will that take?

I took a deep breath. I couldn't really take offense when she was only trying to protect herself. "Fine," I replied. "I'll make an appointment tomorrow. Can I still do stuff to you?"

"Oh, you'd better," she replied, turning around and leading me to her table.

"Hey, Chloe, Logan," I said, wrapping an arm around Nell's waist.

"How was Kavos?" Logan asked, smirking and putting the tray of drinks on the table.

"Interesting," I replied.

"Is it like what you see on TV?" Nell asked, pressing into my side.

Her hand was splayed over my abdomen. I fuckin' loved when she did that.

"It's exactly what you see. I'm pretty sure I lost several hundred brain cells and fifty percent of my liver function, all thanks to alcohol."

Nell shrugged. "Sounds fun to me."

"I didn't say it wasn't fun."

"Ah," she replied. "The women."

"I was smashed the whole time, Nell. Didn't get a whole lot of action. Don't think it'll even work until the booze is out of my system."

Her eyes shone with mischief. "That sounds like a challenge."

Nuzzling her neck, I replied, "It is. Take me to the bathroom."

She laughed, moved in front of me, and looked over her shoulder. "I don't need to do that to prove it still works."

I was about to argue because, more than anything, I wanted us to touch each other up in a restroom stall, but then I realised her game. She pressed that perfect behind against my crotch, and my dick sprang to life.

"I prefer my plan," I growled in her ear as she teasingly brushed against me again. "Keep doing it, and see where it gets you."

If she wanted to play, I was game, but I would win. She knew that, too. Nell loved to play, but when it came to her teasing me, if I'd had enough, we were going to have sex in the nearest suitable place. Half the time, I thought she did it just so I'd drag her off.

Laughing, she picked up her cocktail and took a sip, pretending to listen to what Chloe and Logan were talking about. I took my beer and had a large gulp. Tomorrow, I was going to feel like shit.

Nell moved to the side but stayed leaning against me with half of her body squashed against my chest. I could smell her and touch her. My heart was racing too fast, and my body was buzzing with the need to be naked and pressed against her. I was home.

Chloe dragged Logan, kicking and screaming, to the dance floor.

"What did you get up to while I was away?" I asked Nell.

She pursed her lips and turned to the side, so we could have a proper conversation. I preferred when she was standing in front of me.

"Not much. Worked and hung out with Chlo a lot. That's about it."

No guys. Good.

"So, basically, you spent the whole time pining for me?"

Her eyes narrowed, and she folded her arms. I was goading her, and she knew it.

"Not quite. But there was no one that came along who seemed worth it." She shrugged, and her dark eyebrows knit together into an adorable frown. "You're cocky, and it's annoying. Well, I kinda like it actually, but that's not the point."

"Right. So, what *is* the point, Nell?"

Her left eye twitched. "That you're a cock, but no one does it for me quite like you. Don't let that go to your head."

Smirking, I grabbed her wrist and pulled her closer. "Too late for that."

"Great," she muttered as she glanced up at me.

The look in her eyes took my breath away. It was lust and something else that I knew she had no idea about. She cared more than she wanted to. Nell stared at me like I was a fucking prize. She was all about casual, so I knew she wasn't really aware of how she saw me, but that didn't matter right now. All that mattered was that she made me feel like a fucking god, and I couldn't get enough.

"Want to get out of here?" I asked.

"We've only been here for forty-five minutes."

"So?"

Biting her lip together, she thought about it. I ran my hand down her back, feeling her bare skin. Her lips soon parted, and I felt the electricity between us strengthen and crack.

"Damon…"

She felt it, too—the heat, the straight-up animalistic need to be sweaty and naked together.

Nothing about how much I still wanted her was rational, but I didn't give a shit. All I needed from her was one look, and I was gone.

"What?" I whispered, stepping closer.

The bridge of her nose was level with my mouth. Leaning forward, I kissed her and moved to the side, kissing her skin until I reached her ear.

"I need you, Nell. It's been far too long."

Goose bumps bubbled under my fingers as I moved my hand south, stopping just before I met the material at her lower back. Her body trembled under my touch, making me painfully hard. We would have sex a lot, and in the last two weeks, I'd had sex a grand total of once. The woman was forgettable, and I barely remembered it.

I *needed* Nell. Now.

"Come on. You know you don't want to stay here for another second either," I said, practically panting.

Her body was against mine, and it made it hard for me to think about anything else.

Abruptly, she pulled away and looked over her shoulder. If I didn't know her so well, I'd think she was annoyed off with my advances. But she was looking for Chloe to tell her we were leaving.

Her slow searching pissed me off. Holding her upper arms, I led her to the now heaving dance floor and shoved our way through the crowd.

"Damon!" she squealed as I held her in front of me, awkwardly walking us out.

"I can't wait," I hissed in her ear, sliding my hand down to her hip.

If she didn't want to drive me to insanity, then she shouldn't wear tight little dresses when I hadn't had her in fourteen days.

Laughing, she grabbed my hand to stop me from going any lower and pointed to Logan ahead of us. We pushed past the last few people in our way.

"We're going," she said to Chloe.

Logan smirked, and Chloe wiggled her eyebrows.

"Bye," I said before turning us around and shoving our way back.

Nell laughed and waved to Chloe over her shoulder. *Screw talking and long good-byes.* They knew Nell was safe with me, so we could now get out of here.

We took a taxi back to my place and burst through the door with our lips sealed together and Nell hooking her leg up around my waist.

Fuck, I'd missed her. I'd missed the softness of her lips, her smell, the silkiness of her raven-black hair, the way she'd react to my touch with such hunger and greed. And her eyes, they were the most shocking and beautiful shade of green I'd ever seen.

As she flicked her tongue over my top lip, my lips parted of their own accord. I groaned and hauled her up, so she could get both of those long legs around me.

We were perfectly lined up, and I felt like I was going to lose my mind. My dick was throbbing. I could feel her heat through my jeans, and it was driving me crazy.

"I need you," I growled into the frantic kiss.

Having had enough, I carried her into the living room and collapsed on the sofa. Giggling as her back hit the cushion, she kicked her eyebrow up as I reached into my wallet for a rubber.

"Bet I can make you come before me." She bit her lip and rubbed her palm over my erection.

I arched into her touch and groaned. "Game on, Presley," I hissed.

THREE

NELL

I woke up in Damon's bed with a bloody banging headache.

After having sex on the sofa, we'd moved it to his room. I'd missed him like crazy, and it kinda sucked that we had to be extra careful until he was tested for STIs, but I wasn't going to risk anything.

It wasn't particularly early, but I'd still expected him to be in bed when I awoke. He was nowhere to be seen. I could smell coffee though, so he must be in the kitchen. It was Sunday. Damon had nothing to do, and I'd cancelled my plans with Chloe when I knew the date he would be back from Kavos, so we would have a whole day to catch up on two weeks' worth of sex—condom sex but sex nonetheless.

In the corner of Damon's room was his suitcase, still done up and probably full of his clothes. It would likely stay that way for at least another week. I'd missed him more than I'd thought I would. I'd missed the things he could do to my body, but he was back now, and I was absolutely going to get him to do those things at least twice more before I left.

"Damon," I called.

"Be there in a minute. Don't get dressed."

I had no intention of getting dressed. "Hurry up."

He laughed, and then I heard faint footsteps as he made his way back to his room. Anticipation flooded my body.

Damon and I had been sleeping together for about six years since the last year in high school when he transferred. We'd been at it all through uni, too. I still couldn't get enough. I'd had a few sexual partners, but none of them had even come close to Damon. We fit together perfectly, shared the same sex drive, and could separate the act from ridiculous feelings and emotions.

The door swung open, and Damon stood before me in his birthday suit, holding two mugs of coffee. He was as confident about his body as I was with mine. Actually, he was definitely more of an exhibitionist. I, in no way, thought my body was flawless, but I was happy enough and completely unashamed of what my mama had given me.

My mind short-circuited for a second. So much perfection, dark hair, deep hazel eyes, muscles, ink, and skin were all wrapped up in one now lightly tanned gorgeous package.

I regained my composure, but inside, I was still fanning myself. "Wow, you don't get this kind of service at Starbucks."

"I'm sure old Fred would take his kit off if you asked him."

I had no doubt that the old pervert would. "I'm sure he'd do it even if I didn't ask," I replied, turning my nose up. "But I think I prefer your six-pack to his saggy beer belly."

"Oh, thank you," Damon said, smirking and setting the drinks down on the side table. "Lie down, Nell. This is going to be quick and hard. I don't want the coffee going cold."

Who am I to argue with a pre-coffee quickie?

After spending two hours in bed, we finally got up and got dressed. Damon seemed to be in no rush to get me out the door, and as long as he wasn't looking as though he was bored of me, I wasn't going anywhere.

We were lounging on his sofa, eating ice cream and watching The Godfather movies. It was the best way to spend the day getting reacquainted.

"Are you back at work tomorrow?" I asked.

"Yeah, but I could really do with another week off."

Couldn't we all?

Damon was one of those bloody annoying people who had found their dream job right out of university. I knew he'd worked hard for it, and he deserved it, but I couldn't help but feel like a failure next to him.

"You love your job."

He nodded. "I'd still rather my job was getting you naked at every opportunity."

"How is it not?"

When we were alone, my clothes would come off.

Laughing, he dug the spoon in the tub of cookie dough. "True. Can you blame me?"

"I cannot," I replied, winking. "So, how many girls did you get naked with in Kavos?"

"Two."

"Per day?"

"No, two *total.*"

What? "But Kavos is where you go to get laid. How did you only score two?"

He shrugged. "Don't remember a whole lot of it, to be honest, and actually, I think the last one only took her top off. Pretty sure I was too drunk the entire time. Doug won. He allegedly bagged nineteen."

"Shut up. More than one a day?"

"I think you underestimate how loose everyone is in Kavos. But he could well be bullshitting. Your math is shit hot, by the way."

"I'm thinking he lied. And I know. Shame I don't want to do anything math-y."

"Math-y?"

"I don't know. Teach it or something."

"You won't always be in that job, Nell."

"I won't. I have to remind myself of that thirty thousand times a day. There are millions of people out there who hate their jobs. I'm just one of them for now."

"That's the spirit. If things get too bad, I'll hire you. In fact, I'd hire you right now."

"Ha! No, thanks. Prostitution is illegal."

His eyes darkened. "I wasn't thinking like that…although I am now. I mean it. You're sharp, intelligent, confident, perfectly capable of turning your hand to most things, and seemingly awesome at math. Your business degree is going to waste, and I know for a fact that my boss would want you on the team."

I'd be lying if I said I wasn't tempted, but I couldn't work for or with Damon. No way. We shared bodily fluids and hung out. I liked our arrangement. We slept together and went on with our individual lives, and becoming colleagues would only blur the lines of the carefully crafted relationship we had.

"Thank you, but I don't think it's a good idea. Besides, I want to work my way up independently. I appreciate you wanting to help, but this has to be something I do alone."

He leaned over and gave me a kiss. His lips were cold and tasted like ice cream. I licked mine, which made his eyes smoulder.

"I knew you'd say that. Offer's there, but I get where you're coming from."

I was curious to know what he'd hire me to do, if it were his decision, but I didn't want to tempt myself or end up talking myself into thinking it would be a good plan to take the job. Work and play shouldn't mix. Neither of us was particularly awesome at keeping our hands off each other, and that could be really awkward in a meeting.

"You want to get together tomorrow after work?" I asked.

"I have a meeting at five, but I'll be free by six. Wanna come over?"

"Hmm, my place, I think."

"Sure, I'll bring Chinese."

"Chinese and sex."

"Nothin' better," he said. Then, he nodded to the TV. "Now, watch. I can't believe you've never seen The Godfather before."

I'd tried to watch it once, but I couldn't get into it. My dislike of the film didn't seem to bother Damon. He was more concerned that I hadn't seen a classic than whether I liked it or not. It didn't really matter though because, between the movies and sometimes a quarter or halfway through, he'd stop our watching in favour of something a lot hotter and sweatier.

I was laid out over his chest as the third movie started. We were both as naked as the day we were born and sore in all the right places.

"I hope you're not falling asleep," he murmured.

"You can't seriously want it again."

Is he a machine? I knew his sex drive was high, but this was ridiculous.

"Don't blame me. You're lying all over me, naked."

"Want me to get off?" I said into his toned chest.

I felt his body shake with silent laughter. His hands slid down my back, leaving a trail of goose bumps where they went, and rested just above my butt.

"No part of me wants you to go. I want you to come."

"You are such a pervert," I whispered, all husky and needy.

"Mmhmm."

"I don't know if I can have sex again."

"Sure you can," he replied. "If you want, I'll tie you to my bed and do all the work."

Laughing, I shook my head. "I'm sure my lying there like a sack of potatoes would be so much fun for you."

"I'd be inside you, Nell. You could be up and down like a yo-yo or lying as still as a statue, and I'd still come so hard that it'd feel like my eyeballs were going to explode."

For a good ten seconds, I could find no words. "You feel like your eyes are going to explode when you come?" *Should it feel like that? Am I orgasming wrong?*

"Not usually, but with you, it's something else."

"Thank you very much," I replied. I felt his smile. "Er…you make my eyes explode, too."

His chest shook again. "Maybe I used the wrong analogy."

"No, no, I like the eye thing. Quite original."

"What are your plans for the rest of the night?" he asked.

"I thought I'd hang out here and make up for lost time. Unless you have plans?"

"My only plan involves you lying all over me, naked, for the rest of the night."

"Hmm," I said, lifting myself to my elbows. I grinned down at him. "I can get on board with that plan. But you're still not getting laid until you've proven you're clean."

"There's plenty other things I can do to you again and again and again."

Yep, I can definitely get on board with this.

FOUR

DAMON

The day after Nell had told me that no bare part of me was going inside her before I had an STI test, I'd made an appointment. I was careful, and there had only been a few occasions when I'd not used a condom—all with her—but she'd insisted.

If she'd been to the easy-lay capital of the world, I would have wanted her to get the all-clear first, too. So, this afternoon, I would get the pleasure of pissing in a cup.

I left work ten minutes early to make the appointment on time. I'd only been back for two days after having fourteen off, but the next available appointment wasn't until next week, and there was no way I could wait that long.

My nerves started to kick in the second I walked into the building. A few people sat in the waiting area in front of a wall full of sexual health posters and flyers. *Not doing much fucking luck in here.* It'd be too late by the time you stepped through the door.

"Hello," I said, wanting the world to swallow me whole.

The receptionist looked up and smiled. "Can I help you?"

"I have an appointment in a few minutes. Damon Masters."

She blinked at me twice, smiled, and then tapped away at the computer. "Ah, there you are. If you'd like to take a seat and fill in these forms, you'll be called through in a minute."

"Thank you," I replied, taking the sheets of paper and a pen.

I didn't want to take a seat. I wanted out. It was absurd that I was so fucking nervous. Everyone in here had come for the same reason, and getting tested was sensible. Still, I felt…dirty.

Me, feeling dirty!

But this was in the wrong way.

"Mr Masters," a pretty blonde with a huge rack called.

Things were looking up already.

I nodded. "Yeah, hello," I greeted.

"If you'd like to please follow me. Have you been tested before?" she asked as we turned into the first door past reception.

"No, I haven't." I'd always been very careful when it came to my sexual health.

She took the forms from me. "Okay. Take a seat, and we'll begin."

Begin? Am I not here just to give a urine sample?

"I need to start by asking you a few questions, if that's okay?"

"Absolutely. Fire away," I replied, sitting down. I kicked my feet out, crossing my legs at the ankles.

"When did you become sexually active?"

"Wow, you're straight to it."

She cracked a smile and shrugged.

"I was fourteen."

"And how many sexual partners have you had?"

I winced. "Ballpark?"

She looked up through her lashes and cocked her eyebrow. "That will do, if you're unsure."

Shifting awkwardly in my seat, I replied, "Forty to fifty."

Her sharp looks and manners made me feel like I was under siege, but I could well be dreaming it because I felt like an arsehole.

"All right. When was the last time you had unprotected sex?"

Nell. About a month ago in the front seat of my car, we had been coming back from a night out, and she'd gotten rather horny and carried away. The memory of having her bareback on top of me in a confined space got me hot under the collar.

"Er, that was about four or five weeks ago," I replied, trying to keep my cool.

Nell had better take me in the car like that again since I'm doing this for her.

"And do you think you could have an infection? Are there any changes you've noticed or anything you're concerned about?"

"No, but I was in Kavos last week and thought it's probably time to get checked out."

"Did you have unprotected or oral sex while you were there?"

"Not unprotected sex."

She smiled and nodded her head. "Okay, I'll need a urine sample to test for chlamydia and gonorrhea and a blood sample to test for HIV and syphilis. Since you have no symptoms or changes in your genitals, we don't need to test for herpes."

I rubbed my hand over my face. *Shit.* When someone uttered the word *HIV*, things would become very real. I was nervous and worried even though I knew I'd been careful.

"Can't we do the other one, too? I'd like to test for everything," I said, seriously stretching the definition of the word *like.*

"As you wish," she replied. "Can you please roll up your sleeve, so I can take the blood sample?"

I shoved my sleeve up past my elbow and rested it on the arm of the chair. She removed a needle from a packet and popped a tube in the end. The needle pricked as it pierced my skin, and I watched my blood trickle into the tube, but it was over in seconds.

"All right," she said. She slowly extracted the needle from my vein and placed a cotton ball where it had entered. "Keep pressure on that for a minute, and it should be fine. Unless you'd like a plaster?"

Is she serious? "I'm fine. Thank you."

"Okay. I'll give you a minute to undress from the waist down and lie back on the bed."

My eyebrows shot up in surprise. "Sorry, what?"

"I need to take a swab of your urethra for the herpes test."

I instantly jerked forward and pressed my legs together. "You, what? I thought this was all done by urine and blood now?"

"Most are, but…"

"Oh God, I can't believe I'm doing this," I muttered.

"If you'd prefer not to, that's fine. I honestly don't believe you need this test. We don't usually do it unless a patient has experienced sores on their genitals or anus."

This day just keeps getting better and better.

"Perfect," I said dryly. "It's fine. I'll be happier knowing I'm clear of everything."

"Okay," she replied as she turned around. "I'll give you a minute. Let me know when you're ready."

I would never, ever be prepared or ready for what she was about to do.

Nell better give me the mother of all blow jobs after this.

I put the cotton ball dotted with a speck of my blood down on the chair and dropped my trousers. Hopping on the table, I laid my head back on my arms.

"I'm ready," I said before taking a deep breath.

She was back, eager to do this. "All right, this won't take long, and I'll be as gentle as I can."

Too fucking right she will.

Usually, a pretty woman in a nurse-like getup touching my dick would get me hot and hard, but knowing what was coming had it trying to shove its way inside my body. I felt something on the tip and braced myself. She pushed it inside, and my eyes widened. I grabbed ahold of the sides of the bed and clawed the faux leather material.

"Fuck. Fucking hell, fuck. Get it out!"

"Almost done."

I was positive I saw her crack a smile. She pulled the swab out, and I cowered, covering my area and closing my eyes.

That did not feel good.

"There. Are you all right?"

Do I look all right?

"Fine," I bit out.

There has to be a better way to do that.

She turned around again, and I used the opportunity to get my trousers back on fucking quickly. I pulled up the zip, careful not to let it rub because it still felt tender.

She looked at the details I'd filled in on the forms while I waited. "You'll get your results via text message, like you opted for, within a week. If you test positive, you'll be invited back, so we can discuss the results and plan treatment."

"Okay. Is that all?"

Laughing quietly, she nodded. "That's all."

"Thank you," I replied. I got the hell out of there as soon as I could.

Why would anyone volunteer themselves for that?

Something was very wrong with me. I loved all kinds of sex with Nell and would do just about anything to get her naked, but this was insanity.

FIVE

NELL

I sat opposite Chloe in Bella Italia, enjoying my lunch hour and a break from The Ogre and his offspring. We had just ordered, and she now had her serious face on. Her amber eyes were distant and dreamlike.

"What gives, Chlo?"

"Logan and I are going to Scotland to look at this gorgeous castle you can get married in, and I wondered if you'd come, too?"

What? "Okay, back up. Scotland?"

"Logan's great grandad was Scottish…apparently."

"So, you want a wedding in Scotland because a member of his family that he's never met was—"

"No, that's not the only reason. I want it to be away, somewhere that's not ten minutes down the road."

"A castle?"

She rolled her eyes. "It's not as princess-y as it sounds. The castle is now a hotel, and you can get married there."

"Hey, it's your wedding. Have it where you want. But you really want me to come on your romantic weekend?"

"Well, I thought Damon could come, too."

"Ah, there it is," I said. I thanked the waiter as he gave us our drinks.

She sipped her Pepsi and then replied, "There what is?"

"You playing Cupid. Neither of us is interested in a relationship, Chloe."

She dropped her straw and held her hands up. "I'm not saying you are. I thought it'd be nice to get away for the weekend. I need your help because, if I leave it to Logan..." She raised her eyebrows. "Yeah. Come on, it'll be great. They have a spa, so we can chill, and Logan and Damon can prop themselves up at the bar."

She didn't really need to sell it to me. If she needed help, I'd be there. Plus, I was all over a dirty weekend with Damon.

"So..."

I nodded. "I'm in, and I'll ask Damon later."

"You seeing him tonight?"

"I'll talk to him tonight, seeing him tomorrow..."

"I'm not judging you, Nell. As long as you're happy, I'm happy."

Seeing straight through her fake smile, I asked, "You don't think I'm happy?"

"I can see you are. I just worry that it won't last, not with the way things are."

"It's been six years, and I've not wanted to marry the guy yet. I think I'll be fine."

"But what about Damon?"

I shrugged. "What about him?"

"What if he wants more?"

No. It was simple. We worked, and our situation worked because we were open about everything. If he wanted more, I'd know. And I'd run like the motherfucking wind.

"He doesn't. We're both completely honest with each other, and if at any point things change, we'll deal with it."

"And by that, you mean, if he wants more, you'll end it?"

I gulped. That was not something I wanted to happen—at all—but we couldn't continue if we wanted different things. "Yeah, I would."

She tilted her head. "Nell..."

"I don't want a relationship. Maybe that makes me a freak or whatever, but I don't."

"It doesn't make you a freak. Just be careful. Casual rarely stays casual forever. Be happy."

I nodded. "Happy is the plan."

Happy was always the plan, and there were moments when I did feel happy, but it seemed to be on a surface-only level. I had fun with Chloe and a lot of fun with Damon, but at the end of the day, I was still alone. People were more than capable of being happy alone though.

So, why do I feel like something is missing? It was *my* choice to stay relationship-free, so I should be satisfied with that. Life was a never-ending shit sandwich.

"Good. So, you're at your mum's tonight?"

"Yep," I said.

I went to my mum's for dinner most weeks. When she wasn't with my dad, things were better between us, and I was happy to go over there. I was making the most of her single stints between the drama.

"You doing your fiancé tonight?"

Rolling her eyes, she smiled and then replied, "Absolutely."

Chloe and I finished lunch, and I returned to work to muddle through the rest of the day, all while wanting to tell my boss what I thought of him before I walked out. I could really have done with a night in, drinking wine and watching mind-numbing TV, but I had to get through dinner with my mum first.

I briefly stopped off at home to change out of my work clothes and into jeans and a knit jumper before heading back out.

"Mum," I called, letting myself into her house.

I could smell something cooking in the kitchen, so I headed there. Mum slammed her mobile phone down on the table and gritted her teeth. She then looked up, and her face softened. We looked a lot alike. We had the same shape face with high cheekbones, green eyes, and black hair. But that was where the similarities ended.

"Nell, baby, I didn't hear you come in," she said, gripping her hair, twisting it around her hand, and shoving it in a large brown hair claw.

"No, you were too busy smashing up your belongings."

She made a disgusted noise at the back of her throat and waved her hand. "Your dad called. Arrogant prick wants to come over tomorrow night."

"Mum…"

"I know, I know. We're not getting back together."

I loved both of my parents, but growing up, they had been a nightmare. They'd first broken up when I was about eight, and since then, they'd been on and off. I didn't want them to get back together. They were better apart.

"Well, I hope not."

"I just said I wasn't. Do you want a drink?"

"I've lost count of the amount of times you've said that. Coke, please."

She opened the fridge to get my drink and replied, "I mean it, Nell."

No part of me believed her at all. The last fourteen years, I'd watched them both break their promises not to get back together.

Sighing, I took the glass from her. "Thanks. So, what's new? Work going okay?"

She worked for a private cleaning firm in town, taking care of rich people's houses. She loved that all she had to do was clean and then come home. Mum didn't want any big responsibilities that usually went with a high-paying job. She was happy to earn just enough. Dad was the same. He drove a lorry for nine hours a day, and when his deliveries were done, he'd go home. I admired that about them, but I wasn't the same. Thank all that was holy I wasn't the same.

"It's fine, it's fine. What about you? That man treating you better?"

I turned my nose up and sat down. "It's bearable. I'll find something else soon."

"You deserve the best, Nelly."

I hated it when she called me Nelly. It left a bad taste in my mouth.

Smiling tightly, I replied, "Thanks. Hey, did you decide to give Dave a chance?"

Dave was someone whom she'd met through a colleague at work. I'd heard all good things, but Mum's one complaint that he was "frightfully boring." Personally, I thought she could do with boring. Drama was way overrated where she was concerned, and I desperately wanted her to meet someone boring and normal, so she'd stay away from her toxic relationship with Dad.

"Oh, I'm way past all of that nonsense."

"Mum, you're forty-seven. I don't think you're quite ready to book the retirement home yet. You deserve happiness. Where's the harm in having coffee with Dave?"

"It wouldn't work out."

I narrowed my eyes. She'd been open to new relationships in the past and had a few dates. The only time she would write a man off straightaway was when she was getting back with Dad.

Why can't they just stay away from each other?

"You don't know that. Don't dismiss someone before you've gotten to know them." *Please just give the man a chance.*

"I'll think about it. How come you're so interested?"

"Perhaps because I want my mum to be happy in a healthy relationship."

"We weren't that bad, Nell," she said, lowering her voice, proving that they had been that bad.

I was stunned that those words had just left her mouth. I felt like a little kid again. My eyes watered. I wanted to leave. *How can she say that? How can she just dismiss what'd happened for all those years?* We had all been unhappy for so long, and here she was, telling me it hadn't been that bad. It had been *horrible.*

I turned away from her, partly because I couldn't bear to look at her and partly because I didn't want her to see me struggling to keep it together. I heard her open the oven, and the definite smell of roast chicken wafted throughout the room.

"Have you spoken to your dad recently?"

Why are we talking about him?

Swallowing hard, I replied, "Um, a couple of days ago. He's apparently calling tonight."

"Hmm, that's good," she said, as if he had barely bothered with me since the first of their many breaks.

I was as close with him as I was with her, and he called me just as much. I really didn't understand the point of being with someone you hated fifty percent of the time.

"Mum, are you okay?"

"I'm fine. Do you want onion gravy or plain?"

"Whatever you want is fine with me. You're distracted."

"I'm just having a long week, that's all."

I didn't believe her. My heart was in my stomach, and I felt sick with worry. They were going to get back together, and as always, there was nothing I could do to change it.

Biting my tongue, I helped her finish up cooking.

There was an atmosphere all through dinner. I could barely eat a thing. I was so concerned. Years might have passed, and I might be an adult now and understand more about their relationship, but I still worried just as much as I had when I was younger.

Mum brushed her fringe off her forehead and smiled. She was still so proud that she didn't have a single grey, and I was amazed. I was surprised I wasn't grey already from stressing about my parents so much.

I couldn't get away fast enough after dessert and helping Mum load the dishwasher. I wanted to shout and scream at her and pray that something I said would actually sink in. I wanted them both to stop being so selfish because I could see where this was going, and I was tired and terrified of it.

Neither of their parents had had good relationships, and they'd copied traits from both, which had led to this mega fuckup.

I wanted to be done, but I hadn't managed to wash my hands of them yet. *What will it take for me to be over it for good?* I knew I couldn't take it each time, but I'd still stay for another round.

"I'll see you soon," I said at the front door, eager to get home. I needed chocolate and a hot bubble bath—and possibly a visit from Damon, but I might even be in too much of a bad mood for that.

"Next week, baby."

Yeah, we'll see.

She'd be back with him by then, and when they were together, I had absolutely no desire to be around them ever again.

"I'll call you," I replied, giving her the best I could under the new circumstances. I wanted to be able to fool myself into thinking I was just overreacting and they'd stay away from each other, but that ship had long sailed. When it came to my parents, ignorance wasn't something I could indulge in anymore.

"I love you."

"Love you, too, Mum." I gave her one last smile and jogged to my car just as it started to drizzle.

Halfway home, my phone rang. Damon's name lit up the screen, and part of the nagging worry at the forefront of my mind vanished.

I pressed Accept and said, "Hey."

"Hey, you left your mum's yet?" he asked. His voice filled my car.

"Yeah, almost home."

"Good, because I'm freezing my balls off on your front step."

I was momentarily thrown. "Huh? Did I miss plans?"

"Nope."

"Then, how come you're outside my house?"

"You said you'd probably be home at eight."

"And you took that as an invitation?"

"No, I knew you were just mentioning it, but then I thought about you driving in one of those little skirts you wear, and I got hard."

I'd blush if I wasn't so used to it. "Damon, I'm not wearing one of my little shirts."

"You are in my head."

"Wow, I'm surprised I'm wearing anything at all in your head."

He laughed, and the sound made my heart race. "Me, too."

Shaking my head, I replied, "Shut up, Damon. I'll see you in a few, and if you're really lucky, I'll warm those balls up."

He groaned right before I hung up.

Apparently, I wasn't getting my evening alone to wallow and worry, but the thought of going home to Damon considerably lifted my mood.

I pulled into my drive ten minutes later, and Damon was sitting on the doorstep. He was definitely the best type of therapy.

SIX

DAMON

My balls had frozen in my boxers by the time Nell pulled into her parking space. She would be fully responsible for warming them up whether she had been joking about it or not.

She got out and lifted an eyebrow. "Stalker."

"I called and told you I was here. How is that stalking?"

"Well, maybe you're just shit at it."

With a cold gust of wind, her black hair whipped over her shoulder. She shivered and unlocked her door.

"Maybe I just got horny."

Looking behind at me, she rolled her eyes. "You definitely got horny. Why else would you be here?"

I closed her door, holding in, *Because I like spending time with you.*

Spending time with her was more than physical. We were friends, and I enjoyed her company.

And I loved the sex.

"Touché. How was your mum's?"

Turning her nose up, she discarded her handbag on the floor and replied, "It was good."

She didn't share much, and there was definitely more to it than what she would ever tell me, but we didn't have a relationship where I could probe and get her to talk. If I pushed, she'd pull. Until she was ready—if she ever would be—I wouldn't be getting through.

I took off my coat and threw it on the chair by the door. "Good."

"Coffee?"

"I'll make it. Why don't you go change into something more comfortable?"

She narrowed those pretty green eyes. "Meaning, *get naked, Nell?*"

"I'm not opposed to that idea, but I thought you'd be more up for this," I replied, pulling my T-shirt over my head and handing it to her. "But if you don't want to let it all hang out..."

She bit her bottom lip. "I will if you will."

I lifted an eyebrow. "Game on, Nell."

My hands went to my jeans before she could move. I wasn't at all worried about her not following through because I knew she would. Nell was body-confident, and it was sexy as fuck. She also wasn't shy around me. Whether that was just who she was or because she felt comfortable with me, I wasn't sure, but I'd take either if it meant I got to view her naked form as much as possible.

Giggling, Nell followed suit and removed her clothes. I watched with hooded eyes as she stared at me and dropped her underwear. I'd never seen anything so perfect as her bare body.

"Nell," I said breathlessly. It hurt to look and not touch.

My body ached to be against hers. My hands longed to caress every inch of her soft skin.

"Are you making that coffee or not?" Her voice was too sweet, too innocent.

I knew what she was up to.

"You don't play fair."

Lifting one shoulder in a lazy shrug, she replied, "I don't know what you're talking about."

"Like fuck you don't."

She was challenging me to sit there and sip coffee while trying not to jump her. My dick was already as hard as steel, and my balls felt like they were going to explode. I wanted her, and I didn't want to wait or play games.

But I also didn't want her to win.

I locked my muscles and forced myself to smile. "Sit down, and I'll bring it through."

Smirking, she nodded and turned around. Her walk to the sofa was slow and seductive. I watched the lines of her delicate form, the curve of her arse and hips sway, and the soft tips of her hair brush against her lower back.

Groaning inwardly, I turned to go into the kitchen and took deep breaths. My plan for tonight was to pounce. I hadn't mentally prepared myself for abstaining for any length of time.

I filled the kettle, flicked on the stove, and tried to think about anything other than Nell being naked.

Nell's naked, Nell's naked, Nell's naked!

I wanted my hands and mouth on her, and I'd only take her after she begged me to.

I was supposed to drop to my knees the second her clothes had come off. She'd turned my plans upside down, and she ended up being the one playing with me.

I was pissed.

Slamming two mugs down on the worktop, I filled each with instant coffee, and then I got the milk out.

"You okay?" she called in that sickly sweet voice.

Fucking woman.

I cleared my throat. "I'm fine. Why don't you find something to watch?"

"Already did," she replied. "I really fancy a chilled evening in front of the TV."

Another dig at me, telling me she was absolutely fine with not having sex. I knew different, of course, but she wouldn't ever acknowledge that. It wasn't part of the game.

Making the coffee, I was stirring so fast that I'd periodically spill it over the worktop. I threw the spoon in the sink. She could wipe the coffee stains off the wooden counter. It was her fault they were there in the first place.

"Here," I said, placing one mug in front of her.

From where she was sitting, she leaned forward to pick up the cup, and her mouth was perfectly lined up with my cock.

Jesus Christ.

If I didn't want to win, I would've slammed my drink down and guided her mouth to where I *really* wanted it. She sat back before I could give in, and she smiled up at me. Nell had perfected her innocent-eyes look, but I wasn't buying it.

Taking a deep breath, I put my drink down and sat beside her. As she shifted on the sofa, tucking her legs under herself, her breasts, not so subtly, pressed against my side.

"We play the most pathetic games, Nell."

"Oh, are we playing?"

I glared. "Don't act cute."

Laughing, she returned her mug to the coffee table and straddled my hips.

"Uh-uh, no way are you claiming a win if I take you now! You can't sit on me and expect me to keep my hands off you."

Her smile stretched, and she wrapped her arms around my neck. "I don't expect anything from you, Damon, other than you supplying me with *a lot* of orgasms."

"Well, I think I can handle that."

Unexpectedly, because she never usually backed down, she covered my mouth with her own and maneuvered her hips, making me slowly sink inside her.

I win.

An hour and a half later, Nell was lying between my legs, sprawled over my chest as we watched *Sons of Anarchy*. I loved the post-sex part just as much as the sex itself. She was usually sated and cuddly—unless she wasn't done with me. Then, she'd just tease and do things to me that would make my eyes roll back into my head.

And post-all-clear test results meant that she was back to doing all the good stuff. The herpes test of Hades was worth it.

She sighed. "The things I'd do to Charlie Hunnam."

"Are they the same things you do to me?"

"Hmm, yes, but I might give him a little extra."

"Whoa, whoa. Back up. That's harsh, Nell. Come on, I'm way better-looking than that guy. Look at his hair; look at how disgusting that is."

Honestly, I couldn't give a fuck about what was on the man's head, but there was no way I was happy that he'd get special treatment.

"I like it, something to grip ahold of."

"What's wrong with my shoulders?"

She laughed, and it stirred something inside. Usually, when we crashed in the last position and began watching TV, that would be the end of the sex marathon for the evening. There was definitely going to be more if she kept moving around on top of me, no matter how minute that movement was.

"There is nothing wrong with your shoulders—besides the scratches."

"I happen to like those scratches."

She giggled. "So do I."

"Are you going to tell me what extras Charlie would get?"

"He'd get a threesome. But I haven't chosen the other guy yet."

Well, there was absolutely no fucking way I would be having a threesome with her. "I'm glad you've reserved that for him."

"You wouldn't?"

"I don't like to share."

She lifted her head off my chest and narrowed her eyes. "How is that not what you're doing?"

I didn't want to think about that.

Nell was single and had every right to see whomever she wanted, whenever she wanted. I had no idea if she did that or how many men she'd slept with since we started seeing each other, and I had no desire to ever find out. In my head, it was zero. For my own sanity, I needed to believe she wasn't getting anything else from another man. I would beat the tosser to a pulp.

"It's not," I replied as I turned away.

She sensed that a conversation about who else we might have shared bodily fluids with was not going to happen and followed my lead by watching Charlie ride a bike.

The first spark of erection number three of the evening had well and truly fizzled out. Thinking of her with another man was almost enough to make the pissing thing fall off altogether. I tried to shove it from my mind, but I couldn't help it. Thoughts of another man being that close to her ate away at me. It wasn't even the sex that bothered me the most. It was the possibility that she could be lying with him the way she was with me. I didn't want anyone else to be this close to her. Ever.

I suddenly found myself royally fucked off. Nell wasn't mine, so I couldn't get angry about something like that. Shit, I'd slept with someone on holiday, so I was being a complete hypocrite. Nell hadn't gotten moody with me for that, so what right did I have? I didn't even know if she'd done anything. This was wholly unreasonable.

She pushed herself up. Her slender arms were on either side of my face. Her hair fanned around us, creating a glossy black curtain of privacy. "I'm hungry again. You want something?"

"Are you going to cook for me?"

She grinned a full, toothy smile. "Well, I'll cook for me, but you can have some, too."

"Whatever you're making is good."

Getting off the sofa, she looked at me over her shoulder while putting on my T-shirt that'd been tossed on the floor. Hot girl in a white T-shirt was just about the best thing.

She blew me a kiss. "Don't get dressed. I'll want some after eating."

"Not gonna argue with that."

The very second she was out of the room, I texted Chloe. It was a bunny-boiler question and not one I even wanted the answer to, but it was driving me insane, and I knew it would constantly eat away at me.

Is Nell seeing anyone else?

Her reply came just minutes later.

Just you. Why?

The *why* was obvious. Chloe was fully aware of how my feelings for Nell had changed and evolved. She was the one telling me to tread carefully but to go for it. I wanted to. We'd be great together, we already were, but Nell was so unapproachable on the subject. If I ever dropped so much as a hint of a hint about relationships in general, she would close up and tell me how lucky we were "not to have to deal with that serious bullshit."

The more time I spent with her, the more I wanted in on the serious bullshit. I wasn't looking for wedding bells or anything like that, but exclusive sounded good, really good.

I replied.

Just needed to know.

Chloe let it go and didn't message back, but that must have been very hard for her. Or Logan had confiscated her phone, so she couldn't grill me further. My money was on the latter.

"Damon, I have no food in!" Nell shouted from the kitchen.

"What do you have?" I asked.

She appeared at the door, holding a sorry-looking apple and a jar of Nutella. "What am I supposed to do with these?"

"Eat the apple, then spread the chocolate over your body, and come back to the sofa."

Glaring, she replied, "I'm ordering Domino's, and it's on you."

See? We were pretty much in a relationship already. Very little would actually change if we gave ourselves a title. Without it though, she was safe and unthreatened. When I found out what that was all about, I was going to squash it.

Nell ordered a pizza for us to share since we'd both already eaten. She made me get dressed to answer the door, and then I had to remove my clothes the second it was shut again. We lounged around, eating and touching. When we finished eating, Nell lay back down on the sofa—this time, with her legs over my lap.

"No one thinks this," she said, gesturing between us, "will work. Apparently, casual never stays casual."

"By no one, you mean, Chloe?" I asked. *Where is this coming from? Did Chloe text her after speaking to me?*

Nell scoffed. "Yeah, my sucky best friend."

"She's just trying to look out for you."

"I know that. God, I never realised how annoying it was to have someone looking out for you. Bet she was pissed off at me when I was trying to get her to stop caring about what people thought of her being with Logan."

"You know she was. Now, are you climbing back aboard or what?"

Her dark eyebrow rose. "Maybe I don't want to."

"So, you made me remove my clothes again for no reason?" I was hard again, and I needed her mouth frantically attacking mine while I fucked her into the sofa.

"No, I made you remove them to screw."

"You're such a romantic, Nell."

"Damon Masters wants romance?"

"That depends."

"On what?"

I grinned. "If it'll lead to me getting at least a blowie."

"Wow, you're so charming and so smooth."

"I'm honest."

"Yes, you definitely are that."

Neither of us was ready for anything heavy, like proposals or moving in, but I did want more than what we had. I, at the very least, wanted to know for certain that Nell was sleeping with only me. The rest could come later.

The only issue with that was Nell. I wasn't sure if she wanted a relationship at all. The thought was terrifying because that could only end in disaster. We couldn't keep doing this if the fundamental parts of our relationship changed.

"Seriously though, Nell, don't let it bother you. We're good, and we're not hurting anyone."

"That's what I think, too."

"Good. So, are you climbing on?"

Laughing, she launched herself up and landed on my lap. I groaned, immediately taking her mouth and pulling her body flush with mine.

SEVEN

DAMON

After a full week at work and spending most nights with Nell, I was ready for the weekend. She'd been more demanding, which I loved, but it'd also left me with some serious withdrawals. This weekend, I was visiting family and would have to go two nights cold turkey. I'd started to rely on seeing her though, and that was dangerous territory. We were supposed to make each other's world pleasurable, not be each other's world.

The drive was mostly motorways, so I was able to open the car up a bit and just focus on the road. The weekend was going to be relaxed, and although I didn't really want it to be, it was exactly what I needed.

I always loved going back to my parents' place. It was just over two hours away, so I didn't get to do it often. I missed my family and friends back home. Moving away from the small town was the best decision, but it was good to go back. Plus, my mum would do my washing.

I pulled up to the house and opened the door when my mum ran out like a maniac.

"Damon!" Mum cried, hurtling toward my car.

I leaped out in time to be tackled in an unnecessarily huge hug.

"Hey, Mum."

"I've missed you. Don't you dare leave visits so long again!"

It'd been five weeks.

"I won't. I missed you, too. If you let go, we can get inside and properly catch up."

"Ah, yes. Stephanie is here."

"All right."

Stephanie was a friend from high school. We had gone on a few dates and tried the more-than-friends thing, but it hadn't worked out. I hadn't been feeling it, and I was pretty sure she hadn't either. She hadn't seemed that upset when I broke things off, so she couldn't have been too cut up.

"She's still single, you know."

I slung my arm over Mum's shoulder and locked my car. "Thanks for the heads-up, but that's not going to happen."

"Oh? Because of Nell?"

A few months ago, I'd made a monumental mistake of mentioning Nell to my mother, and now, she was all over it, wanting to meet her and get to know her. But because nothing had happened, she was getting impatient. I had no idea why she was so desperate to marry me off. I didn't even live with her anymore.

"Mum…"

"Don't *Mum* me. You can't mention a girl and have that be the end of it."

"Yes, I can," I said, closing the front door behind us. "Right now, Nell's just a friend, and I don't know if it will go anywhere. When I know, I'll tell you."

She sighed and nodded toward the conservatory. "Everyone's in there. I'm just going to put another pot of tea on."

"All right," I replied, heading out the back.

Sure enough, Stephanie had planted herself right between my dad and grandparents. Her mum was here, too. We'd known her family for years, and my mum and hers had grown close after the death of Stephanie's dad when she was seven.

I'd always known that, deep down, Mum would love for me to be with Stephanie, but she'd never force it. I also knew that the second she met Nell, she'd understand why Stephanie wasn't an option for me.

"Hey," I said, moving farther into the room.

Dad was up first, followed by my sister, Cara, and then Stephanie and her mum, Greta.

"Hi, son. How was the drive?" Dad asked.

I gave him a quick hug. "It was fine. Hey, Cara. How's school?"

"I hate it," she replied, occasionally glancing up from her phone so that she wouldn't walk into something.

Cara was eighteen and addicted to her mobile phone. She was studying hard and planned on attending university in September.

"Hey, I'm so glad we could make it over the same weekend you're home," Stephanie said, leaning in for a hug.

"Yeah, me, too. It's been a while, huh?" I took a step back. "We should hit the bar tonight and see who's around."

"Sounds good, but your mum has this big meal planned."

Great. "Beers here then."

"Absolutely." Steph's blonde hair was considerably shorter now and quite choppy. It used to be long, but now, it was above her shoulders. It suited her. Her eyes were pale green, the opposite of Nell's striking colour.

Jesus, I had to stop thinking about Nell. She drove me crazy, even when she wasn't around. Something was going to end badly there. Every day, I would think about her more and more.

We settled down with the first of many mugs of tea my mother would make. I thought she genuinely believed the hot drink could solve all. I stayed with Stephanie, catching up on what I'd missed from the last eight months or however long it'd been since I saw her last.

"So, you're loving your job? Your mum mentioned you have the chance at co-running the place."

"I love it, but I'm a little ways off from buying into the business. I'm not sure if that's the direction I want to go in yet. I might get more experience and go it alone a few years down the road."

"Wow, that's exciting."

"You'd know. How is the new line?"

Stephanie had always been into fashion, and from the age of fourteen, she'd made all her own clothes. Some of her designs were in local independent shops and boutiques, and she also sold them on her website.

"It's fantastic! Next week, I'm meeting with a rep from ASOS. I love every second of it."

I made an appropriately surprised and impressed face. *What the fuck is ASOS?*

"I'm sure they'll love your designs."

She bit the side of her lip. "I really hope so. Enough about me. How are things with you?"

That felt like an are-you-single question.

"Things are going good. I'll be moving into a new place next month. Now that I'm working full-time, I can afford somewhere nicer and closer to work."

"That's good. It's my plan, too, but Mum has a huge house, and I need a lot of space for stock and dressmaking. Hopefully, things will really take off, and I'll be able to afford to buy my own place."

"It'll happen."

She nodded. "So, do you keep in touch with anyone from school?"

"Not really. I keep up with everyone on Facebook, but you're about the only person I properly talk to still." I kept more in touch with the people I'd met at university than high school.

"Yeah, me, too. We should make a bigger effort to catch up more often. It's been far too long."

"I know, but living two hours away makes it difficult. We'll try harder though," I said.

Growing up, Stephanie, Lance, and I had played out a lot together since we were the only kids on our street.

My phone rang in my pocket, giving me the opportunity to slip away for a second. "Sorry, I'll be back in a second."

"Of course," Stephanie said, turning away and heading for Cara.

"Hey," I said, stepping to the side so that I'd actually be able to hear Nell.

"Hey, are you having a nice time back home?"

"Yeah, it's good. What's up?"

"Okay, this is going to sound weird, but I'm just going to come right out and ask. Chloe and Logan are going to Scotland to look at a wedding venue, and she wants me to go, too. No way I'm going to be stuck with the lovebirds for two nights though, so do you want to come with?"

Finally! Chloe had told me about that a week ago. I had started to think that Nell wasn't going to ask.

"Sure, I'm in. When is it?"

"Next month. It's going to be absolutely freezing."

Turning away, I muttered quietly down the phone, "I'll keep you warm."

"I'm sure you will. So, you want to share a room?"

"Nell," I said. I laughed. There was no point in dignifying that with a reply.

"Right. Okay, stupid question. I'll go and tell Chloe we're in and let you get back to your family time."

"I'll see you tomorrow night," I said.

"Do we have plans?"

"We do now. Bye."

I hung up and noticed Mum had caught me saying Nell's name. She watched me with a giddy smile.

"What, Mum?"

"How is she?"

"She's fine."

"Perhaps one weekend you could bring her with you?"

I would love that, but I doubted it would happen anytime soon.

"Maybe," I replied.

Mum scowled and went back to talking with Greta.

"You never mentioned a girlfriend. How long have you been together?" Stephanie asked.

"We're not together. Me and Nell are…" *Now, how do I explain fuck buddies nicely so that my mother won't be disgusted if she overhears?*

Turned out, I didn't need to.

Stephanie's eyes widened with understanding. "Oh, I get it."

"Yeah, we're *friends*."

"You're not happy about that?"

"No, I am. I'm cool with being friends and seeing how things go, but somewhere down the line, I'm going to want more."

She ran her index finger around the rim of her almost empty wine glass.

When did we move on to alcohol?

"And Nell?" she asked.

Sitting down, I took a deep breath. "Nell is complicated. She's sure that she doesn't ever want a relationship, and I know a lot of people say that about all sorts of different things, but she's so determined that I'm not convinced she'll change her mind."

"What if she doesn't?"

"Well, I'm not going to have half of a relationship forever."

"Maybe she just needs time. You're both still young. I assume she's our age?"

"Yeah, she is. Time is all I've got."

"I hope things work out for you, Damon. You deserve to have everything you want."

"Glad you think that because, right now, I'd like to get drunk in my mother's kitchen. Want a top up?"

She laughed and nodded. "Definitely, and I think you moving on to beer now will do the trick."

Fucking right.

EIGHT

NELL

Damon was at his parents' house, and a girl was there. I'd heard her on the phone. And I wanted to rip her hair out, strand by strand, with my bare hands. Damon and I weren't together in any real way, but I selfishly thought of him as mine. A random on a night out or holiday was nothing; he'd never see them again. A girl from home was a whole different story.

Chloe and I sat in a bar, drinking cocktails.

"Who do you think she is?" I asked.

Obsessing. Yep, I'm obsessing. It was irrational and downright annoying, but I was.

She rolled her amber eyes. "I think she's a friend of his from back home."

"Yes, of course she is! We fucking know that, Chloe, but a shagging friend or a non-shagging friend?"

Laughing, she folded her arms on the table. "Um, shagging probably. Yeah, definitely shagging."

I narrowed my eyes at her and wanted to throw up all over her nice new dress. The cow had said that on purpose.

"No." *That's not it.* Shaking my head, I replied, "No, I don't think so."

"Oh, really? Why's that?" she asked, grinning wide and clearly loving every second of this.

What is there to love? What kind of a backward best friend enjoys things like this?

"I just don't think she is. He would've said something to give it away even if he didn't mean to. She's just an old school friend who's also a friend of the family."

She shrugged. "Okay."

"Do you even understand how annoying you're being right now?"

She grinned again. "Uh-huh. Sorry, but I'm *really* enjoying this. I didn't think I'd ever see you get all worked up about a guy."

I held my finger up. "I am not getting worked up." I was. "I just want to know if I need to demand he goes for another sexual health screening."

"And do you actually believe that?" She did a double take. "Wait, another one?"

"Never mind. He's clear, and I hate you."

"No, you don't."

Yes, I bloody do.

I clapped my hands together. "I vote that we get me shitfaced tonight."

"She's just a friend, Nell."

"Good for him. It doesn't matter what he does. My desire to get drunk has nothing to do with Damon and his little friend."

She raised one eyebrow.

"Fuck off. I don't care what he does."

Wisely, she didn't say anything, but the little cow didn't need to because, this time, both perfect eyebrows rose. The thin strips of hair on her face told me exactly what she was thinking. *It does matter.*

Deep, deep down, I knew that it did, but I couldn't let feelings like that bubble to the surface. It was dangerous, and the last thing in the world I wanted when it came to a man was danger.

"Have you decided what dress you want me to wear for the wedding? Nothing puffy, *please.*"

Laughing, she slumped back in the seat and pouted. "But I've seen this gorgeous peach floral dress with the most adorable ruffles and lace edging."

"I would wear it, Chloe, but I would never forget it. Remember, with you being the first one to get married, you are setting the precedent for how I'll choose your bridesmaid dress." I wanted to add, *If I ever get married*, but that would only make her talk at me about how stupid I was being.

"You know I wouldn't. I'll have to steal you away from Damon to try some on."

"Hos over bros, Chlo-Chlo; you know that. Name a date, and I'll be there. You've probably not got long…"

Her eyes widened. "Don't I know it? Logan wants to do it as soon as possible, and so do I, but he's not the one organising everything. There's so much to do. I feel like I'm already going crazy."

"You're a wedding planner," I said dryly.

"Yeah, I know. That's what I thought, too. *Oh, it'll be easy because I do this for a living.* Not so bloody easy actually!"

"Have a drink. I'll help wherever I can. Do you honestly think she's just a friend?"

Chloe started laughing. "Oh, you don't care at all, huh? Open up, and let him in, Nell. I have a feeling you'll be so much happier when you do."

"To start with, maybe."

My parents had been great at first. I was young when things had been all happy with dancing unicorns and glitter, but then it'd changed. I wasn't confident enough that Damon and I wouldn't change the way they had.

"What does that mean? Come on, talk to me. You've said a million times that we can discuss anything. What can't you tell me?"

What I didn't want to tell her wasn't going to be spit out over drinks in a bar. I didn't ever want to talk about it. I liked that she only knew the mostly strong Nell. Having someone know how messed up my head would get sometimes made me feel sick.

"Look, both sets of my grandparents had a lot of issues, and my parents did, too. I'm not willing to go down that road. Love can be so fickle. You only have to watch *The Jeremy Kyle Show* to know that. People who were once madly in love can turn against each other. I'd rather not do that, especially with Damon. We're friends, and I like having him around. Why would I want a relationship to screw that up?"

"What if it didn't?"

I shook my head. "I don't think I can do that." It was too risky. "Anyway, you absolutely suck at getting me drunk."

She took my conversation change the way she was supposed to, and she shut up about my relationship quirkiness. *Ha, I bet she'd put it differently.*

"All right, prepare to wake up with a mouth drier than a desert and a marching band in your head," she said, shuffling out of the booth and heading to the bar.

Oh, well. At least then, I'll have something to do tomorrow. Spending the day dying with my head over the toilet would take my mind off my absent *special* friend.

When Chloe returned, I raised my glass. "To spending tomorrow feeling like I just deep-throated a cactus."

Two shots and three cocktails later, I was off my face, and Chloe was trying to keep me under control. Once or twice, the staff had looked over when I laughed a little too loudly or stumbled my way to and from the bathroom.

"Honestly, you get a little tipsy, and everyone thinks you're crazy," I said, dropping myself back in the booth.

"Probably because you can't walk in a straight line, and your skirt is tucked into your knickers."

I should've been embarrassed, but I burst out laughing. I had a fairly decent arse.

Ripping my skirt out of the material of my French knickers, I shook my head. "Whoops."

"The old man at the bar got a real good look," she said, laughing along with me.

Brilliant. I would be an old man's wanking material tonight.

I did notice how my *best friend* had let me walk the entire length of the room rather than rushing to my aid and covering my bare arse.

"I think I'm done tonight, Chloe. When the whole bar sees your backside, it's time to call it a night."

"All right, let's get you home. Wait there until I come around. I'll make sure you're fully dressed before you stand up."

"Oh, now, you want to protect my dignity. You're a little too late for that tonight, *sweetheart*."

She smiled as I used Logan's pet name for her. It was cute. It'd started out with him calling everyone sweetheart, but the more he had fallen in love with her, the less he used it for anyone else.

God, they make me sick.

Chloe helped me up, out, and home. She was an angel.

"I love you," I said to my best friend. The alcohol had made me feel warm and fuzzy and in need of telling everyone how incredible they were.

She laughed as she carried me into my bedroom. "Love you, too."

"Chlo-Chlo, I'm going to be hungover for dinner with my mum tomorrow, aren't I?"

"Yes, honey. Probably the day after that as well."

I groaned and gripped my head. "I don't want it for that long. Call Logan. He's a health and fitness freak—for which we all thank him, especially when his top comes off. He'll know some magic anti-hangover cure."

Instead of punching me for admitting that I perved on her fiancé, she laughed and rolled her eyes. "He would tell me to give you water and get you to go to sleep. I don't think you'll have any difficulty with the sleep part."

Neither did I. Every step took monumental effort that I just didn't have in me anymore.

"I'm not thirsty." *Christ, I've just drunk an entire bar.*

"That's not the point," she said as she launched me onto my bed.

I bounced and rolled onto my back, watching the world take a second to catch up.

"You need to hydrate your body, so please stay awake long enough for me to get a glass of water down your throat."

I saluted. "Yes, boss."

Shaking her head in pure amusement, Chloe left my room in search of water. If my body wasn't so heavy and if I had a clue as to where my phone was, I'd call Damon. I wanted to hear his voice whisper unspeakable things to me.

I looked around and saw that Chloe had dropped my bag on the bed, too. I extended my arm, but it was just out of reach. Things had started to swim, and I knew it would only get worse if I moved. My late-night drunken call to Damon seemed as impossible as me having a clear head in the morning.

"What are you doing?" she asked.

She laughed at me as I wiggled my fingers, willing my handbag to come closer.

"Want my phone," I replied.

"That a good idea?"

"Why wouldn't it be?"

"Because doing anything on your phone when you've had eight too many is never a good idea."

"*Ooh*," I said, pointing at her, "you're totally right! Rule one is never use a phone while drunk. Rookie mistake."

"Okay, sweetie, sit up, so you can drink this."

I pushed myself up onto my elbows and waited for the sea-like motion to stop before I fully stayed up. "Thanks," I said, taking the glass. I drained every drop.

"Good girl. Now, do you need help getting changed?"

"Yeah, I can't sleep in my bra."

She laughed. "And your dress, earrings, and shoes?"

"Bra more," I replied, tugging the hem of my dress.

Chloe pulled me to my feet and assisted with getting me undressed and into some pyjamas.

"Now, into bed."

I did as I had been told and snuggled under my quilt. "Chloe?"

"Yeah?"

"She's just a friend, right?"

Chloe sighed and brushed my hair behind my shoulder, so it wasn't falling in my face. "Of course she is. Get some sleep, Nell. You're going to feel like shit in the morning."

"Thanks for looking after me. Sorry I got drunk."

"No, you're not. You asked me to get you drunk."

"You're right. I'm not sorry, but I am grateful for you."

"Anytime. Love you."

She kissed my forehead, and I was drifting by the time she closed my bedroom door.

When I turned up at Mum's for our biweekly dinner, Dad's car was in the drive. My heart fell right down to my feet. Disappointment fizzled in my veins, but I wasn't surprised. I was never surprised, but today, I was too hungover to deal with it. *How many times will they do this?*

Damon had picked a bad weekend to go away. I needed something physical and exhausting to get my mind off of what was undoubtedly going on here. With shaking hands, I grabbed a packet of paracetamol from my bag and popped a couple.

Pulling myself together and praying the painkillers would kick in soon, I blinked the first signs of tears away and got out of the car. Years ago, I'd reached my limit of anger when it came to my parents and their actions, so even though I wanted to scream at them, I knew it would be pointless.

I walked in and found them in the kitchen. Mum was stirring gravy, and Dad was smiling at her from the other side of the island. Dad spotted me first and pushed away from the marble worktop. Seeing them, combined with the hangover, doubled the churning in my stomach.

"There's my little Nelly," he said, rounding the island to give me a hug.

"Sweetie," Mum said, hugging me next.

"Hi," I replied tightly.

I just needed to get through the next few hours, and then I could go home to normality. It'd be a miracle if they didn't bicker or argue over dinner.

"What's going on?" I asked. It was a stupid question and one I'd asked so many times that I'd lost count.

Dad smiled the same way he did every time, like the cat that had gotten the cream. "We've decided to give things another go. I love your mum, Nell, and we're both determined to make it work."

I wanted to whack them around their heads with the boiling gravy pan. "What makes you think it'll work this time?"

"Nell," Mum said, her tone warning.

"No, love, Nell has a right to ask questions. There's never been anyone else for me other than your mum. You know that."

I understood that perfectly. I could also respect it. But that didn't mean they should be together. If there were ever two people who should stay away from each other—preferably by one of them moving to Australia—it was my parents.

"Right," I replied. "Well, let's hope it doesn't end the same as it has before." *Dozens of times before.*

"It won't," Mum said.

She always sounded so sure, and I had no idea how she could after going round in circles for such a long time.

"Now, would you like a glass of wine with dinner? It won't be long. You can have one, right?"

"Sure. That'd be great." Keeping the disappointment from my voice was so difficult.

"Could you get it, please? I need to stir," Mum said to Dad. Then, she went back to making her fucking gravy.

I sat down and watched the picture-perfect scene in front of me with tears in my eyes.

After dinner, Dad went into the living room, so he could catch the second half of the game, and I stayed back to help Mum clean up.

"I know what you're thinking," she said, vigorously wiping the table.

"Yep, so there's no reason we need to talk about it."

"There is if you're going to give me the cold shoulder."

"I'm not. Under the circumstances, I think I've been very civil."

She dropped the cloth on the table and straightened her back. "Things are different this time, Nell. We're both trying hard to get along and talk about our problems before they turn into screaming matches."

I'd only heard that about a million times before. I wondered if she still believed it. *She can't, surely?*

"Really? What's so different this time, Mum?"

"We've been apart for the longest period of time. We've both done some growing, and we want to make it work. We're trying so hard, and Dad's even suggested we see someone."

My eyebrows shot up in surprise. That was a new development. Dad wasn't someone who spoke about his problems to anyone. Still, I wasn't at all convinced that they'd make it work. Until I saw it, I was one hundred percent sceptical. They clashed in the worst way, and unless one of them had had a personality transplant, I didn't think even a therapist would be able to help them sort it out. Some people just shouldn't be together.

Rubbing my head, I groaned. *Why are they doing this all over again?* I just felt so done with it all. I was fed up with the same cycle over and over again. In a few months' time, they would break up and announce they hated each other and that the other one was the worst person in the world, and I'd be back to listening to them bitch about how they should have never put the effort in, only to get nothing back.

Same shit every single time.

"Fine, Mum. You know how I feel. I'll never want you two to be together, but there's never been anything I could do about it."

"Oh, don't be like that. Most kids want their parents to be together."

"Well, thankfully, most kids didn't grow up with you and Dad."

"Hey," she snapped. "I know you're not happy about it, but there's no need to go around, saying hurtful things like that. You don't understand our marriage."

No, she *doesn't understand marriage.*

I held my hands up. "I don't want to argue with you."

"Neither do I, love. Can't you just try to be happy for us?"

Nope, no way.

"I'll pray for the best. That's all I can give you."

"Nelly, have a little faith. This time, we'll make it work. We're older and wiser and all that." She turned back and continued wiping the table.

They had gotten older, but when it came to each other, they'd never been wise.

I helped Mum clean up, and then I made a quick exit. The drive home was horrible. I was in one of the worst moods I'd felt, in a long time.

If Damon were on my doorstep now, I'd tell him to fuck off. The whole stupid world could bugger off. People were idiotic, and I'd never wanted to run away to a remote island more.

Screw work tomorrow.

The second I got inside, I was going to open a bottle of white wine and down the lot.

Thankfully for us both, Damon wasn't waiting for me when I got home. He was probably still at his parents'.

Mum tried calling, but I ignored it in favour of pouring wine right to the top of the glass. My phone vibrated two minutes later, and Dad's name showed up. It looked like she'd told him about our conversation.

I gulped the wine, wincing at the same time.

My phone rang for a third time, and I was just about to launch it at the wall when I noticed it was Chloe's name on the screen. I wasn't really in the mood to talk to her either, but I knew if I didn't answer, she'd only worry, and then she might come over.

"Hey," I said.

"Hey. How are you?"

I'm drowning my sorrows. "Fine. You?"

"Good. Logan's working late tonight, so I'm watching chick flicks and eating chocolate. How was dinner with your mum?"

I snorted. "It turned into dinner with Mum and Dad."

"They're back together?" she asked.

"Yep."

Chloe knew better than anyone else how toxic my parents' relationship was, but she didn't know just how bad things had gotten. I didn't want her to.

"Wow. Can't say I'm surprised. Are you all right about it?"

"Nothing I can do. They're adults…apparently."

"Sorry, hon. Do you want me to come over?"

"Nah, I'm good. Might have an early night."

"Are you sure?"

"Yeah. Thanks though. Call you tomorrow."

We hung up as I dropped onto the sofa. I clenched my jaw and managed to keep my tears at bay for another ten seconds before I broke down.

NINE

NELL

I was in a shit mood, and it was all thanks to my parents. After they'd been split up for a while, I'd stupidly gotten complacent with the feeling of peace. Now, they were back together, and a pit of worry the size of the Grand Canyon weighed heavily in my stomach.

Groaning at the shrill ring of the alarm on my phone, I tapped snooze and covered my eyes with my arms. Sleep hadn't come until the early hours, which did not help. I wanted to redo today already, and I hadn't even left the bed yet.

My mattress was too comfortable, and I had absolutely no motivation whatsoever, so I lay awake in bed until the alarm went off another three times. Then, I had to get up, or I could add being late to work to the list of why today was shit.

I sat up and rubbed my eyes, hating days when I felt like this. They weren't often, but when I felt crap, all I wanted to do was hide away. *Good fuckin' luck to anyone who pisses me off today.*

Grabbing clean underwear and a cream shift dress from my wardrobe, I made my way into the bathroom to get ready.

I'd lain in too late to shower, so dry shampoo was going to have to rescue my hair. I couldn't care less. Holding my long, heavy hair up the best I could, I sprayed the shampoo into the roots, massaged it in, and brushed it. I pinned the front back with slides because I was in no mood to keep pushing it out of my eyes.

I managed to get dressed and do my makeup in time to grab something quick for breakfast—a bowl of cereal and a much-needed coffee. It was almost eight in the morning, and the text message tone went off on my mobile. I knew who it'd be.

Damon clearly wanted to get an early start on the flirting today. Hopefully, it would lift my mood. I waited until I was sitting at the table with breakfast before I opened it, so I wouldn't get distracted.

Our contact over the weekend had been minimal, and I was relieved to have it get back to normal now. I'd tried not to think about his lack of communication being due to the whore he was with. Shaking my head, I resisted the urge to be pathetic and hit myself. Here I was, hating a woman for doing absolutely nothing wrong.

Nice one, Nell. That didn't make me a crazy person at all…

> *Woke up with painful, massive morning wood. Now going to have a cold shower and think of you.*

Shaking my head and smiling at his text, I replied.

> *If only you were here…*

I could do with cheering up, and I knew Damon's body would be able to do that. Even just a text made me feel better and took my mind off all the other crap going on.

He replied seconds later.

> *Fuck's sake, Nell!*

Laughing, I inhaled my food and gulped down the coffee.

The fact that he could cheer me up pissed me off a little. *Shit, I'm such a melodramatic little bitch today.* I should be happy that someone could make me feel better, but no, not me—not completely anyway.

What have I turned into?

If Chloe were here, I'd ask her to slap me even though she'd probably think this was great and offer a high five. If she did that, then she'd be the one getting the slap.

I need help.

Leaving my empty mug on the table, I slipped off the stool and rushed out the door, grabbing my bag as I went past. I was running late, and I knew Reg would be pissed, but he could do one. I had many, many more things to worry about than my arsehole boss.

Driving like a fucking maniac and running like an Olympian meant I managed to make it to work just three minutes late.

Harry cocked his eyebrow as I burst through the door. It took every ounce of willpower not to stick my middle finger up at him.

"Sorry I'm late," I said, not bothering to offer an explanation.

"That's not the first time, Nell," he said, blatantly talking to my boobs.

I stuck my chest out, making him aware that I knew what he was up to and also hoping it would keep him from being a twat about my lateness. *Three-minute lateness.*

Harry—a guy not that much older than me—cleared his throat and finally looked up. "Just see that it doesn't happen again."

I smiled sweetly. "Of course. I'm so sorry."

If the guy didn't pick up on the sarcasm dripping from my words, there was no hope for him at all.

"I'll have a coffee, and then you can come to my office." He smirked and walked off.

Fuck. Have I just led him on? If I walked into his office and he was naked, I would flip out.

My first stop was my office to wake up my computer and put my bag under my desk. My tiny office was depressing and plain. But it could be painted all the colours of the rainbow, and I would still think that. This was the last place on earth I wanted to spend five days a week, but a girl needed shoes and wine, so I had little choice.

I passed the gossiping accounting girls standing along the corridor to the kitchen. I had been late, but they hadn't started work either. If I could handle falling back ten years, I would've pointed it out, but I should probably practice a little more maturity than that. *Probably.*

"Morning," I said.

They replied and turned straight back to their conversation. One-on-one, they were great, but in a group, they turned a bit clique-y. I was having absolutely nothing to do with that. The only girl I liked was Chloe. Logan's sister, Cassie, was cool, too, but we didn't see a whole lot of each other.

I struggled through the morning, feeling rubbish because I'd been shouted at and ordered about by my arsehole of a boss. Lunch couldn't have come soon enough, and I didn't even care that I was eating alone in a restaurant, looking like a proper saddo. I was out of the office for an hour, and that was all that mattered.

My phone rang just as I finished my sandwich. "Damon," I said, trying to sound more cheerful than I felt.

"What colour is your underwear?"

Rolling my eyes, I took a sip of my coffee. "You have an unhealthy interest in the colour of my underwear."

"And an even unhealthier one in what's under it."

"Do you want something, Damon? I don't think I have enough time for a quickie."

My voice was much too loud for an unusually quiet coffee shop, and no less than four people looked up. The young man in the smart pinstripe suit gave me more attention than necessary. If he thought I would have a quickie with him, he was going to be disappointed.

"Christ, people are watching," I muttered into the phone. *Why do I continue to answer his calls in public?*

Damon laughed, as I'd thought he would. "Let's step this up."

"Let's not!"

I'd like to think that if he were here, he would stop, but he absolutely wouldn't. Now, I didn't care what people thought of me, but Damon didn't care on a whole different level.

"Seriously, what do you want?" I asked.

He laughed again and replied, "I just wanted to see if we're still on for tonight."

"We are. Chloe and Logan are meeting us at the restaurant, so we can get together after work and go tomorrow if you want."

"Yeah, sure. I'll come by and pick you up."

"Okay."

"You are okay?"

I frowned, my heart speeding up. "Yeah. Why?"

There was a pause that I didn't like at all.

He cleared his throat. "You just seem different, quieter. I don't know."

"The entire coffee shop doesn't think so."

"Nell."

"Yes?"

Sighing, he said, "Is everything okay? We can talk about that, right?"

No, we couldn't talk about the really personal stuff. That was for couples, and we weren't a couple.

"Everything's fine, Damon. It's just my boss and his son. You know what arses they can be."

"Those jumped-up little pricks will only be sorry when you're gone. When are you thinking about changing jobs?"

I snorted. "About three months ago. I'm going to look into it soon."

"Okay, well, if you need any help…"

My eye twitched. I rarely asked anyone for help, and I hated it when it was randomly offered. People thinking I needed help made me feel weak.

"Thanks," I bit out, "but I'm fine."

"All right."

Sighing, I asked, "So, how was your weekend?"

He instantly brightened, and it'd better not be because of the girl. "It was good. Nice to catch up with the family. What did you do?"

"Got drunk with Chloe, showed the world my underwear, and then went to dinner at my mum's." *I've had the worst day in a long time.*

"Right. How drunk were you?" he asked.

I could hear amusement and concern in his voice and knew he was fishing to find out if I'd gone home with anyone.

"I remember getting to the bar and waking up in the morning, so I'm going with considerably drunk. It was a good night though. I think."

"I've not seen you drunk for too long."

"We'll rectify that soon. Anyway, I'd better go and eat. I'll see you after work, okay?"

"Yeah, see you later, Nell."

I hung up and picked at a slice of lemon cake for the next half an hour, and I pretended it was normal that Damon hadn't sent me a follow-on dirty text. I'd usually get one if we spoke during my lunch break, especially if he mentioned sex or my underwear. He probably realised that he'd made me feel uncomfortable with his offer of help, which was going to make seeing him later awkward.

I grabbed my handbag and headed out the door. A relationship wasn't something I wanted because of the drama, responsibility, work, and the fact that it would probably all go to hell, but I felt like all of that was exactly what I already had with Damon. Our casual relationship was turning into something it shouldn't be, and I didn't know how long I could ignore that for.

Back at my desk, I started filing a pile of invoices; it had somehow become my job.

Damon started texting, and it went on throughout the rest of the afternoon, but my mind wasn't in it, no matter how rude the messages were. After a while, he gave up, and I couldn't blame him. I was determined not to let him think I was a moody bitch and cancel on me, so as soon as The Ogre and his son left—early as usual—I did, too.

Damon's work wasn't far from mine, so it didn't take me long to drive there. Plus, by leaving early, I'd missed rush hour. His building was much fancier than the run-down one I worked in. But then he didn't work for shits either.

"Can I help you?" a pair of breasts attached to a human asked.

If they were real, I was going to kill myself.

"I'm looking for Damon Masters."

She smiled. "Down the hall and second door on the right."

"Thank you."

I walked up the corridor and stopped just before Damon's office. There was a half wall of glass, which gave me a great opportunity to perv on him in his suit. He oozed importance and professionalism. It was a major turn-on. Also, he was wearing a suit. I fucking loved him in a suit.

Feeling warm in all the right places, I sighed and walked in.

TEN

DAMON

Something was up with Nell, and it bothered me that she wouldn't talk about it—not that she really talked about anything of depth. The things that affected her were reserved just for her.

I looked at the time on my monitor. It was 4:58. Thank fuck for that.

Nell would be meeting me here, so we could go to dinner with Chloe and Logan and then back to her place for the night. The back-to-her-place part of the evening couldn't come soon enough.

Whatever I was doing at work, no matter how absorbed I was in a job, she would still be on my mind. Her big green eyes constantly stared back at me. Every time I scribbled something down with black ink, I'd think of her long dark hair. I was a pathetic moron.

"Hey." Nell's unexpected voice carried through my office, sending a thrill right to my dick.

I looked over my monitor and couldn't help but suck in a deep breath. She was absolutely stunning. Her hair hung down around her in black waves. She was still dressed from work in a cream dress that showed off those legs. Her lips were bright red, and I prayed on all that was holy that she had on underwear to match it.

"Hey, you're early."

She walked in, looking around. My office was a decent size with a large desk, bookshelf, seating area, Nespresso machine, and coffee table for meeting with clients. It was light, open, modern and probably much more than I deserved, considering my short time with the company and the fact that I was right out of uni.

"Yeah, Reg and Harry left, so we all did, too. Your office is amazing. Mine looks like a shoebox compared to this."

The people she worked for were pricks. Nell was smart, independent, resourceful, had a shrewd head for business and great vision, but she was also stubborn. She could get a job with me anytime. The company was forward-thinking and believed in investing in people. They would create a job for someone who could take the company to new places. Rich, my manager, had created mine, and now, he wanted me to go into business with him.

But when I'd suggested she speak to the owner and make an appointment with him, she'd turned me down. I had a lot of respect for her wanting to do it alone, but it just seemed crazy to pass up on good opportunities because of who'd recommended them.

"Rich," I called as he walked past my office.

He stopped and came in, scratching his head.

"Everything okay?" I asked.

"Yeah, just on my way to a late meeting."

"Oh, sorry. I won't keep you."

He looked at Nell and said, "No, it's fine."

"Rich, this is Nell Presley. Nell, this is my manager, Rich."

They shook hands.

"It's a pleasure to meet you, Nell."

"You, too," she replied, dropping her hand to point at me with her thumb. "So, you're the one who employed him?"

Rich threw his head back and laughed. "That was me. Best thing I ever did, too. Got great vision and creativity, that one. He's one of the greatest."

I cleared my throat. "One of?"

He winked and touched Nell's arm. I felt a bolt of possessiveness and jealousy. Fucking hell, he'd only touched her. He wasn't asking for a shag.

"I'm hoping I'll be able to rename the company to Brown and Masters soon enough."

"Wow, you two as a team would certainly take the advertising world by storm."

We were a team now. I just had to work out if I wanted that to become legal and official. Starting up myself was exciting, but I'd been here part-time since I was eighteen. This company could be moulded into something that would fit both me and Rich. And if Nell came on board, there would be nothing we couldn't achieve. She'd be able to do amazing things for the company.

"I'm not sure if the advertising world is ready for that yet," I said.

Rich rolled his eyes. "You'll say yes eventually. You know it makes perfect sense. Please excuse me. I don't want to be late. I hope to see you again soon, Nell. It was lovely to meet you."

She nodded. "Likewise."

He wasn't gone two seconds before she asked, "You're going to be a partner?"

I shut down my computer. "Possibly."

"Why would you not want that?"

"I've just started out full-time, and I need to make sure I'm comfortable with the added responsibilities and stress. Now, are you ready to go?"

"Yep. I'm starving. They'd better not be late."

I grabbed my phone and wallet from the desk and slid them into my pockets. "Let's go then." Walking around the desk, I put my arm around her waist and led her out of the building.

She leaned against me as we walked toward my car, her breast brushing my chest. My breath caught in my throat as she looked up, all doe-eyed and pouty lips. She knew what she was doing to me. I felt my trousers tighten in the crotch area and hoped to fucking God that the hard-on she'd given me just by existing would be gone soon.

Chloe and Logan beat us to the restaurant. They were already at a table with our drinks.

"Hey," Nell said, sitting down opposite Chloe.

They launched into gossip at a million miles an hour, so I focused on Logan.

"How's it going, man?" he asked.

"Not bad. You?"

"Good."

Logan and I had effectively done the whole day's catch-up thing in under ten words while the girls were still discussing getting dressed this morning.

"Ordered you a beer, but are you driving?" he asked.

"I am. One's all right though. Thanks." A cold beer, good food, and good company were exactly what I needed. "How are the wedding plans going?"

He shrugged. "I'm not the one to ask. I'll turn up and smile."

"You can be involved," Chloe said, leaning on Logan's shoulder.

He scoffed. "That's not what you told me last night."

"Only because you said you wanted a screen to watch football in the reception room."

"Logan!" Nell said, shaking her head, just before I'd had the chance to argue that it was a perfectly valid request.

Apparently, it wasn't. Weddings went on for ages, and a match was only ninety minutes long. It wasn't like he wanted to spend the entire time in front of a TV.

He raised his hands. "It's not happening. I get that now."

It was nice to see their excitement even though I did think they were both so young still. But I supposed that didn't matter because they were the perfect match. They balanced each other out, and it was plain to see that they were in love.

"Are you having a morning, afternoon, or evening ceremony?" Nell asked.

"I thought about morning, but then I figured…" Chloe said.

Logan and I looked at each other, and he shrugged as they carried on with discussing the wedding plans.

Smirking, he said, "Again, I'll just turn up."

It looked like he was going to have to because, by the time the girls had finished, they'd pretty much planned out everything.

"You suggested Scotland, right? That's almost getting a say," I offered.

He nodded. "Yeah. She ran with it and found a castle, but I suppose it came from me."

"You're not sold on the castle?"

"Couldn't fucking care less, man. We'll see next week, I guess."

"Oh, that's right," I said, nudging Nell's arm. "Dirty weekend next week."

"You're getting *no* sleep that weekend," she replied.

Leaning my arm over her chair, I said, "Didn't plan to."

I drove back to Nell's after dinner, and it was finally the part that I had *really* been looking forward to. Meeting up with Chloe and Logan had been great, but having Nell all to myself was much better. She was driving me crazy, absentmindedly playing with her hair and giving me the occasional flash of her neck—a neck I wanted to be kissing.

"Are you okay?" I asked.

She still seemed a bit distant. Her mind was elsewhere.

"I'm fine. Sorry, just family stuff. Nothing I can't handle though. Parents can be a nightmare sometimes."

"Yes, they can be. Sure you're all right?"

"Absolutely."

We parked in her drive and walked into her place. She wasn't going to share why her parents were a nightmare, and I didn't want to push her, so I let it go.

"Do you want a shower?" she asked, turning around and raising her eyebrow.

"What? Now?"

"Me. You. Wet."

I mentally undressed her and felt a strain against my trousers. "When you put it like that…" Suddenly, it seemed like the best idea ever even if the timing was a little off.

She started unbuttoning her shirt. "Good. I'll rub you down if you rub me down."

Oh, fucking hell. My eyes dilated so much that I could barely see.

ELEVEN

NELL

So, we were flying to Scotland in a plane that looked like a toy. The anticipation of my steamy weekend away turned into pure fear of crashing in the tiny tin can. And not even Chloe shared my fears.

"Nell, will you stop looking at the plane? Everything's going to be fine," she said, stirring her cinnamon spice latte.

We had thirty minutes before we'd need to board, and we were spending it drinking coffee in the café. My cappuccino was doing nothing, and nowhere in here sold alcohol. I was screwed.

Damon put his hand on my thigh under the table. "Relax. It won't crash."

"And how do you know that?"

"I just do. We're going to be fine."

"Okay, I'm gonna need a little more than that."

He sighed and squeezed my leg. "All right, if we crash, I'll lie under you, so I break your fall. Happy?"

Happy? "No, not happy."

"You're being impossible. Has anyone got a Valium?"

"I don't need drugging, Damon."

He flashed me a smile as his hand travelled higher. "It's not for you."

"Oh, how very funny you are," I said, catching his hand before it could go to the inside of my leg.

Out of the corner of my eye, I could see Chloe grinning at us. She was obsessed with the idea of me and Damon being a couple. In an ideal world, that would be great. I really liked the guy; he was fun and killer in bed. But we didn't live in an ideal world.

"I wasn't joking, Nell," he replied. "The plane is fine, and we're going to be *fine.*"

"Okay, but when it's plummeting out of the sky and we're hurtling to our death, I'm so saying, *I told you so.*"

"Go for it. Jesus, I think I'm just going to have to fuck you in the bathroom for the whole hour it'll take to get there."

Logan and Chloe laughed, but I wasn't so sure he was joking on that.

I held my hands up. "I'm letting it go. I'm sure the rickety, old tiny plane will get us there without a hitch. Are we looking around the castle first, Chlo?"

"No, we can check in first and then meet up afterward, save us from lugging our stuff around. I hope it's as nice as it looks in the pictures."

It was a *castle* in Scotland. *How can it not be?*

"I'm sure it is. Are you setting a date this weekend if you love it?"

Logan looked at Chloe for the answer. Bless him, he would do absolutely anything to make her happy. I'd bet he didn't care where they got married. I'd bet Chloe didn't either actually, but they deserved their dream wedding. They'd been through a lot to get together.

"I think so, if we're both set on it."

"Still summer this year?" I asked.

That got a negative reaction from Logan. He wanted to marry her immediately, but Chloe was a little more traditional than that. She wanted to plan a big wedding and celebrate with all their family and friends.

"It depends on the dates. Maybe spring if we can."

"Better," Logan mumbled.

It was February now, so they didn't have long, but that was what they both wanted. I was so damn excited for them. They were adorable together. It was sickening really.

Our flight was called, so my telekinetic powers obviously hadn't developed enough to seriously damage the engine. I took Damon's hand and followed a buzzing Logan and Chloe to our gate.

"Focus on getting hot and sweaty in the hotel room while the snow falls outside," Damon said, trying to loosen my death grip on his hand.

That did sound romantic. Our sex was usually dirty, frantic, and needy, so romance actually sounded…nice.

"Perfect," I replied.

A little too perfect.

We had to walk to the plane and climb the steps. The fucking thing was only about three of me long. Okay, I was exaggerating slightly, but I hadn't thought commercial planes could be so tiny. Not even fifty people could fit in here.

Damon and I took our seats behind Chloe and Logan. I made the mistake of sitting next to the window, so I could see the rickety wings moving in the chilly February wind. Thankfully, there was no snow or ice, but what about on the other end? Scotland was notoriously colder than England. *What if our pretend plane hits ice on landing? We'd have no chance.*

Note to self: If they choose this castle, I'm driving up.

"Do we fly over the sea?" I asked.

Damon lifts his eyebrow. "I'm not sure. Why?"

"Just trying to work out our best chances of survival. The plane is small, so we could make an emergency landing in a field, but surely, the best chance would be on water."

"All right, I'm banning you from talking about the plane."

"You can't ban me from anything."

"Maybe not, but I can make it really annoying if you try."

"How do you—"

"Ba," he said.

"What?"

"Da, da, da."

I took a deep breath. Right, that was what he was doing.

"Are you three, Dam—"

"Nelly, Nelly," he sang until I slapped my hand over his mouth.

Chloe and Logan chuckled in front of us.

"All right, enough. I won't mention it again," I snapped, pulling my hand away.

"So, my folks are visiting next weekend, and they want to meet you," he said casually, as if he were telling me the time.

"I'm sorry, what?"

He rolled his eyes. "I wouldn't introduce you as my wife, so calm down."

I fucking know he wouldn't. "Why do they want to meet me?"

"Last time I was there, I took a call from you, and then the questions started. I guess you, Chloe, and Logan are the only people I've really mentioned since I moved here. Don't look scared. If you weren't phone-stalking me, they wouldn't have wanted to meet you."

I coughed in disbelief. "Me stalking you? I think you put in way more booty calls than I do."

"Oh, that is so not true. Damn, I knew I should've kept a tally."

Chloe glanced over her shoulder and grinned at us through the gap between the chairs. *Bitch.* I almost wanted to stop arguing with Damon, so she'd stop doing that annoying smug face, but there was no way I was going to let Damon win this.

"Damon, you call me more."

"No, I don't."

I glared. *How can we settle this?* There was no way of remembering all the times and who'd instigated them.

"Whatever. Let's just say that I make the calls the most," he said.

"Yes, let's because you do. Anyway, I'll meet your parents, but if you make one marriage joke, I'm out of there."

"Deal. You're not the marrying type, so it'd be pointless."

"What's that supposed to mean?"

In front, Logan's shoulders shrugged like he was wincing along with Damon.

He held his hand up. "That sounded nowhere near as bad in my head."

"What. Do. You. Mean?" I hissed.

"I mean, you make no secret of the fact that you'd rather chop off your own head than settle down. Obviously, I don't mean that no one would want to marry you." He looked rightfully scared.

"That wasn't very obvious."

"Hey," he said, lifting my chin, "I would never think that about you, Nell. If it's not clear that I think you're the perfect woman by now, then you're blind." He extended his index finger and added, "And before you say anything I'm not telling you this just because I want more, I know you don't want anything heavy."

I didn't know what to say to that. I wasn't perfect. Who was? Knowing Damon thought I was though made me slightly more optimistic for a future with someone rather than Cat Avenue, where I was headed right now.

We were thankfully interrupted by the stewardess telling us where the life jackets and exits were—all of which did nothing to calm my jittery nerves.

There was no weirdness as Damon leaned over to double check that my belt was buckled.

Don't worry, buddy. That's the first thing I fucking did.

Our relationship might not be conventional, but I did love how well we got along and how nothing ever seemed to be too awkward to talk about. I had been a little uncomfortable though when he said I was perfect, but that was a reflection on me and not *us*.

I was supposed to be the strong, confident one, and I was, but that also meant I tried extra hard to bury any insecurities I had, which was plain ridiculous because there wasn't one person out there who didn't have any.

"Ready?" Damon asked, smirking.

"As I'll ever be. Do you think they sell wine?"

He laughed. "Probably, but it's not a long flight. I am *not* carrying your drunken arse anywhere."

"Yes, you would. You've done it plenty of times before. Hey, remember when I had to carry *you* home?"

"You remember *why* you had to do that?" he asked.

I bit my lip. I'd ordered doubles for him, and he hadn't realised until the sixth drink. "Whoops."

"Yeah, whoops," he repeated, narrowing his intense eyes.

I sat back as we started to move. Damon's hand soon found mine, and I relaxed a little.

Surprisingly, the flight was passing by quickly. Damon kept me entertained by chatting about absolute crap. Chloe and Logan spent most of it being loved up where Damon and I spent it arguing over who would tire whom out first. I was determined to win.

He flashed me a cocky smile. "I think you'll find that I'm the one who's up for the next round first."

The plane dropped a fraction, and so did my heart.

He laughed and flexed his fingers, telling me to loosen my death grip. "We're landing soon, Nell. We need to be closer to the ground to do that."

"Fuck off," I hissed, making him laugh again.

I closed my eyes as we slowly descended to the runway. *Please just let us make it safely.*

We bumped to the ground, and the fucking thing wobbled. My eyes flew open, and I pressed my face into Damon. If anything happened to us, I wanted to be as close to him as I could get right now. I wanted him to be the last thing I saw, touched, and smelled.

He placed a kiss to the top of my head and whispered, "It's fine. We made it."

I still didn't allow myself to breathe properly until the plane came to a stop, and we were told to unfasten our belts and get off.

Leaping up, I left the plane before everyone else and felt so relieved that I could kiss the tarmac.

We were officially in Scotland.

And it was fucking freezing.

I wrapped my coat around myself and huddled against Damon's side as we made our way into the airport.

"I'm so glad we're not looking at a winter wedding," Chloe said, jogging to get inside.

I shot her a look. "Me, too, or I wouldn't bloody come."

When we got in, Damon and Logan went to wait for our suitcases while Chloe and I found seats, sitting close for warmth.

"Are you excited?" I asked.

She smiled so beautifully that it made me, *Aw*, inside. "I can't wait to get the wedding booked, wherever we choose. I'm *so* ready to be Mrs Scott."

Will I ever be ready to be Mrs anyone?

I couldn't picture it. No matter how hard I tried, I couldn't see me in a marriage. I wouldn't repeat history.

TWELVE

NELL

We arrived at the hotel—*castle*—and I quickly dashed inside, rubbing my hands together in the hopes that it'd bring the numb, motionless icicles I called fingers back to life. I hadn't realised this level of cold existed. Snow looked pretty, and snow covering a castle looked beautiful, but bloody hell, it was freezing.

"I got your case, Nell," Damon said sarcastically as he entered the hotel a few seconds later.

"I can't feel my feet. I'm positive that, when I take my socks off, my toes will still be in them," I said.

He laughed and let go of our bags in favour of holding me. "How about I warm you up when we get to our room?"

Logan made a gagging sound and took Chloe to reception to check in.

"Hmm," I replied, stepping closer to Damon, "I think I like the sound of that."

"Damon, Nell," Chloe called. "Come on, I've got your key."

I sighed and narrowed my eyes. "They'd better not ruin our fun all weekend."

"I think the fun starts after we get that key from her," he said, letting go of me and grabbing the handles of the cases. "Go get it."

Turning on my heel, I stalked toward my best friend. She really doesn't need to try anything stupid, like hiding the key or trying to keep it out of my reach.

Chloe handed it over with a smirk. "Do you want to meet in five minutes to take a look around?"

"No," I replied tightly, glaring at her expression.

Logan shrugged and said, "I'll only need three," which made everyone laugh.

From the few stories I'd managed to pry out of Chloe, he could last a lot longer than that.

Chloe rolled her eyes. "Lucky me."

"Best three minutes of your life, sweetheart."

"You two are so sad," I said, shaking my head. "So…our rooms are, where?"

"Third floor. Lifts are this way," Logan said, taking Chloe's hand and walking to the corridor going left. "Thankfully, our rooms aren't too close though."

"Whatever do you mean, Logan?" I asked, bumping Damon's shoulder.

He smirked down at me. "He means, they don't want to hear you screaming my name all night."

Logan looked over his shoulder. "What he said."

We got in the lift, and since there was an old couple riding with us, we opted for silence. I leaned against the wall and hooked my finger around the waistband of Damon's dark jeans. Of course I knew that I wouldn't win a game of who could feel up whom more in public because he had no shame, but that didn't stop me from doing it.

He raised his arm, and I held my hand up. Okay, this was a bad idea. His eyes were on my boobs, so no doubt, his hand would've been if I hadn't stopped him.

"I'm disappointed, Nell," he whispered.

"Yeah, well, I'm stopping us from being arrested."

"Where's the fun in that?"

"If you spend the weekend in a cell…"

"Ah," he said, grinning. He couldn't spend it in me. "Good thinking. I'm very much looking forward to this."

I gulped and licked my newly bone-dry lips. The temperature had risen *a lot* in the last few seconds. "So am I."

The lift doors slid open. Chloe and Logan walked out with their arms wrapped around each other. Logan called over his shoulder that we'd meet in reception in three hours. Damon took a step back and started to pull our bags along with him. I took a breath and followed.

We didn't see Chloe and Logan again—their room was at the end of the hall—so Damon let us in, and my mouth dropped. Our room was gorgeous. It was actually a suite.

When did he upgrade us?

The bed looked so comfortable I wanted to ditch Chloe's wedding plans and tie Damon to it for the weekend.

It took me a minute to take everything in—the high ceiling, large seating area, bathroom that looked bigger than my flat. When I turned back to Damon, he was looking around also, but he was concentrating on everything he saw.

"What are you doing?" I asked.

"There are at least seven things in this room I'm going to take you on or over this weekend," Damon said in his ultra casual way.

Okay, that's what he was doing.

"Hmm, I'm definitely glad I brought you with me," I replied, wrapping my arms around his neck after he stalked over to me.

He held me flush with his body and dipped his head, stopping just short of my lips.

"Are you teasing me, Damon?"

"Oh, yeah, we're alone for the next three hours, I'm horny as hell, and I want to hear you beg."

His words hit me down south—every single time.

I bit my lip, knowing that drove him crazy. "Oh, you think *I'm* going to beg *you*?"

"No, I *know* you are." He ran his hands down my sides and up my top, skimming the skin just above the waistband of my jeans.

"We'll see."

His eyes were ablaze with hunger for the challenge, and I was pretty sure mine were, too. I loved playing this game with him. It always ended in frantic, raw, selfish sex.

Damon's hands settled on my hips, and in one swift movement, I was airborne and flying backward onto the huge mattress.

"Damon!"

He took his coat off and pulled his jumper over his head. His naked chest took my breath away. He took good care of himself. Real good care. Muscular arms flexed as he removed his shoes. Black, grey, and dark blue watercolour-style ink swirls and blotches covered his right upper arm. It wasn't really anything but awe-inspiring art. The other upper arm was full colour. Damon loved his tattoos, and so did I.

"You're wearing too many clothes, Nell," he said. "I'm gonna need them off now."

I didn't need him to tell me twice. My clothes came off in two seconds flat. As I was lying down after throwing my bra, leaving it in a heap with the rest of my things, Damon's body covered mine.

His soft skin sat over hard muscle. I traced the valley between his six-pack, leading right down to his erection. He sucked in a sharp breath as I wrapped my hand around him.

"I want you quickly, and then I want you in the bath," I said.

Fuck the game. He didn't seem to care for it right now either.

His dark eyebrows lifted, and he squished me against his chest, my breasts almost flattening against him. It was an oddly pleasant discomfort.

"Your wish is my command. But, first, I want to…" He pushed back and sank to his knees.

I didn't have time to really process what was going on before his tongue was on me.

Sweet mother of…

Gasping, I gripped his hair and bucked my hips into his mouth. Surprise tongue was the best. I cried out and tilted my head back.

Damon's fingers dug into the flesh on my thighs as he flattened his tongue and made maddening slow circles between my legs. "I love it when you get all needy," he muttered as I arched my hips again.

My eyes rolled back. It felt so fucking good.

His voice vibrated through my body, making me shudder.

I was so close that it almost hurt. "Damon. Fuck."

Flicking his tongue hard and fast, he pushed one finger inside me, and I clenched around him, flying up on my elbows. I cried out and let my head fall back as I ground my hips against his mouth.

He moaned and sucked my clit into his mouth. I yelled his name and pushed my hips harder. My toes curled, my heart raced, and my hands tightened around his hair, pulling from the roots. It probably hurt him, but he groaned rather than snapping at me to stop.

Damon pulled his finger out and used both hands to lift my butt off the bed. With my hips in the air, he had a much better angle, and he pushed his tongue inside me. My eyes snapped shut, and I shouted out, falling off the edge of the cliff at a million miles an hour. He rode out my orgasm, knowing exactly when I needed him to stop.

My legs felt weak. I let go of his hair and gripped his shoulders.

"Fuck, I love seeing that post-orgasm flush in your cheeks. You're, without a shadow of a doubt, the most beautiful thing I've ever seen," he said, looking up at me in wonder.

I gulped. His words seemed a little too heartfelt, and I liked it so much that it scared me.

"You're not too bad yourself," I replied, trying to play it down.

He lifted his eyebrows twice. "I know, Nell." Sitting up on his knees, he smirked and added, "Where do you want me?"

"Oh, my choice, is it?"

"Thought I'd treat ya."

Rolling my eyes, I said, "I'm honoured."

He grabbed me by the waist and pulled me against his chest. "You should be. Now, how am I fucking you, Nell?"

His bluntness was nothing new to me, but it still made me blush a little. Placing one hand on my hip and the other on my jaw, I pretended to think about it. In all honesty, I kind of needed a minute. His earlier beautiful comment left me with an annoying, weird fucking feeling in the pit of my stomach. Plus, after coming like a train, I was feeling a little sensitive.

Damon's head tilted to the side. "You've got five seconds, and then I'm bending you over that desk."

I grinned. "Well, now, I don't know if I should choose or just let you do that."

"Nell…" His tone was a warning and a threat and such a turn-on.

This was fun. "Sit down on the bed."

He wasted no time in doing what I'd told him. "You're having me?"

"Yep."

He took a deep breath as his eyes travelled the length of my naked body, and he held his arms out. "Well, all right then, do your worst."

"Are you challenging me to fuck your brains out?"

"Absolutely."

His erection stood proud against his stomach, showing me how ready he was to play who could do whom harder.

I got off the bed, pulled the hairband off my wrist, and tied my hair up. Then, very slowly, I stepped toward him. "Game on, Masters."

THIRTEEN

NELL

I lounged over Damon's body, trying to catch my breath.

"Well," he said, breathing deeply, "you certainly know how to rise to a challenge, Presley."

"I'm hurt that you would ever doubt me. Anyway, bath time," I said.

He pressed his lips to the top of my very messy hair. Some of it had fallen out of the hairband while we were rolling around on the bed the last time.

"You're one of the few people I never doubt," he said.

My heart did all sorts of new things, like trying to exit my body through my chest. No one had ever said anything like that to me before. My fingers dug into his chest a little as I tried to calm my stupid heart down. I closed my eyes.

Damon moved from under me, and I let go to allow him to get up. I assumed he was going to run the bath, but instead, he wrapped his arms under my body and picked me up.

Laughing, I held on around his neck. "What are you doing?"

"You look thoroughly fucked, so I thought I'd carry you."

"I am, and thank you. Would've been nicer if you'd run the bath and then come to get me."

He looked down, narrowed his eyes, and turned around.

"Where are you—" I stopped mid sentence and screamed as he dropped me back onto the bed.

"Women are so fucking demanding!" He smiled and shook his head, showing his humour for the situation. "Stay there, and I'll come get you when it's ready, your highness."

I couldn't keep the moronic grin off my face as he bowed and disappeared.

After a few seconds, I heard him sloshing water around in the bath and then a few other bashing and bumping noises that I couldn't figure out. We needed to stop acting couple-y, but as long as we were both clear and honest, we'd be fine.

"What are you doing in there?" I shouted after ten minutes. It didn't take that long to run a bath, surely.

"Almost done. Have some fucking patience, Nell," he called back, making me laugh.

Lying down on the bed, I closed my eyes.

Bringing Damon here was a good idea. We were alone a lot, but it was usually between work or other obligations. This weekend, all we had to do was take a look around a pretty castle with Chloe and Logan, and then we would be free to do what we wanted—that being, each other…lots.

"Ready! Get your arse in here," Damon called.

Scowling, I opened my eyes and sat up. "I thought you were coming back to get me?"

"I'm in the bath."

"What? Why didn't you wait?"

"Because you can walk from one room to another, unaided!"

That was so not the point. "But you said you would."

I heard muttering and the sound of water being moved around far too quickly. *God, what is he up to?*

"Damon?" I said, kicking my legs over the bed and standing up.

He rounded the corner, naked. Naked and dripping and covered in bubbles.

Oh, hello!

My heart skipped two full beats and then raced so fast that I thought I'd pass out. The fluffy white bubbles ran down his arm, occasionally giving me a peek at the ink they were hiding. We would have to have more baths together because... *bloody hell.*

Smirking, he walked toward me like a lion stalking its prey. I licked my lips, still not looking at his face, as bubbles collected along the V. Then, because I was so focused on his naked form, I didn't really register him until he grabbed me. Suddenly, I could see his back—but upside down.

"Damon!" I squealed. "Oh my God, you're soaked."

He didn't say anything at all, which was unlike him.

"Okay, put me down now, and I'll get in," I said as he took me into the bathroom. "Damon, come on, don't throw me in." *That'll hurt, right?*

The tub was full of water, but it wasn't made out of mattresses. I didn't mind being thrown onto a bed, but this was something else entirely.

He swung me back, and my head spun.

I landed back on my feet. "Jesus, I feel dizzy now, you prick!"

Laughing, he gestured toward the bath. "But at least you didn't have to walk all that way from the bed to the bath."

Narrowing my eyes, I stepped in and sat down. The hot water instantly soothed sore—thanks to Damon—parts of me, and I closed my eyes.

The water rose to the lip of the claw-foot tub as Damon got in on the other end and barged his legs around mine. "Fuck, I love it when you're all wet," he hissed.

Is he a machine?

I loved sex, especially with him, but I was achy and definitely not about to get back down to it.

"Well, you can love it from afar. You're not coming near me again until tonight."

"Really?" he said, sliding his hand up the inside of my calf.

"Damon..."

"Nell..."

Glaring, I shook my head. "You don't understand the soreness."

"Yes, I do. I'm just not being a baby about it."

I snorted. "Whatever. You'd still have sex even if your dick was on fire."

He laughed, tilting his head back. "I'll give you that one. Though I am a little insulted you wouldn't."

"You're insulted I wouldn't have sex if I were on fire?"

"I'll fuck you so hard, you'll be on fire."

Rolling my eyes, I said, "Maybe we should have a quiet bath."

"I've got something that'll keep you quiet."

"I wonder what that'd be," I said sarcastically.

"I'll let you do it. If you want, I'll let you."

"I think I'm good with all the sucking for today, but thanks."

"You're very good with the sucking, but you know what would make you great? Practice."

Little prick! Sitting up, I cursed him and splashed water over his smug face. "Fuck you. If I'm not *great* enough, why don't you get someone else to suck it?"

His smile spread, and his hands circled my wrists before I could splash him again. "No one else is here."

"That's it! No more blowies!"

Pouting, he cocked his head to the side and looked far too cute. "Now, that's not very nice."

"Neither are you. What would you do if I insulted your oral performance?"

"Please!" he barked, laughing.

Okay, so maybe I couldn't be serious about that because the man had mad tongue skills, but still, he was a twat.

"There's always room for improvement, Damon."

Frowning, he sat forward. "Right. Lift up your pelvis."

I giggled as he tried to pull my hips upward. I batted his hands and shook my head. "I don't think so. You're good. You know it. I know it. Let's just leave it there."

"Good? I'm *good*?"

Why do I even open my mouth?

"You're amazing, incredible, the best, the king of making women come all over your mouth. There. Happy?"

He lay back. "All right, you sound a bit bunny-boiler complimentary."

"What? What does that even mean?"

"You know, when a girl or guy is embarrassingly cute about their better half."

"Ah, yeah, that does make me cringe. A girl at work is like that. 'Tom is so amazing. Tom is so handsome. Tom is the best thing that has ever happened to me. I love Tom so much.' Ugh, Tom needs to run for the pissing hills. Also, there is no way you found what I said embarrassing. You're probably disappointed that no one was around to hear it."

"You know I think you might be the best kind of woman."

"You *think*?" I raised my eyebrows. "I'm fucking ace, and you know it."

"You'll do."

There was nothing worth coming back with because we both knew we were the most sexually compatible people on the planet—excluding right now because I kind of hurt. I wanted to have a lot more sex this weekend, so I'd need at least an hour to recover.

Although I did love the banter and teasing, with Damon being quiet, our bath was much more enjoyable.

"We need to meet Chloe and Logan in twenty minutes," Damon said, stretching his arms out to the sides of the bath.

"No. I don't ever want to get out," I replied.

Damon, wet and naked and covered in snow-white bubbles, was heaven.

He laughed. "I can't believe I'm even in a bath."

"Think you'll be doing it again?"

"I know *we'll* be doing it again."

Sold!

I stretched my legs out. He took ahold of my heel and started massaging the sole of my foot.

Oh, Jesus. That felt amazing.

I heard myself moan and then the sharp intake of his breath.

"You're not developing a foot fetish, are you?" I joked. Honestly, I wouldn't even care, if it got me regular massages.

"No, I just like seeing you turned on."

"Of course," I muttered. "And that was a moan of appreciation, not pleasure."

"Hmm." His hand slid up the inside of my calf, rubbing with a gentle pressure that I felt *everywhere*. "Really? Just appreciation?"

Narrowing my eyes, I said, "I know what you're trying to do."

"I'm just trying to give you a massage, Nell." His attempt to innocent while his hand travelled further up my leg was pitiful. His eyes were too dark, too hungry, and they gave away his true motives.

I almost clamped my legs together as he reached the top of my thigh, but I just couldn't. Gripping the sides of the bath with both hands, I panted, feeling needy and starved of sex, even though it had only been about thirty minutes since the last time.

He proved, once again, that he was the Tongue King.

FOURTEEN

DAMON

I hadn't had a bath since I was a kid. Relaxing in hot water was a waste of time. I preferred to stand under a shower and get it over with. But Nell had completely changed my opinion. *Who can hate baths when a stunning girl is at the opposite end? Especially when I can get my mouth on her.*

She stood, naked, in front of the mirror, brushing her black hair. When it was wet, the ends reached the curve at the small of her back. My eyes travelled down further to *that* gap, and I took a sharp intake of breath.

Her eyebrow lifted in the mirror. "Enjoying the view?"

I leaned against the doorframe and folded my arms. "Very much. Hey, can you bend down and pick up that towel?"

Laughing, she shook her head and put the brush down. "Now, why would I do that? We're supposed to put them on the floor when we want housekeeping to change them."

"Do we need new towels after one use? I don't think we're being very environmentally friendly," I replied.

"Damon," she said, "we have to leave in about two minutes, and neither of us is dressed. You got my hair wet with all your splashing around, so go and get ready, and I'll do as much bending over as you want later."

I watched in amusement as her eyes widened.

She spun around. "Not like that! You know I don't like that."

"No, I know you *think* you don't like it."

Her eyes narrowed. "You've never even done it."

"But I'm not saying it's not my thing. I'd do anything with and to you."

"Suck my toes?"

Smirking, I shrugged one shoulder. "Sure."

She pointed and then frantically waved her hand. "You're weird. Go get dressed!"

I left her to it and threw on a pair of jeans and a T-shirt. I was ready just as she finished doing her hair. She strutted into the room and walked over to her suitcase, picking an outfit. My heart hammered harder every second I watched her slip into skinny black jeans and a hot-pink knit jumper. Even the simplest of outfits looked amazing on her. I loved when she dressed casual. To be fair, I just plain loved her.

"Okay," she said. "Let's go. We're late."

Standing up, I replied, "I've been ready for—"

"Yes, all right, all right!" Reaching out, she grabbed my hand, and her fingers slipped seamlessly between mine.

I swiped the key card off the side table, and we walked to the lift.

Nell pressed the button and turned around to face me, her hand still firmly wrapped around mine. She pressed her body up to my chest, and I licked my lips.

"Are you trying to get me to pick you up and carry you back to our suite?" I ran my free hand down her side and around to her back, and I pulled her even closer.

Her breasts pressed against my chest. This wasn't a good idea. I wanted her badly. No matter how many times I'd had her, I always wanted more. She was an addiction that I didn't want to break.

The door behind her slid open. She let go of my hand, gripped my T-shirt, and pulled me inside. I also loved it when she took charge.

"As mind-blowing as that sounds," she said, pressing the button for the ground floor, "we have somewhere to be."

Groaning, I pressed my forehead against hers. The harder I fell for her, the more I wanted her to myself. Sometimes, I just wanted to shut out the whole world, so we could be together without any distractions.

We stopped on the floor below, and others got in. I didn't take my eyes off of her.

"Fine, but you're staying my place tomorrow night when we get home."

She shrugged, like it was no big deal, and replied, "All right."

It was a big deal. The amount of time we spent together—at each other's places—was more than casual. Nell was either in denial or completely ignorant about it.

Three other people were with us, so I couldn't do all the things to her that I wanted. Instead, I watched her try to ignore me staring at her. It was fun. She kept her eyes ahead, occasionally returning a smile with the old woman standing next to her.

I meant to just piss Nell off a bit, but I couldn't look away. She was everything I wanted and a whole lot more. She turned to gaze at me, narrowing her eyes for a second, telling me to stop. I couldn't. I didn't even want to.

The woman next to her looked at me and scowled, probably thinking I was stalking Nell.

I turned my attention back to Nell and ran my tongue along my bottom lip. I could see the shock on the old woman's face. Nell bit her lips together, trying to stop herself from laughing. Knowing the lift ride was coming to an end, I decided to step things up. I groaned, dropping my gaze to her breasts, and cocked my eyebrow.

The door opened on the ground floor, and the old woman made a quick exit, followed by an amused but would never admit it Nell.

"You're terrible!" she said, spinning around and shaking her head at me.

Laughing triumphantly, I did a bow.

"How are you so successful? You're a fucking child!"

"I tend to act like an adult at work—mostly. What's the point of life if you can't have a little fun?"

"What's he done?" Logan asked, walking toward us from the bar.

Chloe was on the end of his arm, and they were both smiling like moronic idiots.

"He made an old lady uncomfortable in the lift by leching over me."

I held my hands up. "She didn't need to watch."

Nell jabbed her finger at me. "You didn't need to do it." The humour in her eyes gave her away. She wasn't mad. She was probably annoyed that she hadn't thought to do it herself.

Chloe laughed and pulled Nell's arm, linking it through hers. "Let's go see this hotel!"

The girls skipped off, pointing things out and playing What Shit Will Go Where. Logan and I trailed behind, bored stiff.

"We could just go to the bar, and neither of them would notice," I said as we waited at the entrance of one of the rooms they could have the reception in.

"Tempting, but the second I leave, Chloe will fucking notice. Women have this…gift for noticing the shit we screw up on and not a lot else."

"You're right there. Apparently, everything is my fault, even the things that aren't—like yesterday, for instance. It's my fault that we only got one English Breakfast tea bag each but two Earl Grey. Please tell me how that was my screw-up."

"Oh, it was," he replied.

"What? Whose side are you on?"

Logan tipped his head to the side. "You've got a cock. It'll always be your fault, and the sooner you accept that and learn to nod and repress, the happier you'll be."

"Well, it's a good thing that Nell and I aren't in a relationship."

He raised a light eyebrow. "Of course. That would be ridiculous."

"Fuck off."

Laughing, he shrugged one shoulder. "Damon, just make it official, yeah?"

He made it sound so easy. You didn't *just* do something with Nell unless it was purely physical and made your eyes roll back into your head. The girl was complication personified, and I didn't fully understand why.

"I would. She wouldn't."

"She would. She just needs to stop being scared."

"Hey, if you have any suggestions on how to do that…"

He smiled apologetically.

"That's what I thought. I don't know. If she's going to be with someone, I like to think I'm the one she'd let in, but whether or not she will anytime soon is anyone's guess."

"Sorry, man."

I shrugged it off, but it did bother me more and more each day.

"If it helps, sometimes, people need more time than others. Not everyone's path is perfect and straightforward. Look at me and Chlo. I loved her for years before she started feeling the same way, and even then, it took her months to be okay with it. For whatever reason, Nell just needs time."

"I just wish I knew the reason. You knew with Chloe, which must've made it easier to understand. All I've got is a stubborn woman who drives me insane."

"That'll never change! It did help, especially since I'd been through the same things as her, but waiting to see if she'd ever come around and be cool with us was excruciating."

Excruciating. Yes, that hit the nail on the head.

For so long, I'd been repressing my feelings for Nell and what it was doing to me because being with her wasn't an option. But I could only bury what I felt for so long, and now…

"I don't know."

I had a feeling that things between us would eventually blow up, and that'd be it. Even knowing that, I still couldn't walk away before it turned to shit. I was committed to seeing it through, no matter what the outcome might be. If there was a slither of hope, I was going to stay until I knew otherwise.

"Have faith, man."

That was all I had. There was a chance, albeit a miniscule one. Maybe I could get through to her, help her overcome or face whatever she was hiding.

"How long do you think they'll be doing that for?" I asked, moving on from my failure to properly connect with Nell on any real level.

They both looked very special, holding their arms out to the length of what I assumed were tables and other shit that'd be needed in the reception room.

Logan laughed and took out his phone. "A little while longer, I hope. How dead do you think I'd be if I posted these online?"

I watched him take a couple of photos.

"Really dead and divorced before you're even married."

"Damn," he said, raising both eyebrows. "Guess these are just for us."

"Nell," I called as they went to the far end of the grand room.

No less than six chandeliers hung from the ceiling, and tall windows made the most of the view of the acres of land.

Shit, what do I want her for?

She walked toward me with a content smile. Her green eyes softened the closer she got.

Logan made himself scarce and headed over to Chloe.

"Yeah?" When she reached me, she stepped into my embrace and looked up.

"I'm bored," I said.

"You called me over to tell me you're bored?"

No, I called her over to have her over.

"Yes."

Rolling her eyes, she stood taller and kissed me. I felt everything—every brush of her lips, every time she dug her nails into my back and pulled me a fraction closer, and every lick of her tongue.

Moaning, I curled my fingers into her hair and deepened the kiss. If we weren't in public, I would've pushed her against the wall and slid my hand up her top.

Clamping my arms around her back, I pinned her body against mine and sucked her bottom lip into my mouth. I couldn't get enough. Nell gasped and slid her tongue against mine, massaging slowly and clawing at my back.

I loved her.

I fucking love her!

"Nell," I moaned.

Her heart pounded against my chest at the same insane rate as my own.

How can she not see we belong together? No matter what we had to go through to get there, it would be worth it. I needed her to realise that soon.

"Er, guys?" Logan said in amusement.

Scowling, I parted from Nell and glared up at him and Chloe. "What?" I snapped.

"I think we're done here if you want to…you know," Chloe said, winking.

Nell turned in my arms but kept her body plastered to mine. "Go shopping? Absolutely. I need to get gifts for my parents."

"Sorry?" I said, my arms tightening around her. *Let that be a joke, please.*

"Good luck, Damon," Logan said, laughing. "We're off to meet with the wedding planner. Catch ya later."

"You honestly want to shop right now?"

She nodded. "I thought we could chill tomorrow, so I want to get it over with today."

"Ah, like the walk-around with the happy couple?"

"Yep. I have plans for you tomorrow."

"I like the sound of that. Let's get this over with then," I replied, letting go, taking her hand, and pulling her out of the room.

We walked up a steep hill, following the directions Nell had insisted on getting from the hotel staff. I continued to hold her hand, never knowing how that was going to go down. She didn't look at me as I threaded my fingers between hers, but she did look on, smiling so peacefully that it made me ache.

There was always something she held back, a part of herself that she would never truly open. Even when she laughed so much she could barely breathe, she was still holding back. But now—*fuck me*—she was free, and I wanted to stay here forever if this was what being away did for her.

"Do you know what you want to get them?" I asked.

"Nope. Something tacky that says Scotland on it. Maybe a crap fridge magnet or that dog they all seem to love."

"All right. Looks like there are a couple of souvenir shops ahead. I'm sure we'll find tacky there."

"Cool. Then, you can buy me KFC. I'm starving."

I pulled her hand, making her step closer, and kissed the top of her head. I was in love with the perfect woman, and I was determined to enjoy the next day with her—in bed.

FIFTEEN

NELL

Holding my paper bag filled with tacky Scotland gifts for my parents, I let myself into their house. We'd all safely made it home on the flimsy little plane, and I'd promised my parents I'd visit the day I got back.

Chloe and Logan had jumped in and booked their wedding after falling in love with the hotel. I was really pleased they had because the place now held amazing memories for me. I felt so close to Damon that it hurt. I'd told myself over and over that it was because we were away, kind of like a holiday romance.

Things were back to normal now, and the distance was painful. It wasn't supposed to bloody hurt. I ached to be that close to him again. I wanted to lie in his arms and just kiss for ages. I wanted to hold his hand that fraction tighter than usual.

Taking a deep breath, I swallowed the hollow feeling in my heart and called, "Mum, Dad!"

"Living room, Nell," Mum replied.

I turned the old-fashioned silver ball door handle and almost dropped the bag on the floor. Mum was curled up on the sofa with mascara running down her face.

I froze. "Mum, what happened? Where's Dad?"

"He left."

"What? Where did he go? Tell me what happened."

I put the bag on the coffee table as I walked past and sat down in front of her, tucking my legs under.

"He lost his job again."

"Another one? What went wrong this time?"

"Apparently, it's all their fault."

It always was. He would flit from job to job, depending on what he wanted to do next. I couldn't fault him for wanting to find if there were something out there he was passionate about, but Mum couldn't support them both on her low salary alone.

She took a sip of her vinegar-smelling white wine. She was drinking on her own. My mum was the classiest chick. To be fair though, she wasn't a big drinker at all. The odd bottle of wine would be saved for the many, many times she and Dad broke up.

Clenching my teeth, I took the glass from her. "Mum, put that down, and talk to me."

"I don't know what to say, Nell. I can't get through to him. It's like talking to a brick wall sometimes."

The familiarity kicked me in the stomach. I put the glass down before I dropped it.

"Work wouldn't let him take extra holiday, on top of what he's entitled to, so he quit," she said, throwing her arms up in the air. "Just like that. Like we don't have bills to pay."

"Is that why you're so upset? Did you…did you…argue?"

"When he came home early, he tried telling me that he had a half day, as if I can't read the signs by now. I knew, so I confronted him. He gave me the usual drivel about how I never supported him and said if I was going to constantly be on his back, then he'd leave."

"And you told him to leave."

Their arguments never changed. They might occasionally be about different things, other than Dad's jobs and money, but the cycle was the same.

"Bloody right I did. I'm not asking for mansions and diamonds, Nell, but if we're a partnership, I expect him to pull his weight and do what's best for us both."

And here we go. Time to start slagging each other off.

"You're right, Mum, but you know how he is. I don't see how you can continue complaining about something you *know* is going to repeat itself."

Growing up with my parents had taught me that you had no place to moan about something you weren't willing to change—or at least try to change.

"I thought we were trying," she said, getting defensive.

I felt like bashing my head against a wall until I drew blood. Actually, every single conversation I'd had with her about him was like doing exactly that. My weekend in Scotland had made me feel like I was floating, but thanks to my parents, I'd fallen right back down to the ground with an almighty crash.

"When did he leave?"

"Friday."

"Why didn't you mention it when I spoke to you?"

"You were going away. I didn't want to spoil your weekend."

I would've fainted if I wasn't sitting down. Not once in my life had she ever not bitched about Dad because she thought it would taint anything in my life. They'd both usually let it rip without a care in the world, not giving a shit what it did to me to hear them say such horrible things about the other.

"Oh," I replied. This was new territory, and I wasn't sure how to handle it. *Do I thank her? Tell her not to be silly?* "Have you spoken to him since?"

"I tried calling this morning, but he cut me off. I just don't know what he's thinking, but I know I've had enough."

Right, like I hadn't heard that a thousand times before.

"Enough of your dad's drama though. Tell me about Scotland. Did Chloe and Logan like the castle? Bit fancy, hey?"

I was ready to change the subject, too. It was giving me a headache. "They loved it. The room they'll get married in isn't that fancy really. It's gorgeous, and they're happy."

"Well, that's all that matters in the end. All I got was a rush wedding in a register office."

Smiling tightly, I nodded. *Surely, the* where *doesn't matter. And she fucking said yes!* "Yeah, I'm looking forward to their big day."

"What about that boy you went with? Damon?"

"What about him?"

"Will I get to meet him soon?"

Absolutely no way. I clamped my mouth closed, so I wouldn't laugh in her face.

My family was the definition of dysfunctional, and I didn't want anyone to see that. Pigs would fly, and hell would freeze over before I brought him to meet my parents.

"Probably not, Mum. We're not together."

"I don't see why not."

If she looked in the mirror, she would understand.

Shrugging, I shifted my legs and reached over for the bag I'd brought with me. "I'm young still. I have plenty of time to settle down. Here, this is for you."

She took the bag with a smile on her face. "You didn't have to get me anything. All I want is you home, safe and sound."

"One of them is for Dad, but you can choose which one you want."

She tipped the magnets onto her hand and laughed. How she was genuinely pleased with a shitty fridge magnet, I had no idea.

"Thank you, honey. I'll take the man in the kilt."

I'd thought she might. The kilt was blowing up with the wind. You couldn't see anything decent though.

"You're welcome. Hey, do you want me to go? You look tired."

She put the magnet down on the cushion next to her. When she looked down, the dark circles under her eyes became more prominent. "No, of course not. I'm all right. Just haven't had much sleep over the last two nights."

"Are you sure, Mum? I'm worried about you. What are you going to do about Dad?"

"Oh, I don't know."

I did, so I wasn't sure why I'd even asked the question.

Mum made me dinner and brightened up a little when we got into the kitchen. I started to see a little of how she was without Dad. That version of her wasn't perfect either, but when she wasn't slagging him off, she was a million times better than when they were together.

I left early evening and went home, waiting for the inevitable text to say Dad was home and all was well. By the time I pulled into my drive, I had a message—only it wasn't from Mum, and it was one that put a smile on my face. Damon.

I'm randy as fuck. Talk dirty to me.

I replied with a huge grin on my face.

Bugger off. I'm busy.

The following day, after a full day at work, I was ready to collapse. Since the weekend when everything had been as close to perfect as I was ever going to get, being bossed around by a jumped-up prick and his pervert son had sent me spiralling into one of the worst moods.

But I'd made it through the day, and I kicked my shoes off as I walked toward my bedroom, discarding clothes along the way. I got halfway there and was in my skirt and spaghetti-strap base-layer top when the doorbell rang.

Of course, I knew who it was. We had plans to meet up tonight, but I'd thought it'd be later when I had a chance to change and neck a glass of something.

I'd missed Damon like crazy, so I raced to the door even though his timing was shit.

"You cannot be here right now!" I said, swinging the door open and holding him outside with a palm to the centre of his chest.

He gripped my wrist. "Why not?"

"Because you've given me no time at all. I've just got in, and I haven't even showered."

That was absolutely the wrong thing to say.

His eyes lit on fire. "I can help you with that."

"Damon…"

"It's the perfect solution to both our problems."

I glared. "How?"

"You'll get washed, and I'll get inside you," he said. He released my wrist, trailing his hand down my stomach. "It's been ages."

"It's been twenty-four hours."

"Exactly. Ages."

He stepped forward over the threshold, and because I refused to move, his body was pressed against mine. We were chest-to-chest, both breathing a touch heavier because of the contact. My heart thumped against my chest, and my lips parted.

I wanted him to kiss me. I ached for his touch.

"So, are you going to let me in?" he asked.

"To me, looks like you're already in."

He arched his eyebrow. "You'd know it if I were in."

I gulped. *Yes, I would.*

"Damon," I whispered emotionally as I closed my eyes, "please just take me."

With my eyes shut, all I could do was smell his aftershave and hear the sound of his breath. It did things to me that were so intense that I thought my heart was going to implode.

After an agonising minute, I looked up. His eyes turned fierce as he watched me for a few seconds. Then, he scooped me up in his arms, carried me to my room, and did everything I'd asked.

For a while, I was whole again.

SIXTEEN

NELL

I sat on my sofa under a blanket, watching in amusement, as Chloe paced back and forth across my small living room. She was panicking. The wedding that she and Logan were so excited about, that she'd constantly talked about, was in less than two months.

"You're going to wear a hole in my carpet," I said, laughing.

She stopped on the spot and glared.

"Chlo, you'll be fine. You have a venue and have contacted someone to marry you. Nothing else matters, not really."

She pouted. "I know, but…"

"But you want to be a princess for a day?"

"Yeah." Sighing, she sat down. "Does that make me a bad person?"

I shook my head. "Of course not. This is your and Logan's day, and you can have what you like. As long as I get free wine, I'm cool."

Laughing, she threw a cushion at me and flopped back. "I'm spending fifteen thousand pounds of Logan's savings, Nell. It's his inheritance, and I'm terrified he won't like it."

A few months ago, Logan's great uncle died, and because he had no children, he'd left the money to Logan's mum and her children.

I snorted. "You're an idiot. He won't care about the little details."

"Exactly! So, I should just have a register-office ceremony and go back to the local pub."

"You don't want that, and Logan wouldn't be happy that you weren't happy."

"So, I just spend all his money? It took him years to save for a place, and now that he's inherited some money, he can do something he really wants."

I held my hand up. "Let me stop you right there, you tit. I don't think there's anything he wants more than for you to be his wife. Plus, you're getting married, so technically, it's your money, too. Stop feeling bad. Logan wouldn't have told you to spend more than what he's comfortable with spending. Now, I will slap your skinny arse if I have to. Can we move past this and get the rest of your day planned?"

She leaned forward, taking her glass of white from the table. "You're the best, Nell."

"Yes. So…what are you feeding us? Not something posh and tiny, please!"

"Logan wants fish and chips."

"Sounds good."

"It does. But you should've seen the wedding planner's face when he asked if they could do that instead of something from the menu. Good thing he was wearing that fitted black T-shirt." She bit her lip, her mind diving into the gutter.

In all fairness, Logan was gorgeous.

She grabbed her full folder from the coffee table. "Before we get sucked into this, shall we talk about why you've been quiet the last few days?"

"I thought you liked it when I was quiet?"

"My head does, but it worries me. Is something wrong?"

I ran my finger up and down the stem of the wine glass. Something was wrong, but I didn't want to talk about it. Chloe knew that my parents argued and broke up a lot, but I was trying to keep my mind off their relationship issues.

"Nell," she said much more sternly, "we talk about my problems often, so bloody tell me what's going on!"

"We talk about my stuff, too."

"No, we talk about what you want to do to your flat, how you wish you had a spare room, that your boss is an arsehole, that you want to start your career, and that you have mind-blowing sex with Damon, but we don't talk about anything *real.*" She dropped the folder back onto the coffee table.

Shit, she's getting serious now.

"Talk to me about what you're feeling, and maybe I can help."

No one could help. The only ones who had the power to stop me from feeling like a terrified child were my parents, and they hadn't cared when I was a kid, so why would they give a flying fuck now?

"Nell!"

"Fine! Jesus, you're annoying when you're determined."

"I could say the same about you," she shot back. "Spill."

Tucking my legs underneath me, I pulled the blanket higher. "It's my parents. They were back on, but Dad left after an argument."

"Well, that's not unusual, right?"

"No."

But she didn't know the whole story, so she wouldn't get why I was so distracted with it.

I shook my head. "Yeah, you're right. I shouldn't let their petty dramas get to me, but they're my parents, you know, and I just want them to be happy."

"Their happiness is down to them. I'd like to see you worry less about people almost twice your age and focus on what makes you happy."

She might as well have said, *Focus on Damon*, because that was exactly what she meant. He did make me happy, ridiculously so, but I loved being free, and the sex was out of this world. *What is there not to be happy about?*

I nodded once. "Sounds like a good plan to me." And it was one I had been trying to put into action since I was sixteen. Life just wasn't that clear-cut.

"How are things going with Damon?"

"Good. I'm seeing him tomorrow after work. I hope he has a weekend of bedroom antics—"

Chloe held her hands up. "All right! I don't need to know the details."

"Why not? I wanted to know all the details between you and Jace, and now, you and Logan. You still haven't told me who's bigger or better in bed." I almost finished speaking without laughing.

Chloe's death stare was actually pretty good.

"We will *never* talk about that."

"Sodding prude," I muttered. "Anyway, enough about me and the size of your men's dicks. Let's do this wedding thing."

"Sounds good, but they are not *my* men. Me and Jace have been over for a long time."

"I know. You don't have to say that. So, what are we planning tonight?"

She grinned. "We're researching local florists and DJs."

There was a reason I hadn't chosen a wedding planning career like Chloe. For the next *three* hours, I was bored to tears but happy to help my bestie.

After we narrowed it down to three, based on reviews and a bit of Internet stalking, Chloe left to go cuddle with her fiancé, and I was alone. Being alone when you were stressing and worrying about something was the worst. I tried to put everything to the back of my mind, but I'd never been too successful at that.

A huge part of me wanted to just pack my bags and leave, so I wouldn't have to deal with how I felt about Damon. Running was easier. I'd been running my whole life, but now, I wanted to physically do it, too. Watching my parents do the same shit time and time again was emotionally exhausting.

I felt weak and lost. Those were the two things I'd strived the most not to be. I wanted to cry. My throat constricted around a lump the size of a golf ball. Even if I couldn't run, I could at least hide.

There wasn't one person that I wanted to see—not Chloe or Damon and especially not my parents. I just wanted to be alone and hide under a blanket. Tomorrow, I had work, but at least I knew that, for the rest of the day, I could completely forget about social media or making any type of contact with humans.

Curling up on the sofa, I pulled my fluffy blue blanket up to my head and escaped.

The next morning at work, thankfully, passed quickly, and at lunchtime, I dashed out of the office to meet Chloe at Chimichanga for Mexican food and final—if there were any—wedding plans.

"Hey," I said, giving her a hug.

"Hey, you okay?"

I nodded, and we took our seats.

"You look nice," she said, nodding at my grey trousers and peach silk shirt.

"Thanks. You look exhausted."

She rolled her eyes and picked up a menu. Her amber eyes looked duller than usual, and her complexion was pale. "I am."

"Does that mean the wedding is almost sorted?"

Chloe was super efficient and organised. She'd planned every last detail, but we had a few things on the list to do. I was excited for their wedding but nervous, too. *What if they don't work out?* If Logan ever hurt her, I would do things to his private area that would leave his manhood resembling an omelette.

"Yep, almost. We just need favours and disposable cameras."

I beamed. "Awesome." *Thank God for that.* I loved Chloe and would help her with anything, but wedding planning was dull and felt never-ending. "If you get them and drop them off, I'll add them to the many boxes we're taking."

She tilted her head to the side. "Are you sure you want to drive all that way?"

"If you think I'm ever getting in a rickety, old plane again…"

"All right. I'm glad you are. Having them couriered all that way would've cost a fortune. You're like my little packhorse."

I deadpanned. "Thanks. You're very, very welcome."

We ate tacos, gossiping about the wedding, and then headed our separate ways back to work.

Damon had called during lunch, but I'd silenced the phone. I'd also noticed a text from this morning. I didn't call him back or reply. Dealing with Damon—particularly how I was feeling about him—was too much on top of everything else right now. I felt like everything was slipping from my grip.

I got halfway when my phone vibrated. Shoving my hand in my bag, I rummaged around, trying to feel it. *Fucking thing. Why don't I ever put it in the little pouch* designed *for phones?*

Finally, I managed to grab it, and then I saw the name on the screen and wished I hadn't.

"Hey, Mum," I said, still power-walking back to the office.

"Your dad's gone again."

I stopped dead, making someone behind me have to hop to the side to avoid a collision. He swore under his breath and walked past me.

"What do you mean, gone *again*? When had he come back?"

"Last night. I found him on the sofa this morning, and when I confronted him, he went off, ranting and raving. You know how he does. I don't know what to do with him half the time."

"There's nothing you will do, other than the same thing you and he have always done." I wanted to bash my head against the window of the Starbucks I was standing next to. "I've got to go, Mum," I said, starting to walk again. "I don't want to get back late." *And there is no point in talking about this.*

"Are you coming on Sunday?"

I didn't want to, and I thought about an excuse because I didn't like them together, but I was worried now that they were back in each other's lives again.

"Sure. I'll see you then. Bye, Mum."

We hung up just as I made it back to the office, ignoring a text from Damon.

I wish I could stop caring about my parents or cut them out of my life because I knew they would never change, but it wasn't that simple. No matter how many more times they would do this, I had no choice but to stay on the ride and go through it, too.

"You're five minutes late, Nell," The Ogre said, folding his arms over his enormous belly. His face was red, and sweat trickled down the side of his forehead. "I hope you're planning on making that up at the end of the day."

I gritted my teeth. This was where my idiotic bosses were going wrong. When you hired someone, you were investing in the person. No one wanted to put in that little extra when their employer was an arsehole. Late happened. It was unintentional, and it wasn't like it was thirty minutes.

Don't punch him in his big, fat gut.

"Of course," I bit out.

There were so many things I would change about this place. The way the employees were treated would be first on my list. But there would never be a chance for me to wave my magic wand and make this company more efficient. Besides, Reg, The Ogre, owned it, and he could pretty much fuck off.

"And I'll have a coffee," he added before turning away and going back into his office.

One of the worst parts was no one said anything. So much change was needed, but no one dared to speak up about what was wrong. We all needed to eat, I guessed.

How bad would it be if I put just a tiny bit of poison in his drink?

I walked straight to the kitchen, counting slowly and telling myself to let it go.

"Hey, Nell," Tommy—the only guy I didn't want to stab in the eye—said, finishing up making his tea.

"Hey, how's it going?"

He turned his nose up and chucked the spoon in the sink. "Better when I eventually get out of this place."

"Hallelujah!"

"You're not enjoying it either? I see the way Reg speaks to you. He's done it to all of the PAs he's had. No one lasts long."

"Yeah, I won't last long. I'll either move on soon or kill him."

Tommy laughed. "Well, you won't be alone there—on both accounts. I've been looking for something new for the last two months."

"Yeah? Much come up?"

"Not really."

Smiling, I replied, "Well, that's encouraging."

"Sorry. I'm sure you'll have better luck than me."

He wasn't sure of that at all. He didn't know what I was qualified to do or the experience—or lack of experience—I had.

"I doubt it. But, hey, if we've still not found a job in the next six months, let's set up a rival company ourselves."

Laughing again, he said, "You're on. And maybe we could get together sometime to discuss the business."

That sounded a lot like him asking me out on a date.

No.

A date wasn't going to happen, ever, and I wasn't attracted to Tommy, so sex was off the cards. There was nothing wrong with him. He was relatively good-looking, tall, and stocky with closely shaven brown hair, and he was nice, but I had to really want him.

"What are you suggesting?" I asked, needing him to be crystal-clear here.

He twitched his head. "I don't know. Whatever you'd like. Coffee? Dinner?"

"So, a date?"

"Well...yeah. It would seem we're on different pages..."

Ha, we're in a totally different book.

"No, it's just...I don't date. That whole dating-slash-couple thing is so not for me. Always ends bad and all that."

"Right," he said, averting his eyes.

Well, ain't that just bloody perfect? The one person I could have a normal conversation with without him talking behind my back, I'd just fucked up with.

We were left with awkwardness.

"Sorry," I muttered, reaching for a mug to have something to do.

"No, you don't have to be sorry. We can be friends, right?"

"I'd like that. Everyone else here is..."

Smiling, he nodded once. "I know what you mean. I'll see you later, Nell," he said before walking off.

Groaning, I looked up to the ceiling. *Can this day get any shitter?*

SEVENTEEN

DAMON

I slammed my front door in a foul mood and lobbed my phone and keys on the side. Nell had been off with me for the last few weeks and dodging my calls since yesterday. It pissed me off a lot more than it probably should have. She didn't have to check in, but after Scotland, I'd thought we were moving forward.

My phone rang just as I reached the kitchen, and I almost ignored it, but I turned back and went to see who was calling. Nell's name flashed up.

I picked it up and swiped my thumb across the screen. "Yeah?" I said.

"Are you in?" she asked.

I gripped the phone harder. "Yeah, why?" My tone was harsher than I'd intended, but I didn't appreciate being ignored.

"Um…" She sighed. "All right. I'm sorry, okay? I've had a lot going on, but I should've at least sent you a text."

She should've done much more than that.

"What's wrong?" I asked.

"Nothing really. Work stuff. I just needed to be a hermit for a night. But I am sorry that I didn't say anything."

There was more to it than that. If she needed a night, she would've just said, like she had a few times before. Something was wrong because she'd hidden the need to be alone.

"Right," I replied, gritting my teeth at her lie.

I would prefer if she didn't offer any explanation than lie to me. We didn't need to confide in each other, but I hated that she didn't feel like she could tell me whatever was going on.

"Are you angry with me?"

Closing my eyes, I ran my hand over the top of my head. "No, I'm not angry. You don't owe me anything, Nell. We're just screwing around, so if you want a night off without an explanation, that's your right."

"Wow, you are angry…and kind of a tosser right now," she snapped. "If you're going to be a little bitch about it, just forget I called."

"Oh, I'll wait for you to deem me important enough to reply to."

Shit. Why am I engaging in a stupid argument with her? She sucked me in every time, and I'd end up acting like a fucking teenager.

She snorted. "Get over yourself, Damon. This wasn't about you."

It wasn't myself I needed to get over.

"I can't believe we're having this fight. Do you want to talk about why you ignored me?"

"No."

"What do you want, Nell?"

"I wanted to see if you were up for getting together tonight—something I'm thoroughly regretting right now." Sighing sharply, she added, "Twat," under her breath.

"Perhaps I'd like a night to myself."

"Fine, suit yourself," she snapped before hanging up.

Growling, I launched my phone at the wall, and luckily, it just missed, flying past and hitting the side of the sofa instead.

Deep breaths. Deep breaths. What the fuck is wrong with her?

No one could get me worked up in the best and worst ways like Nell. Half the time, I wanted to hold on to her until we grew old, and the other half, I wanted to throttle her.

Knowing I'd gone too far, I did the walk of shame to my phone, embarrassed at how I'd lost it, and called her back.

"Hello?" she said in that tone that would usually have me shielding my balls and skulking off.

"I'm sorry. I overreacted, and I'm sorry."

There was a good ten seconds of silence while she contemplated what she wanted to do. Nell was stubborn, and if she wanted to hold a grudge, she could do so, very easily and very successfully.

She sighed, and I knew I was forgiven.

"It's my fault. I should've handled it better, yesterday and just now," she said.

"Did you call before because you wanted to come over?"

"I did, but..."

"Come over, Nell."

"Yeah? You sure? You don't want a break from my crazy?"

"Nah, it makes life interesting. And, in all honesty, I think I equally contributed to the crazy back there."

"Hmm...yeah, you kind of did. Fucking drama queen."

"Hurry up, Nell," I said. I hung up, smiling.

Her place wasn't too far, so if she were jumping into her car and heading out, I wouldn't have long to pick up the dirty underwear on my bedroom floor. Nell wouldn't care, past taking the piss, and I never did a big clean before she came over, but I drew the line at her walking over my worn boxers.

I pulled my T-shirt over my head and went to my room. My place was usually tidy, mostly because I didn't own too much. I didn't like clutter. Well, I didn't like to clean, so I kept things minimalistic.

Nell rapped on my door ten minutes later—nine minutes after I'd finished throwing my clothes in the washing machine. I answered the door, and she smiled sheepishly.

"Hey," she said, biting her lip.

"Come in," I replied, stepping aside.

She walked in, much more reserved than usual. We'd argued a million times before, but this one was different. It was about something real.

I kicked the door shut and held my hands up. "Are we cool? You're not planning any revenge, are you?"

Tilting her head to the side, she said, "No revenge, I swear. Arguing with you is kinda fun."

Is it? I liked when we mercilessly teased each other but not when we argued.

"I'm sure it'll happen again."

"No doubt." She turned before going into the living room. "Damon, I'm exhausted—physically and emotionally."

Her words hit me like a fucking freight train. She hadn't come here for sex. She came for comfort. That was a new development.

"Have you eaten?"

"No, but I don't want to."

Nell wasn't the skipping-meals type, so I knew something was really affecting her, and even if she wasn't ready to open up and tell me why, she had come to me for support.

"Go to bed then."

Laughing nervously, she tugged on the sleeve of her jacket. "You don't mind me coming over just to steal half of your bed?"

Jesus, she can be really obtuse sometimes. "No, I don't mind." I actually loved that she was coming to me. Usually, it would be Chloe who got her.

"Thank you," she whispered, her voice thick with emotion.

Something passed between us. My heart raced, and the hairs on the back of my neck stood up. It was a breakthrough, and I wanted to push, but it'd taken her years to get to this point. This was a huge deal to her.

"Are you coming, too?"

"I'll be there in a minute," I replied.

Nodding, she walked off to my bedroom, leaving me calculating the probability of this being a robot or an alien version of Nell. Something had changed for her to come here tonight. I was worried about what that was. She could be in trouble, but I had no idea what she could have possibly done.

Flicking off the lights, I went to the bathroom to brush my teeth and headed in to find Nell. I thought my heart was going to rip right through my chest when I saw her curled up in my bed. She had the covers right up to her chin with her face tucked against the edge of my pillow.

What happened to her?

Her vulnerability was difficult to witness.

"Hey you," I said, slipping my jeans off.

Smiling up at me, she replied, "Hey back."

"Been a long day?"

Snorting, she raised her eyebrows. "Long life."

I sat on the bed, and she shook her head.

"Sorry. I'm being really depressing, aren't I?"

"You don't have to be happy and carefree all the time, Nell."

Her silence told me she thought she did. Whatever she was hiding, she'd been doing it for a long time. She'd mastered the art of pretending everything was fine. I wanted to know it all, but the lengths she went to, to protect her secret scared me.

I clenched my jaw as worst-case scenarios plagued my mind. *What if she was hurt, abused?*

"Hey," I said, lying down and stiffly pulling her into my arms. I needed to snap out of it and focus on taking care of her.

She made a quiet gasping sound, like she was choked up, and burrowed into my side. I closed my eyes. That was better. Having her body tucked against mine felt like the most natural thing in the world.

"It's okay if you're not okay. It's normal," I said.

"Maybe I'm not normal."

Smiling against her forehead, I replied, "Yes, you're definitely not normal, but you know what I'm getting at here. Everyone has bad days, and you don't have to hide them from the people who care for you."

The person who's fallen so fucking much in love with you, it kills.

"I just don't like to be one of those miseries that brings everyone down."

"You wouldn't do that by showing when you're struggling."

"I'm not struggling," she replied, instantly defensive.

"Perhaps that was the wrong word, but you know what I mean, Nell. If you're pissed off and down, *be* pissed off and down. It's fine."

Sighing, she kissed my bare chest and said, "Thanks, Damon."

"Sleep now, okay? And if you want to talk in the morning, I'm here."

She wouldn't want to talk in the morning, of course, but at least she knew the option was there and that I didn't care if she wasn't bouncing-off-the-walls happy.

It was half past six in the evening, and we were in bed. No amount of hunger was going to tear me away from her tonight, not for a second. This was exactly where I needed to be.

Nell slept in long after I got up at six a.m. She flat-out refused to get up before seven. It was now ten minutes to, but apparently, that holy ten minutes was going to be spent with her face pressed into *my* pillow on *my* side of the bed.

We both had work today, and I enjoyed the normality of getting ready together a bit too much—or I would when she actually got up.

"Nell," I said.

She rolled over, leaving a mass of shiny black hair fanned out on the pillow behind her. Her lips pouted, and she groaned. "I don't want to leave this bed. I'm still exhausted."

"I managed it."

"Well, congratulations to you."

I laughed and slipped my shirt on, buttoning it up. "Will you get up for coffee?"

"I'll do anything for coffee."

My hand froze on my button. "Why didn't you say that sooner? I'll get these trousers off."

She bolted upright and put her palm up. "Oh no, you don't, you sex pest. I'm still tired, so there is no way your ultra-randy self is coming anywhere near me until tomorrow."

"Tomorrow?"

With a nod of the head, she replied, "Tomorrow. Come over. Oh, and be nice."

"I'm always nice."

"Fine. Be gentle then."

"That's probably the only time I've ever heard you ask for it to be gentle."

She frowned, and her nose scrunched up at the tip. "And don't you think I'm mad at you for making me want that?"

I laughed and went back to getting dressed, picking out a slim red tie. "Don't be mad. I happen to be very good at gentle, too."

"Well, I look forward to tonight then."

"Tonight? You said tomorrow."

"You look good in a suit, and it's making me hot. Tonight."

"I won't argue with that. We have time now…"

She held her hand up. "Definitely not. I need a shower and time to get ready. I don't want to be sore and late."

"You are no fun in the mornings."

"Fuck off, Damon," she muttered, making her way to the bathroom.

I laughed, enjoying having her here to get ready with me, despite her not being a morning person. She walked a little gingerly into my en suite, still raw from opening herself up and asking for help last night.

"What do you want for breakfast?" I called, finishing fixing my tie.

"Anything. I don't mind."

God, I hated it when women said that. *Why can't she just tell me what she wanted?*

"Bagel?"

"Sounds good," she called back.

The shower turned on, and I had to get out of the bedroom because the thought of water running down her naked body was calling me to go in.

I made coffee and peanut butter bagels topped with slices of banana, reminding me of my childhood. Nell came into the room, looking incredible in a fitted skirt and knit jumper. She'd not done anything with her hair but tie it up, but she still looked like she'd spent hours on her appearance. Beauty came naturally to her.

"This looks good," she said, picking up a bagel. "I've never had peanut butter on it before."

"Really?"

"Really."

"My mum used to make them when we needed to eat quickly before leaving the house. Cara hates it, but it's still one of my and Lance's favourites."

She took a bite.

I waited to get her verdict. "Like it?"

Nodding, she replied behind her hand, "It's good."

We ate the breakfast of kings together and then went to our cars to part ways.

She would stay at my place at least once a week, and visa versa, so it would make sense to keep some things at each other's place, but I knew that if I suggested that, she would freak out. So, we would lug a bag back each time.

I put her small case on the backseat of her car and leaned against the door.

"Well, thanks for letting me sleep over."

"Anytime," I replied. *Literally anytime.* "You free at lunch?"

"I'm meeting Chloe today, but I'll see you tonight. And tomorrow is Scotland, so you'll be sick of me by the end of the weekend."

"Not likely. And, shit, that's come around quick."

Kicking her mouth up at the side in a shy smile, she stepped into my embrace. "I really appreciate last night,

Damon. I don't like to…" Biting her lip, she lowered her eyes. *Show weakness*, was what she was getting at. "Well, just thank you."

I lifted her chin and pressed my forehead to hers. "You're welcome. I'm always here. And I can't wait to get you back in that huge bed in Scotland."

I couldn't wait to have Nell back the way she had been the last time we were in Scotland. She had been so free of whatever demons she carried around.

"Remind me to tie you to it this time," she said with a mischievous glint in her eyes.

"Done."

"Come here," she said, reaching up and pressing her lips against mine.

Groaning, I cupped her neck and deepened the kiss.

EIGHTEEN

DAMON

Nell had insisted that she was going to drive to Scotland rather than fly again. She had also insisted that I fly with everyone else, but there was no way I was going to let her drive alone—or at all. She was a terrible driver.

I was picking her up, and Chloe and Logan stopped by to laugh at us. We were supposed to leave at eight in the morning because it was going to take seven hours to get up there. But it was now eight twenty-nine, and Nell was still rushing around, trying to find a certain top that I'd bet she wouldn't even end up fucking wearing.

"Nell, do you need it? You have enough to wear, and the second we're in the hotel room, you're going to be naked anyway."

Chloe laughed, Logan wolf-whistled, and Nell continued looking, as if I hadn't even said a word. She was either ignoring me or was just so used to it by now. Whether it scared her or not, we were a couple already.

It did scare me, too. The way I felt about her scared me. I'd had no previous idea of what it was like to love someone in that respect, to put them before anything else, to want to do everything humanly possible to make sure they were okay. It was intense and had sort of crept up on me. I was powerless to stop it or control any part of loving her, which sucked for me because she was anti anything even remotely serious.

"Nell, Damon's right. You'll be there for only three nights, and you already have enough clothes. Why do you need this specific top?"

"It makes my tits look awesome," she replied, getting a chuckle out of Logan.

I cocked my eyebrow. "Every top does that. Get your arse in the car. I'm leaving in two minutes with or without you."

She huffed and shoved her hands on her hips. "Fine. Are the bags loaded?"

"Yes, they have been for the last forty minutes."

Chloe and Logan stood up while Nell stood still. All right, she wasn't getting in the bloody car of her own free will, so I was going to make her. I scooped her up, swinging the top half of her over my back. She squealed and gripped my hips.

"Who the hell do you think you are?" she snapped.

"Do you mind locking up, Chlo?" I asked.

Laughing, she replied, "Not at all. Have a safe trip, and we'll see you there tonight. Love you, Nelly."

"You do *not*, or you wouldn't let him manhandle me!" she shouted back as I carried her out of the house.

"I wouldn't have to manhandle you if you'd just gotten in the fucking car," I said, flipping her back onto her feet.

Her hair was as wild as her eyes. She glared. "What. The. Fuck?"

"You're not the one who has to drive for the next seven hours. I want to get going," I said.

"How many times did I offer to drive whole or part of the way?"

I laughed. "I would very much like to arrive in one piece."

"There is *nothing* wrong with my driving."

A loud burst of laughter broke out from the pit of my stomach. "You drive too fast and brake too late."

"But are you dead?"

"I would like to keep it that way."

"You might not have a choice!" she growled.

"It makes me hard when you get all worked up like this."

Her mouth dropped open. She walked around me, got into the car, and slammed the door. That was absolutely worth it. I waved Chloe and Logan off, tried not to laugh at Nell too much, and pulled onto the road.

"Are you ignoring me?" I asked twenty minutes in when she hadn't even glanced my way.

"I'm just thinking."

"About?"

"About how uncomfortable my bra is."

My heart started flying. "Take it off then."

She reached around her back, and her hands went up her top. "Going to. There's no way I can be uncomfortable for seven hours."

"If there's anything else you want to take off to get more comfortable, be my guest."

"Yeah?"

"Absolutely."

Her hands left the back of her top and went to the zip of her jeans.

"Nell!" I said, swerving to the side in shock and almost crashing the damn car. "Are you serious?" *Oh God, please be serious.*

"Keep your eyes on the road! You can't complain about my driving and handle the car like a knob at the same time."

"You're taking your jeans off. What do you expect?"

Every few seconds, I'd glance back to see if she was actually going to take them off.

"I expect you to get us to Scotland in one piece."

"Maybe we should find somewhere to pull over."

"Why?"

"I'm not driving for the next seven and a half hours with blue balls."

Rolling her eyes, she pointed to the road. "Look ahead. I'm changing into shorts for the drive."

"Why couldn't you have just worn them to begin with? This isn't fair."

"Because it was cold outside, and I had to wait for the car to heat up."

"Do you think I'm an idiot?"

Turning her head, she laughed. "Do you want an honest answer? Contrary to what you believe, I don't stay up at night, planning different ways to torture you."

"No, that just comes naturally," I muttered.

"In a minute, I'm just going to go to sleep and let you drive the whole way in silence."

"That would be lovely, Nell. I'd appreciate seven hours, nag-free."

She gasped. "I do *not* nag!"

"Think back to five seconds ago when you were telling me how to drive."

"*Anyone* would have told you to watch the fucking road!"

"Most people wouldn't have been taking their clothes off in my car."

Growling, she slapped my arm.

"What the fuck, Nell?"

Her eyes filled with tears, and she bolted upright in horror.

Shit, what just happened?

"What? What's wrong?" I asked, looking around.

"I'm sorry," she mumbled, looking at my arm.

Had we stepped into another dimension? It wasn't as if she'd stabbed me. We teased and play-fought all the time. Granted, it was more wrestling than slapping, but it was on the same level to me.

"Hey, don't worry. I think I'll live."

"I'm so sorry," she repeated.

"Nell, seriously, forget it. Why are you so spooked by this? It's not the first time we've messed around like that," I said, flicking my eyes between her and the road.

"I know. I just don't want to hurt you."

"That didn't hurt."

She raised her eyes to look at me. "Are you sure?"

"Real sure. I'm not that much of a pussy."

"I know you're not. I just…"

Her eyes glossed over again, and then she was so far away that I could barely breathe.

Is this linked to why she's so closed off? If someone has hit her, growing up, I'll fucking kill them.

"Hey, would you rather have sex with a family member or have your vagina sealed shut?"

Bursting out laughing, she covered her face with her hands. "What's wrong with you? You're disgusting."

Just lightening the mood again. We had a long way to go, and I didn't want to spend the trip with a subdued and moody Nell.

"Which one, Nell?" I asked, grinning.

"Sealed shut, you weirdo! Who would pick the other one?"

"You'd never be able to do me again."

"I don't care! That's so gross. I feel like I need a shower now. Wait…what would you choose? Family or penis drops off?" She looked scared to ask.

I shrugged. "It'd have to be a sexy cousin."

"Oh my God, what's your damage, you fucktard?"

Laughing, I replied, "I'm kidding, and I don't have cousins—not any who are sexy anyway."

She turned her nose up, making me laugh again.

"Do you want to play the number-plate game or make each other pick between horrendous situations?"

"Number plate," she replied instantly.

The entire way there, I exchanged banter with the old Nell again. She was funny, rude, and downright annoying, and I loved every second. A few miles from the hotel, she changed back into her jeans, almost making me crash again.

I'd promised her that, as soon as we got everything up to our room, I'd spend the rest of the day making her scream. We'd never checked in or moved so many bags so quickly.

I spent the entire evening making good on my promise.

NINETEEN

NELL

My best friend was getting married today. I was unbelievably excited and happy for her, but I also envied her for having something so amazing. I guessed I just felt a little sad that I couldn't have this—or have it so easily. The thought of getting married made my head spin.

"Chlo, you absolutely have to drink on the morning of your wedding. You're not following the rules," I argued when she pushed away the glass of champagne for the second time.

"She's right, darling," Chloe's mum, Bethany, said.

I gave her a smug smile. "See? I'm right. Drink up."

"I'm not getting drunk before I marry him."

"Can anyone even get drunk on one glass of champagne?" I asked.

"Fine," she said, holding her hands up. "*One* is all I'm having until after the ceremony."

"That's all I ask," I replied, handing it to her again. "Bethany?" I said, holding one out for her.

She took it like a real sport, her eyes filling with tears.

Uh-oh, proud mum coming up.

I was a proud best friend, too.

Chloe and Logan's journey hadn't been easy, but they'd made it, and they were happy now. And Chloe looked beautiful. Her hair long brown hair was styled with big curls and a crystal-encrusted silver comb pinning back one side. Her gown hugged her body, giving her the perfect figure.

"Chloe," Bethany said thickly.

"No, Mum. No way. You can't do this to me right now. I've just had my makeup done."

The makeup artist had left a few minutes ago, and she'd done an amazing job of accentuating Chloe's natural beauty. Her amber eyes looked bigger, and the subtle dark eyeliner made them stand out. She looked incredible, and I almost wanted to marry her myself.

The makeup artist had also done mine and Bethany's, and we looked bloody good, too. My eyes appeared bigger and brighter, and I couldn't help but take the occasional peek at how awesome they were. Tomorrow, when I would try to re-create the same thing, I'd look a mess.

"I'm sorry," she replied, fanning her face and taking a sip. "You're just beautiful. I'm so proud of you."

"Mum, seriously!" Chloe said, glancing up and blinking.

They looked absolutely ridiculous, and I laughed.

"I can solve this problem. Chloe, who's bigger? Jace or Logan?"

"Nell!" she snapped, her mouth popping open.

Bethany pretended to be shocked, but she laughed and ruined the act.

"Bet you don't feel like crying now, huh?" I said.

"You're the worst maid of honour ever."

"But your makeup is still flawless. You're welcome."

"I think I'm just going to see how your dad and the boys are getting on," Bethany said.

I put my glass down. "Wait, Bethany. I'll go and order them around. You stay and have a few minutes with your daughter. If she starts getting teary, just bring up the size thing. Works every time."

She smiled and shook her head, discouraged. "Thank you, Nell."

The guys had a room down the hall. They didn't really need one since they didn't do the getting-ready-together thing, but Damon had insisted, so they could have a few drinks together before the ceremony. There had also been talks of cigars and card games, but I hoped that was just a joke.

I walked down the hallway and knocked on their door, but over all the laughing and what I assumed was teasing of Logan, they didn't hear. If I walked in there to find strippers, I was going to lose my shit.

Pushing the door open, I crept in. It was fine—no strippers, just lots of booze—so they would get to keep their privates.

"Logan, you'd better not get drunk!" *Jesus, now, I sound like Chloe.*

Damon was the first one to look up. He froze, and his eyes widened. I did look pretty damn great. My hair was naturally wavy and messy, but it'd been curled and ruffled up. It was similar to Chloe's, but I didn't have anything fancy in mine. I'd probably lose it anyway. I wished I could afford a hairdresser to come and do the same thing for me every day.

"Nell," Logan said, "you look incredible. And, no, I'm not getting drunk. I've only had two pints."

"Good. Keep it that way, or Chloe will have your balls," I replied, trying to keep my eyes on Logan. I could *feel* Damon close by, *feel* that his eyes were fixed on me. It gave me butterflies.

Usually, Logan would say something crude, but Chloe's dad was in the room, so he wisely chose to do nothing but laugh.

"How is she? Not planning her escape?" he asked.

"Oh, she's already gone. That's what I came to say."

A few of the guys laughed, and Jace shoved Damon's arm. Damon barely moved. His eyes were still fixed on *me*, not on my breasts.

"You're really not funny, Nell," Logan said, narrowing his eyes.

ine. She looks amazing, and you're going to lose it e her."

His grin lit up his light eyes. "Yeah? Is she nervous?"

"She's not showing it if she is. I'm forcing champagne down her neck, so that'll squash any last-minute nerves if she has any."

"You're a true friend," he said dryly.

"All right," I said, cracking my knuckles, "line up, guys. I need to fix your sorry attempts at tying the cravats."

It looked like they'd tied them the way they did their shoelaces. Chloe wanted the perfect big wedding, and she was bloody well going to get it.

Jace appeared in front of me first, smirking back at a now glaring Damon.

Men.

"You're crap at this," I said, undoing it and tying it again.

"Good thing you've come to the rescue then."

"It is. Are you excited for today?"

"That your way of asking if I'm going to ruin the wedding?"

"No, that was me asking if you were excited. My next question…well, not really a question, was going to be a death threat along the lines of, *I will bury you in the grounds of this castle if you mess this up for them*," I said, smiling sweetly.

He laughed as I finished and dropped my arms. "I got over Chloe a while ago, Nell. I'm happy for them both."

"Good answer. Now, move along. I've got another six of these things to do."

Jace walked away, and Damon was up next. After briefly shooting daggers at Jace's back with his eyes, he turned to me. His lips parted, and he looked at me through hooded eyes.

"Hi," I whispered, my heart flying in my chest.

He tilted his head to the side and took a deep breath. "Hey," he replied, taking hold of my upper arms and pulling me against his chest.

We didn't really have time for this, but I couldn't help it. He was like a magnetic force that I was powerless to withstand.

I felt light-headed. With shaking hands, I reached around the back of his neck, lifted the collar, and then removed the badly tied cravat. Damon's hazel eyes pierced into mine with a thousand promises that I wanted.

"You look good," I said, focused on the task at hand so that I wouldn't let the things I was feeling right now consume me.

"I can't..."

I looked up, amused to see him at a loss for words. It didn't happen often.

When I met his gaze, the look in his eyes stole my breath. Neither of us said a word. Everyone in the background faded until their conversations were merely a background hum. I could smell Damon's aftershave, a smell that instantly made things better, and hear his slightly heavy breathing. And my heart...my heart was racing in my chest, beating so fast and so hard that I was certain he could hear it, too.

"There," I said so quietly that I barely heard myself. I patted the cravat. "All done."

Damon didn't say a word in reply, and I was becoming concerned about what was going through his head, but I had a feeling it was the same as what was happening up in mine. Something melted away inside me, and I fought to grip ahold of what I needed to do in order to avoid repeating history. For the first time ever, I understood why my parents couldn't easily walk away.

"You are so beautiful, Nell," he whispered. His voice was hoarse and sexy and turned my insides to mush.

I licked my lips and smiled. "Thank you. I'm glad you like the dress."

"It has nothing to do with the dress."

Blowing out a deep breath, I said, "I have to finish fixing everyone else up and get back to Chlo." What I really needed though was a strong drink.

"I know," he replied before cupping the side of my neck and kissing me.

He didn't let the kiss turn wild or deep, and it only lasted a few seconds, but it was still the most poignant kiss of my entire life.

He smiled, and I saw a glimpse of the old Damon back.

"Fuck, I need a drink." He gave me one last kiss and then walked to the table that looked like a bar had exploded all over it.

I bit my lip as I watched him walk away, and when I turned to tie the next cravat, I found Logan standing before me with his arms folded, his eyebrow lifted, and his lips smirking.

"Don't even fucking say it!" I hissed in a whisper, making him laugh.

I left the men when they were acceptably dressed, and I headed back to Chloe's room. My heart hadn't slowed down after my moment with Damon, so I was desperate to get back and have something to take my mind off it.

When I walked in, Chloe and her mum were hugging. Neither was a blubbering mess, so their chat had been successful in that right.

Chloe turned as she heard the door close. "How are they?" she asked.

"All fine. Logan can't wait to get you down the aisle." She beamed, and then it hit me. "You're getting married soon!"

We shouldn't even be old enough to do this shit yet.

"I know. I can't wait." She took a deep breath. "Thank you, Nell."

"For what?"

"For all those kicks up the butt when I was trying to work through my feelings for Logan. You helped me see a lot of things much clearer."

That was why she was pushing my relationship with Damon. She thought I was in the same place as her. There was a big difference between us. She was able to give Logan everything he wanted, but I couldn't do that for Damon.

"You're welcome. I'm just glad you saw sense."

She rolled her eyes. "Me, too. Are we ready to get me married?"

I linked my arm through hers and grinned. "Absolutely!"

Bethany, still with tears in her eyes, stepped forward and handed us both our flowers. "You girls look beautiful. Chloe…" She waved her hand, fanning her face. "Okay, I can't say another word, or I'll cry again. I'm going to find your dad and send him to your room, and then I'll see you in there."

"Thanks, Mum."

I watched them interact and wondered if I could ever have that with my mum. We weren't close, but I was sure that if I ever got married, she would be excited. I hoped she would anyway. It was pointless thinking about it. She was too wrapped up in her relationship with Dad, and I wasn't going to get married.

"Any last-minute nerves?"

"No. Was Logan really okay?"

"He's fine. Just anxious to get a ring on your finger."

Her smile warmed my heart. I loved how much she let herself love him.

"Okay, good. I was worried."

"You think he'd call off the wedding?"

"No." She shook her head. "I don't know. You'll understand what I mean when you get married."

Rather than bite her head off at being yet another person who thought I didn't want to tie the knot just because I was still young, I smiled and gave her a hug. No one needed to know my past or the shit I carried around with me.

"Can I come in?" Bill said, knocking on the half-open door.

"Of course, Dad," Chloe replied, turning to face him.

His face lit up when he saw her. "Chloe, you look…"

I wrapped my arm around my best friend's shoulder. "She's gorgeous, right? Logan is going to be uncomfortably hard the whole day."

"Yes," Bill said, shaking his head in grossed-out amusement. "Thank you very much for that, Nell."

Chloe didn't even go red like I'd hoped. I guessed there were only so many times you could do things like that before it stopped being embarrassing.

"You're welcome, B. Now, let's get this show on the road."

I let go of Chloe and kissed Bill on the cheek.

"You look beautiful, too, love," he said.

"Thank you. I'll give you a minute, but you literally have, like, sixty seconds before we need to get our arses down that aisle."

They both nodded, and I left them alone. Chloe was an only child, so I knew it was hard for him to see her all grown-up. I rounded the corner and saw a flash of something black before I was shoved against the wall.

I gasped and went to knee the guy between the legs but got caught when he clamped them together, pre-empting my move. Looking up, I saw an amazing pair of familiar eyes looking back at me.

"What's wrong with you?" I hissed, slapping his chest.

Damon pressed me harder into the wall with the weight of his body. "You."

"Me? What have I done?"

Groaning, he ran his hands down to my hips. "That dress, the legs, your hair—everything."

Oh, looks like Logan isn't going to be the only one hard all day.

"I haven't been able to think straight since I saw you," he said, trailing one hand lower.

My dress was knee-length, which seemed to be agreeable with Damon. When his fingers skimmed the skin of my thigh, I gripped his arms.

"What are you doing?" I asked, looking back and forth down the hall.

We were in a public place, and Chloe and Bill would be walking past here any second. He moved up, and I groaned as he brushed the lace of my French knickers.

"You *can't* do this here, Damon," I said the words, but I so didn't mean them.

The thrill of being caught turned me on more than it should have. He made me feel free and unashamed. But still, I didn't want my best friend's dad to catch me getting fingered in the hallway.

Damon tilted his head to the side. "You don't mean that."

No, I don't. "Come on, we—" I gasped and shoved him away as I heard Bill's and Chloe's voices drifting down the corridor.

Damon laughed, grabbing my wrist and pulling me back. At least we weren't still pinned to the wall when they appeared. He kissed the side of my head, and I felt my heart leap.

"I'll see you after," he said before walking off.

Smiling in pure fucking hope that I wasn't flushed, I said, "Let's get you married, Chlo!"

She squealed and hugged her dad's arm. "Promise me you won't do a stupid dance down the aisle, Nell."

Grinning far too wide, I winked at her dad.

"Nell Presley!"

Holding my hands up, I said, "I swear, I'll be good."

"She will," Logan's sister, Cassie, said, pulling my arm. She'd been in the ceremony room all morning, making sure it looked perfect.

"See? Cass will kick my arse if I'm bad."

Taking a deep breath, Chloe nodded. "Okay. I'm ready. God, I am *so* ready for this."

"Then, less chatting and more walking, sister!" I said, pulling Cassie toward the door.

We were going in first, and then Chloe would follow.

"You're not really going to dance, are you?" Cassie asked as we lined up beside the open door, ready for the music, which would be our cue.

"Oh my God, you don't even know how tempting it is since she forbid it."

Cassie laughed and shook her head. "If it wouldn't ruin her day, I might've done it."

"What? You?"

Gently slapping my arm, she said, "I can do crazy, spontaneous things, too."

"Oh, really? Perhaps you should prove that tonight."

"How?"

"I'm sure you'll think of something—or someone."

Her mouth popped open, as if I'd just suggested she should walk down the aisle, naked. It was going to be interesting to see what she'd come up with because casual sex was clearly an alien thing to her.

The music started, and I gave Chloe an encouraging smile before walking into the room with Miss Spontaneity in Training.

TWENTY

NELL

Cassie and I walked down the aisle at the designated pace. Heaven fucking forbid we messed up the timing.

"Almost there," Cassie whispered, smiling a bit psychotically.

That basically meant, *Don't dance or skip or do anything but carefully put one foot in front of the other.*

When people really didn't want me to do something, it was very hard not to. Perhaps, one day, I'd be a grown-up.

We reached the end and stood to the side, waiting for Chloe. Her extra-special music started, and she appeared in the doorway with her dad. I watched Logan as he first caught a glimpse of her, and my heart melted in a puddle.

Chloe beamed as she watched Logan and walked toward him. Cassie was already crying. I didn't feel like crying even though I was mega happy for her.

The venue was grand, but they'd opted for a short and sweet ceremony that I really appreciated. I wasn't anti-love or anything, but having people harp on about love and marriage for an hour, like they did in church weddings, made me want to stick my head in a blender.

Everyone's eyes were glued on the happy couple—everyone but Damon's. That little shit stared at me like I was

ESPN. I could feel him watching me, and it made me self-conscious. I didn't mind him checking me out—in fact, I would have been insulted if he hadn't—but this was on a whole new level of creep that I wasn't used to. And maybe I kind of loved it a little bit.

Chloe and Logan led the way out of the ceremony room as husband and wife, and Cass and I followed. We went to the reception room next door for drinks and photos before dinner. I headed straight for the free alcohol.

"Thank you," I said as I was handed a glass of champagne.

A hand—which I knew belonged to Damon—wrapped around my waist from behind. "You look fucking edible," he growled into my ear.

Chloe's great-grandmother's mouth popped open, and she walked off, very slowly and very offended. Damon didn't even seem to notice, and I didn't particularly care.

"Am I now?" I sipped the champagne.

"If I didn't think Chloe would kill me, I'd drop to my knees right now."

Turning in his arms, I glared. "Let's not do this now. We have a whole afternoon to get through before I can have my wicked way with you."

"Your wicked way with me, huh? What do you have planned, Presley?"

"Now, that would be telling, but I do know there's chocolate mousse for dessert, and I don't plan on eating it off the plate."

His breathing got a little heavier. "I think I'm going to like your plan."

"You most definitely will. Do you want champagne?"

"I'd rather drink piss, which isn't too unlike champagne. I'll go to the bar and grab a beer."

He let go of my waist and took my hand. I guessed I was going, too.

"Do you want anything else?" he asked.

"Nah, I'm good with champagne. Thanks."

"You're not fussy as long as it gets you drunk, are you?"

"Not one bit."

Laughing, he tugged me closer to him and kissed the top of my head. I liked that a lot. It made me feel cherished.

"How long do you think the photos will take?" I asked as we propped up against the bar.

This was pretty much where we'd stay until we had to go in for dinner.

"Fucking ages. You're going to have to be in a lot of them."

"What?" I groaned. "Seriously?"

"They're probably going to want their *bridesmaid* in the photos," he said dryly.

Frowning, I took a gulp of champagne. "Think I could convince them to just get one and Photoshop me in the rest?"

"Because that'll look great," he said to me, and then to the bartender, he said, "Beck's, please."

Logan's parents had paid for an open bar—big, huge mistake if you didn't want people getting wasted and falling over or fighting and one in which I intended to bankrupt them with. At least I was a lover when I was under the influence, so I wouldn't embarrass them—unless I got a little too lovey.

"I can't believe she's married," I said to Damon as we watched on at the photographer ordering them to stand together and clink glasses.

Wrapping his arm around me again, he took a long swig of beer. His thumb rubbed circles on my hip, making it harder to concentrate on anything else. "They look happy."

"They do." Every time I saw them, I wanted what they had. "Think it's inappropriate to get drunk yet?"

Smiling down at me, he nodded. "Maybe we should wait until after the meal to get you good and drunk, hey?"

I turned my body into his, pressing against him. "Are you going to get me very drunk?"

His intake of breath made me hot all over. "Yes."

"Hmm...then what will you do with me?"

"Wouldn't you like to know?"

I couldn't decide if I wanted to or not. Knowing what was coming would drive me wild, but so would the unknown. Whatever it was, I would be eating my pudding off his chest first. That was certain.

"Now, can we have the bridesmaids with the bride and groom?" the photographer called out.

Damon grinned and raised his eyebrow. "It starts. Have fun."

"Fuck off," I said as I put my glass down before leaving Damon laughing at the bar.

As much as I didn't want to stand around and have my photo taken hundreds of times, I would suck it up for Chloe.

"Hey," I said when I reached her side.

We hadn't had a chance to talk after the ceremony with so many people congratulating her and then the photographer stealing her.

"I'm married!" she squealed in a whisper.

"Oh, *that's* what that was."

Rolling her eyes and trying not to laugh, she hissed, "Just shut up, and look pretty."

"Yes, boss." I posed in the position instructed and smiled.

Behind the photographer and right in my line of sight was Damon at the bar. I kept my eyes on the camera and focused on making Chloe's wedding photos something she wouldn't kill me for afterward.

"Great, and now, just the bride and her bridesmaids."

Logan looked relieved to get a minute off and reached straight for a pint of beer his dad was holding for him.

Cassie moved closer to Chloe as she had been on the other side of Logan, and just when I went to smile again, I noticed some slag muscling in on Damon.

Who. The. Fuck. Is. She?

I didn't recognise her, so I wasn't sure if it was someone on Logan's side of the family or one of his old friends. Whoever she was though, she needed to move and do it quickly.

Instead of acting like she appalled him, Damon smiled and started a conversation.

And who the hell does he think he is?

"Okay, look this way," the photographer said directly to me.

Can he not see that I'm in the middle of a crisis here?

I held no claim over Damon, but he was mine, and other bitches could back off. Just because he was allowed to sleep with other people didn't mean he could do it in front of me. That was rude.

David Beckham could walk in right now, and I wouldn't jump on him because there were certain standards you had to follow, or you were just a dick.

In Damon's defence, he kept his distance. But, at the same time, he wasn't telling her to do one.

I smiled while the photographer clicked the button over and over again, but my mind was somewhere else—a place where Damon had a girlfriend, and I had been thrown away like a used condom. I wasn't sure what I was more disgusted with—the idea of Damon seeing someone exclusively or comparing myself to a spunk-coated condom.

"Thank you," the photographer said. "Now, bride and groom and his parents."

Wasting no time at all, I headed straight back to the bar. Neither of them noticed me approaching, and as I walked, I considered how best to handle the situation. The *me* side of me wanted to kick the backs of her knees, so they'd buckle, and she'd fall to the floor, but the rare rational side told me to act with more dignity and maturity.

As I got closer, I still wasn't sure which one I was going to listen to.

"Hey," Damon said, *finally* noticing I was there.

"Hi," I replied, standing a smidgen too close to him and turning my head to her. "I don't think we've met."

She smiled and leaned her disgusting tiny hip against the bar. "I'm Miranda, Logan's cousin."

Ah, I knew she was on his side of the family.

"Nell. I'm Chloe's friend."

"And bridesmaid," she added. "The dresses are so cute."

My eye twitched. I knew that *cute.* It was as fake as her eyelashes. *Seriously, Damon was attracted to her?*

"I know, right? I wanted these little pink ones that sat about two inches above the knee, but Chloe flat-out refused."

Miranda's dress was orange and short, but she didn't seem to get the connection between what I'd said and what she was wearing.

Since when do you wear club-slut clothes to a wedding? I would never wear anything that would flash my intimate area for all to see, if I bent over, to a fucking wedding.

She shrugged. "Shame, but it's Chloe's choice."

"Absolutely," I replied. *Why is she still standing here?*

"You want another drink, Nell?" Damon asked.

Oh, I'm going to need a lot of drinks. "Please. Miranda?"

"I'm fine. Thank you. Damon just got me one."

Low blow, bitch.

I turned to him, and he frowned.

Is he really doing this in front of me? Please say I'm just overreacting.

"What do you want?" he asked, sounding confused and scared and like he was about to protect his crotch.

"I'll have a double vodka and lemonade, please."

"Doubles already, huh?" he said, using his flirty voice.

Damon was back. But why wouldn't he act normal when he could go off with another woman right now, and it would be fine?

Well, when I say *fine,* I meant, I would want to slaughter him, her, and probably a few innocents, too, but he had no obligation to be faithful to me. I hadn't been to him over the years.

Although I had for almost the last year.

Fuck. I haven't slept with anyone else in almost a year!

"Nell, are you okay?" Damon asked, gripping my wrist.

I shook my head but answered, "Yeah."

"Well, I'll see you both around," Miranda said, finally taking the hint.

"Oh, okay," I replied. "It was nice to meet you."

Smiling, she walked off without another word.

"Hey, do you think you could cram any more sarcasm in there?" he asked.

Standing my ground, I put my hands on my hips and nodded once. "I wasn't being sarcastic. She seemed nice."

Damon deadpanned. "Oh, really? You spoke to her for three seconds."

"And in those three seconds, she seemed lovely."

"Yeah, she was actually."

Wanker.

I gritted my teeth. "Good. Want me to mingle, so you can chase after her?"

If he said yes, I was going to smash his glass over his head.

Curling his hand around my hip, he pulled me forward. "Now, why would I want to do that when I have you to keep me entertained?"

"Good choice." *Very, very good choice.* The stress and insane jealousy ebbed away.

Arching his eyebrow, he replied, "Well, I think so."

"Would it be totally inappropriate if I jumped on you right now?" I asked, pressing my body against him, thankful that Chloe had chosen dresses that were fitted around the bust and waist.

"It would, but let's not let that stop us."

Logan stopped by, slapped Damon's shoulder, and said, "Please let it stop you."

I stuck my tongue out. "Party pooper."

"It's my party, and Chloe would kill you," he said, shaking his head. Smiling, he walked off.

"He is no fun at his wedding." I pouted.

Damon lifted one shoulder. "It's all right. It'll be dinner soon, and I'll just finger you under the table."

My face slowly dropped. *Lovely.*

Letting go, I turned around and headed to the remaining champagne glasses on the table across the room. Behind me, Damon laughed and laughed and laughed.

The photos went on for ages, but we were fed canapés while we waited. Plus, free bar.

I made up with Damon after his fingering comment, and he behaved himself through the meal. Chloe had been between guests the whole time, so we didn't get much time to chat, but that was cool because Damon was keeping me busy.

"So, we have, what? Two hours until we have to be back here?" Damon asked, pushing the sleeve of his suit jacket up to look at his watch. "Now…what can we do in two hours?"

"Take a nap. Continue to drink the bar dry." I still had my dessert, so I knew we'd be having sex very soon.

He lifted both eyebrows. "I think you know what we'll be doing, Presley."

"Right. Drink. I think it's a good idea."

"Nell," he said warningly.

"Fine, fine. You're doing what I want. This is going to be all about me."

He snorted and draped his arm over the back of his chair. "When isn't it?"

My mouth dropped open. "You utter bastard. It's not always about me! You get so many blow jobs that I'm surprised it's not fallen off."

"If you want to try again to make it fall off…"

"I really don't know why I bother talking to you."

"I'm sorry," he said, not meaning it at all. He leaned forward to whisper, "Tell you what. Since I'm such an arsehole and clearly need to make it up to you, I promise to make you come again and again and in as many ways as I can think until you tell me to stop."

I gulped.

"After that, I'll bring you downstairs, get you drunk—like you want—dance with you all night, and then carry you back to our room to continue where we left off."

His breath blew down my neck, and the softness of his voice made me shudder.

"Whatever I want in the bedroom and lots of alcohol and dancing in the ballroom?"

"Mmhmm," he mumbled into my shoulder. He placed a kiss at the base of my neck. "It's all about you."

Chloe was the one who had gotten married, but I was definitely the happiest woman in the castle today.

TWENTY-ONE

DAMON

Bright light streaming through the fucking curtains woke me with a burn to the eyes. We'd been preoccupied when we burst through the door last night, but now, I wished we'd taken a second to close the curtains.

Groaning, I rubbed my eyes and looked over at Nell. Her makeup was smudged, the back of her hair was matted, and she slept with a small frown on her face. She looked like she'd had the best night of her life.

"Nell," I whispered.

She would undoubtedly have a hangover, and I didn't want to make it worse—well, a part of me did because, you know, revenge, but she'd probably kill me.

She mumbled something that sounded very much like, "Go to hell," and rolled over, so her back was to me.

"I take it, you're feeling a little delicate this morning," I said.

"Damon," she growled, saying no more.

I'd take that as a yes.

"Do you want me to get you water and painkillers?"

Making a fake sobbing sound, she nodded her head. "Everything hurts."

"That's what happens when you drink all of the alcohol in a castle."

"I'm not leaving this bed today. Can you order anything and everything that's greasy on the room service menu, please?"

I rolled onto my side and kissed her naked shoulder. Her skin was so soft and so perfect that it did wild things to my heart. Just being near her made me feel complete and gave me a level of happiness I'd thought was only possible in sappy chick flicks.

"So, what do you want to do in bed all day?" I asked, running my fingertips over her arm and shoulder.

She made a quiet moan of appreciation and leaned forward, giving me better access to her back.

It was moments like this that I felt invincible, like I could achieve whatever I wanted and be whomever I wanted. She did that to me. She made me strong.

"I want to *die*," she groaned.

I laughed and kissed her neck. "How about we get you fed and hydrated? Hmm…or you could roll over, and we could get me fed?"

"Oh my God!" she moaned, pushing me away. "Are you ever not in the mood for sex?"

"Are you?"

"Yes, when I'm exhausted after going at it for ages and when I'm hungover. If you're randy, go have a shower, and get your right hand out to play."

"I don't think I like it when you're hungover."

"Not doing cartwheels about it over here either. Coffee. Please. Find. Coffee."

"Get up, and get dressed, and we can go down to breakfast," I said, grinning at the prominent frown on her forehead that I could just see while leaning over her.

Even when she looked grumpy, she was still stunning.

She shifted to look over her shoulder. Flicking her eyes open, she glared. "I don't want to. I want you to get up, go downstairs, and bring me coffee back."

"Oh, do you?"

Nodding once, she replied, "Yes. I know I'm being demanding and borderline unreasonable, but I don't care. If I don't get coffee soon, someone is getting cut."

I fell down flat on my back and laughed. "Fuck, you're dramatic."

"You try getting much out of any woman before coffee, and you'll see that I'm perfectly normal. Are you going for me?" she asked, sticking her bottom lip out.

Looking over, I sighed. "Fine."

Her eyes lit up at the thought of coffee.

"You owe me; you know that, right?"

"Whatever," she muttered, slurring over the word. "Coffee now, please, or I wont be able to repay you with sexual kindness because you'll have no danglies."

I laughed and shook my head. "Danglies?"

"Yes, your parts that swing when you do your thing will be *gone*."

"Right," I replied, getting up and getting dressed. "You're special, Nell."

"Fuck off."

Chuckling to myself still, I left Sleeping Beauty in search of something that'd make her less violent. I didn't want to lose my *danglies* now.

I made my way to the lift as it opened, and Logan stared back at me.

"Er, you're doing a runner?" I asked, stepping inside.

"Nope. Chloe sent me out for herbal tea."

"Fucking hell. That must be a woman thing. I'm going for proper coffee."

"Oh, she doesn't really want it. I don't think she even likes it, but it's the only one not in the room, and I think she needs ten minutes to throw up."

"*O-kay…*"

He shrugged. "She won't let me hear her be sick, not that I particularly want to. Women are weird."

"Yeah. Manage to consummate, or were you too drunk?" I asked.

"Of course I managed," he replied, sounding offended.

Laughing, I leaned back against the wall and closed my eyes. I was getting a banging headache now. "Me, too. Not consummate, but you know what I mean. I gave it to her good."

Logan chuckled under his breath. "Good night all round then."

"What's the plan for today? You and Chlo doing anything?" I asked as the lift stopped on the ground floor.

We headed to the bar.

"She needs food, so after not drinking the herbal tea, we'll come down for breakfast. After that, we'll probably see off the people who are leaving today and then spend the rest of the time in bed."

"Sounds very similar to my plan."

I ordered three coffees and an herbal tea for Chloe to throw away, and we went back.

"Any developments with Nell?" Logan asked, pressing the button in the lift for our floor.

"Who knows? Things between us are changing, and I know she feels it, too, but what she'll do about it is anyone's guess."

"She'll get there."

I hoped so. The lift stopped, and the doors slid open.

"See you later, man—if we can still walk after today," I said, winking.

He scoffed, "Twenty quid I have more sex than you."

"Oh, it's on, brother!" I said, backing out of the lift and watching a smug-looking Logan walk down the opposite end of the corridor to his room.

I opened the door and put the coffee down on the bedside table.

Nell was fully under the covers, but she pulled it down enough to reveal her eyes. "Coffee. Oh God, coffee, I love you."

Of course, the coffee, she loves. Fucking woman.

"Drink up. I'm calling room service for breakfast, and then we're spending the whole day fucking."

Cocking her eyebrow, she replied, "Are we now?"

"Logan thinks he and Chloe can do it more."

She sat up, winced, and reached for the coffee. "I'm going to need painkillers. Get ordering, and then get naked."

Fuck, I love her.

Nell and I had spent all day in bed, ordering food to the room when we needed it. After the first time, it'd stopped being about beating Chloe and Logan, and it'd become about us.

We were free of expectations and the looks of people who assumed we'd announce we were exclusive soon. We didn't have to do anything but whatever the hell we wanted.

The sun was setting, and we kept the curtains open, watching the sky darken. Neither one of us was dressed, but the quilt was pulled up to my waist and, unfortunately, just above Nell's chest.

"Five years' time, where will you be?" I asked.

She took a second, licked the ice cream off the spoon, and said, "New York, working for some super huge and super powerful company that I helped to turn around. I'll have a flat…or *apartment* that overlooks Central Park and drink cocktails after work every night."

I could see her doing all of that. "Dreaming big."

"Only way to do it. What's the point in aiming low?"

"Hey, I'm with you there. Room for me in your suitcase?"

"Want to conquer the advertising world in America?"

"I'd planned on the world, but America is a good start, I suppose."

She sighed. "I doubt I'll ever get to New York."

"Not with that attitude. Where did that come from anyway?"

"I'm not saying I wouldn't smash it. It's just that I couldn't *not* have quick and easy access to Cadburys, and I think getting blank looks when I used the words *bellend*, *tosser*, and *wanker* would piss me off."

Laughing, I leaned over and kissed the side of her head. "Fair point."

"What about you? Five years?"

"Mansion. Inside pool. Ten-car garage."

"You're such a guy."

"Yes."

I had hoped that she would have mentioned something about wanting to be with someone—me—or engaged by five years' time. Not Nell. But that was probably because, in her head, she'd still be single in five years. *What will it take to get through to her?*

"Ten years?" she asked. "You know, when you're old and past it."

"Ah, well, I'll still have the mansion, cars, and pool, but I'll be sharing it with a woman who'll keep me young."

She turned her nose up. "You're disgusting. You're going to be one of those old men with a really young wife, aren't you?"

"Tempting but perhaps a little too cliché."

"Cougar?"

"Why do I either have to have a child bride or a granny?"

"Because someone your own age isn't funny."

"Thanks. What about you? Sugar daddy?" *Me!*

"I don't do marriage or any of that shit."

I wasn't sure what to say. Biting my lip, I looked away. There was nothing I could do to make her want more, want me, and there was nothing I'd want to do. It hurt. I swallowed the sting and looked over.

"Lie down."

"I am lying down," she said.

"Lie down more."

"Why?"

"Jesus, Nell, just lie the fuck down!"

She was so infuriating sometimes. If she were lying naked next to me, I'd do just about anything she asked with no question.

Giggling, she put the ice cream on the bedside table, shoved the quilt off her body, and pushed herself down on the bed, so she was lying flat. "All right, do your worst."

I was momentarily stunned by her beauty. Her long jet-black hair was splayed out on the pillow. Full breasts sat pert on her chest, leading down to a slender, toned waist. Hip bones peeked out in the sexiest way. The gap between her legs sent my heart wild, and the miles and miles of legs begged to be wrapped around my shoulders.

"Nell…" I groaned.

Fluttering her eyelashes, she trailed her fingers up her stomach and around the swell of her breasts. "Yes, Damon?"

Her face looked innocent, but her actions were anything but.

I loved her. I loved her so damn much, and I didn't care that it was going to rip me apart one day.

TWENTY-TWO

NELL

Damon slept beside me with one arm slung over my waist. He was gorgeous and exceptionally so when he was sleeping. I ran my hand through his hair and bit my lip.

The sex last night had been different. Amazing and scary different. It'd meant…something. It had been painfully perfect.

His eyes flicked from side to side under his eyelids, as if he were dreaming. I wanted to kiss them, but I didn't want to wake him, not yet.

Just watching him made my heart race. I could feel it, hear it, going crazy in my chest. My breath caught in my throat. What I was feeling was overwhelming, and a tear escaped, rolling down my cheek.

No! I loved him. I'd gone and bloody fallen in love with him.

Chloe was right.

Pressing my face into the pillow, I cried silently because loving him was the most incredible thing in the world, and that *hurt.* I wanted to shout and scream at how unfair it all was, but that'd get me nowhere.

Turning over, I wiped my eyes and stared up at the ceiling. The lump in my throat felt like it was the size of a watermelon. I had so many conflicting feelings that I wasn't one hundred percent sure what to even think. I tried not to move as I cried. I didn't want Damon to feel the movement through the mattress and wake up, but I didn't want to rush to the bathroom in case that might wake him, too, and then he'd see me.

Pull. Yourself. Together.

I wiped my eyes a few times and took a deep breath. *Everything is going to be all right. I can do this. I can be in love with him and not have it change anything.*

Damon sighed, and his eyes fluttered open. "Hey," he said, a grin breaking out across his sleepy face.

Gulping, I replied, "Hi."

His smile gave me so much. I wanted him to be happy. I only ever wanted to see that smile. A tidal wave hit me again, and I wanted to kiss him until I couldn't breathe, to tell him how much I cared for him.

I tried to focus on what Chloe had said about not being too hard on myself. Everyone had hang-ups and issues. I wasn't alone. I wasn't a bad person because I couldn't do something others did so easily. *So, why do I feel so fucking awful about it?*

"Sleep well?" I asked.

The air felt thick and heavy, so I tried to keep things between us light.

"Yeah," he whispered. "You?"

Best sleep ever. I'd never felt so safe and well rested. "Yep. Want me to take advantage of you in your sleepy state before we go down for breakfast? We have an hour before they stop serving."

A slow lopsided smile pulled at his lips. "Not going to say no to that."

I rolled him onto his back and kissed him long and deep.

It was our last day in Scotland. Neither of us had a hangover, so we were going to explore a little.

His breath tickled my neck as he brushed his head against mine. "Hurry up," he said. "I'm hungry."

"You can't be."

"I can. I've been burning a lot more energy than usual, and I'm going to need a truckload more for tonight."

Tonight was our last night. Tomorrow morning, we would be driving home and going back to separate beds and booty calls. It sounded horrible, but it was exactly what I needed to get things on track with our boundaries firmly back in place.

I turned around in his arms. "Yeah, what are you doing tonight?"

The look he gave me, all wild and wanting, told me exactly what *we* were doing tonight.

"Really?" I said, arching my eyebrow.

"Oh, really," he replied. "Hurry up, and take some bloody pictures. We're stuffing our faces in five minutes, and then I'm taking you back to the hotel."

I was absolutely not going to argue with that. Snapping a few pictures, I shoved my phone in my pocket and took his hand.

Damon, not one to break his word, kept me in the bed all day. I managed to pry him off me long enough to meet Chloe and Logan for dinner, and then it was back upstairs.

I thought he knew this was it. All too soon, we'd be back to reality, and things would be different between us again. The last few days had been incredible, and I wished they didn't have to end, but they did, so for the next eleven hours, we made every second count.

I woke up with a heavy heart, and the desire to block out stupid reality and stay in Scotland where we could pretend our closeness was purely because we were on holiday. We packed in silence and checked out in silence. Physically, there was no distance, but no matter how close I stood to him, I felt like we were on different continents.

The shittiest part was, I didn't know if I could ever get past not wanting anything serious. I had no idea if I would ever feel such peace again.

I was so sad to leave Scotland. The wedding had been amazing, and spending so much time with Damon had been more than I could have ever expected. We'd gotten along so well, and I had fallen in love. Now, I was scared that, when we got home, something—or *someone*—would come along and ruin what we had.

He deserved to have everything he wanted. He'd eventually want something real.

Chloe and Logan still had a few more days before they would be flying off to Italy for a fortnight. Most of the wedding guests had already left, and now, Damon and I were packing up the car, ready to head home.

"I don't want to leave," I said, pouting at him.

Leaning over and chuckling, he tried to bite my lip, but I managed to arch my back away from him before he could reach.

"We could stay. I wouldn't mind having you to myself for longer."

"Appealing," I said, straightening my back and giving him a kiss. So unbelievably appealing that it hurt to think we couldn't do it. "But I have to get back to work, and there are things I need to do first."

"What things?" he asked, clamping me in his arms.

My heart raced as I fitted against him in the best way. He was comfort, and I was getting greedy.

"Seeing my mum, seeing my dad, sorting out all the clothes from this weekend, redecorating my bedroom."

"Redecorating?"

"I don't like the purple wall anymore. It needs to go." Call me crazy, but I wanted the colour of the walls in my room to be the same colour as the walls in the room where I had fallen in love with Damon. Yeah, I was crazy. But I couldn't have him the way I wanted to now, so I wanted whatever I could get.

"You need help with that?"

Would he have offered if we hadn't had this weekend to grow unbelievably close?

We began out as acquaintances, had unbelievably amazing sex one night at a party that led to the friends-with-benefits pact, started spending time alone together around booty calls, and become friends. But we wouldn't really hang out unless sex was involved. We'd invite each other on nights out or to come over, but it was so that we could have sex.

This offer was decorating help. It was different. But we were friends, too, and friends helped.

The logical part of my head was screaming at me to tell him that I was okay to do it alone because the line between casual and so-fucking-not casual was too close to see. But my heart…Jesus, my heart wanted to see him at every opportunity I could get.

"That'd be great. Thanks."

I was being too hard on myself again. We were *friends.* I didn't have to keep him at a distance because, by definition, we were supposed to help and support each other.

Oh, yeah, no part of that is bullshit I'm saying to justify this to myself.

TWENTY-THREE

DAMON

We started the journey, flirting shamelessly and making plans to decorate her room and go out—and *in*—a couple of nights. But the more distance put between us and Scotland, the more distance appeared between *us*. I had known this was coming, but I wasn't ready for it.

The way I saw it, I had two options—one, try to find out what was behind her absolute reluctance to commit and risk her backing off completely, or two, go along with what we'd had before Scotland. Neither sounded that appealing, if I was honest.

"My family is coming to my place tomorrow night, but they'll be gone by nine, if you want to come over?" I asked.

The plans we'd made so far meant I wouldn't see her for two days. It wasn't really a long time, but it felt like it. I also wanted to get on the topic of family and their past.

She looked over and smiled. "Sure."

I had no doubt that she would turn up a little after nine to be on the safe side.

"You're not cooking for them, are you?"

I rolled my eyes. "I'm not that bad."

"Right—with dishes that have no more than two ingredients, like cheese on toast or frozen pizza."

"I make a mean cheese on toast. They're lucky they're getting fed."

She smirked. "You're ordering in, aren't you?"

"Yes. Unless you want to come and play chef, I'm ordering Chinese."

"I'd make a rubbish chef, but feel free to save me some Chinese."

"Oh, I can't promise there will be any left. You want chow mein, you arrive on time."

Her mouth dropped. "You told me to come at nine!"

"No, technically, I told you my family would be gone by nine."

Would she be willing to come when they're here? That would be huge for her, but I wanted to be sure she wasn't just playing the game.

"You said I could come after if I wanted."

Sighing, I gripped the steering wheel harder. *Fuck, she winds me up.* "You're more than welcome to come earlier, Nell."

She bit the inside of her lip, clamping her mouth together. It was something she was considering.

Well, fuck me, I'd expected a flat-out no from her. Meeting the parents was a big step, and we both knew full well that we'd passed the stage of being able to pass it off as a friend-meeting-a-friend's-family thing.

"Um…" She frowned.

I could see her internal debate. I wasn't going to help her get out of it, but I wasn't going to push her either. This was her decision to make. I just hoped she would make the right choice.

"Is that a good idea? You don't have one of those mums who plans a bloody wedding whenever you mention a girl's name, do you?"

Yes, I absolutely do, and Nell is the only girl I've mentioned to her, too.

"She won't be trying to marry us off," I said. *Because I will give her about three thousand warnings beforehand.*

"Okay," she said, visibly uncomfortable and unsure. "I'm in then."

If we weren't stopped at a traffic light, I would probably have crashed the car. Nell saying yes to meeting my parents was about the last thing I'd ever expected.

"Great," I replied, too stunned to say more.

It was a major breakthrough. After this weekend, I had known things would continue to change between us, but I never expected it to happen so soon. She was trying, and that meant everything.

I relaxed, knowing that although there was more distance now, she seemed to be willing to work on whatever it was holding her back. It gave me hope, and when it came to Nell, hope was all I had.

For the first time in three days, Nell and I had been apart the previous night, and I was so ready to have her with me again.

My parents were due over at any minute, and Nell looked nervous as she leaned against the worktop, chewing her lip to bits. I was sure she wanted to bolt, but she wasn't doing it, so that was a good sign.

I handed her a second glass of wine, and she smiled gratefully. Part of me wanted to reassure her, but that felt like it would be a couply thing to do. After all, this was just supposed to be a friend meeting a friend's parents. She was a flight risk, and I wasn't about to highlight the fact that this was so much more than an innocent meeting.

"What time are you ordering dinner?" she asked.

"Are you hungry?"

She shook her head. "Just wondering. Am I dressed too slutty?"

"What? Where the fuck did that come from?"

"I don't know. Sorry."

I put my beer down and walked over to her. "Nell," I said, lifting her chin, "you don't look at all slutty. You never do. Not gonna lie. You look edible, and I'm having to remind myself every two seconds that my parents will be here soon, so I can't bend you over the worktop."

Her eyebrows shot up.

"But you definitely don't look slutty. Relax, okay?"

She was wearing a dress, but it was very casual and very maddening. Her long, toned legs kept pulling me in, begging to be caressed and then wrapped around my waist. Her hair was messy and curly, just the way I loved it.

With my hands on her, I had little self-control. I lowered my head and teasingly brushed my lips against hers. "You look beautiful, Nell."

Before she had the chance to react, I sealed my mouth over hers and kissed her. She reacted to that quickly enough and gripped the sides of my T-shirt. I groaned into the kiss as she pushed her body against mine.

I took a step forward and placed my hands on the worktop on either side of her waist, blocking her in. She whimpered and hooked her leg up around my backside. The best parts were all lined up, and I didn't care that I was supposed to be exercising some control right now.

I gripped the back of her thigh, kneading the flesh with my hand. *God, she's fucking amazing.* "Nell," I growled into the kiss, feeling harder than I'd ever been before. I needed her so badly.

Running my hand further up, I almost came in my fucking boxers. She was wearing lacy French knickers. If they were white, I wouldn't care who came knocking at the door.

"Damon," she said, panting, as she pulled back and gripped the wrist of the arm that was working its way to the front of her underwear. "We can't. Your parents will be here any second."

I groaned in pain. "I don't care. We'll pretend to be out if they come." Nothing was going to stop me.

I dropped to my knees, and she gasped.

"What are you doing? You can't!"

Oh, I fucking can.

The underwear was white. My nostrils flared, and my dick strained against my jeans. I lifted her dress higher, so the bottom of her stomach was exposed. There was nothing in this world better than having my hands on this woman.

"Hold it up," I ordered, handing her the fistful of material.

She instantly did as I'd said, even going as far as lifting it higher so that I could just about make out the bottom of the matching bra.

Gone was the Nell who had worried about being interrupted. She moved one leg to the side, giving me much better access, just as the doorbell rang.

I shook my head. "No. No, no, no, no, no. This cannot be happening." I'd never hated my family before. "Be quiet," I said.

She clamped her legs together as my hand travelled up the inside of her thigh.

"Don't stop me."

"You're *kidding*, right? Your bloody parents are two walls away!"

"So?"

Her mouth popped open, and I groaned.

"Don't do that when I'm so close to blowing already."

Turning her nose up in mock disgust, she stepped to the side, leaving me desperate, worked up, and still on my knees.

She took a composing deep breath and fluffed her hair. "Rain check."

"We *will* pick up where we left off," I growled, standing up.

"I know. I don't like your parents," she grumbled.

"Yeah, I'm not too keen on them now either."

"Okay. You'd better let them in then."

"You'll be here when I get back? You're not planning on climbing out of the window, are you?" I asked, rearranging myself.

Rolling her green eyes, she replied, "Bloody go and let them in!"

I left Nell in the kitchen, not wholly convinced that she would stay. It certainly looked like she wanted to run. Opening the door, I tried to smile genuinely, but they'd just stopped me from getting inside Nell.

"Hey, Mum, Dad," I said through gritted teeth.

"Damon!" Mum instantly went in for a hug. I kept my distance but hugged her back. "Where is she then?"

God, my mother was so excited to meet Nell, and I was certain that she'd say something embarrassing—or many things—but I was on too much of a high that Nell had agreed. Today was a huge deal, and that was all I was focused on. Plus, I was still coiled too tight to give a shit.

"Your mum's been talking about this since you said Nell would be joining us," Dad said, rolling his eyes.

"Great," I muttered sarcastically.

I walked my parents into the kitchen where Nell was nervously chewing that lip again. She was going to bite it off if she kept on like that. She was leaning against the granite worktop with one leg crossed over the other. As soon as she saw us, she stood properly.

"Mum, Dad, this is Nell. Nell, my parents, Hannah and Nick."

"Nice to meet you," she said, giving them a million-dollar smile.

There was no way they wouldn't fall in love with her.

"You, too, Nell," Mum said, stepping forward and giving her a hug.

Nell hadn't been at all prepared, and even though she did hug Mum back, it was a bit robotic, much like mine had been.

"We've heard a lot about you. It's nice to put a face to a name," Dad said.

He needed to stop saying shit like that right now. I gave him a stern look. I'd given Mum a warning but not Dad. He wasn't supposed to need one.

"And you," Nell replied, shaking my dad's hand and maintaining that killer smile. "Can I get you a drink since

Damon isn't offering?" she said, gesturing to the liquor and wine on the side.

Mum laughed and nodded, and I knew she was won over already. "Red would be lovely. Nick will just have coffee since he's driving. Damon, put the kettle on then."

I felt like I'd stepped into an alternate universe. Nell had taken her place as my girlfriend whether she'd meant to or not. Probably not. You didn't offer your fuck buddy's parents drinks in his home.

"Damon," Mum said again.

I peeled my eyes off of Nell and looked up at my grinning mother. "Kettle. Right."

TWENTY-FOUR

NELL

I knew what I was doing was against everything Damon and I stood for, but here I was, sharing a drink with his family. We'd probably broken almost every single rule we'd made when we started sleeping together.

If there were an award for the Most Unsuccessful Friends with Benefits Agreement, we would be short-listed. And then we'd probably win. Still, I didn't leave. I didn't even leave when Damon's mum kept giving me secret smiles.

How invested in us is she?

People weren't supposed to want more for us. It'd just lead to disappointment. If Damon had told her something he shouldn't have even been thinking about, I was going to have his balls—and not in the way he'd want.

"Oh, come on, Nick," Hannah said, shaking her head.

They were having an argument about when their first date was. From the amusement on Damon's face, I guessed it was something that came up often.

"Do you remember when your first date was?" Nick asked me.

I'd never been on a date, so that was easy. Damon's body stiffened, and he looked like he wanted to murder his dad.

I didn't want to make a huge deal out of it or let it get in the way of having a good night, so I shrugged and replied, "Nope."

"See, Hannah? Not everyone remembers," he said to his wife.

"I remember," Damon said.

What?

"You do, love?" Hannah asked.

"December sixteenth."

I call bullshit. "Please!" Rolling my eyes, I added, "You just made that up."

Laughing, he leaned back against the worktop. "Fine, I did."

"Damon!" Hannah scolded. "Do you not remember your first time with Nell?"

A slow grin spread across his face that made me cringe inwardly, knowing what was coming. "First time, yes. First date, no."

He remembers our first time? I remembered the alcohol and waking up beside him, but that was it.

Also, he'd just told his parents that we had sex. They had known, of course, but I was sure they hadn't wanted it confirmed.

"Damon," I hissed.

It hadn't embarrassed me, but it really hadn't needed to be announced.

He laughed and shrugged. Neither of his parents seemed to be bothered at all, which made me like them both that much more.

I didn't really want to start making friends with them. We couldn't have a close relationship even though being around them gave me a family feeling, something I hadn't felt in a *very* long time. It was comforting, and I wanted to dive headfirst into their arms.

Bad. Fucking. Idea.

"Anyway," I said, "another wine, Hannah?"

She handed me her empty glass. "That'd be lovely."

Biting my lip, I held Hannah's glass and mine out to Damon and smiled. "Here."

"Oh, of course I'll get you both a drink."

Hannah waved her hand at him and wrapped her other arm around my neck. "Good boy. Come on, Nell, let's sit down and let the men sort out dinner, which I assume is takeaway."

Damon rolled his eyes and turned to get our drinks.

"I like that idea. Damon, bring our wine in when you're done, yeah?" I said. I didn't look back at his reaction, but I could imagine.

"So, what do you do, Nell?" Hannah asked.

Damon hasn't told her that? "I'm a PA, but I studied business at uni, so I'm looking into new jobs." Plus, my boss was an arsewipe, so I would have to get something else ASAP.

"That's a good idea. There's no point in having a degree you're not properly using."

Tell that to potential employers.

"I'm sure I'll find something new soon."

"Here, have you thought about the company Damon works for?"

I clenched my jaw. *Has the fucker been talking to his mum about that?*

"Damon's mentioned something about me meeting with his boss, but landing a new job is something I want to do alone."

She sat back and smiled. "Your independence is admirable. I wish I'd had the opportunity to do that at your age."

"You couldn't?"

"Oh no, my family was traditional, and we didn't have the money for me to go to university. My parents barely had enough to stretch clothing around for four children, and I couldn't get finance. I left school at fifteen and worked at the corner shop my parents owned. By eighteen, I was married, and three years later, I had Lance. Enjoy the opportunities you have."

"I will. So, what's the age gap between Lance and Damon?"

"Just under four years. All through his childhood, Damon tried to act the same as Lance even if it was something he physically couldn't do. Cara is just eighteen."

"They're close? He doesn't talk about Lance much—well, besides telling me he hated him after the holiday. He's mentioned Cara a few times."

She laughed. "They're close, and they argue something rotten. I don't know what happened on that holiday, but I have a feeling I don't want to."

"I don't think I want to either."

"Oh, Damon wouldn't cheat."

I licked my lips. Damon couldn't cheat because we weren't exclusive. But I didn't really want to tell his mum that we just had casual sex. For some ridiculous and annoying reason, I didn't want her to think badly of me.

"I know, but I'm sure a lot went down out there."

"I think Lance has a tattoo," she said.

Damon walked into the room. His eyes widened, and he froze, confirming that his brother did have a tattoo.

"Is that a bad thing?" I asked.

Snorting, Damon handed each of us our wine. "Here we go," he muttered.

"Both my boys are handsome the way they are. They don't need anything marking their skin."

"Er, you have seen Damon's arms, chest, and back, right?"

"Back?" She gasped. "Damon, you have a tattoo on your back?"

Wincing, I looked at Damon and mouthed, *Oops*.

"Thank you, Nell," he said darkly. "No, Mum, not really. It's just a little from the arm."

"On your back?" she said.

"Yes, it goes over to my back. Drink your wine." He turned and left, and I couldn't help but laugh. "I can hear you, Nell," he called into the room.

Biting my lips together, I tried to stop.

"Lance had better not have one as well," Hannah said. "Do you have any?"

I shook my head and opted not to tell her that as soon as I was sure of what I wanted, I would go for it.

"Damon says you're an only child?"

"I am."

"Was it lonely, growing up?"

Totally and completely. I'd needed someone so much, but I couldn't be selfish enough to actually wish it. One fuckup was enough. We hadn't needed to spread the bad luck and selfish gene any further.

"It was okay actually. I didn't know any different, and I had Chloe. She's practically a sister."

"I would've loved to have had another daughter. You know, I bought one dress when I had Damon, and I used to put him in it when he was first born. Then, I had Cara, and of course, she hates anything girlie."

"Fuck's sake, Mum!" Damon shouted from the kitchen.

I burst out laughing and held my glass very carefully. "That's golden! Tell me you have pictures."

"I do, but I fear I'll lose a son if I show anyone."

Damon frowned into the room. "Why do you feel the need to do it? And you can rip it up, or I'll move to America."

Her mouth dropped. "You wouldn't!"

I sat back as Damon quipped with his mum about how he would move to the other side of the world, and Hannah hit back by telling him that she'd follow. I felt warm and safe and accepted. There wasn't one moment where I was on edge, and I didn't have to worry about any arguments—other than Damon and Hannah's stupid little ones.

This was how a family was supposed to be. My heart ached for the feeling of belonging, and it also hurt as I realised just what I'd missed out on while growing up.

Two hours later, and his parents had left. Hannah had made me promise to be over the next time they were here. I'd said I'd try, not wanting to promise something I wasn't sure I could deliver.

"So, you okay?" Damon asked as he loaded the dishwasher.

"Yeah," I replied, surprised that I was.

Meeting his family had been so much more fun than I'd thought it would be, and although there had been a few awkward—for me—moments, I'd enjoyed spending time with them.

"You?"

His smile gave him away. "I'm good."

He was more than good, and it made my heart flutter. I licked my dry lips and pulled my dress over my head. Things were starting to get heavy, so I needed to lighten it again.

Damon did a double take and dropped a glass into the top rack of the dishwasher. "Well, hello."

"Want to take me to bed now?" I asked, popping my bra strap undone.

"That was a rhetorical question, right? You don't need me to answer that."

"Absolutely don't, Masters. Bed. Now."

I expected him to order me in there. What I hadn't expected was the sudden force of his body crashing against mine and slamming me back into the wall. My head hit the plasterboard, but I didn't give a single shit because his mouth attacked mine, his hands gripped my butt and lifted me, and his erection lined up perfectly between my legs, making me whimper.

I kissed him back with equal hunger and dug my fingers into the muscles on his shoulders.

Squirming against him, I tried to arch myself enough to get him inside. I needed the release so badly. "Damon," I murmured against his lips. My gut twisted, and the pulsing between my legs made me delirious.

"Fuck," he hissed as he sank to his knees.

My breath caught in my throat. He really was picking up where we'd left off. Yanking my underwear down, he hitched my leg up and threw it over his shoulder. He was wasting no time, and it drove me insane.

"Damon, stop teasing," I said as he slowed down and planted featherlight kisses up my inner thigh. His lips burned wherever they touched. "Please..."

"If you keep begging, we're skipping this part," he muttered against my skin.

"Right now, I don't care. I just need..."

He ripped away from me, and I fell forward with the force before correcting myself. I was soon slammed back against the wall the second his jeans hit the floor.

"I fucking warned you," he said, hitching my dress up again and sinking into me.

Calling out his name, I closed my eyes and wrapped my legs around his waist. I wasn't going to complain because, as much as I loved having his mouth on me, I *needed* to feel all of him.

"God, you feel incredible, Nell. Every. Single. Time."

I looked into his hooded eyes and clenched around him. His pleasure was a total turn-on, and right now, he looked like he was in heaven, and I was right there with him.

Pushing me against the wall, he thrust harder, faster, relentless in his pursuit to get us both off. My head fell back, banging gently on the wall. I ground my hips against him and cried out. The angle was perfect; his pace was perfect. He always felt too good. My body responded to everything he did in a way that no other man had achieved.

I felt everything inside me tighten as he pounded harder, breathing heavily into my ear.

"Shit, Damon." I was close, so close.

He moaned and smashed his lips to mine in a primal, passionate kiss that had my toes curling and nails biting into his skin. Tightly clamping my legs around his waist, I exploded and moaned his name against his mouth.

Suddenly pulling back, he tossed his head back and groaned, "Ah, fuck." Calling out, he buried his head in my neck and spilled inside me. "God, Nell, I could do that all day. I'll never have enough of you."

"Back atcha, champ," I said, flopping forward and laying my head on his shoulder.

Damon laughed quietly and started to walk us to his bedroom.

"Are you planning on doing it all night now?"

"Always," he replied before kissing me.

Damon laid me down on the bed, slowly pulled out, and lay beside me. "So, did you like my parents?"

"They're great," I replied. "Your mum is awesome."

He raised an eyebrow. "Hmm…"

"Oh, she is! It was fun to see you around your family."

"We're close even though they drive me insane, her especially."

I laughed, remembering many of their little arguments. "She loves you like crazy—anyone can see that—even if you broke her heart when you inked your skin."

He rolled his eyes. "She's a bit psycho with the perfect skin thing."

"I kinda think it's perfect with the tattoos."

Wiggling his eyebrows, he said, "You think I'm perfect?"

I deadpanned. "I'm so *not* getting into this with you."

"Fine. So, what else do you want to do? Are you ready for round two yet?"

"Bloody hell, you're a machine! I'm tired. Sort yourself out this time."

It wasn't late, a little after ten, but being around his family and having it bring up things I tried to bury had left me drained.

He laughed and splayed his hand over my stomach. Usually, that would be enough to get me to go again, but I was emotionally and physically exhausted, and there was no chance of me moving until morning.

"Wait, you're really going to sleep, aren't you?"

"Mmhmm."

Sighing, he kissed my forehead. "If you wake up first, climb aboard."

Smiling with closed eyes, I replied in a whisper, “Will do, cowboy.”

TWENTY-FIVE

NELL

I felt all kinds of confused when I left Damon's house the morning after meeting his parents. Too close, too much. The firm rules I'd wanted back in place after Scotland had clearly not happened, and it was my fault. I was the one who had agreed to meet his parents—against my better judgment.

There wasn't one part of me that wasn't ridiculous. I should just keep to myself and be a hermit, and then I couldn't make stupid mind-screwing choices.

On the top of my to-do list today was the thing I should've done before—reset boundaries. Being close to him was amazing, but that had to be over now, and I only felt half-sad about it. Some people never got even a second of what I'd had. Four days had been incredible, especially since I had been so sure I would be one of the never-get-it ones. I hungered for more, but I was also grateful for what I'd had.

I walked into my office, and reality smashed me in the face with a mallet.

The Ogre was sitting on my desk with his arms folded over his chest. "We need to chat," he said, scratching the stubble covering his double chin.

"Um, okay," I replied, doing a mental inventory of all the things I'd done that this chat could be about.

There was nothing that he could have found out—well, that I knew of. Occasionally, I'd indulge in a little Internet shopping during work hours, but I'd never failed to get my work done.

"What's up?"

"You're having too many days off, Nell."

"I haven't been sick since I started." *What the hell is his problem?* I put my bag on my desk and defensively straightened my back. "The only time I've had off was booked as holiday, and as far as I'm aware, I'm entitled to take that."

"We have an understanding here that we don't take time off too close together. We're constantly busy, and it doesn't help when an employee takes a few days off here and there every month."

"Okay, first, no one has ever told me that. Second, I don't think you can dictate that unless it's in my contract, which it isn't. And third, why was my request signed off by management if you didn't allow someone to have blocks of holiday close together?"

His chubby face turned red. He hated knowing that I was right, and he couldn't say a thing. "You deliberately went to Harry to sign the request off because you knew I'd done the last one."

"No, I didn't. My friend set the date of her wedding. It was only five weeks away at the time, and you were away, so I asked Harry because I knew I wouldn't see you until Monday."

There was absolutely no way I was backing down.

"Harry, come in here for a minute," Ogre snapped.

His voice boomed through the offices, and everyone looked up from their desks.

Great.

I had never felt like telling him to shove his job more. The weekend had been perfect, but I was still a little delicate over losing what I'd had with Damon. This made me want to scream, punch Ogre and Harry, and cry—in that order.

"What's wrong?" Harry asked, folding his arms in the doorway.

"You signed off on Nell's holiday form?"

Harry blinked rapidly and then said, "I did. She never mentioned how long it'd been since the last time."

"Why should I have?" I snapped. "That rule was never made clear to me."

"Nell!" The Ogre bellowed. "Harry, that's all."

Oh, bugger.

Harry made a swift exit, happy that he'd covered his own arse even though I was the innocent party here.

"Yes, Reg?"

His neck was dripping with sweat. "If you ever talk to a member of management like that again, you'll be out. Consider that your verbal warning." Without another word or giving me a chance to defend myself, he walked out and slammed my door shut.

My heart raced in the worst way. His approach scared me, and then what he'd had to say/shout plain pissed me off.

How dare the bastard yell at me for sticking up for myself! What I'd said was right.

With shaking hands, I sat down. My ears rang, and it took every ounce of self-control to stay. They wouldn't push me out. As much as I wanted to, I wouldn't leave without another job to go to. They could keep paying me.

I turned my computer on and waited for it to boot up. My phone rang just as the screen popped up. Thankful for the distraction, I rooted around until I felt it at the bottom of my bag.

"Hi," I said to Damon, trying to be cheerful when I was so close to tears.

"What's wrong?" he asked.

"Nothing. Why?"

"You sound…upset. Has something happened?"

All I'd said was hi. *How could he know I was upset?* "I'm fine. It's just my boss."

"Tell me."

I explained the whole thing to Damon, careful not to talk too loudly in case anyone heard. It'd look great now if one of them came in and saw me chatting away on my phone. When I finished, Damon spent a full two minutes listing swearwords and telling me in three different ways how he was going to kill The Ogre.

I said, "Calm down!"

"Calm down? He had no right to talk to you like that even if you had done something wrong—which you hadn't!"

"I know that, and he knows that. It's over now, really."

"It's not fucking over. He's been a prick to you since you got there, and he can't get away with it."

"Damon, I really don't want to ever bring it up again. It's finished, and I want to move on. Things are pretty unbearable here as it is, so I just want to keep my head down until I find something else."

"You've got a job here," he said.

"You know I don't. I'm going to go now and get something done before his coffee demands begin."

"Lazy wanker," he muttered.

"I'll speak to you later, okay? Please let it go now. I don't want to think about how he made me feel anymore."

Damon practically growled down the phone. I'd bet he was pacing his office and rubbing his forehead.

"Fine. I'll pick you up at lunch," he said before hanging up.

We didn't have any lunch plans, but he was coming here. I made a mental note to leave a few minutes earlier, so I could wait for him outside. There was no way I wanted him to come in when he was angry. Things here were shit, and having Damon yelling at my boss would not make it better.

I put my mobile back in my handbag and opened Google. The very first thing I was going to do was search for another job—on The Ogre's time, on his computer.

Fuck him.

Of course, I knew I needed my job and should keep my head down, like I'd just told Damon, but the anger simmering under the surface and the longing to be anywhere else told me it was a fabulous idea.

Twenty minutes later, I had emailed five job possibilities to my personal email address to follow up with later.

By summer, I *would* have a new job and finally be working my way to where I wanted to be.

With the emails sent, I felt lighter. For too long, I'd been standing still and getting on with it while I should have been making things happen for myself. Things were looking up, and I was so positive that I didn't even care when The Ogre started calling for coffee.

I was so engrossed in making Harry a spreadsheet that I didn't notice the time.

Harry was knocking on my door. "Someone's here for you," he said.

"Oh," I replied, grabbing my handbag in a fluster. I wasn't prepared for Damon or his anger toward my boss and his shithead of a son. "I lost track of time."

"Perhaps, in the future, you could have your men meet you somewhere else," he sneered.

Cheeky bastard.

He'd made it sound like I met up with someone different every day.

"Who the fuck do you think you are?" Damon spit.

I couldn't see him yet, but I sure as hell would soon. I leaped out of my seat and ran to the door just as he stopped in front of Harry.

Holding my arm to his chest, I tried to stop him from getting closer to Harry. "Damon, it's fine. Let's go."

"It's not fine, Nell."

The Ogre came stomping over, and I groaned inwardly. "What's going on here?"

"I was just letting Nell know that her friend had arrived," Harry replied.

"You arse-kissing little prick," Damon said. "You know exactly what you said to her."

"Now, listen here," Ogre said, "I don't know who you are, nor do I care, but I won't have you coming in here and talking to my son like that."

"You don't seem to give a shit about how you and your son talk to Nell."

"She's an employee," he said.

That was clearly not the right answer for Damon—or me. I put my hand on his chest as he stepped forward, tilting his head in an aggressive manner.

"You what? You hired her, so that gives you the right to treat her like shit. Is that what you're telling me?"

"I'm not telling you anything. I don't need to justify anything to you or anyone else."

Damon's body tensed under my hand, and any other time, it would have turned me on.

"It's not about justification. It's about not being a tosser. You treat her with the respect she deserves, or I'll be coming back."

"Damon, please," I whispered. I was so goddamn pissed off with him for coming in here that I wanted to kick and punch him.

"Are you threatening me?" Ogre asked, trying to straighten his back, but the weight of his gut prevented him from moving too much.

"Yes," Damon replied, not missing a beat. "What the fuck else could I have meant by that?"

Sighing, I closed my eyes and fought the urge to cry for the second time. Crying made me feel like a helpless, scared child, and I didn't ever want to feel like that again. A dark cloud wrapped its way around me, and I felt sick.

I'm okay. I'm not a kid anymore.

"Come on, Damon," I snapped, pushing him toward the door.

I looked back and winced.

The Ogre's face was bright red as he added, "Back by one, Nell," as if I'd suddenly forgotten when my lunch break ended.

I didn't reply or look back again as we left the building. "What the hell was that?" I yelled the second the door closed.

Sighing sharply through his teeth, Damon threw his hands up. "I'm not sorry, Nell. I wasn't going to do that, but the more I thought about it, the more it pissed me off, and then I heard what he said. He has no right to treat you that way."

"I know he doesn't, but I can handle it. Damon, shit, I need this job."

"No, you don't."

"I can't live off hopes and fucking dreams, can I?" I hissed, throwing my arms in the air.

He caught my hand, and I felt him instantly calm down a fraction. "How many times do I have to tell you that there's a job where I work? Can working with me really be worse than what you put up with here?"

"Of course not, Damon, but…"

"But what?"

"Things would get complicated if we worked together as well as slept together. You said yourself years ago that there were certain rules to making this work."

He looked at me like I'd grown another head. We were both comfortable with being friends and hanging out, but we didn't want to cross the line by putting ourselves into positions we couldn't easily get out of, like not sharing student accommodation when we had gone on to the same uni and working in the same place.

"Yeah, back when we were sixteen and still feeling our way through the boundaries that worked for us. Things have changed, Nell. We're older, more mature, and I'd like to think we're capable of working for the same company without killing each other—or whatever else you assume might happen."

I *assumed* that being around him so much would make me need more than I already did, and when that all blew up, I'd be heartbroken and still have to see him every day.

Narrowing my eyes, I pulled my wrist free of his grip. "That's not the only reason. I don't want help to get wherever I go."

"It's not always a bad thing, Nell. You shouldn't turn down great opportunities just because of some misplaced pride. You might hear about the job through me, or I could recommend you, but at the end of the day, getting the job and working your way up would be on your own merit. Jesus, why are you so fucking difficult?"

"Me?" I asked. "You're the one changing things without talking it through."

"Like what?"

Like making me fall in love with you, you bastard! Instead of the whole truth, I went with, "Duh, the work thing."

He sighed in frustration. "Fine. I think we should change the work rules."

I narrowed my eyes. That wasn't exactly what I'd had in mind. "Look, I'm getting hungry, and I need to be back by one. Can we please go and argue over lunch?"

"Absolutely," he replied, gesturing to his car.

Actually, I had hoped he'd apologise for shouting at my boss and tell me he didn't want to argue anymore. For the hour I got away from work, I didn't want to talk about it.

Damon drove us to a nice restaurant five minutes from my office, and we were shown to a table. The place was just starting to get busy with the lunchtime rush, but we'd managed to get there just in time.

Once we ordered, it was time to continue our argument.

"So," he said, "are you going to finish being a brat about me wanting to protect you?"

"I was not being a brat. Excuse me for not wanting the guy I fuck to threaten my boss."

His eye twitched, and his shoulders stiffened. "And excuse me for giving a shit about you. Obviously, I made a mistake."

He pushed his chair out, but before he could get up, I reached across and grabbed his wrist. My heart leaped in the worst way. The fear and panic I felt at him leaving killed me.

"No, don't leave. Please. I'm sorry, okay? That came out badly. You know what I mean though. This could cause more issues at work."

Looking up, he closed his eyes and blew out a deep breath. I didn't know which way this was going to go, but I knew I hated the thought of him walking away from me right now.

Finally, he lowered his head. "Maybe it will, but you can't let them talk to you like that."

"I like a roof over my head, Damon. I found a few jobs to apply for, and I *will* leave sooner rather than later, but until then, I have to be earning money."

"Have you handed your notice in yet?"

I smiled shyly. "No, I kind of planned to tell him to shove it one day and walk out. Completely immature of me, I know, but it's something I've wanted to do for a *long* time."

"Well, I fully support you."

"I know you do. Thank you for having my back."

"But?" he asked.

"But please speak to me before you go rushing in and shouting at the people who pay my wages."

He raised his eyebrow and took a sip of his beer. "Just to let you know beforehand, or so you have an opportunity to stop me?"

"Damon!"

Putting his glass down, he laughed and held his hands up. "All right, fine. I apologise for the way I handled it."

"Thank you."

"Hey, can I talk to you about something?"

"Sure. You want to get together later? Feeling randy?"

He deadpanned. "No. Well, yes."

"What's up?"

Licking his lips, he looked me dead in the eyes. "Do you still just see me as the guy you're fucking?"

The waitress, having the most impeccable timing ever, placed Damon's plate down with a fire-engine red face. She didn't look me in the eyes as she put my pizza in front of me. "Can I get you anything else?" she asked timidly.

I bit my lip and looked away. He could call me immature all he wanted, but I couldn't talk to the woman without laughing.

"No, thank you. We're fine."

I actually did want ketchup, but I wasn't going to ask for it now.

"Enjoy your meal," she said, hightailing it off the second she'd finished talking.

"Did you see her coming?" I asked.

Nodding, he flashed me a guilty smile.

"You arsehole! The poor girl was so embarrassed."

"She works in a restaurant, Nell. I bet she's overheard worse."

I cut my pizza into slices and picked up one. "Not the point."

"Are you going to answer the question?" he asked.

"Oh, that wasn't just to make the waitress uncomfortable?"

He rolled his eyes. "Of course not. I was asking it anyway and decided not to stop just because she was there."

Like normal people would have.

"No, I don't just see you as the guy I'm fucking. I like to think we're friends since, you know, we're friends."

He blinked a few times and then cleared his throat. I thought he was going to say something else, but he tucked into his steak without another word. Whatever was going on in his head, it was clearly eating away at him. Usually, he'd be joking around and flirting shamelessly.

I watched him concentrate too hard on his food. He cut the meat a little too vigorously, chewed a little too hard, and held himself a little too rigidly. There was no denying he was pissed off, but even with the tension in his eyes and his hostility, I could barely take my eyes off him.

To me, Damon was perfect. I loved everything about him, even his protective tendencies.

"You okay?" I asked after an unbearable few minutes of silence.

"Mmhmm, I'm fine. Your pizza good?"

It was, but suddenly, I didn't feel at all hungry. Nodding my head, I forced in what I could. The shift from Scotland

Nell and Damon to normal Nell and Damon was harder than I'd imagined it would be.

"Are you sure you're okay?"

He dropped his knife and fork on the plate, making me jump at the clattering sound. "What do you want me to say, Nell?"

I had absolutely no idea.

"Forget it," he said, shaking his head. "Can we please just enjoy lunch?"

With a twist in my stomach, I nodded. "Yeah, sure."

I couldn't enjoy lunch. There was a dark, heavy feeling that enveloped me, making me want to skip the rest of the day and hibernate at home.

TWENTY-SIX

DAMON

Lunch yesterday had been a disaster. Not only had Nell and I argued, but she'd also just cemented what I'd known all along. Nell wasn't going to want more. Shit, even if she did, she'd never let herself have it. Something was really wrong because no one just decided to be alone when they didn't want to.

I put in a fairly fucking desperate-sounding call to Chloe. Nell had claimed my heart and every other piece of me, so if there were even a glimmer of hope, I was going to run with it.

"Damon," Chloe said. "Now, what could you possibly be calling me about?"

"Very cute," I muttered dryly, earning a laugh.

"Go on. What's she done?"

"Nothing. She's not done anything. Nell's perfectly okay to keep on the way we've been for years. I know full well that it's what I signed up for, so I can't complain but—no, fuck it, I want to complain."

"Please do."

"I love her. I want everything. Hell, I'd marry her right now if she were willing."

"Er, you probably shouldn't say things like that to her."

I laughed humourlessly. "Don't I know it? How do I get her to open up? Do you even know why she's so bloody stubborn when it comes to relationships? If anyone knew, it'd be you."

"Not really. All I know is that her parents had a rocky marriage, and it put Nell off. I kind of thought that, as she grew up, she'd get out of the physical-only phase and realise she could have something real. God, last year, she said she wanted more but very quickly changed her mind."

"She did? She's wanted that before?" *Hope, hello, you beautiful bastard.*

If she'd been open to it once, no matter how briefly, then there was a possibility she could again.

"Yes, but not for long. I think she was trying it out, just considering it."

And there hope goes. She couldn't even get past considering it.

"Right," I said.

"Look, Damon, if you really want to know, I think you need to be having this conversation with Nell."

"I know, but what if…"

"If she doesn't want anything?"

"Yeah."

"What would happen then?"

Wincing, I rubbed the ache in my chest. "I can't keep doing this. We said as long as there were no real feelings, and it has gone way past that now. How am I supposed to have her that close to me but have no real part of her?"

Chloe sucked in a deep breath. "Are you going to break things off with her?"

"I don't think I have a choice, Chlo."

"I do understand where you're coming from. There is no way I could have a casual relationship with Logan. But I'm worried about what this'll do to her."

"So am I. Don't get me wrong. I think I have to put myself first right now. I want her so bad. I want to go home to her, wake up to her, be the one she goes to for help and support, cook with her, have her steal my side of the bed, have her girlie shit all over the place. But she won't give me that, and I don't know how to be around her, knowing that. Loving her like this is killing me."

"God, I hate to be the one to say this because I love that girl, but if you carry on, you're both going to end up getting even more hurt. Just please, please tell me, so I can be there for her."

Things got very real, very fast. Chloe's words were like a bucket of ice-cold water being tipped over my head. I already missed Nell, and I hadn't made my final decision yet—even though I knew full well what I needed to do.

"All right. Thanks for the chat, Chlo."

"Of course," she replied softly. "And you know if you want to talk more first or if there's absolutely anything I can do to help before…well, you know, then just pick up the phone."

"I will."

We hung up, and I felt like I had a fucking truck parked on my chest. And the only person I wanted was the one person who was shredding me from the inside out.

Nell walked into my flat with two Domino's boxes, a six-pack of Beck's, and a bottle of wine. It was times like these, where we were so much like any normal couple, when it was easy to get lost and think it was real.

"How was your day?" she asked as she put the boxes on the worktop and got a wine glass out of my cupboard.

She was comfortable enough to help herself around my place and treat it like her own, and she had absolutely no idea of what that really meant, which was probably a good thing at the minute.

My conversation with Chloe was still at the forefront of my mind, fucking me up further.

"Not bad," I replied, flipping the box lids open and popping the top on the bottle. "Yours?"

"I didn't kill my boss and his son, so the day was a success."

Gritting my teeth, I asked, "They still giving you shit?"

"Yep. Nothing I can't handle though."

"Sure?" I wanted her to say no and ask for my help. There wasn't much chance of that, especially after the last time I'd paid her boss a visit.

She took a sip of wine and sat beside me at the island. "I'm fine, honestly. I won't be there forever. God, I'm so starving. I think I'll take your slices bet today."

"Ah, will you?" I said.

"I'm eating you under the table, mister."

I laughed at what she'd said. "Not going to say no to that."

She rolled her eyes. "Oh, funny. After pizza, if you're lucky…"

My heart thumped, and I felt a stir in my pants. "I'm suddenly not at all hungry."

"You're such a pervert, Damon. Eat your pizza."

"Are you staying over tonight?"

"I can," she replied.

"Well," I said, running my finger along her thigh, "I think that's a good idea."

She raised a jet-black eyebrow. "So do I. Maybe you should eat up, so you'll have enough energy for me later."

I would make a joke about how I wouldn't need to eat, but that wasn't true. Nell was a demon between the sheets. I adored how much she loved sex and how unashamed she was about what she liked. It was the sexiest thing about her.

"Eat up, Nell."

My phone rang as Nell elbowed me in the side, smiling up at me in a way she hadn't done before. For a second, I forgot the phone and the fact that we were only supposed to be friends. Hell, I forgot my own fucking name because Nell was looking at me like she loved me.

She clicked her fingers in front of my face, and I blinked. "It's your mum."

I took the phone off her and gulped before answering the call, "Hey, Mum."

"Hi, darling. How are you?"

"I'm good. Just eating dinner with Nell."

"Oh, sorry, I didn't realise you had company." The way she'd said *company* made me press the phone to my ear harder in the hopes that Nell wouldn't hear. My mother was just waiting for me to tell her that Nell and I were exclusive.

"No, it's fine. Is everything okay?"

"Everything's great," she replied. Her voice had risen suspiciously after finding out Nell was here with me. "So, how is she?"

I looked over and saw Nell smirking at me. "She's fine." *Soon going to be* very *fine.*

"Can I speak to her?"

"Er, she's eating, Mum."

Nell mouthed, *Speakerphone.*

My mum could be a little overenthusiastic sometimes, so I was reluctant, but I wanted Nell to get along and be comfortable with my family.

"Hold on, Mum," I said. I put her on speaker. "We can both hear you."

"Nell, how are you, darling?" Mum asked, sounding a lot happier to talk to her than to me. She was bloody desperate to marry me off.

"I'm great. Thanks. How are you?"

"Much better now. What has Damon cooked for you?"

Nell laughed and then pouted at me. "He didn't. I brought pizza with me."

"Damon!"

I rolled my eyes. *Here we go…*

"She offered, Mum."

"You can't let your girlfriend live off pizza."

Fuck.

Panic sparked in Nell's eyes.

"Mum," I said warningly.

"I mean it, Damon. I raised you better than that."

"Mum," I snapped, "I have to go. I'll call you later."

An icy pit settled in my stomach. Nell didn't talk or move as I hung up.

"Sorry about her. She gets a little…*mum* occasionally."

She licked her lips. "It's okay." Her voice was low and reserved.

It was definitely not okay.

"Are we cool?"

"Yeah, as long as we know this is what it is, and it won't turn into some fairy tale."

Wow. Her words plowed into me like a fucking freight train.

"Right," I said. "Just casual."

She put the pizza crust down that she'd been holding stiff in her hand since Mum's bloody girlfriend comment. "Yep, just casual."

How can I do that when I'm so overwhelmingly in love with her? Shit, I couldn't fool myself into thinking that casual sex with the woman I'd fallen in love with would be enough. I wanted everything with Nell—commitment, house, marriage, hell, even kids one day. But she didn't want any of it.

She wasn't ready, couldn't give a big enough part of herself, or just plain didn't feel anything for me. Whatever it was, I couldn't stick around to find out.

I was in this, and she wasn't. That meant I couldn't have any of it.

"Nell," I said, already half-regretting my decision, "we can't see each other anymore."

Her posture immediately became defensive, the way it would whenever a subject was getting heavier than she was comfortable with. "Why not?"

I can't believe I'm doing this. "I think that it's obvious why. I want more than this, and you don't." Each word was like a jagged cut deep in my flesh. I was ripping my own heart out, knowingly, *willingly*.

A fleeting look of pain passed her eyes so quickly that I almost missed it.

"Um…" She looked around, completely and utterly lost. "How can you do this to me? We had a deal, Damon. You can't just change your mind."

Now, she was the one doing the stabbing with her words.

"Can't I?" I said. This hadn't been the plan. Believe me, I never wanted to fall in love with her, but I couldn't help it.

"We agreed on casual." She shook her head. "You can't just change your mind," she repeated a little more forcefully.

"Yes, I can. Jesus, I'm *in love* with you, Nell."

She sucked oxygen in like it was going out of fashion. She looked stunned and then downright terrified.

"No." She shook her head, and her eyes filled with tears. "Stop. Damon, don't. You can't."

"I don't really get a choice, do I?"

"Yes, you do. Casual. We agreed on casual, and I don't care what you say. You can't just—"

"Can't just, what? You don't get to control who you love. Not everyone can switch it off like you can. Is it me, or is it all men? You can tell me if I'm just not someone you could fall for." *I think I can take it.*

"I don't want a relationship," she said.

"I know that. You've mentioned it quite fucking often, but that's not what I asked."

"You can't see me sexually or at all?" she asked, completely changing the subject.

I gulped and closed my eyes. "At all. It's too hard. I can't stop wanting everything with you."

She pursed her lips and turned her head away. It almost looked as if she was going to cry, and then I saw a tear.

"What am I going to do without you?"

"You'll be fine," I whispered. I wouldn't be. My gut was in knots.

"We're friends. Aren't we?"

"Nell, we are so much more than friends."

She shook her head. "We're not. We're what we agreed to be."

"I knew you were closed off, but I never thought you were blind. How many men have you slept with since the weekend before Chloe and Logan moved into their house?"

Her green eyes were so cold. "That's not the point. There wasn't anyone I wanted to sleep recently…"

"Wow," I said, trying to pretend like that wasn't killing me. "That's real classy, Nell."

"Don't you *dare* judge me. I *never* led you to believe anything else. Why do you get to sleep with whomever you want, but I can't?"

She had me there, but that wasn't the point, not really.

"I don't want to argue with you. I just want this to be done. Unless you can give me something right now, a reason to stay that's not just great sex, I'm gone. It doesn't have to be some big commitment, just *something*, so I know we could work at getting there. I don't want to lose this, but this can't be all we have." I was begging, and I didn't even care. I would get on my fucking knees if it would make a difference.

"This is all I have in me to give," she whispered. "I'm not like Chloe."

"I don't want you to be like Chloe. I want you to be you but *with* me. Let yourself open up to me, please. If you can't even tell me you're willing to work on something, I'm gone. It's too hard, and I really can't do it anymore." Gulping, I swallowed the rising urge to cry. Thick emotion clogged my throat.

She stood taller, and I had a moment of blind panic. *What is she doing?*

I loved her so much. She was the other half of me, everything I wanted.

But I couldn't force her to stay. If she wanted to walk, there was nothing I could do.

"I'm so sorry," she said. "I really don't know what I'll do without you. You're a friend."

A tear rolled down her cheek, and I wanted to brush it away, but she was breaking me, and I could do nothing but watch on in horror.

"What you're asking of me isn't something I can give."

So, that's it.

I took a deep breath as the dagger pierced my heart. "Then, you need to go, Nell." Turning around, I walked into my bedroom and didn't look back.

TWENTY-SEVEN

NELL

In a complete daze, I walked out of Damon's flat. It hurt. *So* bad. Turning him down, hurting him, leaving him gave me the worst feeling I'd ever experienced. I tried, unsuccessfully, not to cry as I got in my car and put even more distance between us.

The drive home was dodgy. I remembered absolutely nothing of it only because I could barely see through tears I shouldn't be shedding over a guy in the first place.

When I parked outside my little flat, I leaned against the window and closed my eyes. All I had to do was forget about him and move on. I could do that, and when I did, things would be all right again.

We were never permanent. I had known that better than anyone. From our very first night after the agreement, I had known there would come a point when we'd have to stop.

I hadn't been prepared for how much it would crush me.

Love is a bitch.

A few minutes later, I couldn't hold off on getting out and going inside anymore, and people were starting to look at me lying in my car. I got out and dashed inside before anyone could ask if I was okay.

I slammed my front door, kicked off my shoes, and stumbled in a messy, sobbing state to the sofa. *Why does it feel like my insides are falling out and my lungs are constricting? How can a feeling affect you physically?*

After twenty minutes of crying my heart out, there was a knock on my door. I ached for it to be Damon. Dragging myself off the sofa and to the door, I yanked it open to see Chloe smiling sadly back at me.

She gasped, so I knew I looked like absolute shit.

"Nell, come here," she said, wrapping me up in a big hug.

I fell into her, sobbing on her shoulder. Chloe was good enough to let me get tears and mascara all over her nice cream jumper and not bitch at me over it.

A few minutes later, I let go of her and ran my hands over my face. "Sorry," I muttered. I didn't break down, especially not in front of humans, so I was embarrassed that Chloe had seen me like that.

"Don't be silly." She sighed. "What am I going to do with you, huh?"

"He called you, didn't he?"

"Yeah. I'm sorry, Nelly."

I shrugged and closed the front door. "Not your fault," I replied, leading her into the living room.

Great, my smudged mascara face was all over my cute sage scatter cushion, too. Damon owed me new soft furnishings.

Curling up on the sofa, I hugged my ruined cushion. "I don't like missing him," I whispered.

Chloe tilted her head to the side, and her long, straight hair fell in front of her shoulder. "You don't have to miss him. That's the part I'm still unclear on, Nell. Anyone can see how you feel about the guy, so why are you denying what you both want?"

"You know you sound a lot like me when you were running from Logan last year."

She licked her lip. "Yes, I do. I was terrified because I'd fallen in love with my dead boyfriend's brother. What's your excuse, sweetie?"

"Jace wasn't dead," I grumbled, picking on the one thing that didn't make this about my issues.

"Thank God. Though that doesn't change the facts. I thought he was dead, and when he turned up, it only added to the problems. You're not getting out of this. Talk to me, and maybe I can help."

"No one can help."

I—*we*—needed help years ago. My parents never wanted help.

"You're scaring me. Are you in trouble? Did something happen? Nell, I need to know."

"Nothing happened. I wasn't beaten or abused. I've just seen a lot of marriages turn to shit, and I'm not about to enter into that. Can we not talk about it tonight, please? I either need to eat a lot of junk or get blind drunk. You choose."

"I'll get the chocolate."

Damn, I was hoping for the other one.

I pressed the cushion into my stomach as she got up and went to the kitchen. Everything still ached. I was so done with that feeling already and just wanted it over with now.

"Here," Chloe said, coming back with a tub of ice cream, a large bar of Cadburys, and a box of Maltesers. "Will these make you feel better?"

I glared. "They should."

They wouldn't. I wasn't quite dumb enough to believe that getting over Damon would just take a little—or a lot—of sugar. But it was a good start. I would follow what they did in movies—eat junk food, and drink booze.

"If you're going to be like that, you can leave. I don't need to hear how much of a twat I am, Chloe. I already know it."

"I love you, Nell, and I'm never going to judge you. But you totally have the power to un-twat yourself right now, and other people messing up isn't a good enough reason. You know full well that you control your own life. You've been doing it for long enough. You're not your parents. You're uniquely bloody stubborn, and no one is going to make you change into something you don't want to be."

I understood logic perfectly well—I wasn't broken—but I couldn't separate that from what I'd been through. If someone would like to give me a pill to change that, then they could be my bloody guest. I'd take it gladly.

"Take a few days, and see if things are clearer then."

Things were perfectly clear now. I knew what I wanted, but I didn't know how to have it. Shit, I needed a shrink, like yesterday.

"Yeah," I said, conceding so that we could move on for a while. "So, what did he say when he called?"

"He just explained that he told you he wanted more, and you couldn't, so you're not seeing each other anymore."

"How did he sound?" I asked.

"What do you want me to say to that?"

"The truth. I always want the truth from you."

"He sounded crushed."

I couldn't help the little gasp of pain at hearing how much I'd hurt him. It killed me. Every instinct told me to protect him, to make it better. It was hard to fight what I wanted to do, right down to my bones. I wouldn't forgive myself for hurting him, but I could live with it a hell of a lot easier, knowing we'd never become what I'd witnessed while growing up.

"Oh, Nelly, I hate to see you like this. Do you think you should talk to him and see if you can work something out?"

"Work what out? We want different things. There is no way I can go back to what we had, knowing he wants more, even if he could. I'm not that heartless."

"I know you're not. No one is saying you are. You're allowed to want different things, if that's really what this is about."

"It is," I replied. "I like him, Chlo, but I can't give him what he wants, so we can't do this, any of it."

She smiled sadly. I could tell she was a little disappointed that I couldn't get my act together to be with him, and honestly, a part of me was, too. Insecurities and self-doubt were supposed to get smaller as you got older. No one fucking told you they'd only grow.

"What's the plan now then?"

I shrugged. "I guess I just carry on. I'll work at getting a new job and having the career I want."

"And after work, what will you do?"

"I have no idea." *Go back to how things were pre-Damon.*

I could barely remember before him. He had been such a big part of my life, and I hadn't realised how much until he was no longer there.

"Is there anything I can do?"

"Unless you can change me, there's nothing you can do but bring the wine."

"You can change you," she said, giving me a sympathetic smile.

"Yeah? Tell me how, and I'll do it."

I didn't have the first clue on what it took to make a relationship work. Screwing one up? That I could do in a heartbeat. I'd seen enough of that. *How am I supposed to be successful at something I don't know?* It scared me, and it was a much bigger risk than jumping into a new career or a change of hair colour. Relationships had the power to completely crush a person, to turn them into a shadow, and I wasn't prepared to break another person or be on the receiving end. Too much risk.

"You could start by talking."

"I don't know what to say. I've not had the best role models, and I'm scared. There, I admitted it. I'm scared."

"We all get scared."

"I *love* him."

"God, Nell," she whispered, her eyes tearing up. "Talk to me, and let me help. I want you two to be happy, and I know you can be happy together. Let me in. Or better still, let Damon in. I bet he can help you overcome whatever it is that's got you so terrified of giving yourself to him."

"If he can't?"

"Then, it'll be sad, and you'll cry, but you'll both be okay."

"Would you be okay if you and Logan broke up?"

She looked away and bit her lips together.

"See? I might not have firsthand experience, Chloe, but I'm not stupid. When you really love someone, you open yourself up to all sorts of heart-breaking things that can change you forever."

"You sound so much like me before."

"I know I do. It's really annoying actually. Hey, maybe I'll get to where you are one day."

"You will. Just take it one day at a time, and *please* just consider talking to Damon."

Smiling, I nodded. "I'll think about it."

I wouldn't. I *couldn't.*

TWENTY-EIGHT

DAMON

Going out, getting fucked up, and *getting fucked* was all I cared about right now. Doubt chipped away at my very core.

What if Nell will come around? If I had known she'd be ready in six months—hell, a year or two even—I would've kept going the way we were. But there was no guarantee, and I couldn't spend another second out there in the unknown.

I sat at my desk, counting down the minutes until I could leave for the day. I'd made so many mistakes today and been somewhere else completely that I was surprised I hadn't gotten a warning about my performance.

"You all right?" my manager, Richard, asked. He hadn't said anything, but he knew there was something up.

I pushed my swivel chair out and ran my hands through my hair. "Yeah, I'm fine. Sorry, I've just had a shit couple of days."

"I hope everything's okay."

It wasn't, and I couldn't see a way out. Right now, there was just endless darkness.

"I'll be fine, Rich. I just need to pull my shit together."

"We all have things troubling us in our personal lives from time to time. Try not to be too hard on yourself. If you need to take a few days…"

I shook my head. "I don't, but thanks." My relationship with Nell had screwed my personal life, but I wasn't going to let it affect my professional one.

"Okay, we'll go through the Cecil and Graham account next week."

"Did you want to do it now? I'm fine to," I said.

Rich shouldn't have to wait until I was on top of my game to discuss a campaign. If I wanted the option of going into a partnership, I would have to do better than I had been.

He held his hand up. "Sandy wants to go kitchen-shopping this afternoon, so I'm leaving a few hours early. There is no way I'm wasting all weekend on it. If you need to leave a bit earlier, too…"

"Thanks, Rich."

With a smile and a nod, he turned around and left. I thought he saw a little of his young self in me. He'd said a few times that we had the same drive and determination. Right now, I'd bet he was regretting taking me on right out of uni and giving me the responsibilities I had.

I pulled myself together long enough to put an hour of decent work in, and then I left an hour and a half early. Rich had already gone, but I knew it wouldn't be a problem. He'd offered after all.

Taking the steps down to the ground floor two at a time, I prayed no one would stop me to chat. I'd not been here long, but most of the people who worked in the building were very friendly. Right now, I wanted cold beer and easy women.

Driving home was quicker than rush hour. I came to a crossroads and wanted to turn right to Nell's, but I forced myself to go left. Running back to her wouldn't do any good. She would probably just tell me to do one anyway. I hated that we were in different places right now.

Why can't I have met her years later when she'd dealt with whatever is holding her back? Why can't I suck it up and stick it out until that happens?

I pulled into my drive, and a surprise was sitting in a car next to mine.

"Steph?" I said, getting out at the same time as she left her silver Mini. "What are you doing here?"

"I beat your brother. He's meeting me here in about twenty minutes."

"That doesn't answer my question," I said, slamming the door shut.

"Lance and his woman, Ivory, are coming, so we can cheer you up, obviously. I'm sorry about what happened with Nell."

Shrugging one shoulder, I locked my car and lifted my chin toward my house. Stephanie followed, her high silver heels clicking on the concrete floor.

"You guys didn't have to come all the way here. I'm doing fine."

"Being honest here, you don't look fine, Damon. You look like shit."

"Thank you, Stephanie," I said over my shoulder as I let us into my flat.

I knew I did. Sleep had abandoned me for most of last night. I'd lain awake for hours, playing over my conversation and good-bye with Nell. My bed had felt too big, and I couldn't sleep on my side since she'd claimed it.

If this was what everyone went through after breaking up with someone they loved, then I didn't understand why people would take the chance again with someone new. Then, I realised that perhaps that was how Nell felt.

Has something happened before me? She's not mentioned a guy, but why would she? Chloe will know though, surely?

"Do you want a drink?" I asked, flicking the kettle on so that I could make a strong coffee before going out.

"I'd love a tea. Thanks."

"So, what's the grand plan then? How are you lot cheering me up?"

"Well," she said, taking an apple from the almost empty fruit bowl and spinning it in her hand, "we planned to surprise you, get you fed on takeaway curry, and then get you hammered at a club."

"Sounds very similar to what I was going to do anyway."

"Yes, but now, you don't have to be quite as pathetic since you won't be doing it alone."

"Compliments just keep rolling in with you, don't they?" I said sarcastically, leaning against the worktop.

"Do you want to talk about what happened with Nell?"

"Nope."

She rolled her eyes. "It helps to talk things through."

"Didn't with her."

"Are you sure you can't work it out? There's not much you can't work through if you both want to."

Raising my eyebrows, I shook my head. "Won't happen. The only way we could go back to the way it was, is if I settle for casual sex."

"Most men would love that," she said bitterly.

"I used to love it. Things change. People grow—people who aren't Nell, that is."

"Whoa," she said. "That came from a bad place. You're not usually like that."

"Sorry, I don't take rejection well." That wasn't true. This wasn't the first time I'd been rejected, but it was the first time I had been rejected by someone I loved, someone I wanted more than anything else in the world.

"You'll be okay, Damon. We've all had our hearts broken before. What doesn't kill you only makes you stronger; remember that."

Like that bullshit was going to help. I knew I wasn't going to keel over just because Nell didn't want me, but that didn't mean I was okay. Fuck, I was sick of thinking about her all the time.

"You got any single friends?"

"Damon…"

"What? You want me to move on, so help."

"Rebound isn't moving on."

"Of course it is. Rebound is the first stage."

She shook her head. "If you think I'm letting you use one of my friends like that, you're seriously mistaken. Sort yourself out."

Grabbing the Jack Daniels out of the cupboard, I took a swig from the bottle. She was right. Getting into another casual sex situation with someone else was a fucking stupid idea. There was no way I wanted history to repeat itself.

"Fine. I'm sorry, okay?"

She sighed, put the apple down, and grabbed the bottle from my hand. "Lance and Ivory will be here soon."

"They can't see me drinking?"

"No, they can't catch us doing this."

Slamming the bottle on the worktop, she captured my lips in a frantic and domineering kiss. I stood still, frozen, as she gripped my shoulders. It was strange, kissing her, and I didn't want to, but that didn't stop me.

I grabbed her around the waist, turned her around, and lifted her onto the worktop. Stephanie wrapped her legs around my waist and stuck her tongue in my mouth. The kiss was all over the place. I had no idea what she was going to do, and I didn't particularly like it. She wasn't a bad kisser. She just didn't kiss like Nell.

Leaving her hips, I trailed my hands down to her skirt and shoved it up. Moaning, she arched her chest against mine, and my dick finally woke up. Tugging on my jeans, she managed to get them to fall to my knees. That gave me enough room to move.

"Condom," she muttered against my lips as she reached over for her handbag.

With her mouth away from mine, it gave me the time to realise what I was about to do. Stephanie was a friend and not one I could have a casual relationship with even if I wanted to.

She tore the packet open and rolled it down my erection. She'd made the first move; she understood what I was looking for, so I didn't feel bad for thrusting forward and filling her.

"Oh God, Damon," she groaned, tilting her head back.

I compared everything to Nell—every kiss, every time Stephanie muttered something, the way she'd cling to my shoulders without digging her nails in. I'd loved the sharp cut of nails in my flesh when Nell got wild. It was the hottest thing and never failed to get me off.

Stephanie cried out as she came, and I followed, tucking my head in her neck. I stayed there for a minute while she held on around my waist.

Fucking her was nowhere near unpleasant, but I felt guilty.

Feeling bad for doing nothing wrong pissed me off. I was mad at Nell. I wanted to shout at her, smash something, anything, and move away to where I'd never have the possibility of running into her. I wanted to forget she existed, but I knew I'd never be free of her.

I pulled out of Stephanie and dumped the condom in the bin.

"There," she said. "Rebound sex over. Now, can we get on with the night?"

Smiling through gritted teeth, I nodded and swallowed the sinking feeling. I'd just made a big mistake.

TWENTY-NINE

NELL

It'd been three days, and I was so mad at Damon for changing things between us. Everything had been perfect before. Well, it had been as perfect as that situation could have been. He wasn't supposed to fall in love with me. No one was.

Work sucked even more because I wouldn't get naughty texts from him at random points throughout the day. All that was gone. Everything was gone, and I was living in a Damon-free zone. I hated it.

"Nell," The Ogre snapped. He'd really picked a bad day to step up his arsehole game after his standoff with Damon. "I need that file now."

"I gave it to you this morning," I replied, trying not to shout back too loudly. Stepping into his office, I used every ounce of self-control I had and smiled. "It should be on the top of your In tray."

He snatched it off the pile, and his mouth thinned. "Got it."

No apology, he dropped his eyes and opened the folder.

I need my job. I need my job. This is temporary.

Man, I wished I didn't need to eat because that wanker would be getting yelled at right now. *Ignorant bastard.*

As soon as I found something new, I was going to tell him to stick it. Today, I would follow up on the applications I'd filled in and emailed off. I would beg if I needed to.

It was five minutes to twelve, but I couldn't wait another second. I grabbed my bag and headed out for lunch. I'd not eaten at work since my first week. As soon as Reg had shown his true colours—Ogre green—I spent every second out of the office that I could get away with.

I called Chloe on my way to KFC. Today, I was going to eat fried chicken and two portions of chips. It was necessary, and I didn't care. Counting calories could fuck off, too.

"Hey, Nell," she said, all cheerful.

I was happy her world was all sunshine and rainbows, but I still wanted to cut the bitch.

"Hey, you free for lunch today?"

"Sorry, I can't do today. I'm on my way to meet a bridezilla."

"Ha! Have fun with that."

"Oh, I'm sure I will. How are you?"

"I'm perfect," I replied sarcastically.

Chloe laughed. "Things will work out if you work on them."

"I'm supposed to be the strong one, and you're supposed to be the weird emotional one. What happened?"

"You are strong, but even the strongest people have weaknesses, Nell. It's nothing to be ashamed of. Everyone struggles, and everyone makes mistakes as they go. Look at me! You'll work things out in your own time. There's no rush."

She was right, of course. We all put so much pressure on ourselves to be perfect and be everything others expected of us. Perfect was impossible. I was a glowing example of that.

"Yes!" I said, throwing my free hand up. "I'm Nell, and I'm imperfect, but I've never committed murder, so get over it."

Chloe laughed. "You can't compare not wanting a relationship to murder."

"Yes, I can. Murder is worse."

"Not denying that, but—"

"Uh-uh! Don't mess with my mojo here. I got this, Chlo."

"All right, fine. As long as you're back to your old self, I don't care what ridiculous methods you use to justify things."

Neither did I because I was human, and everyone else could fuck off.

For the first time since Damon had cut me out of his life, I felt relatively hopeful. I still missed him much more than I'd even thought possible, but in time, I'd be okay. That was how it went, right? You had someone, you lost them, and you moved on. All I had to do was focus on other things until it didn't hurt to think about him. I could do that.

"I'll speak to you later, Chlo," I said, pushing the door to KFC open. I wasn't okay enough to swap greasy chicken with a healthy wrap or sandwich.

"Bye," she said, still laughing a little.

My perky mood lasted until I got back to work, and Reg started to be a prick. All afternoon, I spent running around after him, usually making coffee and booking dinner reservations. Dinner. That wasn't work-related, so why did the lazy shit think it was okay to get me to do it? I hated him more than normal, and I knew it was because of the whole he-whom-I-didn't-want-to-think-of situation.

When I got home, I walked out of my shoes, dropped my bag and jacket onto the floor, and headed to my bedroom to change into some pyjamas. I was done with the day and just wanted to do nothing but lounge on the sofa and eat.

When I was in my Fair Isle onesie, I slumped down with a share-size packet of crisps and flicked on the TV. There was just shit on, but that was okay because I didn't want to be engrossed with anything. For a while, I just wanted to exist.

Ten minutes in, I decided—against my better judgment—to Facebook-stalk Damon. I would just check my News Feed, and if he were on it, I would allow myself to visit his profile. *Yeah, that's perfectly reasonable. Yeah.*

I scrolled down the list of people sharing random shit—a few unexplained rants, two people letting the world know what they were eating, and Chloe checking in at some restaurant Logan had taken her to.

Nothing from Damon. *Has he deleted me?* I wanted to check. I shouldn't break my own only-if-he-was-in-the-feed rule and check. But who was I kidding? I typed his name in and clicked his profile.

What have I become?

We were still friends. I scrolled down and noticed his last activity was being tagged in Stephanie's photos. He was standing too close to her, looking buzzed on alcohol. His dark hair was messy, and I didn't want to know why.

The post was dated the night after he'd ended things with us. He'd gone out the night after he'd told me he loved me.

What the fuck is that?

I was angry. Real, pure, irrational, steam-coming-from-my-ears anger. I tried to suppress it, but I couldn't and felt like crying. *He isn't mine, never has been, but if he can move on so quickly after confessing love, then what does that say about me?*

Of course I was being absolutely idiotic right now. So, he had gone out. He was hurt and letting off steam. But I never wanted to hurt him, and I knew he wouldn't want to fuck someone else yet. Well, I hoped he wouldn't.

Flicking through the photos extinguished some of my anger but filled the void with guilt. He looked miserable.

Why can't I be normal?

The last picture made my stomach roll. I wanted to hurl my phone at the wall.

In the background of Stephanie and some other girl's selfie was Damon with his tongue down another woman's throat.

I swallowed what felt like a fucking rugby ball, and scalding pain spread through my entire body. He was under no obligation to be faithful to me, never had been, but I'd expected more from him, I guessed. I hated that it was the last picture, too.

What happened after? Did he take her home?

Curling into a ball, I stared at the picture, unable to stop punishing myself and look away.

Did she wake up in his bed, wrapped in his naked body?

I scrubbed my eyes and took a few shaky deep breaths.

Because I was hurt and angry and not at all thinking like a normal person right now, I dialled his number. There was no doubt that I would regret this tomorrow, but right now, I needed to tell him how I felt.

"Nell," he said, greeting me like an old acquaintance.

"Did you fuck her?" *Oh, way to go, Nell.*

Somewhere between losing my clearly tiny mind and calling him in the first place and snapping the word *fuck*, I started to cry. It felt like an explosion of emotions that I'd never experienced before, and I didn't fully understand it. All I knew was, it'd had to come out, or I'd combust.

"Excuse me?"

"The girl you were trying to swallow in the club. Did you take her home?"

"What girl?" he snapped back.

"The one in the picture on Facebook."

He was silent for a minute, and I wasn't sure if he was going to talk to me about it, tell me it was none of my business and hang up, or question my sanity over checking up on him. I was going to do Option C the second we got off the phone.

"You've been checking up on me on Facebook?"

"No, of course not," I said, as if he'd accused me of wanting to sleep with his dad. And I was lying through my teeth, but I couldn't admit to him that I was totally keeping tabs on him. "Jesus Christ, Damon, a few days ago, you were telling me you wanted to settle down."

"And if I remember correctly, Nell, *you* told me you didn't want to."

"That's not the point. *I've* not been out mashing my face against some guy's!"

He groaned, and I felt the sound shake my very soul. I hated hurting him.

"Why are we doing this? You have no right to confront me for kissing someone else," he said.

It was true, but his words cut deep and kicked me in the stomach. Big, fat tears rolled down my cheeks.

"I know that." Of course I knew, and that made it worse somehow. I wanted the right, but I couldn't take it. "I just…" *Just what?* There was no suitable answer for that, not one that wouldn't hurt us both even more anyway.

"I'm sorry," I said, silently crying in defeat.

"Don't be sorry, Nell. Just figure out what the fuck you want. If it's not me the way I need us to be, then delete me from your life and social media."

"So, this is really an all-or-nothing deal?"

"I love you, for fuck's sake!" he shouted. "How am I supposed to be your *friend*?"

God, I wished he wouldn't say that. It made me whole and tore me apart at the same time.

"I shouldn't have called. I won't do it again," I said, pressing End Call just in time to fold over and sob into my poor, poor cushion.

THIRTY

NELL

I hated missing Damon. I hated myself for not being able to get my love life together—or even my life together. I hated that he could be with another woman. And I hated my parents.

Everything felt colder and darker. I'd had no idea how much happiness and light he brought before he was gone, and it was too late.

I sat at my dingy desk after making The Ogre his second coffee of the hour. I'd never felt so low or like such a complete failure before.

Opening my drawer, I got my phone out to check my personal emails to see if anyone had offered me an amazing job for ten times what I was earning here. No such luck.

And nothing from Damon. Not that I'd expected it. Ending things was ultimately my idea, but here I was, hoping he would make contact. I was desperate for something. *Anything.*

Chloe had spoken to him a few times. She hadn't divulged much, and that'd made me want to shine a bright light in her eyes and demand that she told me every little detail. But I was afraid. Afraid that she would tell me he was coping and afraid that she would tell me he wasn't. I'd hurt him, but I couldn't hear someone tell me how much, not again.

I gripped my phone in my hands, wanting to reach out to him. If I could flick a switch and have everything go back to how it had been before we parted ways, I'd do it. When he'd walked out of my life, he had taken something with him, something big, and I wasn't sure how I was supposed to live with that.

Not wanting to be *that* woman, I pushed the longing from my mind, put the phone down, and carried on. I didn't *need* anyone. My chest might well feel hollow, but my heart still pumped, and I still breathed. I'd be fine.

Ten minutes into sorting The Ogre's diary for the next week, I got a call on the phone I was trying to ignore. No one called me during work hours. And my blood chilled when I saw it was Nan calling.

"Hello?" I said.

"Nell, it's Nan," she said, still in times where you didn't have a screen to tell you who was calling. "Where are you?"

This was now officially weird, and I felt slightly sick. Her monthly catch-up call wasn't due for another week, and she always preferred to call me on the landline rather than mobile.

"At work. Why? What's going on?"

"Okay, love. I'm going to come and pick you up," she said softly.

"Why?" I asked, standing up. I had a pit in my stomach the size of the Titanic. Something wasn't right. "I don't need picking up. I have my car. Why would you need to pick me up?"

"Love, I really think it's best if I come and get you."

"O-okay," I whispered, placing my hand on the desk as I felt my body sway.

Nan hung up, but I kept the phone to my ear. Ice pricked my skin. She didn't live far from my office so she wouldn't be long—if she was coming from her house.

Lowering the phone, I let it drop on the desk and then walked through to The Ogre's office.

"Reg, my nan's coming to pick me up," I said, curling my fingers into my palms.

"Why?" he asked, frowning. His forehead wrinkled, creating deep waves of skin.

I shook my head. "I…I don't know. Something's really wrong, but she didn't say."

Why I'd thought I'd get any comfort from telling him, I had no idea. I wanted and needed someone to tell me that I was panicking over nothing and that the ice-cold fear I felt was unnecessary. Reg was never going to do that for me. I knew whom I needed, and he was the one person I couldn't call. He'd told me to stay away.

"Well, let me know before you leave."

Wanker. "Sure," I said in a daze. I turned around, going back into my office.

Something's happened, and I think I know what. I've always known, so why am I in shock?

I sat down at my desk and carefully placed my phone in my handbag. Gripping the handles between my fists, I watched the clock tick by. She wouldn't be long. Soon, I would know what'd happened. Soon, my worst fears would undoubtedly be realised.

"Nell," Harry snapped. "Someone's here for you. In the future, can you save personal calls for your lunch break?"

I completely ignored him as I stood from my desk and walked out. At the minute, I didn't have the energy to worry about them.

Nan was outside reception. She looked awful, had clearly been crying, and was pacing back and forth.

"Nan," I said, bursting through the doors, "what's happened?"

Which one of them?

"Oh, Nell," she said, falling into my arms and sobbing. "I'm so sorry, darling, but it's Mum."

I went through the motions of pulling her back and asking what'd happened. I got in the car with her, put my seat belt on, and turned the dial to full heat. I was so cold that I couldn't stop shivering.

"Nan, I need to know what happened," I said calmly.

"There was an incident."

There's always an incident.

"They were upstairs when things got out of hand. I don't know what happened next, but your mum fell down the stairs."

They were throwing punches and didn't think about where they were.

"Fell? She fell?"

"Love, I'm so sorry."

The air was sucked from my lungs, and I doubled over. It hurt so much that I felt like I was being ripped apart. "No…no, she can't be."

"Nelly…"

My mother is dead.

I squeezed my eyes closed and leaned against the window. It hurt so bad.

"But…fuck! Why? I don't understand why they couldn't just stay away from each other. I asked them, pleaded with them, so many times," I said, breaking into chest-rattling sobs. "She can't be dead."

"Shh, lovey, you're going to be okay," she replied, forcing her words through thick emotion.

"What happened?" I sobbed.

"They were arguing, and it got out of hand. Dad…your dad is in custody."

Fucking hell.

"I promise, you'll be okay."

How can that be true?

One of my parents was lying on a cold slab of metal, and the other was behind bars. I had no idea how to handle the situation or what I should feel, other than utter despair. There were so many questions flying through my head, so much guilt I carried for not doing more to make them stay apart.

My parents had been okay on their own, but together, they had been toxic, and they hadn't cared about anything or anyone around them—not even their own daughter.

I sat in Nan's car, trying to piece everything together. *How did it happen? What will happen next? How am I going to get through losing them both? How will I find the strength to say good-bye to my mum and even accept that I won't see her again?* Every painful question had the same agonizing answer. *I don't know.*

Mum was dead. Dad was responsible. And the only surprising part to me was that it'd taken this long to happen.

"Are you okay?" Nan asked, periodically wiping her eyes as she drove.

"No, I'm not." I was having an out-of-body experience. I was crying while I felt robotic and somewhat detached. "You?"

She shook her tightly permed head. "I just can't believe it. We'll get to the bottom of this."

Get to the bottom of it? We knew the basics. We knew enough to understand what had happened. They'd fought all the time. They would get so violent that this was the only place it could end.

Is she more concerned about Dad when her daughter-in-law is dead?

Right now, no matter what the circumstances were, I couldn't care less about Dad. I just wanted to be with my mum.

Nan pulled into a parking space at the hospital as close to Accident and Emergency as she could get. Mum had come in through A&E, so that was the best place to start. We didn't know if she might've been transferred to the...morgue yet.

We raced through the automatic doors, and then I froze up. The rushed journey here had given us something to do, but now that we were here, the last step would be seeing Mum dead. *Is that really how I want my last moments with her to be?*

Things were strained when I would go over for dinner, but we'd have a laugh, say *I love you*, kiss on the cheeks, and have a hug. That was better than crying, not hearing *love you* back, and kissing a cold cheek.

I felt like I'd been plucked out of the air and thrown out somewhere, cold and alone. No one was here to tell me what to do for the best, for the best for me. Nan had her son at the forefront of her mind. If she were allowed to see him, I doubt she would be here now.

Shivering, I wrapped my arms around myself and looked around. People in white coats walked past. Patients milled around, waiting to be seen. The receptionist talking to Nan spoke with her head at an angle—the sympathy angle. I'd bet I looked really odd, standing in the middle of the entrance with my arms wrapped tightly around my middle.

Everyone moved so gracefully through the entrance of the hospital. I'd expected rushing around, shouting, blood and gore, but there was none. Everything around me was so calm, and although I stood still and peaceful, I was anything but.

They were all so completely absorbed in their own lives. No one noticed me at all. I had never felt so alone in my whole life. *Am I an orphan, or are you only given that title if you're a minor? Is there even a word for adults who have lost their parents?*

I hadn't lost my dad, not really. But in every way that felt real, he was gone.

It'd been a very long time since I'd hero-worshipped the man, but what was left of my heart bled for him.

How could either of them let it happen? Why didn't they just stay away?

My skin felt too tight. I didn't want to be alone in this anymore. Nan was here, but we weren't particularly close. There wasn't one time in my life when I'd confided in her or looked to her for comfort.

The only person I could rely on was my best friend.

I pulled my phone out of my bag and sent Chloe a text message. It was short, blunt, and to the point.

Dad killed Mum. I'm at the hospital.

Less than twenty seconds later, it was ringing.

"Nell?" Nan said, now back with me and looking at my ringing phone.

Huh, when did she get back over here?

"Do you want me to answer that?"

I held it out to her.

Where's Mum?

"Hello? No, it's Nell's Nan."

Chloe must be speaking because Nan listened for a while. I'd bet Chloe was ranting and stumbling over her words, frantic to find out what my text was about. I should've called her, but I wasn't sure I could have said the words aloud.

"Yes, it's true. There was a fight, and she fell down the stairs." Nan placed her hand on my cheek and said the words for Chloe to hear, but they were all for me, "She hit her head hard on the wall, and that…well, it killed her instantly."

She died instantly? Please say that is true. How would Nan know that? Dad told her maybe?

I nodded, and as I blinked, a wave of tears rolled from my eyes.

It made me feel a tiny bit better that my mum hadn't suffered. *But did she know she was going to die?* I couldn't bear the thought of her being terrified of death as she had fallen at the hands of a man who should've protected her.

None of it made sense to me. I could count on one hand the number of people I loved, and three of them were only because I was duty-bound to, and I knew I could never, ever hurt them.

"Yes, I think she would want you here," Nan said. She told Chloe we were in the waiting room of A&E.

Won't we go to the morgue soon?

"Okay, bye." She hung up, handed the phone back to me, and kissed my cheek.

"Nan," I said as she took my hand and led me…somewhere, "where are we going?"

"That's up to you. Do you want to see her? It doesn't have to be now, if you're not ready."

"When, if it's not now?" It wasn't like we could grab coffee next week. *When the fuck will I see my mum?*

"The funeral home, lovey."

I stopped dead in my tracks, making her stumble. The funeral home after they'd cleaned her up and made it look like she were sleeping. They would cover cuts and bruises as best as they could. I wanted to see my mum when she looked like my mum.

"I want to do that. I don't want to see her now." I didn't ever want the image of her looking broken in my head.

"Okay, we can arrange that. Whatever you want, Nell."

"Chloe's coming, isn't she?"

"She said she was, but I can call her back and let her know I'm taking you home."

"No!" I snapped, taking a step back. "I'm not going anywhere."

Her speckled grey eyebrows knit together. "Why?"

"Because…I can't." I looked around, panicked. *Can security make me leave if I'm not here with a purpose?* "I can't leave her here, Nan."

"Oh, Nell." She wiped her eyes again. "You can't stay here, love. You need to go home. There's nothing we can do right now. Let me take you home and wait until your friend gets there."

Where is she going after?

Actually, I knew that one. The second she got a chance, she'd ditch me to go to the station.

"No, thank you. I'm staying here. I'll wait for Chloe." *And stay with Mum for as long as I can.* "You go and do what you need to."

"Sweetheart, he's my son. And he's your dad. Whatever you think, he loved your mum, too."

That isn't love. It's obsession and habit and selfishness. Calling it love is an insult.

"I understand," I replied, pursing my lips. "I'll speak to you later."

"I can't leave you here by yourself."

"I won't be by myself for long, and if I'm honest, I wouldn't mind sitting down, alone, for a while."

"Nell…"

"Please, Nan. This is what I want. Will you tell me what's happening with Dad when you know?"

"Of course," she said, gripping me in a warm hug. "I love you, darling."

Why do I never feel like I'm whole and complete when my family say that? I knew they loved me, in their own way, but the only person whom I'd really, really *felt* it with was Damon.

"Love you, too," I replied, trying to sound as sincere as I could.

Nan left, and I walked over to a quiet area near the side of the doors in A&E. People chose to be closer to reception, probably so they could keep an eye on who was coming and going to make sure they weren't overlooked.

I didn't want to be noticed, and I was already freezing right down to the bones, so sitting by a chilly door wasn't going to make any difference to me.

My cloak of invisibility was lifted when a nurse knelt in front of me. "Are you okay?" she asked.

"I'm waiting for my friend," was my reply.

She nodded, stood up, and walked away.

Then, I was alone again. It wasn't an unfamiliar feeling, and the realisation made me feel sick. My whole childhood, I'd felt alone. I'd had Chloe, but because I couldn't let her in and tell her what was going on, I never really felt like I had anyone. She knew now, and I'd have to tell her everything.

The pain of opening up and baring it all took my breath away.

THIRTY-ONE

DAMON

Life without Nell was pure shit. I knew I'd made the right decision for us both, but no part of it felt good. I'd spent the whole morning snapping at everyone, and I was pretty sure I'd screwed my chances at becoming a partner.

Melissa, my joint assistant, poked her head around my door. "Can I speak to you for a minute, please?"

I wanted to tell her no, and that if she spoke to me again, I'd fire her on the spot. But I didn't. Grinding my teeth, I gestured to the chair. "Sure."

She walked into the room and sat opposite my desk, her heels clicking against the polished concrete floor. "I know it's not my place, but I just wanted to ask if you're okay."

"I'm fine," I replied.

"Well, I'm glad about that…"

"What's going on, Melissa?"

"The email you sent me yesterday had a few mistakes in it, only minor things. I was able to check your contacts to find the correct addresses of the clients, but it's unlike you. I'm sorry. I just wanted to see if there was anything extra I could help with?"

Sighing, I ran my hands over my face. "No, I'm sorry. My head's been all over the place lately. I should've double-checked the details. I apologise for making more work for you."

"It's no problem. I was hired to assist you and Rich. I just want you to know that if you need extra support at work, I'm willing and capable of taking more on."

"I know you are, Melissa. Thank you. I appreciate that. Can you move my four o'clock to next week? I'm going to leave early today."

"Of course. Is there anything else?" she asked, standing up and flattening her tartan pencil skirt.

"No, but maybe in a week or two, we can look at your responsibilities."

She beamed, her bright red lipstick cracking with her smile. "That sounds wonderful."

Hell, if she wanted more shit to worry about, then she could have it. Rich gave her much more than I did because I hadn't been full-time for long, and I'd wanted to experience everything. But I was confident I knew enough now, and I was—usually—shit-hot at my job, so Miranda could take some of the load off.

As soon as she closed my heavy wooden door, I closed my computer down and got my phone, which had a booty-call text from a girl I'd met last week. I was done for the day. I was going to go home, get laid, and forget everything that had been driving me insane for a while.

Emma threw her head back as she came, digging her nails into my thighs. It was enough to make me follow suit. I held her hips still, pressing deeper into her. As soon as it was all over, I felt empty. Emma was a good girl—sweet, funny, killer in bed—and she knew the score.

But she wasn't Nell.

She groaned and lifted off, kissing my chest and lying beside me while she caught her breath. "I have to meet the girls in half an hour," she said. "I'd better be able to feel my legs soon."

Laughing, I looked over and raised my eyebrow. "If you come back, I'll finish the job properly."

"Damon!" she chastised, lightly slapping my arm. "I don't think I could go again for a while."

Neither could I—but for a completely different reason.

I wanted to be able to slot back into my pre-Nell life, but she'd been around for so long, and it was hard to readjust. There had been a few girls while Nell and I were fucking around, too. It had never been as good, never felt as right as it did with her, which was why I'd barely gone there, but I had still been able to do it then without all this *guilt.*

Today was my third time with Emma, and I knew that would be it. Things with Nell had started as a couple of nights when her friends merged with mine, and there was absolutely no way I would get myself into another situation like that.

Emma rolled off the bed and started getting dressed. I went to find my clothes.

My suit jacket was lying by the door, and the pinstripe shirt was near it. My charcoal trousers were beside the sofa, so I dumped the condom in the bin, slipped the trousers on, and waited for Emma.

"Okay," she said, swiping her heels from the floor, "I'm ready."

She didn't look ready. She looked like she'd just been fucked. Her hair was no longer sleek and styled from where she'd been throwing it around, her mascara had smudged, and her cheeks were flushed.

I nodded and walked to the front door. "Take care of yourself," I said.

She smiled and then kissed my cheek, knowing that we were done now and sex for us was off the menu. "You, too, Damon."

My phone started to ring behind me. I gave Emma one last nod of the head, closed the door, and went to answer.

I took a breath before I picked up. "Hey, Logan."

"Hey," he replied, sounding stressed. "Look, I know you and Nell aren't seeing each other anymore, but I think she needs you."

My heart started to race. *Why?* "What's going on? Is she okay?"

"She's fine—physically anyway. Her mum died today…at the hands of her dad. She's at the hospital still. Chloe's going up there now."

I swallowed hard. "Her mum? Shit! Okay, I'm leaving now. Do you know where in the hospital?"

"Her mum was taken to A and E, so I assume there."

"Okay, thanks for letting me know, man."

"No worries. I'm glad you're going to her."

I loved her, so I would always go to her, no matter how much she'd hurt me.

"Of course. Speak later."

"Bye," he said before hanging up.

For a second, I was frozen. *How will Nell be?* I didn't even know if she'd want me there, but there was no way I wouldn't go. Even if she told me to turn around when she saw me, I was still going to try.

My muscles finally unlocked, and I grabbed my clothes up, dashing to the bedroom. I chucked the old ones to the side and threw on a pair of jeans and a T-shirt.

Guilt burned me from the inside out. While I had been fucking someone else, Nell was at the hospital, dealing with her mum's death. I would never forgive myself. She needed me, and I had been having it away with a girl I'd met a week earlier. My chest felt tight as I dressed as quickly as I could and ran my hands through my hair. Thankfully, it didn't show that I'd just been fucked the way Emma had. But I could smell her still.

There was no time for a shower, so I sprayed deodorant and aftershave and hoped for the best.

It took me twenty minutes to get to the hospital, and I called Chloe, who was also just arriving.

"Damon!" she called, running toward me from the opposite side of the car park. "I'm so glad you came, too."

"Have you heard from her?"

Chloe nodded with tears in her eyes. "She texted me, and I spoke to her nan. I was on my way back from viewing a venue with a bride, so I just got here. I can't believe it."

Neither could I. Logan only knew the basics, nothing in depth that told us what had gone down there.

"What happened?" I asked as we walked through the sliding doors into the building, both heading toward the desk halfway down the large reception and waiting room.

"I'm not sure. Her nan just said that her parents had an argument that resulted in her mum falling down the stairs. Apparently, she died instantly but was brought here. I don't know if we should be here or at the morgue, so we need to find someone."

"Jesus." *That's rough.*

We were almost at the desk when I heard my name being called. I stopped dead in my tracks. It was Nell's voice, but it was so low and broken.

"Nell," Chloe said, spinning around and darting back the way we'd come.

I looked over, and Nell was sitting down to the left of the entrance, staring up at us. She looked so devastated that it took my breath away.

Chloe dropped to her knees in front of her and whispered Nell's name.

All I could do was watch for a second. I was so completely in love with Nell that it physically hurt to see her in pain. Unable to stand back any longer and just needing to try to make things better, I walked toward her and prepared to be whatever she needed me to be.

THIRTY-TWO

NELL

I didn't know how long I had been sitting in the hospital, but it'd turned dark outside. That was also around the time Chloe and Damon turned up. If I'd known Chloe was so far away, I…I would've waited here anyway. I was fine to be alone, but I wasn't ready to be alone all by myself.

I sensed Damon before I saw him, as stupid and ridiculous as that sounded. I just knew he was there. I croaked his name out, half-expecting him to be a figment of my imagination.

Then, Chloe was rushing over. "Nell," she said from the floor in front of me, lifting my chin, "are you okay?"

Damon knelt beside her, in front of me, too. He put his hand on my knee, and I wanted to collapse in his arms.

He's here. He's here. He's here.

I shook my head. "No."

"What happened?" Damon asked, squeezing my leg.

"He finally killed her," I replied, not meeting either of their eyes.

"What?" Chloe whispered, pushing herself up and sitting down beside me. "Nelly, what exactly does that mean?"

"It was always going to happen."

"What was? You're scaring me, Nell," she said.

Chloe didn't know the truth. She knew that my parents argued, and growing up with that had been hard for me, but she had no idea how volatile it'd gotten. The violence between them had been horrendous. I didn't remember there ever being even a week of peace. They'd bruised, broken, and bled each other, but nothing had changed. Every few years, Mum would leave and tell me everything was going to be fine. Then, they'd get back together, and it would start again.

"They didn't just fight verbally, Chloe. This was always going to be how it ended."

"Oh, Nell," she said, "why didn't you tell me things were that bad?"

I felt a big, fat tear run down my cheek. "I didn't tell anyone. I was ashamed. You know, I knew this would be where we all ended up. When they'd finished fighting, I would plead with them both to either just end it or get help because one of them would kill the other. Apparently, I was being dramatic, but look what's—" I took a rugged breath and wiped my eyes. "I don't even know why I'm surprised. I'm not surprised."

"Hey," she said, sitting closer and wrapping an arm around my back.

I leaned my head against hers, grateful to have my best friend here for support.

Damon hadn't said a word. He hadn't even moved. I didn't know what that meant, but right now, I didn't have room to worry about it.

"Can you tell me what happened?" she asked. "Only if you want to."

"They were fighting, the neighbours called the police, but by the time they arrived, Mum was at the bottom of the stairs. She died instantly. Dad's been arrested, and Nan is trying to see him. That's all I know at the minute," I said, telling her everything Nan had told me.

Chloe stroked my arm. "Do you want to see him?"

"I don't know."

She bit her lip and nodded. "Okay, whatever you want. Should I take you home now?"

"I will," Damon said, talking for the first time since he'd turned to stone.

I stared at him for a second. The green in his hazel eyes was more prominent as he watched me with a mixture of pain and worry.

Chloe looked up, surprised, and then arched her eyebrow at me, silently asking what I wanted.

I wanted him. Of course I did.

"It's fine, Chlo. Go home to Logan, and I'll catch up with you tomorrow."

"Are you sure? I don't like leaving you like this, not after..."

"Not after my mum died," I said, filling in her blank.

Wincing, she looked down. "Sorry."

"No, it's all right. Honestly, I'll be fine with Damon. I just want to sleep now anyway. Come by tomorrow when it's all sunk in, and I'm a total mess."

Smiling sadly with tears in her eyes, she kissed my cheek. "I'll be over first thing. You call me if you need anything. I don't care what time it is or what you need."

"I will. Thank you."

She stood up and gave Damon a stern look. "Take care of her."

He rose to his feet, too. "I will."

Chloe gave me another unsure look before leaving.

Damon held his hand out. "Let me get you out of here, Nell."

I stared at his hand. I was on the verge of spilling more tears. The sound of his voice was like coming home. This was the worst day of my life to date, but he made it that tiny bit easier. I hadn't thought I'd see him again, not with him willingly coming to me anyway.

I placed my hand in his, stood up, and almost fell into him. He caught me.

"I don't want to go home," I whispered.

"I know you don't. I was going to take you to mine."

God, he was standing so close that I could smell his aftershave and feel the warmth from his body. It was so much more comforting than I could have ever imagined.

"Damon," I whispered.

"It's okay," he replied, pulling my body flush with his. "I've got you now. Is there anyone you need to tell you're leaving?"

I shook my head.

"Your nan? Where is she?"

"She is at the police station, trying to see my dad."

She was his mum after all. She was more concerned with her son than her dead daughter-in-law or granddaughter.

He clenched his jaw. "Right. Let's get you out of here then."

We slowly walked out of the hospital, and Damon practically put me in his car. I was useless.

"Do you want to call your nan and find out what's going on with your dad?" he asked as he backed out of the parking space.

"Not tonight. Do you think he'll go to her funeral?"

Funeral. That hit me like a ton of bricks, and I wrapped my arms around my chest, as if I were stopping something from falling out. I was going to have to bury my mother.

Squeezing my eyes closed, I let the tears fall freely. It was so unfair.

Why couldn't they have just gotten help? Why couldn't they have been normal? Why wasn't I enough for them to get straight for?

It was getting late, so there wasn't a lot of traffic on the road. It wouldn't be long until I could curl up in Damon's bed. I was so grateful that he hadn't tried to take me to my place. I couldn't face it right now. I didn't want to be where my mum's picture was on a wall.

Damon reached across and squeezed my hand. I gripped back, holding tight.

"I don't know. Don't think of that now. Let's just get you back to my place, so I can look after you."

"I don't expect you to look after me."

"Have you ever expected anyone to look after you?"

I licked my lips. "They looked after me. I had food and clothes and toys. But when the violence started, it was like they were consumed with anger. Any little thing would set them off once they'd opened the dam. I quickly learned to do things for myself, like get my own breakfast and lunch, as they often overlooked it when they were fighting. They were there but never really there. The only time they really wanted much to do with me was when they'd split, and I would have to pick a side."

"How old were you when it started?"

"Four."

One hand gripped mine harder, and his other tightened around the steering wheel, turning his knuckles white.

I had known that I was too young to take care of myself, but so were a lot of kids out there.

"Why didn't anyone help you?"

"I wasn't about to tell anyone. I think they were ashamed of what they were doing. Whenever they saw me getting my own cereal or making a sandwich, they'd be so apologetic. Then, they'd each blame the other one for overlooking feeding their child, and it would start all over." Telling him this felt like cutting myself open. Just a few words exhausted me. "I need to sleep," I said, rubbing my eyes with my free hand. Even just a few short hours where I was at peace would be welcomed.

"We'll be home soon."

Being around Damon again felt right. He was the only person I wanted to be with when I was so lost and afraid. I'd accidentally made him everything.

What I felt for Damon, I had never felt before. It was so pure and so real. I loved him with all my heart. If he never wanted to see me again after tonight, that would be all right because he'd given me something that I never thought I could have. I cried harder for my mum, for the situation, for Damon. He let me love selflessly.

"Did Chloe call you?" I asked between unattractive sobbing.

"No, Logan did. She called him and was frantic, trying to get to you as soon as possible. I guess she called Logan, and one of them decided he should call me."

"Chloe decided. Definitely Chloe." My meddling best friend would have been the one to tell her husband that her best friend needed the guy she loved. And for the first time in forever, I loved her for being right.

"Yeah, probably."

"What were you doing?" I asked.

"Nothing. Just having a drink with a friend."

The fact that he'd started that sentence with the word *nothing* meant that he had been with a girl. I already felt like I was holding on by a thread. Adding Damon being with someone else to the mix would have me falling.

"Okay," I replied, looking out the window.

His hand became stiffer as he realised that I knew what he'd been doing. Seeing other people was his right.

He sighed. "Nell…"

"Don't," I replied, loosening my grip.

He didn't let me get away, clamping his hand around mine. The journey back to his place was taking far too long. I closed my eyes and prayed I could get through this.

THIRTY-THREE

DAMON

It was just after eight thirty when I finally got Nell back to my place. She was tired and withdrawn, and I had no idea what to do. It didn't help that I was shit at lying, and she knew what I'd been doing before I'd received Logan's call.

Carrying her to bed and making her scream wasn't going to help this time, and that was about all I knew what to do with her. That was how we'd worked. If one of us was having a bad day, the other one would use sex to make it better. Our relationship—or however it was defined—hadn't dealt with anything serious. I was feeling my way through this one as best as I could.

"Do you want anything?" I asked, letting us into my place.

She shook her head, wrapping her arms around her chest and kicking off her shoes. "I just need to sleep."

"Okay, take my room, and I'll stay on the sofa. The spare room still isn't done yet."

"No, I can sleep on the sofa."

"Not happening, Nell."

"Just because my mum died doesn't mean I need to be treated like a fragile princess."

I didn't know what to say to that, so I ignored it. She probably didn't even know what she was saying anyway. I wasn't treating her like she was going to shatter. I would have given up my bed for her in any other circumstance.

"Take my room," I said.

She bit her lip, reached out, and grabbed my hand. "Wait. Stay with me. I'm sorry. I know how things are, but I don't want to be alone. Please, just sleep beside me?"

I brushed her long dark hair behind her shoulder and cupped the side of her jaw. "Of course I'll stay. Let me take a quick shower, and I'll be in soon."

Smiling, she stepped back. "You're giving me time to change, aren't you?"

"I'm happy to watch, but I thought you'd want a minute." And I need to get all trace of sex with another woman off me.

"I don't care about you seeing my body. I just don't want to be alone. I feel like I'm about to fall apart."

I wasn't sure if she realised that she'd just admitted to being the fragile person she apparently hadn't been thirty seconds ago, but I let it slide. Whether she liked relying on other people or not, she needed me now, and I was going to be there.

I need to shower.

But how could I argue against that?

"And you know you won't fall apart in front of me because you don't want me to see your weakness."

Her jaw clenched.

"Everyone has weaknesses, Nell. It's nothing to be ashamed of."

"Yeah? What's your weakness?"

My weakness was something I'd been obsessing over for quite a while now. It was something that made me feel on top of the world and completely fucking lost at the same time.

"You," I replied.

She lowered her head and let her hair fall in her face. "I'm sorry, Damon."

"Don't be sorry. Come on, let's get you to bed. You look like you're going to collapse at any second."

I took her outstretched hand, and she finally raised her eyes.

How much can someone take before it changes them? Nell was strong, much stronger than what she gave herself credit for, but things were pretty shitty right now. Not only was she dealing with the loss of her mum, but her dad was also responsible for her death—intentional or not—and he was facing prison time.

Nell immediately started stripping as soon as I closed the bedroom door. For the first time, I didn't want to chuck her on the bed and get hot and sweaty for hours. I wanted to curl myself around her and take away every ounce of pain she was feeling. I wanted to look after her.

She got herself completely naked and then put on one of my T-shirts that was lying on the floor. I realised that I'd been watching her, and I was still fully dressed, so I yanked my top over my head so that she wouldn't know. Thinking I was perving on her wasn't what she needed now. I didn't want her to think I was after anything.

"Are you getting in?" she asked, claiming my side.

We'd slept in the same bed plenty of times before, but we'd just fall asleep in whatever our last position was, usually her lying all over me. Under different circumstances, I'd roll her over and take my side back.

"Yeah," I replied, slipping off my jeans and suddenly wishing I'd worn underwear, not that it really mattered though. She was used to finding nothing under the denim. I quickly got into bed and covered up. "How are you doing?"

She shrugged one shoulder under the quilt. "It's not a shock that it ended this way, but I'm still shocked. That doesn't even make sense."

"It does. I understand what you mean."

"Dad might have been stronger, but Mum was more violent. I always expected it would be the other way around, that I'd have a call telling me my dad was dead."

The fact that she'd even expected a phone call like that was disgusting. I fucking hated what they'd done to her, what they'd forced her to witness. She deserved much better than that.

"I'm so sorry, Nell," I said, pulling her into my arms and kissing her forehead.

"It's okay. Some kids experience worse."

"Doesn't make it okay."

"Maybe not, but I can't do anything to change it. I just wish I had been enough to get them to change."

Oh, no fucking way. "Don't even go there. Not ever."

"I'm not playing *poor me*, Damon, but you're supposed to do the best for your child."

"The fact that they didn't is a reflection on them and not you."

Sighing, she pressed her face into my chest. "I'm tired."

I pulled her closer and tucked her head under my chin. Things were going to get harder before they got easier, but I was going to make it okay, whatever it took. "Sleep."

"Thank you for taking care of me," she whispered.

"Anytime." *Always.*

I woke up to an empty bed. In Nell's absence, I'd rolled back over to my side. She was in the kitchen; I could hear her clattering around. Groaning, I ran my hands through my hair and then chucked my jeans on to go and find her.

"Morning," she said when she saw me walking into the kitchen.

She had two pans going, one sizzling with bacon and the other looked like it was heating beans. Under the grill was a full pack of sausages, and she'd gotten out four slices of bread to make toast.

What is going on?

"Hey, what's all this?"

"I wanted to thank you."

"You said thank you last night."

"Okay, then I wanted to do something to thank you."

I rounded the island and wrapped my arms around her from the back as she resumed cooking. "It's not necessary, but it smells good. How are you feeling? You going to eat?"

She leaned back into me. "I'm not at all hungry, but I'll try to have something."

It didn't go unnoticed that she hadn't answered my question about how she was doing. Nell hated to let people see her vulnerable side. I got it. No one liked to burden people or have anyone think that they couldn't cope with life stuff that was inevitable for everyone. No one escaped hard times and loss.

"Go and sit down," she said. "I'll bring this over in a minute."

I rounded the table and sat, so I was facing her. She worked a little too efficiently, keeping busy so that she wouldn't have time to think.

"Nell," I said as she busied herself with plating up breakfast, "talk to me about how you're feeling."

She dropped the bowl of scrambled eggs and braced herself on the worktop. Lowering her head, she broke down in big, heavy sobs.

My eyes widened in alarm. *What the hell have I done?* "Hey," I said, leaping up and striding over.

I put my hand on her back and started to pull her toward me. When she felt me touch her, she turned and sank into my chest.

"It's okay," I whispered. "You'll be all right, I promise. You don't have to do things alone anymore, Nell."

Her slender body shook as she cried for the loss of her mum.

She should never have had to deal with what she saw while growing up, let alone doing it all by herself. I couldn't even imagine how scared she must have been when her parents fought and how worried she had been that things would turn out exactly how they had.

I felt guilty for the incredible childhood my parents had given me. Nell deserved to be cared for and adored the way all children should be by their parents.

Her weight increased as she collapsed a little more against me, but she held back. After everything, she still held back from completely giving herself to me. She knew I wouldn't drop her. That wasn't what she was worried about.

"Let go, baby. I've got you," I whispered in her ear.

Her body rocked harder, and she shook her head.

"Stop it, Nell. Please trust me. I won't let anything happen to you. Let go, and let me in. I promise, you'll be fine after."

"Don't make me, Damon. I can't," she sobbed.

She cried harder as her fingernails cut into my skin through my T-shirt. Whether she was controlling it or not, she was letting go. All too slowly, she put more weight on me and off herself. I wanted to take it all.

"That's it," I said. "I've got you. I won't let go."

She let everything go. Her sobs were harder, louder, and more devastating when she finally opened herself to me. It was a huge breakthrough. Relying on someone else wasn't easy for her, but she'd done it. I had my foot in the door, and I wasn't about to step back and allow her to shove me out and slam it shut.

I turned the gas and grill off, picked her up, and carried her through to the living room. My stomach was eating itself, but I couldn't eat a thing at the minute. I laid us both down and curled my legs around hers, holding her safe inside.

There were so many things I wanted to say, but nothing would make her feel any better right now, so I did nothing but hold her, kiss her head, and stroke her hair.

Nell was absolutely everything that was right in my world. She filled all the parts of my life that had been missing or incomplete, parts that I hadn't even realised were missing. I would do whatever was needed to heal her heart and make her smile again.

"Sorry," she said, her breath hitching.

"Don't ever be sorry with me. I need you to be able to cry on me when you need to. Please don't fear asking anything from me, Nell, because I'll give it to you."

She pressed her face into my chest and said, "I'm not scared of you saying no. I'm scared of me saying yes. I don't depend on anyone. I don't need anyone."

"Maybe you don't, but things are a million times easier when you do. You can't be a one-person team forever, as much as you want to."

I ran my hand through the endless mass of wavy black hair. She made me only want to be with her. I'd thought I'd seen her vulnerable before, but this was on a completely different level.

This Nell closed every door that led to me wanting a shag with anyone else ever again. I loved her so much, and I was hers—exclusively.

It was day two with Nell at my place, and I didn't know what to do with her. She was so broken, and I felt lost.

This morning, she'd started to apologise for getting in the way. She was the exact opposite of in the way, and that was kind of the problem.

Chloe knew what to say better than me, so I was grateful for each time she popped over.

"Do you need me to call work for you?" I asked.

Nell stared at her untouched coffee. "I called already, but thanks," she replied. "I'll get out of your hair today."

"You're not *in my hair*. You can stay for as long as you like. I want to help."

She finally looked up and smiled. Her now dark green eyes almost looked the way they used to before she'd lost her mum. "Thank you. I really appreciate it, Damon, but I should go home." She sounded regretful.

"Why don't you stay here today? And I'll take you home tonight, if you still want to go." There was absolutely no reason

I couldn't take her back now, other than I just didn't want to, so I hoped she wouldn't ask.

"You want me to hang around your flat all day? I'll drive you insane."

She already did but not in the way she was talking about.

"We've hung out plenty of times, and I've not wanted to strangle you yet. Stay here, and I'll drive you back later."

"Thank you." She wrapped her hands around the mug and bit her full lip. "I don't know how to arrange a funeral."

"It's okay," I said. "You won't be doing it alone. Chloe is on top of things. I know she'd take over completely if you couldn't do it."

She didn't have anyone on her mum's side of the family who could do it, and her dad's family was less than forthcoming.

Nell shook her head. "I can't expect her to do that."

"You're not expecting or asking. She's offering. We all just want to make this as easy on you as possible."

I grabbed the mug from her hand, and she let go.

"This is cold. I'll make you a fresh one," I said.

I hated how much she was hurting and wanted to demand she stopped looking so fucking sad. I flicked the coffee machine on and made Nell a cappuccino.

"Why are you being so nice to me?"

She was able to see me from the living room, but my back was turned to her, and it was a good thing. My jaw snapped together, and my fingers tightened around the mug. I couldn't deny that she'd broken my heart, smashed it into tiny fragments, but I loved her, and nothing was going to change that.

"Why do you think?" I asked, trying to keep the anger from my voice.

Shaking her head, she replied, "I honestly don't know anymore, Damon."

"Guilt? Sympathy?" I asked, turning around.

She lifted one shoulder and let it drop. "Maybe."

"It's neither of those." Guilt was one, a small part of it. I was looking after her because I wanted to.

I continued making two cappuccinos, glad to have a few minutes to myself. It pissed me off that she could think I was doing this for any other reason than because I cared and wanted to help.

I went back in after composing myself and put her drink on the coffee table.

"Thanks," she said.

Her head was still a bit of a mystery to me. I understood her reasons now, but that didn't mean I had fuck all clue about anything else.

"Are you ready to talk about it?" I asked, sitting on the sofa at the opposite end.

There were so many times when she'd looked like she was going to open up, only to turn her head away and build another layer of bricks around herself.

"I think so," she replied, curling her legs up under her. "But you need to promise me one thing."

"What's that?"

"Don't pull the sympathy face."

Raising my hand, I replied, "Deal. Tell me when things started to get bad at home."

She looked so young as she opened her mouth, closed it again, sighed, and then launched into the whole thing. "They always argued, for as far back as I can remember. I recall lots of shouting. I used to curl up beside the sofa when they screamed at each other. They would get right up into each other's faces."

A tear rolled down her cheek, and I had to stop myself from reaching out and wiping it away. I didn't want to touch her in case it ended her share session.

"I was four when their fights turned physical. I remember it so clearly. It was the summer holiday. I was off from preschool, and Dad had lost his job, so we were all home. It'd gotten progressively worse, and it was only a couple of weeks in."

She licked her lips and curled her legs up to her chest. "It was raining, so we were inside. I was playing on the floor with my Barbies, trying to fix one of their legs that'd broken off. Mum and Dad started arguing over Dad's lack of employment. He accused her of being unsupportive because he was trying, and she told him he was lazy. I got up from the middle of the room where I had been playing and ran to my hiding place, wedging myself between the wall and the side of the sofa. I was wearing a pink Barbie nightdress with a sparkly, frilly neckline. It was long, so I pulled it over my legs and down to my feet. I felt safe when all of me was in it." Laughing with no humour, she added, "How stupid is that?"

"It's not."

"They were in my direct sight, but they didn't see me. I remember holding on to my Barbie so tight that her tiny fingers were imprinted on the palm of my hand. I was so scared when Mum threw the first punch."

It came as a surprise that her mum had been the first one to cross that line when her dad was the one who had taken it way too far.

"I'm sorry, Nell."

Ignoring me, she continued, "At first, I was stunned, and so was Dad. I had been taught not to hit. They'd never spanked me, so it was completely out of the blue. She didn't apologise. Instead, she told him he wasn't a real man because he couldn't support his family. It didn't take him long to start up, and he started saying, 'Go on, do it again. Batter me, you bitch.' I had no idea what *batter* meant at the time, but it was terrifying."

She shuffled on the sofa and frowned. "I was shaking and crying. They screamed some more, calling each other names and threatening divorce. I knew what divorce was by that point; they'd mentioned it so many times. I felt really cold and really alone. I wanted Nan to walk through the door and take me away, but no one came. Mum hit him again and called him gutless. That was when he shoved her onto the sofa and stormed out."

Jesus, what the fuck had that done to her?

"Almost every argument after that would result in physical abuse of varying degrees. I watched them hit, kick, and punch each other. I saw my dad pull my mum's hair, and my mum throw things at my dad. Not once did they ever stop when I screamed, cried, and pleaded with them to. I got used to it and could read the signs before they struck first. When they both vibrated with rage, I'd run to my hiding place and cover my ears. It never occurred to me to close my eyes or leave the room. I don't know why, but I guess I was scared that if I didn't look, one of them would disappear forever, and I wouldn't know where. As I got older, I had to push the sofa out a little, so I could still fit there. It's still in the same position I moved it to when I was thirteen, and I think I can still fit in it."

I moved off the sofa, feeling the pull this woman had on me. She was hurting, and I needed to be there, to make it better, but I didn't have the first idea as to how to do that.

"Did they ever...hurt you?"

Looking over at me now beside her, she shook her head. "No. Never me."

Thank God.

"They might as well have though. Watching it hurt no less than what they were doing to each other. I hated growing up in fear. I knew, one day, they'd go too far. When they broke up last year and stayed apart for five months, the longest they'd gone, I thought they'd finally broken the cycle. But then they went back to each other, and...well, you know how well that ended."

"You shouldn't have had to go through that."

Her pretty green eyes were full of sadness. "No one should. When I was a little older I tried talking to Mum because I didn't understand why they hurt each other. God, I was so innocent. I said, 'Mummy, why did you hit Daddy when it's naughty?' How stupid. It wasn't a parent punishing a child with a tap on the butt. It was domestic violence."

"You were *four*, Nell. You didn't know. Shouldn't have known."

"I felt angry after that. They wouldn't talk to me about it, and I didn't understand. I was terrified of my parents, and neither of them took the time to try to make me feel better about it. There was no apology. Just a feeble, 'It'll never happen again, honey,' which was a complete lie. I stopped believing anything they said shortly after that. They never kept their promises."

What can I possibly say to that to make it better? My heart bled for a small child cowering in the corner, afraid of the two people who were supposed to protect her.

She gulped, and I could tell she was struggling to keep it together.

"I don't know what I'm supposed to do now. My head is fried, and there's so much to sort out. I don't even know how to start to accept that she's gone, and I won't see her again. I should be crying right now, but I'm not. Why am I not? And what do you think will happen to my dad?"

"Hey, hey, hey, calm down. You've had a huge shock, Nell, so don't you dare start judging yourself for how you're coping. You're doing amazing. I'm not sure about your dad, but if you want, I can try to speak with the officers dealing with his case."

"Okay. Thank you. He's going to prison, isn't he?"

"I don't know all the details, but I think it's safe to assume that he will spend some time in prison, yes."

Her eyes welled up again. "Yeah. He should. I think he should. Or I think that I think he should. Does that make sense?"

I nodded and replied, "It does."

I wasn't sure if I believed she meant it. It sounded like their fights were pretty even. Neither was more in the wrong than the other. He'd pushed her, and she had fallen down the stairs. They were as bad as each other, no question, and the fact that her mum had died in a mutual fight might mean that her dad would have a chance at getting off or at least getting a lesser sentence. But the justice system was flawed and inconsistent, so really anything could happen.

"Things got better when I was old enough to go out alone," she said, drawing me back into her childhood. "I spent almost all my time at Chloe's. I don't know what I would've done if it wasn't for her. For years, I had been barely hanging in there."

"Did you want to tell her what was going on?"

"I nearly did."

"What stopped you?"

"I was scared of what she would think, what everyone else would think when they knew. I was scared that my parents would get into trouble and scared that people would think something was wrong with me because of them. And I was scared that Social Services would take me away. They were crap parents, but they were still my parents. I didn't want to go into care and be moved from foster home to foster home. So, I stuck it out, kept it a secret, and counted down the days until I left for uni."

Everything made sense—the way she was, the way she'd turned arctic when the word *relationship* was uttered.

Reaching over, I took her hand, and her shoulders lost some of the tension. I loved that one simple touch from me could do that for her.

"Nell, what's your biggest fear?"

"After one of my parents murdering the other, you mean? That would be turning into them. All I know is how to argue and fight. I have no idea what it takes to make a relationship work, and that terrifies me. I won't become them."

"I know you won't. For starters, you know what it's like, so you'd never want someone else, your own children, to go through the same thing."

"But that's not a guarantee. How many people repeat the same mistakes of previous generations? My dad's parents were abusive to each other, and my parents repeated that. I'd bet they said they wouldn't do it, too. They probably spoke about it and said they'd never do anything to hurt each other.

Fast-forward to adulthood…I'm petrified that I'll fall into the same pattern."

"You won't."

Her jaw twitched, and her eyes narrowed.

"I won't let you."

"Damon…"

"Nell…"

She dropped her eyes. "You know…"

"Yeah, I know the score. Don't worry. Everything's going to be okay."

"Promise?" Her eyes widened, pleading with me.

The promise she wanted wasn't just getting over her mum's death. It was so much more. I knew why she didn't want anything real, and I knew that I'd smash down every brick in the protective wall she'd built around herself. She was beginning to allow me to.

We were going to be together soon—whether she fucking liked it or not.

THIRTY-FOUR

NELL

I woke up at five in the morning, feeling like my skin was alive and crawling with millions of bugs. It itched in the worst possible way.

My worst nightmare, the thing that kept me up at night, had been made real. Mum was dead, and Dad was responsible. It was always going to happen.

I quietly got out of bed, so I wouldn't wake Damon and went into the bathroom. He'd convinced me to stay the night again, not that it had taken much convincing, and I now regretted it.

This was how it was going to end, and I'd told them a thousand times. Each and every time, they'd told me I was overreacting, and things weren't that bad—well, that is, the only times they'd actually dignified me with a reply and not just ignored me.

Fuck's sake! I scratched my upper arm and paced beside the bath.

Damon's bathroom was large, and I could usually avoid the long mirror when I was feeling a bit crap about myself, but today, I wanted to look. I felt different and needed to know if that was visible.

I stopped to take in my reflection. It was a mistake. I winced. Somehow, every single one of my features looked duller. There was no colour to my cheeks whatsoever. I couldn't stand what I saw. I wanted to leave, to get out of town, out of England, and just be someplace where I could hide and pretend nothing had happened. And I wanted the itching to stop.

The past few days, Chloe and Damon wouldn't let me be alone to collect myself, but Chloe was home with Logan, and Damon was still asleep. If I was going to get the hell out of here—and that was the plan—then I would need to leave *now*.

I couldn't stay. I didn't want to be around anyone, especially someone who cared and felt sympathetic. Sympathy was useless. It didn't bring back my mum, it didn't change the fact that my dad was the one who had taken her life, and it sure as hell didn't diminish the guilt piling higher every second because I hadn't done more to make them stay apart.

My body was buzzing in the worst possible way. I had to leave. My mind was cracking, and I had to be alone.

They were each their own person, but I could've done more. When they'd broken up, I could've taken Mum away somewhere for a while until she gained proper perspective.

As aware as I was that it wasn't my fault, it didn't stop the what-ifs.

I gathered my clothes from on top of the washing basket and put them on, leaving Damon's T-shirt and joggers inside the basket. Usually, I'd go home in them, wash them, and bring them back next time, but I wasn't sure if or when a next time would be.

Slipping my shoes on, I managed to get my bag and get out of there before he woke up. Now, all I had to do was get home before he woke up. We'd come in Damon's car, so I would have to walk, which was fine because I had to do something to keep busy. It wasn't far, so I pushed myself faster and faster until I was power-walking home.

The closer I got to my house, the lighter I felt. Being around people left me struggling for breath, and the thought of having to have actual conversations with Damon—or anyone—made me feel like I was being suffocated.

I was a people person, loved being social and having a good time. Never had I wanted to be alone since I was little, and alone was all I felt. But, now, I didn't even want to look at another human.

Quickly making it home, I locked and bolted my front door and closed every blind in my small flat. When Damon and Chloe came around, because they would, at least they wouldn't be able to see me, and I would be able to ignore them.

I kicked off my shoes, suddenly feeling like I weighed fifty stones, and collapsed to the floor.

Everything was gone, and I was left hollow.

Pulling the edge of the sofa, I managed to crawl up and curl into a ball on the cushions. All I wanted was for sleep to take over and allow me a breather from the crushing pain and feeling of absolute helplessness.

My phone rang in my bag by the front door, and I knew it was likely to be Damon, having woken up to an empty house. Not wanting any interaction with anything today, I ignored it. He rang again and again. I assumed he'd probably called Chloe, too, because, for five straight minutes, my phone rang almost constantly.

I prayed the battery would run out soon because I had no energy to get up and put it on silent. Curling up as small as I could, I cried into the same pillow I'd ruined when I told Damon I didn't want anything with him.

Finally, the calls stopped, and they'd either given up, or my phone had. Whichever one it was, I didn't care. Silence was welcomed with a sense of relief. I was alone for now.

The sense of calm didn't last long because, shortly after the missed phone calls, there was a knock on my front door.

"Nell!" Chloe shouted, followed by Damon telling me to open up.

So, he had called her, and now, they were here.

I squeezed my eyes shut and pressed my head into the cushions on the sofa. *Just leave me alone.* I appreciated that they cared and wanted to help, but I couldn't be around people right now.

"Nell, open the door!" Damon shouted.

"Come on, babe, we just want to make sure you're okay," Chloe added.

That was fair enough. I dragged my overly heavy body off the sofa and padded toward the door, being sure not to make too much noise. They knew I was in here, but I didn't want them to hear me.

I pulled my phone out of my bag and saw that it was them that had given up, probably because they had both been coming over. My phone had twenty-three percent left.

I put the phone on silent and shot them a group text.

> *I'm fine. Please let me be alone for a while. It's what I need.*

Cradling my phone to my chest, I went back to the sofa and pulled a thick blanket over me. I felt like I was sick and resting, but there was no cure for what I was going through. Time was supposed to be the magic that fixed everything, but I wasn't sure how it was going to heal anything here. I wasn't just dealing with the death of my mum.

Damon replied first.

> *I need you to let me in.*

I replied a simple, *No*, and left it at that.

To believe me, he'd want to see that I was okay because I'd not been all that open before, and I would pretend I was okay a million times over before I admitted I wasn't.

Chloe's reply came shortly after mine.

> *We just want to make sure you're all right. You're scaring us. We're worried. If you won't let us in, please answer Damon.*

My phone rang. He'd given me just enough time to read Chloe's message.

I answered and said, "I'm fine, but I need to be alone." Then, I hung up before he could say a word.

There. I'd given them what they'd said they needed to believe me, so they should leave now. *Please leave now.*

I would be fine, but I had to get my head around it, and the only way I knew how to deal with things was alone. My family never talked through problems. This was the only thing I knew.

Chloe sent a text.

> *Okay. Call when you need me. I love you. X*

Damon didn't reply, and it was probably because I'd dented his male pride or something ridiculous. He wanted to fix things for me, and I loved that he did, but this was all on me. No one could get me past Mum's death and whatever was happening with Dad. I would have to do that for myself.

THIRTY-FIVE

DAMON

"Have you heard from her?" I asked Chloe.

Two days later, and Nell hadn't gotten in touch. I'd passed on calling—she wouldn't answer—but I'd sent a few texts. She wanted to be alone, and that was understandable, but she couldn't just cut us out and not let us know if she was fine. I couldn't imagine what she was going through, and I had no idea how she was coping or if she was even coping at all.

The whole thing was scary and out of my control. I liked control, but when it came to Nell, I'd never had it. It bothered me more now that I knew she needed me.

"I tried calling this morning, but she didn't answer. I don't know what to do. I want to give her the space she clearly needs, but I'm worried sick that she's not coping. There's so much more to her family than I ever knew. I know how to deal with death, but this is different. Her dad did this. That's the part I'm struggling with. How do we get her through the death of her mum and everything with her dad? I don't know if she'll want to see him or what'll happen. Does she hope he'll get off or go down?"

"I think you're getting ahead of yourself, Chloe. Although those are things I've been asking myself. I just want to see her, to know what she wants and how I can help."

"I think we help by doing what she's asked, but it's hard because I don't want to stay away. I want her to cry on my shoulder, get angry and yell. God, I just want something. She was there for me through everything with Jace and then Logan, and it kills me that she won't let me do the same."

"I'm going over there," I said.

Half the time, Nell didn't know what she needed. She'd speak about wanting to let people in, and then she'd push them away.

"Do you think that's a good idea?"

"I don't really care right now, Chlo. We can't sit around and wait for her to come to us because we'll be waiting for a fucking long time. She doesn't ask for help often."

She sighed. "That's true. Let me know how it goes, okay? Tell her I'm just a phone call away, and I'll be stopping by tomorrow, regardless of what she wants."

"I will. Speak later," I said before hanging up.

Raking my hand through my hair, I groaned. It was time I went over there—I knew that—but I was still worried about how she'd react. Worrying about Nell was a full-time job now, and avoiding us was hers.

She'd not been in contact with work since she'd called to let them know what was going on. No one knew if she was going back, and I suspected she wasn't. Everything that'd happened had probably put a job she hated into perspective.

That then left money for her to worry about on top of everything else. She wouldn't take any from me—that, I was sure of—and I didn't know if her mum had had any kind of insurance that would help Nell financially until she got back on track.

Stepping into my shoes, I left my flat and drove to hers. Dealing with Nell was like walking a tightrope. I had to constantly figure out how much to push her, how far I needed to back off, and when I needed to do it. I was exhausted from just thinking about what to do when it came to her.

I parked outside her place and noticed the blinds were closed again. It was morning, so it could just be because she was asleep, but I had a feeling she was trying to keep out more than just the sun.

Walking to her door, I prepared myself for a fight just to get her to talk to me. If Nell didn't want to do something, it was going to take a lot to get her to do it.

I knocked on the door and blew out a deep breath. Minutes later, I was still met by silence.

"Nell," I called. "Come on, it's been two days, and I'm not leaving until after you've let me in."

She would've heard me. Her whole building would've heard me. Now, it was a battle of wills, and I was *not* going to give up. If I had to wait here until she eventually left her place, which she'd have to do at some point, I'd do it.

"Nell!" I shouted, hammering on her door. "Open up!"

The door flew open, and she scowled. "What the *fuck* are you doing?"

"What the fuck are you doing?" I asked. "You've been ignoring my calls and texts. Chloe's, too. We're worried, and frankly, this shutting-us-out thing is getting old. If you need time, that's fine, but you can't just drop off the face of the earth and expect us not to worry. Take months, if you need it, but check in, give us something, so we're not lying awake, scared shitless that you're doing something stupid."

"I'm not going to top myself, Damon."

"How do we know that? You've never been one to overshare, but you've also never locked yourself away for days. We know nothing about how you're coping."

"I'm coping fine," she growled, gripping the edge of the door in her hand.

It didn't look that way. She was pale, her cheeks were sunken, and her eyes were bloodshot and tired.

"Are you?"

"Yes."

I pressed my palm on the outside of the door because she looked seconds away from slamming it in my face.

"Then, let me in for a minute."

"What for? You asked if I was okay, and I told you I am. You said you'd give me space if I wanted it."

I closed my eyes. She was hurting. The spark in her eyes was gone.

"Please. Please just let me come in for a minute," I said, defeated.

Can't she see how much I need to take care of her?

Sighing in frustration, she stepped aside and opened the door. "Fine. Five minutes, but I really don't know what difference it's going to make. I'm not drowning my sorrows in booze or shooting up in the bathroom. I just want to be alone. It's my way of dealing."

"I get that," I said, taking a look around.

The place wasn't particularly messy, but I could tell she'd not done any cleaning in a little while. It mostly looked like no one had been here, like she'd not done or used anything in the last few days.

"Do you want a drink?" she asked, slamming the door. Her whole demeanour was hostile, and all she wanted was for me to leave, which was clear from the slight glare she'd had for me since she opened the door.

"A coffee would be great. Thanks."

After pursing her lips, she nodded once. "Fine."

I followed her into the kitchen, fighting the urge to grin at her stomping around.

"Have you spoken to Chloe about the funeral arrangements?"

I knew she hadn't. Chloe was getting concerned that if Nell didn't get in contact soon, she'd have to choose things, like her mum's outfit, flowers, songs, and which coffin to buy. The venue for the wake and catering was something Chloe could take care of, and she was, but the personal things should be selected by Nell.

She shrugged and flicked the kettle on. "I'll call her tomorrow. We have time."

There was longer than usual time because the nature of her mum's death required a postmortem, and the police were investigating the circumstances, but time was still running out.

"Okay. If you want, I can go with you to choose the outfit and to the funeral home."

Turning around, she licked her lips. "How am I supposed to decide that? Would my mum want casual clothes or something a little fancier? White coffin? Or light or dark wood? We never talked about stuff like that, so tell me. How the hell am I supposed to choose?"

I walked closer to her, and she shook her head, telling me to back up. Her eyes filled with tears. She could tell me to leave, but it wasn't what she wanted. She wanted comfort.

"Damon, don't," she said sternly, giving me a warning look.

"Shh," I said, stopping right in front of her. I dipped my head and pressed my forehead against hers. "It's going to be okay. I'm here, baby, so you don't have to do it alone."

She gulped and closed her eyes, spilling tears. "No—fuck. Damon, I need you," she whispered.

Fucking hell.

Her words and the pain bleeding from each one of them cut me open.

"Everything's okay," I said, finally wrapping her in my arms. "I'm not going anywhere. Ever again."

THIRTY-SIX

NELL

Damon carried me into the living room and went back to make the coffee. I'd felt totally bare when I told him I needed him but strangely lighter, too. He was willing to share the burden of what I had to deal with and the choices I would need to make. I loved him so much more for it.

"Thank you," I said when he'd finished covering me up on the sofa and making us drinks.

"How are you doing, babe?"

Now, that was a good question. "Some minutes are easier than others. I spoke to my dad's lawyer yesterday. He's pleading guilty."

"That's good, right? He's taking accountability for what he did."

"*Good* isn't the word I'd use, but yeah, I'm glad he's accepting responsibility for his part. Not sure if that means he'll do time or not."

"I guess that's up to the judge. There's no point in you worrying about that now. It's completely out of your hands."

"Right—except that he's my dad, and I kind of can't help from worrying. But I'm locking it away in a box until I have to deal with it...until he's sentenced."

"Okay. Let's focus on your mum's funeral first and give her the good-bye she deserves."

He was right. I had to make sure Mum got a good send-off, and avoiding it was pointless.

"A coffin. You'll come with me?"

"I'll text Chloe and get her to arrange going in later today or tomorrow. You cool with that?" he asked.

I took the mug off the coffee table and held it close. "Yeah, okay. Maybe ask her if she'll come with me to pick out my mum's outfit, too? No offense, but I think she'll be more helpful."

He smiled, slung his arm over the back of the sofa, and brushed his fingers through my hair. I leaned into his hand and closed my eyes. Being on my own wasn't what I'd needed. It was him. When I opened my eyes, he was watching me. I saw in his eyes what he felt for me, and I no longer felt alone.

"You're probably right there. I'll text her now," he replied, pulling his phone out and typing slowly with his left hand while the right one cupped my jaw and stroked my skin.

"Thanks. Think she'll be annoyed with me for ignoring her?"

He stopped tapping on the screen and looked up. "No, definitely not. No one is annoyed, Nell. We were just worried and want to help. Chloe hates seeing you struggle through things alone, the same as me."

"I don't deserve either of you."

He clenched his jaw and gripped the phone. His fingers froze on the side of my face. "Don't *ever* say that again. What a person deserves isn't based on perfection or dealing with something in the most socially acceptable way. You deserve everything good that happens to you because you're a good person who struggles with life's shit, the same as the rest of us."

I licked my lips. He was right, but I still didn't feel good enough. I'd hurt him and pushed him away. Maybe I deserved to be happy, but right now, I just felt guilt and loss.

Sipping my coffee, I watched Damon text Chloe with a smile on his face. No doubt he was telling her I'd let him in, and she was pleased I'd ended my hermit stage.

"She said of course she'd choose an outfit with you, and we can swing by this afternoon to pick out a casket. You okay with today?"

I wasn't really okay with ever doing it, but it needed to be done. "Today is good. Thank you for taking care of me…again."

He ran his hand from the back of my head, along my jaw, and across my bottom lip. "I told you, anytime. Forever."

Forever. I liked the sound of that.

"Yeah? You mean that, after everything?"

"Our path to each other might not have been straight and smooth, but the end result is the same, and that's all that matters."

"Wow…who knew you could be all romantic?" I teased, kissing the pad of his thumb.

"I'm practically cupid, baby."

I put my drink down and crawled into his lap. "Damon, I promise that, from here on out, whatever drama we go through won't be from me. Well, I can't actually promise that. It might be, but I mean that it won't be me running from us drama, okay?"

His arms tightened around me like a vise. "That's more than okay. You talk to me, and if you need space, you can have space. I can give you that, but what I can't do is be shut out."

"You scare me."

He paled. "What?"

"I hurt you, and you're sitting here, like it never happened. I know a lot of other shit has gone down, but that doesn't mean the past is healed. I'm scared that you'll resent me. Do you want to talk about it?"

"I don't need to talk about it, but if it'll put your mind at rest, let's do it. Having you worry that I'm secretly pissed at you still isn't good for us."

"Us…" My heart leaped in a good way. "Wow."

"Not us?"

I shook my head, paused, and then nodded. "There is an us…"

"Slowly?"

"Please."

"Right," he replied, smirking. "We'll take it slow."

"I'd very much like to do this properly. Like, old-fashioned properly, not my version."

Pouting adorably, he pressed his head against mine. "I happen to like your idea of proper."

"So do I, but I'm feeling kinda vulnerable here."

"How do we get you to feel as confident and comfortable as you were when we were just fucking?"

"Romance over," I muttered, making him laugh. "Dates and talking are both a good start. I've not done anything exclusive before, so I need to feel my way through this as we go."

"Feel whatever you want, baby."

I rolled my eyes. At least he wasn't treating me any differently, so right now, I knew there was no resentment. "Thanks!"

"All right. How about we get through your mum's funeral, make sure you're really okay, and then I'll take you out?"

"Sounds good. Mahogany."

His eyebrows shot up. "Mahogany?"

"The coffin. Mum had god-awful mahogany furniture in a lot of the rooms. I think she'd want to be buried in that."

He grazed my lips in a soft kiss. "Okay, mahogany, it is. I'm sure they'll have a good selection there."

Fuck, it was so surreal to choose the last thing someone you loved would rest in, something they'd be in for eternity. The pressure to get this right was ridiculously high. Mum wouldn't have given a single fuck. She was gone, and her spirit or whatever wouldn't stand around her grave, scowling at the choice of coffin. But it was important. It was so important that I wanted to run from it again. But I wouldn't.

Enough running. It was time to face my problems, issues, and heartbreaks head-on. It was time for me to *live.*

THIRTY-SEVEN

NELL

Four days later, Damon still wanted us to be together, and I was all for it. But he seemed too keen for it to be real, and I couldn't help but worry that he was still hurt from before.

It was so fucking unlike me to worry when I'd been reassured...

I'd give anything to fix that broken wire in my brain, so I could take what people said at face value.

Right now though, I had to bury my mum. It was something that I couldn't quite comprehend. She needed to be lowered into the ground, and I had to accept that was it. Letting go was hard. It was so sudden, and I expected a call from her to invite me over for a Sunday roast.

Coming to terms with my mum's death was hard enough without trying to make a relationship work, too. Christ, just going to the shop for milk was too much right now. Still, I was determined not to let her death completely consume me. She wouldn't want that. As crappy as a parent as she had been, I knew she loved me and would want the best for me.

It had been six days, and I'd called work to let them know I would be back the Monday following my mum's funeral.

I left my bedroom, still in my pyjamas, and made a coffee. Without Damon to talk to and concentrate on, I was left with my thoughts again.

Did she know she was going to die? Was she scared? Was it really instant? Did Dad try to help her? How had their argument started? Who had initiated it?

At nine, there was a knock on my front door, and I knew it'd be Chloe. She'd done everything with the funeral, completely taken care of it all, because I couldn't. I was not looking forward to the funeral. I didn't know if Dad would be there. I knew he'd applied or whatever he had to do to ask permission since he was locked up, but I didn't know if that had been granted.

"Morning," Chloe said, tucking her brown hair behind her ears. She gave me a hug. "How are you?"

"I'm okay. Come in. You want coffee? I just made a pot."

"Yeah, thanks," she replied, following me into the kitchen. "Was yesterday with Damon okay? You didn't call."

I got her a mug and made her drink. "I was fine. We talked a lot."

"Yeah? That's great. We've been so worried."

"I know, and I'm sorry for doing that."

"It's okay. Are you and Damon…"

I smirked at her. "We're good. Really good. It'll take time, but I think we'll get there."

She beamed. "You definitely will."

Yeah, we would. I was sure of that now. I handed her the coffee and sat opposite her at the island, wrapping my hands around my mug.

She nodded and took a sip. "You don't just have to rely on Damon, you know. You can call if you need me."

"Thank you. So, I was thinking about my mum's outfit this morning, and I don't need to go through her wardrobe. I know what she'd want to wear."

Her favourite casual dress. The second the summer hit, she would be in it until the weather turned again. She'd loved it, and she'd looked amazing in it. She'd once told me it was the only thing that she felt beautiful in, and I wanted her to feel beautiful for eternity.

"That's great. We can swing by and pick it up later, if you want?"

"Sure. The funeral director said he wanted it today if possible."

"Okay."

"So…is everything set?" My mother's funeral…I had no idea how I was going to get through that yet. There were things I had written down to say, but the thought of standing up there and saying them made me want to throw up.

"Yes, everything's done. Logan and I will pick you up and come back after the wake, too."

"You don't have to do that."

She gave me a stern look, her brown eyes narrowing a fraction. "I do, and I want to."

"Is Damon coming?" I asked.

"Why would he?"

She didn't even get a full head tilt before I said, "All right, that was stupid. He knows when it is, but I didn't exactly ask him."

"Why not?"

"Because then he would come."

"Right." Frowning, she said, "Isn't that the point?"

"I don't want him to feel obligated to come."

She groaned my name, shaking her head. "Nell, stop. He wants to be there for you, and you know that."

"I hurt him, Chlo. He's been amazing, but I don't want to push him."

"What's he said?"

"That he wouldn't let me become my parents. He's all for us making a go of it, but right now, I have other things to concentrate on. I'm not sure what will happen with Damon yet, but when my mind is clear and we both want to, I'll work at it then."

She put her mug down. "You are nothing like them and never could be. You're not selfish," she said, concentrating on the first part of what I'd said.

"Aren't I? Look at what happened with Damon."

"What happened? Come on, you both understood perfectly what the deal was between you. You were always clear about what you wanted from him. He fell for you—of course he did—but you didn't lead him on. Just continue to be honest about how you feel and what you want."

"And what if the way I feel now is too blurry?"

She rolled her eyes. "It's not blurry, and you know it. You love him. You're just too afraid to admit it, and frankly, Nell, you need to give yourself a break. A lot has happened, so stop worrying about Damon. Focus on healing after your mum's death, and let the rest happen naturally."

I managed a smirk. "Do you ever wish you'd taken your own advice when you were working through things with Logan?"

"Oh God, all the time. Things would have been *a lot* easier on us both if I'd stopped panicking and overthinking so much. You need to do the same."

"Yes, sir," I replied. "Hey, you think you can help me pick something out for the funeral? I don't know what to wear." *What's the appropriate outfit for saying good-bye to your mum?*

Her face softened, and she put her drink down. "Of course I can. Show me the options."

"Shouldn't you be working? Or spending time with Logan?"

"No, and no." She held her hand out. "Come on, this outfit isn't going to pick itself."

"You're the best, Chlo." I took her hand and stood up. Tying my hair up in a band I'd had on my wrist, I led her into my room.

"You redecorated," she said, looking around at the cream-and-chocolate-covered walls.

When I fell in love with Damon. "Yeah," I replied, opening the wardrobe.

"I like it." She poked her head around my shoulder and immediately tugged on a knee-length black dress. "This is nice."

"My mum didn't like black." I turned to her. "Do I have to wear black?"

"Of course not. Wear whatever you like."

"Her favourite colour was blue."

"Okay, how about the royal dress?" She picked it off the hanger and handed it to me. "Try it on, and see what you think."

On nights out, Chloe and I would have wine, turn music on, and help each other choose what to wear. I never imagined I'd be doing the same thing—minus the MTV channel and booze—for Mum's funeral. Although I could really do with a drink.

Chloe looked through my wardrobe as I shed my PJs and put the dress on. I felt ridiculous. Dresses usually made me feel sexy. I had no make-up on, my hair needed a wash, and my legs were starting to sprout tiny hairs. And I had no desire to rectify any of that today.

"Does it look okay? Suitable?" I asked.

Turning around, she smiled with tears in her eyes. "Absolutely. You look nice in blue."

It was calf-length and a little flowy with short cutoff sleeves and a high neckline. "Okay. Thanks. This one then, I guess."

That hadn't taken as much time as I'd thought it would. Now that the outfit was done and the funeral arrangements were sorted, Chloe would probably want to go home to Logan soon. I couldn't blame her, but I wanted to keep her here a little longer. The rest of the day stretched out in front of me.

"Do you want another coffee?" I offered as I changed back into my comfortable PJs.

"Sounds good. I'll make them. You go sit down. And call Damon about the funeral. It's only a few days away. I have no doubt that he'll come anyway, but I think you should ask."

I thought he would be there regardless, too. But over the last few days, I'd handed over so much of myself to him that I was scared to give more. The last people I'd relied on had let me down in a huge way, and I was terrified that history would repeat itself.

Chloe left after a while with the promise of coming back or at least talking on the phone later. I felt bad that her week had been consumed with checking in on me and not enjoying time with her husband.

I promised her I would call if I needed her. I wouldn't.

Sitting on my sofa, I dialled Damon's number. "Hey," I said, mentally preparing myself to ask him to let me lean on him even more than I had already.

"Hey, how are you?"

"I'm…okay. I wanted to ask you something."

"What's that?"

I licked my lips, knowing that this was it. You asked your boyfriend—someone you were serious about, not a casual friend or fuck buddy—to go with you to your mum's funeral. I shook my head at myself. Damon was so much more than that.

"Mum's funeral is coming up…" *Obviously.*

"Yeah, I know. Are you okay? Want me to come over?"

"I'm fine. That's not why I called. I…" *God, why is this so hard?* "I wanted to know if you…shit, Damon, will you come?"

"Of course," he replied. I could hear the smile in his voice. "I was going to come anyway, Nell, but I'm glad you asked me."

Right. He had this new I-love-it-when-you-need-me thing that I was only just starting to become semi-comfortable with. "Thank you."

"No need to thank me. Do you want me to come over?"

"No, I'm fine." My plan, which I knew was idiotic, was to cry as much as I could today in the hopes that I'd be able to keep it together when the funeral came around. It wasn't a solid plan, but I wanted to be able to give my mum the send-off she deserved.

"Are you sure? I hate to think of you upset and home alone."

When he said things like that, I desperately wanted to be with him. His arms around me made me feel safe. But he needed to work, and I had things here I had to get done.

"I'm sure. I'll be okay. I'll see you tomorrow."

"You will. Take care of yourself, Nell. I mean it. Call me if you need me."

"I will. Bye."

He sighed and whispered, "Bye, Nell."

I dropped my phone onto the sofa and picked up a photo I had of me and my mum. I was nineteen. It was the one and only Christmas where she wasn't with Dad. It was the best Christmas with her I'd ever had.

There was no shouting or fighting, no forgotten charred turkey or mushy veg. We'd cooked together, drunk wine, exchanged presents, and watched Christmas movies. It was perfect, and that day, she had been a proper, normal mum who made it about me and her, not her and her fighting husband.

The picture was my favourite. The ones of me, Mum, and Dad before the abuse had started were tainted with what had happened next, but that one was so pure that it meant everything to me. We both had on knit Christmas jumpers and a colourful paper hat from the crackers. I'd held the camera at arm's length, and Mum held me close, smiling one of her rare genuine smiles.

I gripped the photo frame hard, turning the beds of my natural nails white. Swallowing a lump in my throat, I kissed the picture with tears in my eyes.

"I love you, Mum," I whispered. Then, I fell apart on the sofa, clutching the only memory of when I'd felt properly loved by my mum.

THIRTY-EIGHT

NELL

Three days later, and it was the morning of Mum's funeral. It was much harder than I'd ever imagined, and I hadn't even gone inside yet. Chloe and Logan were being amazing and waiting outside with me. We had a few minutes left, and I didn't want to spend a single second in there longer than necessary.

The service would start soon, so I knew we should go in, but something stopped me. Chloe was here, but I still felt alone. That was new. Deep down, I understood why. There was someone else who made me feel too much. He was the only one who could help me right now.

Logan turned around and touched Chloe's back. "Let's go in, sweetheart."

Chloe frowned, but then understanding crossed her face, and she squeezed my hand before leaving with him. It only took a second for me to realise why they'd left me.

Damon was walking up the path.

I could breathe again.

He wore a sleek dark grey suit with white shirt. It was similar to what he would wear at work, but it was a little more casual today with the top button undone and the lack of tie. I almost ran to him.

How can a person feel like home?

My chin wobbled as he approached.

"Hey," he whispered.

"Thank you," I replied, gulping.

He pulled me into his arms and rested his head on top of mine. "I got you."

"I don't really know how to do this. All the singing and readings and—"

"Shh. Nell, you're getting ahead of yourself. Right now, we're just going to go in and find our seats. Don't worry about the rest yet."

"You'll sit with me?"

He pulled back, and his eyes were burning. "I won't leave your side."

I wanted him to promise not ever, but that would be asking too much. I looked up at him, and honestly, I had no idea how I had even gone a week without seeing him or speaking to him. I didn't want him to be that important to me, but he was.

Reaching up with trembling hands, I ran my fingers along his jaw, and his lips parted. "You really have no idea how thankful I am that you're here."

"I think I do, beautiful," he replied, taking hold of my wrist and kissing the palm of my hand. "Let's get inside."

Damon led me into the packed church. I didn't have many family members. Mum's parents had died a long time ago, and she was an only child. Dad's side of the family hadn't turned up, which wasn't at all surprising under the circumstances. Still, I did hope Nan would at least come to support me. Thankfully, Mum had had a lot of friends.

Even though it was warm outside, it was still cool in the church. Goose bumps spread across my arms. With Damon's arm around my waist, I felt strong enough to say good-bye to my mum for the final time.

Chloe had saved us seats at the front. I wanted to hide in the back, but of course, I couldn't. Being the only person here related to Mum, I had to be right beside her. She deserved that much.

I mouthed, *Thank you*, to Chloe and sat beside her.

Damon's arm stayed around me, keeping me right at his side. He didn't need to. I would've stayed anyway.

Father David started the funeral by saying a few words about Mum. I'd told him the good things about her. It did seem a bit wrong to make her out like the most incredible person ever, but this was her good-bye, and in the end, she deserved a positive farewell.

"I don't know if I can do the reading, Damon," I whispered to him, laying my head against his arm.

Soon, it would be my turn to say something. I'd managed to get this far without breaking down, but I wasn't sure that I could keep it up. Mum was lying in the mahogany coffin to my right. It was torture to know she was there, unmoving.

Chloe had helped me write something down, but that was the easy part. Standing in front of a packed church and reading it to my mum in her coffin would be something else. This was the worst day of my life. My heart weighed down heavy in my chest, and I sniffed back the threat of tears.

"Do you want me to?" Damon asked.

He couldn't. I was leaning on him. I needed him.

"I don't want you to leave."

"Hey," Chloe said, taking my hand. "Just say the word, and we can have Father David read it. He offered, and no one expects this from you. Or I can if you'd prefer that."

"You would?" I said, sobbing over my words, choked up at her offer.

She knew me, knew I wanted my last words to my mum to be personal.

"Of course, I will."

I squeezed her hand as she was blurred beyond recognition by my tears. Chloe was the best friend anyone could have—I'd known that all along—but I hadn't quite realised just how incredible and kind she was before.

My name was called, but Chloe stood up and walked over to Father David, whispering in his ear. He nodded, smiled at me, and stepped aside.

Chloe approached the microphone and said, "Nell has written a few words for her mum, and I'll be reading them for her."

She gave no more explanation, didn't tell anyone that it was supposed to be me but I couldn't do it. I loved her.

"Mum," she started.

I buried my face in Damon's chest. My heart broke all over again.

"*We had our challenges when I was growing up. And I concentrated on the negative things right up until the moment I found out you'd left me. Now, the moments I remember the clearest are you singing so, so badly the year you bought me a karaoke machine for my birthday. I remember your smile and the way you used to do my hair for school photos. Every year was the same pigtails until I realised that I could take them out as soon as I'd left the house.*"

Chloe sounded choked up, but she gracefully read on. I couldn't have done that. Damon's arm held me tighter. He took a ragged breath and pressed his lips to the top of my head.

"*When I was eight and wanted to be an astronaut, you told me not to listen to anyone when the kids at school had told me it was only for boys, so I could never do it anyway. You knew I wouldn't. You knew that it was just a phase, but you still bought me the books and told me you'd be there with balloons when I returned from my first mission in space. When I went off to university, you were so proud that you cried on the phone with me for a week.*

"*You might not have realised it, but you taught me so much about who I wanted to be and what I wanted to do. You also taught me to be so painfully stubborn that failure wasn't an option. Everything I told you I would achieve, I will, and I'll do it with a smile, knowing you're right behind me with a big bunch of balloons. I know you're with me every day, probably telling me to redo my hair how you like it. Sleep tight, Mum. I love you.*"

I tried to be as quiet as I could while I cried against Damon. My eulogy to my mum was very one-sided. I'd picked things to talk about from the times when she had been single and had time for me. But everything was true. I knew who I did and didn't want to be because of her. I loved her, and I was going to make my dreams come true.

When Chloe took her seat, I let go of Damon and hugged her until the end of the service.

The coffin was carried out of the church. We waited a second and followed. I clung to Damon and stayed close to my best friend. Mum's grave was around the back of the church. I stopped by the side and led my friends to a bench.

"What are we doing, sweetie?" Chloe asked.

"I don't want to watch her coffin disappear into the ground. I didn't say good-bye in the hospital because I couldn't have that be the last time I saw her. I don't want this image either."

"Okay, whatever you want," she replied.

"Thanks. I'll just wait here until they're finished, and then we can head to the wake."

Damon kissed my temple. "Just tell us when."

"Chloe…" I said.

She nodded her head, pushed Logan down on the bench, and sat on his lap. There was only space enough for three. "You don't have to say anything, Nelly. I know."

Of course she did. She was my best friend so she knew how much her support today and always meant to me.

"How are you holding up?" Logan asked.

I looked up to the bright blue sky. "Not sure. Okay, I think. Part of me wishes Dad were here. When will he get his chance to say good-bye to his wife?"

"Hey," Damon said, "the officer handling the case said he would probably be allowed to visit her grave, remember? We'll do everything we can to make sure that happens."

I hoped so. My opinion of my dad wasn't particularly high—and it hadn't been for a long time—but he hadn't meant to kill her, and he should get the chance to talk to her. It must be killing him.

"Thank you, all of you," I said, staring back up at the sky.

For a little while, I just wanted to sit still and think about my mum without the pain of watching her being buried. For that twenty minutes, I felt oddly peaceful. She was in a better place. She would be okay, and so would I.

THIRTY-NINE

DAMON

The funeral was nice, for what it was. It was a real celebration of a flawed woman's life. Nell, understandably, cried through most of the service, but she calmed down during the wake. Watching the woman I loved so upset was a new kind of pain I wasn't used to.

She leaned against the wall with Chloe and two of her mum's friends, swapping stories about the woman they'd just said a final good-bye to.

"How are you doing?" Logan asked, handing me a bottle of Beck's.

I gratefully took it and downed a mouthful. "Thanks. I'm all right. Wish I could fast-forward to the part when she's okay again."

"She's going to be fine. She has a lot of people looking out for her."

"Not family."

Her nan had barely spoken to her, and she'd pretty much lost her dad, too.

"Not all family is blood, Damon. Chloe and Nell are as close as sisters."

"Yeah, I guess. I just don't want her to think she has to do this alone."

"She doesn't think that. Stop worrying about things that you don't need to worry about."

He was right; I was being a dick about every little thing.

"I know. It's just…"

"Hard to chill the fuck out when it's the woman you love?"

I shrugged one shoulder. "That about sums it up."

"Relax, man. Nell's doing all right, and if she needs something, she has a lot of people ready to help her out."

I knew everything he was saying was true, and I needed to relax, but I still wanted to skip to a time where Nell didn't cry every day.

"Chloe was talking about taking Nell away one weekend, back to that cottage for some hot tub relaxation. Maybe we should do it sooner rather than later, give Nell something positive to look forward to," Logan said.

"Yeah, I'm in. I'll see when she wants to go."

Nell and Chloe made their way over, and my girl smiled.

"Do you think you could take me home now? I know I probably shouldn't leave before everyone else, but I'm exhausted," Nell said.

"Hey," Chloe said, "you do what you need to. No one's judging. We'll stay and clean up afterward."

Nell teared up. "I don't know what I'd do without you."

They hugged, and I put my beer down after just two sips.

"Call me if you need anything," Chloe said when they stepped back.

"I will. See you tomorrow."

I pulled Nell in close and led her toward the exit. Her mum's friends smiled as we left but didn't say much. Nell kept in close, still feeling bad for needing to leave early. Chloe was right. No one was going to think Nell was rude for splitting, and if they did, I'd punch them in the fucking mouth.

"So, yours or mine?" I asked.

"I've stayed at yours a lot."

"That's not what I asked," I said, leading her toward my car.

It wouldn't bother me if she fucking moved in. I was still ready for more with her, but now was not the right time to say so. I didn't know if, when things were better, she'd go back to wanting nothing.

Her mum's death had probably made her more cautious of relationships. Whether she liked it or not, she was letting me in, one step at a time.

"I feel like you think you're obliged to help me."

I stopped her and spun her around to face me. "I'm here because I want to be here. I don't expect anything in return, and I'm not doing it out of guilt. You mean a lot to me, and I want to do what I can to get you through this."

She stepped forward and wrapped her arms around my waist. "Thank you. In that case, I'd prefer to go to yours, but can we stop at mine, so I can get some clothes?"

"All right," I replied, hugging her back and kissing her forehead.

She smelled like cherry shampoo.

Nell was the answer to everything, to every question I'd ever had and the ones I hadn't even thought of. Nothing made more sense than being with her. Things between us were hard, but it was worth it. I wouldn't take the easy way out again.

When we got in, Nell changed out of the blue dress and curled up on the sofa in her baggy pyjamas. Her black hair was tied messily on the top of her head. She'd never looked so goddamn beautiful before.

"How are you feeling now?"

She shrugged against my side. "I'm okay, I suppose. Everything still feels a bit surreal. I can't believe I'll never see or speak to her again."

"I know. It's not easy. You're going to be okay though."

"Yeah, I will be eventually. You move on, right?"

I frowned. "You move past things. I don't know if you ever really move on."

"Have you ever lost anyone?"

I weaved my fingers through the hair draped from her ponytail. "No, not in that sense. I'm lucky there."

"I'm glad. Do you think I should speak to my dad?"

"I think that's a decision only you can make. There is no right and wrong answer, Nell. It's not a black-and-white case; there are so many grey areas. I don't believe your dad meant for her to die."

"Neither do I, but it happened, and I don't know how to face him. What would I say? What would he say? Nothing can take it back, so what's the point?"

"Maybe the point is, just to understand exactly what happened that night. It'll never make sense, but it might give you closure just to know. Don't worry about it yet. You don't have to make a decision now."

"No. I suppose he isn't going anywhere for a while yet."

He'd been refused bail. Well, actually, he'd refused it. I didn't think those were the actions of a callous, evil man. He cared. In his own fucked-up way, he loved his wife. And Nell loved them both.

"I don't know if Mum would want me to see Dad."

"That's not her decision to make. Your parents made you choose for too long. They slagged each other off and put you in the middle. If you want to see your dad, then go and see him."

She ran her hand over her face and took a deep breath. "I don't know why I brought all that up today. Can we please talk about absolutely anything else? I need to not think about it right now."

"Sure. Hey, do you want to go somewhere tomorrow? A change of scenery and not having to deal for a while might clear your head a little."

"Where would we go?"

"Wherever you'd like. The coast? You never got to make sand castles at the beach when you were a kid, so let's do that."

She tilted her head up and raised an eyebrow. "You, a grown man, want to go and make sand castles on the beach?"

I almost got a smile then. I missed that smile so much. "Why not? I'm not afraid to be immature."

"I know. I've seen some of the Kavos pictures."

"Funny. So, are you in? We can invite Chloe and Logan, too, if you want?"

"No. I mean, yes, to being in, but I don't feel all that social now. I think I'd prefer if it were just us."

Just us.

When she wanted to be a hermit, I would've thought she would only want to see Chloe. I wasn't quite sure when that person had become me, but there was no way I was going to question it.

"All right, I'll sort it."

"Are you really going to make sand castles?"

I'd stopped wanting to make them when I was five, but Nell had never done it at all. Her parents had even fucked that up for her. Every kid should know the simple pleasure of making a house out of sand and destroying it after.

"You're really having a hard time with that, aren't you?"

"I just can't picture it. You, all manly and covered in tattoos, sitting in the sand, filling up a bucket." She shook her head. "Even my imagination rejects the image."

"Hey, castle-making is a very manly exercise."

"How?"

"Oh, you'll see." *Great, now, I have to think of ways not to look like a dickhead.* "Are you hungry?" I asked.

"I don't think I can eat. I just want to sleep, but it's far too early."

"No, it's not. Come here," I said, shuffling so that she could lie on me better. "Sleep here for a while."

She fell asleep quickly. Her breathing became heavy against my chest, and I wished I'd removed my T-shirt, so I could properly feel it. I dozed off now and again, tightening my arms around her whenever I woke, and she was tucked into my side.

Nell was gone when I woke up, but I could smell the coffee she was making, the scent traveling through the house. I'd expected her to be sleeping still, but it was a good sign that she'd gotten up early. She was coping well, but she'd not spoken about it much.

I got up and walked through to the kitchen. She stood against the worktop, wearing nothing but one of my T-shirts. There would be something under the black material, no doubt, but I could pretend she was naked.

"Hey," I said when she didn't look up.

Her eyes were focused on the black liquid pouring into the pot.

She glanced up and smiled before returning to the task. "Morning."

"You're up early."

"I couldn't sleep any longer. I think I've slept so much over the last few days that I could go a week without. Coffee?"

Nodding, I rounded the island and wrapped my arms around her waist. She settled back against my chest.

"I'd love some coffee. Want me to make it?" I asked.

"I can do it."

"I know you can, but I want to look after you."

Tilting her head up, she looked into my eyes. "I know, but I'd actually like to do this one tiny thing for you. You've been my human box of tissues most nights since my mum died, and you've blown off your friends to stay in with me. I think I can make you a drink."

I hadn't been out, not when I was invited on a lads' night or when my dad and Lance wanted me to go and play poker. Nell needed me, and that was the most important thing right now. She was everything, and there was nowhere else I wanted to be.

"I don't want or need anything in return, Nell."

Looking back at the coffee machine, she replied, "I know you don't."

It seemed like she wanted to say a hell of a lot more, but her body tensed. I could feel her pulling away even though she hadn't moved an inch.

"How do you feel today?" I asked, laying my head on top of hers.

She looked better. Her eyes held less pain, and her smile was a fraction wider.

"Actually, I'm doing okay. I miss my mum, but I know she wouldn't want me to lie in bed and cry all the time. She'd roll me out and tell me to get on with it. If there's one thing my mum was good at, it was getting on with it."

"How are you planning on getting on with it then?" What I really wanted to know was, how long she would be staying. I had a feeling, if she said seventy years, it still wouldn't be enough for me.

"Going back to work, and getting out of your hair," she replied, pouring coffee into two mugs.

"You're not in my hair."

"That's sweet of you to say, and you know I appreciate it, but I feel like I have to go home and get back to normal, you know?"

She didn't want to take advantage even if she knew that wasn't how I felt.

"I get it. As long as you know that you're welcome for however long you want."

"I do. Thank you."

Letting go of her, I sat on a stool and watched her work. She was okay when she was busy doing something. Nell had an addictive spirit, and people loved to be around her. But I'd not seen her lightening smile, been on the end of her teasing, or heard her laugh in too long.

"I'll go home after the beach tomorrow."

"All right."

Fucking hell, I already missed her.

Rubbing my forehead, I sighed. "You feel up to it? Going home again, I mean."

"I've been living alone for a couple of years now. I'll manage, I'm sure."

Right, but the last time she had been alone, she'd closed herself off. It had only been a few days, and I wasn't sure if she'd be strong enough to carry on as she was now when there was no one there to pull her back.

"Yeah, but I'm worried. Every day, I see more of the old you, but I worry when you're on your own."

I expected her to shut me down. Recently, she'd opened up about how she was feeling, but now that she was getting back to normal, I assumed everything would go back to how it had been.

Standing and waiting for her reaction was nerve-racking.

Finally, she dipped her head in a small nod. "I understand," she said much quieter than usual. "The last week and a half, I've made a couple of bad choices and pushed everyone away, but I don't want that. For most of my life, I've kept myself locked away, so I wouldn't get hurt, but I got hurt anyway. I'm tired of half-living and not having people close. Chlo and I are close, but I see how she is with Cassie, and I want that, too. They share real, deep stuff that I would never dream of telling another person."

"What do you want from life, Nell?"

Frowning, she bit her lip. "I want…God, everything's changed, and it's a little scary. I'm trying to get my head around it, and I'm trying not to listen to the nagging voice telling me that I'm going to end up like my parents."

I reached across the island where she sat down, and I took her hand. "You won't, and I'm glad you're not letting your doubts control you anymore."

"I'm working on it. I want normal, healthy relationships and the ability to actually tell people the truth about where I'm at and what's going on."

I couldn't believe we were having this conversation. For once, Nell was talking about what she wanted, and it wasn't just the same old lots-of-great-sex comments. These were real things about her future. That didn't mean she wanted me in the picture when she spoke about her new start though.

"You'll get there."

"Damn straight. I'm trying not to rush myself. Right now, I still revert back to thinking that relationships equal carnage. But it's a start that I know I want to change, right?"

I ran my thumb over her knuckles. "It's a great start. I'm so happy to hear you say that. All I want is for you to be happy."

"What about you?"

"Me?"

"Yeah. These last few weeks have all been about me, and while I appreciate you being there, I would really like not to talk about my life for a little while. What do you want? You know, besides cars, mansions, and pools."

"I just want to be happy, wherever that is. Maybe it's because I'm growing up—I don't know—but I want to share my life with someone. I want to be as happy as Lance and Ivory, and Chloe and Logan. I used to pity people in relationships, having to consider someone else all the time, but when I see them together, I see the work is worth it. I want to be solid with someone."

I want to be solid with you.

She smiled, and her face softened as her eyes brightened. "Sounds nice, huh?"

"It does. One day."

The air between us thickened, and she seemed to breathe a little shallower. Silence stretched in front of us, and even though we didn't talk, a thousand words were spoken.

We'd made progress. We might not be jumping into anything major, but even though we hadn't spoke, a thousand words were spoken, we were committed to making it work.

FORTY

NELL

Damon drove us to the coast. I was very ready to get away for the day. He was right; a change of scenery was exactly what I needed for a while. He'd chosen a beach that wasn't popular with tourists, and there was even a picnic in the back. Everything had been thought through.

We parked on the seafront, and Damon grabbed the picnic basket and blanket. He then got two hot-pink buckets and spades out of the boot. For the first time in what felt like years, I laughed.

"When did you get those?" I asked.

"About ten minutes ago, in the garage we stopped at for petrol."

Why didn't I immediately see that and take the piss?

"Well, the colour suits you," I teased.

He grinned. "I know."

He took my hand, and we walked down the footpath toward the sandy beach. Seeing such a masculine man with a fully toned body and inked arms and back holding a picnic basket, a red blanket, and pink buckets gave me the lift I so desperately needed right now.

"Where do you want to sit?" I asked as he walked us in a zigzag along the sand.

"Not sure yet. A little further up, away from the car park."

The beach was relatively clear with only a few people milling around and the odd kid running along the edge of the sea. Damon finally found his perfect space and laid the blanket out. He held his hand out, gesturing for me to sit down, and followed me, sitting opposite.

In such a normal and romantic picture, no one had ever looked more out of place than he did.

"You want to eat before we build a manly castle?"

I tilted my head. "How exactly is it going to be manly?"

His eyes lit up with humour. "I'll build a big moat around it."

"Oh, of course. A moat cancels out you making tiny castles with sand in bright pink buckets." I narrowed my eyes. "You're doing this because you secretly want to do this, aren't you?"

He cocked his eyebrow and pointed at me. His gaze turned intense. "I'm doing this for *that* reason."

"What reason?"

Reaching across, he brushed his thumb along my bottom lip. "For that smile."

Oh.

He dropped his arm and flipped the lid open on the basket. Inside was a bucket of chicken from KFC, chocolate, crisps, and Coke.

"Wow, that's some picnic, Damon."

"I don't bake or shit. This is about as good as it's going to get."

"This is perfect. Who needs healthy?"

"That's what I thought," he said before taking a bite of a wing.

I ate quickly, too eager to get to the part where he'd be collecting damp sand in a pink bucket to make his manly castle.

"Have you thought any more about visiting your dad?" he asked.

I shook my head. "Well, I have, but I can't do it yet. I feel bad because I know he didn't want her to die. The guilt he must be feeling…but I'm not ready to face him yet. Is that selfish?"

"Nell, I think after what they put you through, they have no right to ask anything of you. They've been selfish your whole life."

That did make sense, but it was difficult when I felt like I should go to my dad. I had two conflicting emotions, and right now, I wasn't thinking clearly enough to choose between them. So, I'd do what Damon had said—for once—and give myself time. My dad owed me time.

"Yeah, thanks. Now," I said, handing him the bucket, "fill this up, and let me laugh at you."

He sternly looked at me. "No pictures of this are to be taken."

Saluting, I grabbed my own bucket and stood up. For the next few hours, I wasn't going to think of everything I had lost or still needed to do. I was going to have some immature fun until we went home and got back to reality.

Right on time, Logan knocked on my door. Chloe had mentioned that he *might* pop by on his way home from work. By that, she'd meant that he most definitely would because she'd instructed him to.

"Hey," I said, opening the door and standing aside so that he could come in.

"Hey, you okay?"

"I'm fine, Logan. You don't have to check in on me."

"Yes, I do."

"You don't. I'm doing fine."

He nodded and walked to the living room area. "I know. That's exactly what I said to Chloe, but she threatened me with a sexless month, and there's no fucking way I'm doing that. So, I'll put the kettle on, and you can tell me all about what's happening with Damon."

I groaned and followed as he turned, walking through to the kitchen. "Did she also tell you to ask about that?"

"Nope," he replied over his shoulder.

"So, why do you want to talk about it?"

"I like you, and I like Damon. I think you two could be happy if you let yourselves."

I rolled my eyes. "You're being one of those annoying in-a-relationship people."

"Because I want you to be happy?"

"Yes. I think I prefer bitter singles—or bitter people in relationships."

"Come on, Nell, you're not fooling anyone anymore."

I glared. "Fine, *arsehole*, I like him."

Logan laughed and flicked the kettle on. "Sweetheart, you love him."

See? It was cute when he called Chloe sweetheart, but it was just plain patronising when he called me it.

Narrowing my eyes, I stuck my middle finger up. "I like you less and less."

"No, you don't. You were Team Logan from the start."

I dropped my hand and shrugged one shoulder. "You're hotter than your brother."

He beamed. "Thank you."

Why did I even say it? "Anyway, I do not love Damon. I care about him a lot, and every day, I feel myself truly believing that I won't turn into my parents. But how can I be in love with someone whom I've never been with?"

I was lying through my teeth, but admitting it to a second person would mean I couldn't live in my protective little bubble. Until I was ready for it to pop, he and Chloe would be on my case about it.

Logan cocked his eyebrow. "Do you believe all the shit that just spewed from your mouth? Weren't you the one telling Chloe that she loved me before we were together?"

"That's different."

I really didn't know how right now, but it was different.

"Nell, why are you not admitting the truth to yourself? Or have you?"

Sighing, I dropped down onto a chair and banged my head on the table. "Because, even though I know I would do absolutely everything in my power to break the abusive-relationship cycle in my family, there's still a chance. I can't guarantee it won't happen, and that scares me."

"There's a chance with anyone then. Your parents and grandparents fucked up big time, but they could have gotten help and got out. They *chose* not to. You get a choice, too."

I knew he was right, but sometimes, it was hard to take that leap from safety to the unknown. My grandparents had hurt each other until they couldn't even be in the same country anymore. My dad had lost his freedom, and my mum had lost her life. Those were my only experiences with relationships. Abusive people had been my role models, growing up, and I was terrified that I had that in me somewhere deep down. After all, my mum hadn't been abusive before my dad, and visa versa.

"Look, your fears and reservations are understandable—fucking hell, are they understandable—but that guy worships you, and he would never let things turn out the way it had for them. Trust him, Nell, because no one will ever love you as much as he does."

"You have no idea how much I hate it when you're right."

"You sound so much like Chloe."

I smiled as he placed a mug of coffee in front of me. "Thanks. How is married life?"

"I love it."

"Nothing's changed, has it?"

"No, not at all. I was going to be with her forever, no matter what a piece of paper said or what was wrapped around our fingers. I love knowing that she has my surname and the boring legal shit, like next of kin, but it hasn't changed our relationship. Not a single fucking thing could do that."

"You're so sweet."

He shrugged. "I just say shit as it is."

"And such a smooth talker."

"Now that, I would never claim. Apparently, I say *fuck* a lot."

"No?" I said sarcastically, faking shock.

He held his hands up and tilted his head. "So, what are you going to do about Damon, Miss Presley?"

I bit my lip and wrapped my hands around the mug. "I want us to be together, but I don't want to jump into it. We're going slow."

"Where's the problem with that?"

"Well…he broke things off with me before because I didn't want anything serious, so what if what I can offer right now isn't enough?"

"Have you spoken to him about what he wants?"

"Not recently." *He said in the past he's cool with slow.* "I hurt him a lot, and I think he's healing from that. I don't want to keep bringing it up. He wants us to be official—I know that much—but what if he wants to move in together? Or…I don't know."

"That's not something I can answer, but Damon can. I'm willing to bet my house on him still being okay with taking things slow for as long as you need. You're already giving him everything by opening up enough to properly let him in. He's not going to push you."

I knew all this.

Damon was amazing, and he would never try to push me past what I was ready for, but because he'd ditched me, I was second-guessing the things I'd already known. Shit, I hated being in this situation. I had not had nearly enough sympathy for Chloe while she had been agonising over her feelings for Logan. One minute, I was sure we could make it work, and the next, my head was all over the place.

"Why can't things ever be straightforward?" I asked.

"Ah, the million-dollar question. Want to know my theory?"

I nodded. I'd take anything right now.

"Life's a bitch."

I deadpanned. "That's it?"

"That's about the best you're likely to get. Life is a constant battle. There's far too much to ever understand. No one will be able to have everything straight. Hold on to the things you know, like your feelings for Damon. You love him, Nell, so focus on that, and the rest won't be quite as much of a headfuck."

That was what he thought. Loving Damon was the headfuck. Not loving him would have been easy. But stopping was impossible.

I wanted to pour the hot coffee over my head.

"How long did it take you to know that you wanted to have a go at things with Chlo?"

He leaned back against the worktop. "About five minutes after meeting her."

"Come on. After you thought Jace had died, how long?"

Blowing out a deep breath, like I'd just asked him to tell me the meaning of life, he put his drink down. "About a month after I dragged her arse up out of bed. She'd spent too long not existing after we thought he'd died. When we started hanging out more and she was looking like she'd re-joined the world of the living, I knew. I don't remember exactly when or how long it took to fall for her. I was too busy beating myself up about it. I thought my little brother was dead, and I couldn't stop wanting his girlfriend."

"But that was a while before all the what-the-fuck-should-I-do stuff."

He dipped his head in a nod. "It was complicated. I thought I could ignore it the way I'd done for too many years before. When I started to realise she was having feelings for me, too, I knew there was no way I could stop it. But I was ahead of her. I'd dealt with the guilt for longer, come to terms with more. Chloe was just starting, and I remember how fucking awful it felt at first. I had to give her time. Is that what you need?"

"I'm not sure if there's enough time in the world that would help me get a grip on what happened and trying not to repeat it."

Time wasn't what I needed. It was courage. Taking a leap of faith was scary but necessary. I didn't want to stand still, hiding, anymore. I had to trust Damon and myself.

"I don't think you're right there. You already know what you don't want to be, and you've been taking steps to avoid that for years. Now, you just have to work out how to continue avoiding that with someone."

"We argue."

"Who doesn't?"

"Fine," I said, narrowing my eyes and then sighing. "Fine, I know. I'm being an idiot."

"You are," he replied, picking his drink up. "Stop being a dick, and talk to him. My sex life depends on this!"

Leaning back, I laughed and wiggled my eyebrows. But I would talk to Damon.

FORTY-ONE

DAMON

It had been six weeks since Nell's mum died, and she was doing well. Even though she had only been with me for a few days, I'd gotten used to her being there, and now, I didn't like being alone.

How the fuck can you miss someone who wasn't even with you for one week?

As well as those first few nights, she'd also crashed at my place or had me stay at hers a couple of times when she'd had a real hard day, dealing with her mother's death. That hadn't happened in the last week though, so things were looking up.

I was meeting Nell after work for a quick drink before she went to dinner with Chloe, and I went to Logan's for beer, pizza, and Xbox.

"Hey," I said, sitting down at the table Nell was at.

She smiled up at me and pushed a pint my way.

"Thanks." *Shit, she's the perfect woman.*

"Hey. How was work?"

"Good. You?" I asked, raising my eyebrow.

She turned her little button nose up and flicked her hair over her shoulder. "I'm seriously considering putting laxatives in their coffee again. It's all right though because I have two interviews next week," she said proudly.

"Yeah? That's great. We'll celebrate when you land one of them."

"You're getting ahead of yourself, but you're on."

"So, do you have a date yet?" I asked.

She knew what I meant. Nell had finally decided to visit her dad. He'd refused to apply for bail, so he was waiting for sentencing after pleading guilty to manslaughter.

I was glad she'd decided to visit. She had questions she needed answering and things she needed to say. He had to know what they'd done to her.

"Eight days' time," she replied. "I'm not looking forward to it, but right now, I'm spending the evening with friends, and I don't want to cry in the middle of a bar."

"So, we should talk about something else."

"That'd be good. Tell me something I don't know about you."

"You're the first girl I fingered."

I watched her wish she'd never asked.

She slowly placed her arms on the table and leaned in. "You, what?"

"It's the truth."

"But…how?"

I shrugged. "I'm shit-hot with my tongue."

She blushed and smirked. "I remember. So, really? I was the first?"

"And the only actually."

"Ah, so you didn't treat your Kavos conquests to some finger love?"

Laughing, I shook my head. I loved it when she was as crude as me. It didn't happen often.

"No, that was just drunken sex that I barely remember, and you know the second one just blew me."

"Charming."

"They knew the score."

She held her hands up. "Wasn't judging. We were doing the same."

Ouch. What we'd been doing wasn't some big commitment, but it was more than a one-night stand.

"We weren't doing the same, and you know it."

There was no way she didn't feel anything for me at all.

"Sorry. It was more than your holiday shags," she said.

"Can we put them on the do-not-discuss list, too?"

"Sure," she said. "Are you positive you and Logan don't want to join me and Chlo for dinner?"

"And listen to girl gossip? No, thanks. Anyway, you've not been out with Chloe for a while." Not since her mum had died. "But if you want, I'm up for having you stumble into my flat later tonight."

"What do you have planned?" she asked, narrowing her eyes, all suspicious and accusing.

"You sleeping in my bed, but if you're offering more, I'm not going to say no."

"You're so easy, Damon."

I'd only ever been able to tell her no once, and that hadn't ended well. There was no way I was going to fuck up that badly again. From now on, we were doing shit my way. Her past had clouded her idea of what a relationship was, so I was taking the lead.

"Can I ask you something?"

"Yes, I will do *that* thing," I replied.

She rolled her eyes. "Fine, forget it."

"No, go on."

"I know I've been a big, huge bitch, and I've hurt you."

Hurt *is a small word to describe it.*

"I want to make things right between us. I'm not saying that I want to…" She frowned.

I realised that, probably for the first time, she had absolutely no idea what she wanted to say. She'd always known what she wanted, what she was going to do, what her life would be, and what she would have to do to get it.

What she wanted to do to protect herself was now colliding with what she wanted in order to be happy, and I could see her struggling. I wanted to leap in and rescue her, to tell her not to worry, that we'd feel our way through as we went. But I really needed to hear her express what she was feeling to me. I knew how she felt, but now, it was time to hear it.

Clearing her throat, she looked to the ceiling. "I don't know what I can offer you, Damon, but if you're willing, maybe we could start up where we'd left off?"

An icy chill stabbed at my spine. I thought we'd decided on slow, but now, she wanted no-strings sex? "You want to start the casual sex up?"

"Well, yes, but no. I want us to be how we were—you know, hanging out and stuff. The sex, too, but"—she licked her lips—"without the other people."

"Go on."

She glared when she realised I wasn't going to let her off easily. She was going to have to be very clear with what she wanted.

"You don't want to be fuck buddies anymore, Nell?"

"If you call it that again, I'll shove this cocktail stick right down the end of—"

"Ah, all right," I snapped, squirming and pressing my legs together as best as I could. I could feel the pain just from her words. That was the reaction I had been after though. She didn't want to think of us as that casual anymore. *Finally.* I also knew never to get on her bad side. "I'm sorry."

"You said when I was sorted, you'd take me on a date." Biting her lip, she smiled. "A proper date. And…well, I guess I'd kinda like for that to happen."

A slow smile spread across my face, and my heart beat faster for her. "Okay. Nell, will you come out with me this weekend?"

Flashing me a shy smile, she nodded. "I'd love to. But you're sure, right? Because I don't know how much I can give you."

Bullshit. "Yes, you do. You can give me everything."

Her chest expanded as she took a deep breath, and her eyes widened in alarm. That terrified her.

"I know the idea of eventually giving yourself to me completely scares you, but I promise I would never let you become your parents. I would never lay a hand on you in that way. We'll be fine. You have my word, Nell. Please trust me."

Gulping, her eyes filled with tears. "If you let us hurt each other, I'll do that thing with the cocktail stick."

"We're going to be fine," I repeated. *Believe me.* "One step at a time, okay?"

"Yeah," she replied. "Starting with a sleepover at your place."

Don't make a cocky comment.

I smiled and was pretty certain that my eyes were telling her exactly what we'd be doing at the sleepover. I was more than ready to have my hands and mouth all over her again. Although, under the circumstances, I should probably wait for the green light rather than just pouncing the way I was so used to. If we were working toward something, I should take it slower than ripping her clothes off and dragging my tongue all over her soft skin.

Fuck, I'm hard.

"Damon…"

I looked up to see her eyebrow arched. I guessed it looked like I was inside her, too.

"Sorry," I muttered, not in the slightest bit sorry. "Can't help it."

"Maybe you can save it for later."

That's the green light, surely?

"Okay, we need to finish up and get out of here before I drag you to my bedroom and make you miss your night out with Chlo."

Her lips parted, and her eyes darkened.

Jesus! She's actually considering it.

I couldn't let her, of course. She'd made plans, and she was really looking forward to being *normal* for the evening.

Fuck me and my newfound morals.

FORTY-TWO

NELL

Eight weeks after Mum's funeral, I was starting to feel more and more like myself. I loved my mum and missed her every day, but she'd taken a lot from me growing up, and I didn't want to undo the hard work I'd put in to get my life straight. My parents weren't great, but there was nothing I could do or could have done to change them.

So, I chose to love them both and be happy.

Visiting my dad was hard, and I didn't really get any answers, none that I hadn't already known. They'd fought the way they'd done a million times before, and Mum had fallen. It was an accident—one that my dad was going to pay for with prison time for the next five years.

Things had also changed between me and Damon. We were closer on a level that wasn't just physical. As much as it scared me, I had faith that we wouldn't be anything like my parents. We still weren't together officially, but that was okay because we were taking things slow and healing what had been damaged. He'd taken me out a few times, and I loved hanging out with him on a more intimate level.

Now, I was ready to make things with Damon official. The only problem was him. I didn't know where he was at, and the last two days, I'd only seen him for five minutes. He'd said he was busy with work, and because some campaign was about to start, he had been putting in extra hours. I didn't doubt him, but I doubted myself.

I kept busy with getting ready to start my new job. I'd finally left The Ogre and his little shit of a son. Starting Monday, I would be working for an awesome company that was young, fresh, and forward-thinking.

Tonight though, Damon was supposed to be coming over, so I hoped we could sort things out and finally be happy together. I sprayed my hair, ruffling it up at the roots to give it extra bounce, and I slicked my loose silk tank top down.

He was due anytime now, and I was nervous. It was stupid because I was ninety-nine percent sure I knew Damon would be all for giving us the girlfriend-boyfriend title, but this was new ground for me.

The doorbell rang, and I jumped. Giving my appearance one final look, I dashed to the door, ripped it open and felt my heart soar as his hungry eyes landed on mine. The effect he had on me took my breath away every single time I laid eyes on him.

"Hey," he said, walking forward, making me step back. He kicked the door closed and pulled me toward him. "I've missed you. A lot."

"I missed you, too," I replied.

Jesus, if he kept saying things like that, my heart was going to implode. He was standing so close that I felt a little drunk and delirious.

"How have you been?" he whispered.

I smiled, trying to make it convincing. "I've been fine." I hadn't really been fine. I'd missed him so much that I'd been agonising over what to do with us. "What about you? Work all sorted?"

"Things will be slowing down now, so no more overtime for a while. Means I get to spend more time annoying you," he said, reaching out for me. His hands started on my hips and then slid around to my back.

I stumbled into his arms, resting both hands on his muscular chest. "I don't think that'll ever happen."

He swallowed audibly, and his grip on me tightened a fraction. "I'm willing to give it a go if you are?"

No. What the fuck is he asking? Is he really about to piss on my fireworks? "Damon...what exactly does that mean?"

Lowering his head, he brushed his lips against mine, and I stopped breathing altogether. A fire started in my belly and soon spread south as his tongue grazed my bottom lip.

"It means, I want to spend all of my free time with you. These last couple of days have been pretty unbearable. I thought it'd be fine because I'd be working late and going in early, but you were always on my mind. I constantly worried about you. I constantly wanted to see you. Look, I know that you're still healing after what happened, and there are things you haven't figured out yet, but—"

"I love you, Damon."

His eyes widened, and his jaw dropped. "What? You...you, what?"

I couldn't help but laugh at his surprise. I grabbed the front of his top and pressed my body against his. Our mouths were still so close, and I ached everywhere to kiss him.

"I love you. I'm still scared, but I'm less scared when you're standing beside me. I want us to be official—if you do, of course."

"If?" He gripped my upper arms and lifted me, and then his mouth was on mine.

I squealed against his lips and wrapped my legs around his waist.

"I love you, Nell," he murmured into the frantic, needy kiss.

I cried out as we bumped into the corner of the wall. Neither of us broke the kiss, too caught up to care about anything else. I'd never wanted him as much as I did right now. It was more than sex. I wanted to be as close to him as humanly possible. If it were possible to crawl inside him, I would.

Kneading the tops of my thighs with his fingers as he carried me, he stumbled into the bedroom and laid us both down. He pulled out of the kiss and trailed his lips over my jaw with a feather's touch.

I shuddered and groaned deeply, feeling it everywhere. "Damon," I whimpered. I was so turned on that I could cry or scream.

His touch was softer, and his kiss was slower. It was maddening and perfect and everything I needed it to be right now. The throbbing between my legs made me moan. I was on fire, desperate to feel him inside me.

"I love you," he murmured against the edge of my jaw as he pushed my leggings down.

I arched into his hand as he rubbed me through the lace of my underwear.

"Shit, I can't wait, Nell."

His voice was so husky that it made me shudder.

I sat up, shoving him back an inch, and reached for his T-shirt. "There's a time for foreplay, and this is not it," I said. I made it my mission to get him naked in record time.

"God, I love this side of you. Actually, I love all sides of—"

I kissed him, shutting him up. Groaning, he sat back on his knees and pulled me onto his lap. His tongue slid over mine and then circled it. I let him control the kiss. I really didn't have much choice because it seemed he was determined to get me off just from his mouth on mine. If he kept going like that, he'd do it, too.

I clamped my legs around his and clawed his back, pressing my chest against his. I was burning, and the need to come suppressed everything else. My nails dug into his back. He groaned, roughly tugged my top over my head, and removed my bra. His trousers went next.

Bloody. Hell.

Not being able to stand it anymore, I crushed my body back against his and ground into him. With his erection lined perfectly between my legs, I got the best friction as I circled my hips. My nipples rubbed against his chest, setting every nerve ending in my body on fire.

"No foreplay you said," he growled, lifting and sharply entering me.

I cried out and let my head drop back. "Oh…oh God, that feels…"

"I know," he bit out as he gently laid us both down.

He took my hands in his and very slowly started to move inside me. Gasping, I closed my eyes at the incredible feeling of him filling me as I thought of how much he meant to me. I was in love—totally and completely and eternally.

Sensing that I was on the verge of tears, a complete emotional wreck, he kissed me, gently brushing his lips against mine, as he made long, slow strokes. I wanted to wrap my arms around his back, but he pinned my hands above my head. Not being able to do anything somehow made it feel better.

I whimpered against his mouth. I really, *really* needed him to move now because I was so close that I felt everything inside me tighten. Damon's lips curled against my own, but he didn't go any faster, like he'd usually do when he knew I was about to come.

Bastard.

Pulling my arms, I tried to get free, and when he didn't let go, I pushed my hips harder, only to have him pin me deeper to the bed so that I couldn't even wriggle. And he didn't stop kissing me, so I couldn't scream at him.

My body was so worked up that it was shaking. The emotional feeling of him inside me heightened everything. I clenched around him as he circled his hips, pushing hard. He groaned into my mouth, and I fell apart, clamping around him. My body felt like an explosion, and the orgasm rolled on and on until my legs went numb. Damon followed with a growl, burying his head in my neck and whispering over and over that he loved me.

Having sex with someone you were in love with was nothing like meaningless sex. Damon had always been killer between the sheets, but this time was on a whole new level. It was perfect and beautiful. I'd been missing out on so much by keeping him at arm's length.

He rolled beside me, pulling me into his arms, and ran his fingers through my hair. "How are you feeling?"

"I feel kind of like I'm floating. I'm pretty sure my legs have turned into jelly. But I'm happy. Really happy."

His smile made my heart swell. "I'm so glad to hear that, Nell. You have no idea."

"Please, you know you're good in bed," I teased, knowing full well what he meant.

"Oh, I do know. Your screams, pleads, and back-clawing confirmed that years ago."

Rolling my eyes, I snuggled closer, so our bodies were pressed tightly against each other.

"I'm happy, too," he said. "Looking forward to the rest of our lives."

"Funny, a few months ago, that would have scared the hell out of me. But I finally feel ready to give you everything you want and deserve."

"I never needed any promise of marriage, mortgage, and kids. Through my teens and uni, I was fine to mess around because I was young, and I saw friends settling down as early as seventeen and eighteen. I was doing well in school and had my dream job lined up a year before I finished uni. I had success from an early age, but as I watched my mates falling in love, I realised what really mattered in life. Success is great, but what's the point if you're alone? All I've ever *really* wanted is you."

With the back of my hand, I slapped his chest and then wiped my eyes. "You dickhead, you made me cry!"

Damon laughed and kissed my forehead. "It's nice to know how you feel, too."

"You know how I feel, I told you, but I don't know where to even begin describing how much. I'm not that good at the whole verbal thing, never have been, but I know that as long as you're by my side, I can face anything and be happy doing it. I love you so much more than I ever thought it was possible to love another person."

His lips parted. "I don't think you're doing too badly with the whole verbal thing. It's nice to know you feel the way I do. More than nice actually. There was a time when I didn't think this would ever happen."

"Me, too. I'm sorry I put you through that."

"No, it's okay. You didn't do it to hurt me, and hell, you were hurting, too."

"It still kills me that I caused you pain. I wish I could have gotten it together before. God, it took my mum dying to make me realise that I'm in control of how I turn out."

He ran his fingertips over my bare shoulder. "Yeah, but seeing what you did, growing up, left a pretty big scar. You've come a long way, Nell, and as far as I'm concerned, the part where you run is done with. We're past it, and I don't want you feeling guilty for something that you shouldn't feel guilty for. No one else. We can do this."

That was easy for him to say. We hadn't been exclusive, so I hadn't broken any rules—technically, *he* was the rule-breaker—but that didn't change what'd happened.

"Well, I'm all for putting the past behind us and moving forward," I said, trailing my fingernail down his chest.

His eyes dilated as I traced each bump and groove of his muscles.

"Yeah," he replied, licking his lips. "And how do you want to move forward?"

"I'm thinking we should start with me cooking for you tonight and you taking me out tomorrow."

That wasn't what he was after. His pout was adorable.

"Then, later, you get to decide how we move forward," I said.

He brightened immediately and got out of bed. "All right, deal. I'll make drinks, and you cook. Where do you want to go tomorrow?"

I watched him with a big moronic grin on my face. *How the hell did I get so lucky not only to have him fall in love with me, but also to have him give me another chance?*

He was still wearing nothing but his white gold watch, and I was very much enjoying the view. He picked up a pillow and frowned.

My heart skipped a beat. I'd not looked at that for a while. I kept quiet, hoping he'd throw it down and let it go. Keeping a pillow stained with your mascara and tears from the breakup with your ex-fuck buddy was too pathetic to admit.

"What did you do?"

My quilt covered me, but I felt totally bare. "I cried on it a lot."

He rubbed his forehead. "Oh. Why do you keep it?"

"It's a reminder that I never want to hurt us that badly again."

"Wait, you cried on this pillow over me?"

I sat up, pulling the quilt with me. My efforts to protect my modesty were in vein as Damon tugged on the bottom, uncovering my breasts.

"Yes. A lot actually. Just because I was…"

"Being fucking impossible?"

"Going through some things," I corrected. "That didn't mean that I didn't want to be with you. Every time I thought I could give it a try, I would think about my parents and what I didn't want to become. To me, it was a risk I couldn't take. *Ever.*"

"I know, and I understand now. We could've saved ourselves a lot of hurt if you had opened up and told me from the beginning. There was something wrong there—I knew that—but I thought I could eventually get you to open up and let me in. I hate that you went through so much alone."

He walked toward me, and I bit my lip as my heart went wild with his slow descent to the bed.

"I wasn't alone," I whispered.

"You had Chloe, but you wanted and needed me."

I nodded, confirming what he clearly knew. He was the one I wanted to hold me when everything had gone to shit.

"Well, you have me now, and I'm not going anywhere. Neither are you, so don't even think about getting scared and running away from me again because I won't let you go."

Usually, someone telling me what to do would piss me off, but Damon telling me I was stuck with him really didn't.

"Bring it on," I replied.

He cocked his eyebrow. "Are you going to try running from me?"

"What would happen if I did?"

"Oh, Nell," he said breathlessly, his eyes intensifying.

I didn't have time to blink before I was lying flat. His lips covered mine, and I was lost for the next hour.

FORTY-THREE

DAMON

Nell walked out of the bathroom, wearing a fitted royal-blue silk shirt and a black pencil skirt that gave Pippa Middleton's arse a run for its money. She had her hair up in a sleek ponytail.

I stopped getting dressed. *Fuck me, she's stunning.*

She looked up halfway through smearing gloss over her lips. *I hate that shit.*

"What?"

"You're beautiful," I said, not even pretending I wasn't ogling her like a pervert.

Taking a deep breath, she dropped the lip gloss on the bed and made her way over. "I don't think I'll ever get used to the way you make me feel, especially when you say things like that."

"Good," I replied, pulling her into my arms where she belonged. If she got used to it, then I wasn't making her feel the way I'd sworn to make her feel every day of our lives. "I love you."

I heard her breath leave her lungs much too quickly. "I love you, too."

That was getting easier for her to say. She'd had a difficult time with finding her way back to me, but we were there, and we were happy.

"You'll pick me up after work, and we'll go straight there, right?"

I kissed her forehead. "Right. Are you sure you want to spend the weekend with my parents?"

"Of course. I love your parents."

"Yeah, but you love them based on spending a few hours with them three times since we got together. A whole weekend is—"

"Damon, will you chill? This is going to be great. No commitment fear anymore, remember?"

"You sure about that?"

"Maybe I worry sometimes but not because I think we'll turn out like my parents. We won't. I know that for sure."

"Then, what do you worry about?"

"You leaving me," she whispered.

I almost laughed in her face, but thankfully, I managed to pull it back at the last minute. "Come on, Nell, be serious."

She defensively folded her arms over her chest. "What? *You* asked!"

"You honestly think there's even the slightest possibility that I'd leave you?" I asked.

"I do. I can't help it. You're the best thing that's *ever* happened to me, and I'm so sure that I must be dreaming here."

"Funny," I replied. "I feel the same."

"When we ended things before, it hurt more than I could have imagined, but I know if anything happened now..." She looked away, and I saw a tear trail down her cheek.

"Hey," I said, lifting her chin. "Baby, look at me. I love you, Nell, and I always will. Whatever happens in the future, we'll be okay because we'll work at it. You're stubborn as fuck, so as long as you're willing to hold on and not let go, we'll be just fine."

She let her arms drop, and she fell into my chest.

I wrapped my arms around her and leaned my chin on the top of her head. "Do you trust me?" I asked.

"More than I trust myself."

"Then, believe me when I tell you, I won't let anything happen to us. You're stuck with me for life."

"Yeah?"

I nodded against her. "Yeah. Now, have we finished this discussion and fought off your doubts?"

"Mmhmm," she breathed into my chest.

"Good. Let's get to work then."

I dropped Nell off and headed to my office. Today had better pass quickly because I was really looking forward to spending some real time with my girl and my parents. I loved how she integrated in my family, as if she'd always been there.

Nell was waiting outside her office when I picked her up that afternoon. Unlike when she'd worked for those last pricks, she had a big smile on her face. She loved her new job, got the respect and recognition she deserved, and was making good changes for the company. I loved to see her happy in all aspects of her life.

She opened the door and dropped in the seat, lobbing her bag in the back. "Hey, baby," she said, leaning over for a kiss.

"Hey, you okay?"

"Very okay, but it was a long day. We walked around the whole warehouse, offices, and workshop. We've made great progress, and both Harold and Margaret listened to my ideas. Oh, and I bought a new desk."

Nell worked for a company that made and sold upcycled furniture and home furnishings. She spent at least twenty percent of her wages there and loved one-of-a-kind things. Thankfully, so did a lot of people. Mass produced flat-packed shit was on its way out, and people wanted quality. They needed to expand quickly, and Nell had been hired to plan and oversee that.

"We might need to look for a bigger house."

She grinned. "That's exactly what I was thinking. Three bedrooms will do."

There were two of us, and we shared a room, but of course, we needed an extra two.

"Well, I look forward to paying out hundreds more a month, so all your new stuff can be stored."

"They're working to restore a retro pinball machine…"

My eyes flicked to hers as I pulled up at a red light. "You're trying to get around me with man toys?"

"Absolutely. Oh, and sex. I plan on having lots of sex with you in each of those three bedrooms."

Who was I kidding? There was no way I was pushing for a smaller place if offers of arcade games and steamy sex were up for grabs.

"Fine. Start looking for bigger places then."

Squealing, she pulled out her phone, no doubt hopping on Rightmove to start the search right away. I couldn't care less. As long as we could comfortably afford it, it didn't matter to me where we lived or how much space we had. I'd live with her in a hostel if it meant we could be together.

Nell had come so far, and she deserved everything she wanted. *We* deserved it.

Two hours later, we pulled up at my parents', and I went to get the bags out of the boot. Nell had been organised and packed the night before, so we could go straight from work since we'd be travelling at peak time.

Mum answered the door and hugged Nell first. I hadn't realised that, when I got a girlfriend, I'd be bumped down on the favourite list. But I loved it.

"Hi, darling," Mum said, crushing the life out of her.

Nell laughed and squeaked a, "Hey."

"Will you put her down?" I said, laughing. I kissed my mum's cheek once she'd let Nell go.

We walked inside, and I headed to the living room to find Dad. No doubt he'd be watching football. I rounded the corner, and sure enough, I found him waving his hand at a footie match.

"Hey, Dad," I said, dropping down beside him.

"Hi, son. Nell not with you?"

"Mum stole her."

"She never had a girlie daughter. I'm surprised she's not in there, combing Nell's hair."

Cara was not one bit girlie. The one time Mum had bought her a dress and asked her to try it on and see if she liked it, Cara had taken it out in the garden and burned it.

"How is C getting on at uni?" I asked.

"She's not called, asking for money, in a week, so doing better, I think."

"I remember those days." I laughed and kicked my feet up on the coffee table, same as his.

We'd both get told off for it, but we still did it every time.

"How are things going with you and Nell anyway?" he asked.

Dad was the only one of my family who knew the whole story with Nell. There was no way I was telling Mum. I'd only get my ear chewed off about the correct way to treat a woman—being, not to have casual sex with them. It wouldn't matter that it had been a mutual decision between two adults. It'd be my fault.

"Great," I replied, trying to stop the aching grin I got when I spoke about her or even just thought about her.

My colleagues must think I'd lost it with the amount of smiling to myself I did.

"That's good. Not thought about the next step yet? I knew your mum was the one after the first date, and soon after, I got a ring on that finger."

"Oh, did you?" I asked sarcastically. The amount of times I'd heard that story...

"You're not too old to put over my knee."

I'd heard that a lot, too.

"Are you proposing to that girl or not?"

Mum and Nell chose that exact moment to walk in the room. My eyes widened. The last time Nell had overheard one of my parents saying something stupid, it'd ended badly. Mum looked as worried as I felt, but Nell sat beside me and placed her hand on my chest.

"I doubt he could afford the rock I've got my eye on," Nell said to my dad.

Dad laughed, and I felt like I was dreaming. There was no panic in her eyes. She'd spoken about our engagement so calmly.

"What?" I said, looking at her, stunned.

Nell smiled. "I'm only joking. I don't expect a two hundred thousand pound ring."

I would've choked if I wasn't still so surprised that we were having this discussion. "Um…"

"You're not freaking out on me, are you?" she asked, smirking.

What? "Have we switched places?"

"Looks like it," she replied to me. Then, she turned to my dad. "How are you?"

"Much better now that there are two beautiful women in the house."

I rolled my eyes. He was such a charmer—or so he thought.

Nell laughed and poked me in the chest with her thumb. "Uh-oh, I think we broke him."

Broke wasn't the right word, but I definitely felt…something.

Nell even being able to joke about our future cemented my belief that we could make this work. It eradicated every last niggling worry I'd had about her doing a runner.

"I'm not broken," I grumbled.

"Are you scared about the proposal jokes?"

"The opposite." *Don't propose to her when your parents are watching your every move like a hawk.* If we were alone, I would've blurted it out by now.

Mum made an excited squeaking sound and clenched her fists. She wanted me to get down on one knee—right here, right now. Nell deserved for it to, at the very least, be in private.

Silence stretched into minutes, and Mum, finally accepting that I wasn't doing it here, got up. "Tea everyone?"

"Coffee for me, please," I said.

Nell kissed my cheek and stood up. "I'll give you a hand."

Dad looked over his shoulder as they walked out. "Look at that. She followed Mum into the kitchen rather than hightailing it out the door."

"You're hilarious, Dad."

"Looks like the only person stopping you from popping the question is you."

"No, I think that was you and Mum. Anyway, there's no rush. We've not been together long."

Dad looked at me and cocked his head to the side. "Now, who are you fooling? From what you've told me, you've been together a lot longer than you let on. If you're sure you'll make it, then what are you waiting for? Whether you marry her now or in five years won't change the fact that you'll grow old and grey together."

"Lance and Cara should be here to witness you giving good advice."

"Nothing wrong with my advice, lad."

If I'd done half the things he'd said growing up, I probably would've been arrested. He was the dad who told me to punch them back until they couldn't get up, and small lies on your tax returns weren't illegal because the police didn't have enough resources to arrest and charge everyone who had done it.

"I need a ring."

He cracked the biggest smile I'd seen since I passed my driving test. "That's the spirit. But don't ask me to re-mortgage the house to get her that two hundred thousand one."

"Not much chance of that."

My job paid well but not that well. Besides, Nell wouldn't really care what the thing cost. I was more likely to get shit for it being too expensive.

"You two need to learn to whisper," Nell said, leaning against the doorframe.

"Shit!" I closed my eyes.

There was no chance of this proposal being anything that even resembled romantic now.

She laughed and then bit her lip. I wanted to drag her off upstairs. My old room was still as I'd left it, minus the few boxes of junk that kept finding their way in there. She pushed off the frame and moved aside for Mum to get through with the tray of drinks and biscuits.

"Don't worry. I'll pretend I know nothing."

I felt like shit. She could not talk about it all she wanted, but we both knew it was going to happen. We both wanted it, so it couldn't be forgotten. I wouldn't get to surprise her. It was like knowing what you had for Christmas before the day.

So, I decided to do the one thing she wouldn't expect. I wasn't going to ask her to marry me.

EPILOGUE

NELL

"This one is much better," I said, looking out the window in the departures lounge at our massive plane.

We were lining up, ready to board. The plane looked sturdy, unlike the pretend one we had flown to Scotland in.

Damon rolled his eyes.

"But this one has a lot further to go," Chloe said. "More time for things to go wrong."

I shrugged. Flying didn't bother me. I felt safe and confident flying. But when I was in something that looked like it belonged to a toddler, I would start to get erratic.

It was a year, just over, since Chloe and Logan had gotten married, and we were all on our way to Vegas. I was so excited, I could pee. We'd not had a holiday since Scotland, and it didn't count to me unless I actually left the UK. So, technically, this was my and Damon's first holiday together.

Since we'd made us official and decided to give it a go, I felt an inner peace that I hadn't even known existed. I just felt like I was home, and I belonged somewhere. It wasn't easy. I had a lot of hang-ups, but together, we made sure that we both felt safe in our relationship.

Letting myself love freely and openly was the best thing I'd ever done. I was surrounded by people I loved and trusted. If I had a problem, I knew I could go to Damon, Chloe, and even Logan, and I'd be listened to and never judged. Opening up was hard, but I was learning, and each time I asked for help or advice, it would get that little bit easier.

And my sex life was still just as explosive. Being in a relationship had not slowed us down. It just made everything more intense.

We made our way to the front of the queue and handed our boarding passes over before being let through.

Damon's hand slipped into mine, and I was suddenly ten times more excited.

"I can't wait," I said, smiling up at him.

He'd booked business class tickets, too, so we would have extra room and free booze on tap.

"Neither can I. What do you want to do first?"

I wiggled my eyebrows and then frowned. "Actually…I'll probably want to sleep first."

"Oh, you definitely might want to sleep first…" he muttered as we approached the door.

A very smiley air steward welcomed us and pointed us in the direction of our seats.

"This is posh," I said, looking at the large pod-type seats.

We could properly lie flat, and I intended to. We had a long eleven-hour flight, and I'd barely slept last night because I was practically bouncing off the walls.

"Worth every penny. Or it will be when they come around with beer," he replied.

I rolled my eyes and pointed to our seats. "I call window!"

Shaking his head and smiling in amusement, he replied, "Of course you do."

Thankfully, our flight was direct. I had no desire to get off this plane and onto another one. I wanted to lie down—after sampling a lot of free wine—and sleep until we hit Vegas.

Chloe and Logan were in the two seats on the other side of the aisle. Chloe looked as excited as I was. She sat in the chair closest to me, so we could gossip. I'd have to lean over Damon, but I wasn't going to give up my window seat until we'd taken off. I loved to watch cars and people on the ground turn tiny.

"It's not even night, and I'm tired," I said, buckling my seat belt the second my arse had hit the chair.

"The journey ahead exhausting you?" Logan asked in a condescending but playful voice.

"No, Damon nailing me to the bed until three in the morning exhausted me."

Logan laughed, and Chloe did, too, while hiding her face. Damon...well, he smiled proudly and put his hand on my thigh. He had this thing where he assumed that, just because we were both on the same plane, we'd be joining the Mile High Club.

It was tempting. Even the thought of it made me hot under the collar, but the toilets on planes were gross, and the whole thing was just a bit overdone now. We'd already started out as fuck buddies. There was no need to add to the cliché.

After being shown emergency procedures and had the exits pointed out—which I had known already because I'd pre-booked the seats closest to them, we sat back and waited for the pilot to get this show on the road.

Once the seat belt lights went off, the alcohol began. A beautiful angel brought drinks whenever we asked. Damon ordered a beer for himself and a wine for me, and we relaxed into our long journey.

"Wow," was the first thing to leave my lips when Damon pushed open the door to our gigantic room—a fucking *penthouse* suite. "When did you do this?"

He had previous deception with the secret upgrades, but this one had been so completely unexpected that I wasn't sure we were in the right room.

"Soon after you booked the other room. I asked them not to send you a confirmation and spoil the surprise."

Turning around, I wrapped my arms around his waist. "I love you, Damon."

He held me close and pressed his forehead against mine. "I love you, too, baby. Just so you know, this isn't the only surprise on this holiday."

"Oh? What else do you have planned?"

"Something tomorrow afternoon. Something big."

"Something big that is…"

"You remember a few weeks back when Chloe took you shopping for dresses to bring?"

I turned my nose up at that experience. Chloe had been like a drill sergeant that day. Nothing had been good enough for her, but we had ended up with killer dresses that would make Damon's and Logan's heads spin.

"I remember it vividly." I'd never known tired until that day.

"Are you happy with the dress you got?" he asked.

"Yeah…"

I loved it—like, really loved it. The white dress was knee-length with lace detail on the bodice and a slight kick to the skirt. The strapless sweetheart neckline perfectly showed off my assets. Chloe's dress was equally gorgeous, all blood red and a similar style but without the lace.

He gulped. "For a while, I've been thinking about our future…"

Frowning, I rubbed the knot in my stomach. "Okay…"

"Nell, I've planned our wedding, which is tomorrow at one o'clock, by the way."

My eyes bulged. I'd heard three words that sent my mind spinning—*our*, *wedding*, and *tomorrow*.

What. The. Fuck? We are here to get married?

"What?" I whispered, feeling too cold, despite the heat.

"Don't freak out. I can cancel it if you want. Nell, there is *no* pressure."

"Huh?"

Nothing made sense. *He's planned our wedding? He hasn't even bloody proposed yet!*

"I know how much you think and stress about things like this, and if we'd had a long engagement and planned a wedding, you would have overthought until you were sick."

"So, you took that away?" I wasn't sure if that was sweet or downright stupid.

"Yeah. Plus, after that weekend at my parents', I was pissed that I wouldn't get to surprise you."

"Well, you've certainly made up for that," I squeaked.

He shrugged and kissed my forehead. "I love you so much, Nell. You're the other half of me. You're all I need—now and forever. And if you decide you don't want to do this tomorrow, I swear to you, nothing will change. We'll do this however you want, whenever you want."

"Fuck," I whispered.

Tomorrow, I was all booked in to become Mrs Masters. The thought made my heart jump. It was something that terrified and thrilled me. Damon knew me well. I would have freaked myself out if I'd had months to plan a wedding.

He pressed his lips to mine and firmly wrapped his arms around me. With my head squished against his shoulder, I had no room to move, but I didn't want or need to move away from him—ever. I was overcome with emotion so thick that it choked me.

Damon was my forever, and I would never run or hide from him again. The thought of being his wife filled me with joy and excitement. Knowing it would just be us and our best friends was perfect.

"I'm in," I muttered.

He stilled. "What?"

"I'm in. Let's get married tomorrow."

Pulling back, he flashed the brightest smile I'd ever seen. "I bet you cry before I do," he challenged.

I narrowed my eyes. "Game on, Masters."

ACKNOWLEDGMENTS

Thank you so much to my husband for his support while I spent hours and hours writing, editing, and reading this book.

To Zoë, for her many, many kicks up the butt when my daily word targets weren't really going to plan.

To my PA, Chloe, for freeing up a lot of my time, so I could write.

And lastly, to everyone who read *Second Chance* and told me they wanted Nell and Damon's story. I hope you enjoyed it.